The Travel Mate
Mark David Green

Copyright Page

Cover artwork by Anders Design
Proofread and edit by Storywork Editing Services

Copyright © June 2017 Mark David Green

This book is a work of fiction. Characters are a product of the author's imagination. Any resemblance to actual persons, living or dead, is entirely coincidental.

No part of this book may be used or reproduced in any manner without the written permission of the author. He is reputed to be a reasonable guy, however, and therefore might respond favourably to polite email requests!

www.markdavidgreen.co.uk
md_green@btinternet.com

Acknowledgements

I owe a big thank you to a few special people who helped make the writing of this book possible:

To my mum and dad, Christine and Norman, for the extra tuition in my early years, and their ongoing support and encouragement.

To my wife Nicky, for enduring two years (and more!) of a rather vacant, preoccupied and hermit-like husband. Thanks also for the treat fund – lifesaver.

To my nan, Irene for her bequest which helped enormously with the research trip . To my granddad, Cliff, for his enthusiasm and financial assistance during the lengthy rewriting process, which kept me in ink cartridges and paper.

To Colin and Lesley Watson, for their help sustaining my writing during the bleak post-Christmas period.

To Jon at JW Electrical Services, for several weeks' worth of work over the last few years that has quite literally helped to keep my head above water.

To David Wailing at Storywork Editing Services, for his tireless enthusiasm, attention to detail and insightful suggestions to improve the story. Truly awesome!

To the friendly and optimistic people of Cambodia, who Nicky and I met during our travels. Despite everything the recent generation has endured, you amaze and inspire by continuing to smile.

To the anonymous reader mentioned in the author's note, who suggested I write the story of how Madge and Bozzer met – thank you for the idea – I hope this book, (and those that follow) satisfies your curiosity!

And finally, to all the fantastic readers over the years who have encouraged me to keep writing by taking the time to post a review, or email me with their invaluable feedback. Please don't stop getting in touch – good, bad or indifferent, it's always incredibly helpful to know what you think of my work.

md_green@btinternet.com

About the Book

Twenty-six year old Maddie has it all. A fiancé with a well-paid job, a comfortable home and several exotic holidays a year. But when Rupert drops a bombshell six weeks before the big day, Maddie realises that her lifestyle security comes with a heavy price tag. Taunted by Rupert on a Thailand holiday that she wouldn't last a week living on a minuscule budget, Maddie rises to the challenge. On a hungover whim, she leaves him at Bangkok Airport, swapping her suitcase full of designer clothes for a pair of boots, a backpack and a four-week travel itinerary.

But Maddie hasn't anticipated the rigours of life on the road, or the romantic alternatives on offer. She soon finds herself contending with the attentions of a charming and attractive humanitarian, and a crass, annoying Australian. As if these distractions aren't enough of a complication, there's the small matter of Rupert and a ruthless debt collector pursuing her around Cambodia, each intent on reclaiming something of enormous value …

This book is the second in a series of four:
Book # 1 – The Travel Auction
Book # 2 – The Travel Mate
Book # 3 – The Travel Truth
Book # 4 – The Travel Angel

Author's Note

The idea for *The Travel Mate* originated back in October 2015 when I began rewriting my first self-published novel, *The Travel Auction*. Thanks to receiving positive reviews and feedback from helpful readers, I began to wonder if there might be a sequel to the original book. At the time I wasn't sure I had enough material for a follow up, but a suggestion from one particular reader encouraged me to consider writing about how two supporting characters from *The Travel Auction* had got together. Unfortunately, despite several searches through my email folders, I've been unable to find that message. So to that wonderful, anonymous person, please accept my heartfelt thanks.

For those who have already read *The Travel Auction*, in particular the dedication at the end, you'll be aware that this isn't the first time I've had a stranger to thank for inspiring me to sit down and write …

Once I'd completed the rough draft of *The Travel Mate,* I realised that a third book was bubbling away in my creative subconscious. This would have neatly completed the journeys of the four main characters in a trilogy of books. Somewhere during the writing process however, I realised that the third book was evolving into a fourth. One character in particular had such a strong-willed personality that I found myself with no choice but to allow them the extra space they needed.

Book three in the series, *The Travel Truth* and the fourth, *The Travel Angel*, continue and conclude the journeys of all four main characters. There may be some surprises ahead for them …

Mark
May 2017

One

Shafts of daylight peeked between gaps in the blind, creeping across the pristine vinyl floor. Bozzer twitched in the chair, scrunched his eyes and edged away, lifting a hand to shield the glare. He yawned, stretching as he pushed himself up. Shuffling over to the window, he eased a corner of the blind aside with a nicotine-stained finger. 'Another day, another …'

He turned to face the bed. Crisp, white linen sheets were tucked up under Madge's chin, only a few shades lighter than her pale complexion. Bozzer gazed at her sleeping form, examined the regular rise and fall of her chest beneath the covers. Then he lifted his red-tinged eyes, following the thin plastic tube that trailed over the covers, supplying oxygen through her nose. Other tubes and wires dangled between the bed and an array of monitoring equipment lining the wall. He sank down beside her onto the chair's slippery leatherette covering. Plucking a tobacco tin from his pocket, he carefully pinched then sprinkled wiry strands into the thin paper.

Bozzer glanced up at the waft of air from the door, shoved open by a glowering Simon Black: YouTube presenter, dealmaker and, today, ball-breaker.

'Your friends have dumped you in the shit!' Simon lifted a foot, placed a leather deck shoe on the side of his suitcase and hoofed its black plastic bulk across the shiny floor, the wheels skidding towards Madge's bed. It thumped into the side, jolting the metal frame.

'Whoa, easy mate!' yelled Bozzer, leaping up and scattering tobacco off his lap. He scowled at the suitcase, shoving it aside. Then he leant over Madge, studying her flickering eyelids.

Simon turned towards the door, which hissed sedately against the pneumatic retainer. He wrapped his fingers around the thick wood, attempting to wrench it shut. Instead, the door merely expelled air slightly louder and faster as it gradually closed. He glared at it, then clasped his curled fists onto his hips. 'You really think I'd peel off a cool quarter-mil, and lie back to be shafted?'

Simon snatched the remote control off the bedside cabinet and pointed it at the flatscreen television on the opposite wall, channel-hopping until the image settled on CNN. 'You see that?' Subtitles ticker-taped in yellow font across the bottom of the screen. Bozzer frowned, scanned the text, flicking his eyes between it and the sea of faces outside the Iguazu Falls Airport.

Simon jabbed his fingers at the television. 'That's *my* story!'

Bozzer studied the tentacle-like veins emanating from Simon's throbbing jugular, spreading across his face like an ordnance survey road map. 'You sound stressed, mate. Wanna smoke?'

'I *want* my fucking exclusive!' Simon spat the words out, swaying back slightly as Bozzer sighed and took a step forwards.

'You need calm down, buddy. Anger is for outside.' Bozzer's features tightened, his knuckles clenching as he stared into Simon's bloodshot, purple-shaded eyes.

'They've screwed me over!'

'You're not making any sense ... what's happened?'

'They played me, got booted out of Brazil! Haven't you seen the news?'

Bozzer shook his head, then turned back to the television. The camera zoomed in on the crowd, framing a young couple who both wore white tee-shirts with a photographic image printed on it of Angel and JC, lying on a gently sloping pebble riverbank and kissing passionately, their torsos partially in the water. The scene was reminiscent of the 1950s movie poster: *From Here to Eternity*. Below their picture were six Portuguese words, the penultimate of which had been pixel-blurred out.

Bozzer grinned. 'Fair play.'

'*Fair* play? Try sexual sabotage!'

Bozzer shrugged. 'So what.' He glanced down at Madge, her breathing light and regular, unaltered at the intrusion. 'That's not her fault, or mine. You tried to meddle with the rubrics of someone else's journey. So they socked you right back in the chops. Life is loose, chief. Let it go, enjoy the ride.'

'Let it go ...? Listen, you happy-snappy-hippy – two hundred and fifty *thousand* pounds!'

'Yeah, but you've not actually paid that, have you?' A smirk darted across Bozzer's lips. 'They didn't gain from your deal. But you did – massively. All that advertising revenue, in exchange for what ...?

Pocket change Bolivianos for the minibus victims and a few days tax-deductible treatment for Maddie.' Bozzer lowered his voice, a hint of menace in his tone. 'You got off lightly, chief.'

Simon turned back to the television. He appeared momentarily mesmerised at the glimpses of JC and Angel, exiting a police van. Their heads bobbed between adoring fans, all clamouring for their attention. Jonathan held up their passports, to a rapturous cheer from the crowd. He steered Angel through the mob of well-wishers, escorted by several police officers as they meandered towards the departures hall entrance.

'How's she doing?' Simon muttered absently, folding his arms across his chest, still focused on the television.

'Doc says they'll reduce the medication soon, bring her round properly—'

'But she's gonna be okay, right? Because she's in a private hospital. Funded by *me*.' Simon half-turned, made eye contact with Bozzer.

'I'm sure she'll thank you herself, when she's better,' Bozzer replied, tight-lipped.

'It's thanks to me that she bypassed the morgue. My generosity and their stupidity.' He pointed at the television. 'They owe me. Meaning I own you.' Simon reached for the door. 'But I don't think you get that concept, do you, sport? It's time to find out who pays the bills around here ...'

Bozzer watched Simon heave the door open, leaving it sighing slowly behind him, hissing air. He knelt down to sweep up tobacco with his palm. 'Going outside for a smoke, Madge,' he murmured. 'Don't go getting any ideas about escaping without me – the doc'll have my balls for Christmas baubles.'

He stood up, tipped tobacco into the tin and wandered over to the door, pulling it open. He paused, turning to stare at her stationary form, sucking air sharply through his clenched teeth. He shuddered, shoulders slumping as he stepped back and allowed the door to glide shut behind him.

*

Wisps of smoke curled skywards, drifting sporadically with the downdraft of traffic trundling by. Cars and buses splashed sedately through puddles. Windscreen wipers squeakily smeared the remnant drizzle. Bozzer leant his head back onto the cool polished granite, pressing his bare arms onto its surface, his skin leaching the cool sensation. He lifted a hand robotically, took another contemplative pull on the roll-up stub, holding the smoke in his lungs for several seconds.

'Mister Johnson?'

Bozzer exhaled slowly. He turned, his glazed eyes blinking at Doctor Mario.

'You need to come. Now, please …'

*

Bozzer stepped into Madge's room. Simon stood by the window, his mobile phone clamped to his ear. He turned, glanced dismissively at Bozzer, still engrossed in his conversation. 'Relax, Francis. This is *me*. I got them originally, I can get them back …'

Doctor Mario held the door open to allow his nurses to enter. Bozzer glanced between Simon and the first nurse, fussing around Madge's bed, unplugging monitoring equipment.

Simon listened for a moment, a thin smile creasing his pursed lips. 'Excellent. I'll be in touch. Ciao.' He flicked his wrist, snapping the protective cover over his smartphone. Then he buried both hands in his pockets and flexed his wrists, flaring the crumpled cotton as he leant back, popping his spine and wriggling tension out of his shoulders.

'You're looking far too smug to be safe.'

'From what? You play by my rules now, hotshot.'

Bozzer followed Simon's eyes as he flitted them at Madge. 'Meaning …?' He watched the nurses complete detaching the monitoring equipment. The older one nodded at Doctor Mario, then released the brake on the bed's wheels. Doctor Mario latched the door open and stepped aside to allow the bed to be wheeled out.

'What's happened, why are you moving her?' Bozzer glared at Simon, who flexed up on his toes, whistling leisurely.

'Oh, they're not moving her far … only to reception.'

'Why?'

'She's being released.'

Bozzer turned to Doctor Mario, who dropped his eyes, offering a tiny shrug. 'I'm sorry Mister Johnson. I tried to argue for Madeline to stay, but …'

Simon held up his thumb and first finger, rubbed them gleefully together. 'No moolah, sunshine – no médico. *Comprende?*'

'No. You can't. You wouldn't.'

'Wouldn't, shouldn't …' Simon shrugged, 'done.' He raised his chin, twitched his downturned lips into a *such is life* pout, flicking his eyes at the ceiling. 'Never trust someone your friends have shafted.'

'That's it? Your conscience gonna handle that?'

'Chaos and cash, my friend, never have a conscience. I'll be in the hospital canteen for the next twenty minutes, enjoying a double hit of caramel mocha. You need a hand figuring out what happens next to Princess Madeline, you come find me. Or, go it alone. It's your choice. I'm sure there's another empathetic and generous sponsor out there with deep pockets.' Simon lifted his wrist, made a show of squinting at his watch. 'But make sure you find your new guardian angel fast. Call me uninformed, but Madeline doesn't look the picture of health right now.'

Simon waltzed past Bozzer. He virtually skipped through the doorway, his tuneless whistle echoing down the corridor.

*

'You're a fucking snake.'

Simon glanced up from scrolling through commands on his smartphone and considered Bozzer through narrowed eyes. 'Right now, dingo dick, I'm *your* snake. Sit down, have a coffee. We've got a lot to discuss.'

Bozzer held Simon's stare for a long moment, then shook his head wearily and pulled out a chair. He sank down at the table, opposite Simon. 'I can't believe this crap. What about Madge? Her treatment …'

'They'll keep an eye on her, for an hour.' Simon glanced at his watch. 'Make that forty-five minutes.'

'Then what?'

'There's other private hospitals in Buenos Aries. Take your pick. Unless, we strike a new deal.'

Bozzer slumped his elbows onto the table and crumbled in the seat. 'Haven't you creamed in enough already to—'

'*Enough?* What dippy-hippy planet are you on, chief? This is show *business*. I have overheads, investors.'

'The deal was—'

'The deal was with those same-name waterfall fuck-buddies. So where's my exclusive interview, reality travel-mate documentary? Maddie isn't the only injured party here – I'm bleeding hard currency.'

Bozzer sank his head into his hands, deflating into a hunched-up posture. 'You fucking arsehole,' he said in a muffled voice.

'Yeah. And …?'

Bozzer rubbed his eyes and slowly lifted his head up. 'What is it you want me to do?'

*

Bozzer stared down at Madge. His shoulders lifted a tiny bit higher with each electronic beep as the nurse reconnected the monitoring equipment and array of tubes and sensor wires.

'This is good, much better,' said Doctor Mario. He smiled at Bozzer, clasping his shoulder.

Bozzer continued to stare at Madge, his breathing settling, shadowing her own light, regular rhythm. He sank his hands into his pockets, slowly shaking his head. 'I had to scrape together the cash for my travel insurance. I deliberated, thinking *It won't happen to me*. But we're not lucky like that, my family … don't s'pose she gave it a thought. Her trip wasn't planned, it just sorta happened.'

Doctor Mario studied the heartrate monitor, then noted the readings on a clipboard chart, which he replaced at the end of the bed. 'She is lucky, to have you and your friends.' He leant over Madge and gently lifted an eyelid, pointing a pen torch, scrutinising.

Bozzer watched Madge's finger twitch. 'She moved – is she coming round?'

'Soon … maybe a day or two. She is doing well.' The Doctor accepted a small squeezy bottle from the nurse and dripped fluid into Madge's eye. 'This is to keep them from drying.'

Bozzer nodded. 'Can she hear me? I read about some coma patients being aware …'

'Most patients wake with no sense of time. Three days, three weeks, three months … it will be as if no time has passed. But some do remember conversations, others have dreams. Very occasionally, they are immersed in memories.' He glanced over at Bozzer. 'You have been together long?'

'Seven or eight weeks. But travel time is …'

'Intense, yes?'

Bozzer nodded.

'Then she may be enjoying exotic faraway places, while she waits to wake up.' Doctor Mario trickled a droplet into Madge's other eye, then shone his pen torch. The light danced across her pupil. 'Or perhaps she will recall your time together, and be comforted by these fond recollections.'

*

The light flickered, distant yet bright, forming a halo of yellow and orange around the perimeter of a small, glowing sphere. Like a miniature sun radiating red, orange and bluey-green tints at the fringes. The colour spectrum glinted and dispersed, leaving a brief kaleidoscope of watery rainbow colours, ebbing away into the darkness. Something familiar lingered, like a distant memory perhaps. Tantalisingly vivid, yet not quite within reach … as if hovering at the edge of her subconscious, waiting to be reclaimed …

Two

Soft moisturised fingertips with immaculately manicured nails slowly rotated the gold ring, until the finely polished stone reappeared. She drew her hand closer, peering at the cool turquoise, yellow and azure reflections of light dancing within the diamond's precise, rigid contours.

A girl's best friend, or ...

'Maddie?'

Her head lifted, richly dyed shoulder-length blonde hair trailing over hazel eyes. She swept the strands behind her ear, squinted and replaced the sunglasses on her nose. Beyond the row of sun loungers and parasols, tiny waves swooshed. Miniature white frothy bubbles were sucked into the fine ivory-coloured sand, leaving clear pastel-blue water drifting lazily back a few feet, into the deeper twinkling shades of turquoise.

'I'm saying ... the trouble with you, Madeline, is you don't see beyond your own little bubble.' Rupert Sullivan squeezed a dollop of creamy white suntan lotion onto his belly. He scooped the blob out of the folds of his skin, smearing it across his stomach in a repetitive squelching motion. 'The rules of *engagement* have changed. Tradition has had its day.'

Maddie turned away from the gently sloping shoreline, allowing her gaze to traverse up the perfect bleached white sand and palm tree-fringed beach. She watched ridges of gooey froth form between his chubby fingers as he smeared lotion across his business entertainment gut.

'I'm confused ... marriage is *all about* tradition, isn't it?'

Rupert snapped the cap back on the suntan lotion. 'It's a contract, Maddie, with stipulations and penalty clauses, just like any other. And I have expectations – don't you?'

Maddie stared at her reflection in the greeny-yellow tint of his wraparound Oakleys. She turned away, frowning behind her classically styled sunglasses. 'Of course I do. Conventional expectations. Anything else would feel a bit clinical.'

'Not clinical. *Sensible.*'

She looked away, drifting her gaze out over the vast expanse of sea. 'So let's discuss – you go first.'

Maddie glanced back. She watched his hands work the remaining lotion into his wobbly thighs. 'I thought the vows would take care of our expectations. Love, honour—'

'Obey?'

'*Respect.* Like normal people, entering into a lifelong commitment.'

'Bit outdated.' Rupert didn't look up from his stooped posture as he rubbed lotion into his shins. 'I mean, sure, we can nod our head to all that traditional nonsense, for our family and friends. But between us, we could agree to a more …' Rupert straightened and hunched forwards, peering over the top of his Apollo 13 shades. '… relevant arrangement.'

Maddie stared at him. 'What sort of more *relevant* arrangement?'

'Something contemporary. More reflective of the … how can I put this delicately? *Openness,* of modern society.'

She swallowed, wincing at the dryness in her throat. 'Openness …?' she croaked.

'Sure.' Rupert smiled, swung his hairy legs speckled with white globules off the sun lounger and perched on its edge, his basketball-size belly hunched over his lap. 'Openness, Maddie, equals marital longevity. It allows us to avoid future arguments over money, lifestyle, custody of the kids … all the middle-age divorce crap we'd have to deal with if one of us accuses the other of infidelity.'

'You want a *get out of jail free* card?'

Rupert smiled and cocked his head, gazing at her over the top of his sunglasses. 'I'm merely suggesting a more pragmatic approach, before we sign on the dotted line.'

He flicked his legs back onto the padded lounger and lay back, stretching his arms skywards, linking his hands behind his head. Maddie stared at him. A cold shiver twitched through her spine, causing her to wrench her eyes away, panning her gaze out across the beach.

An attractive bronzed couple in skimpy swimming costumes sauntered past, water lapping against their ankles. Maddie watched the couple link hands as they strolled. Beyond them, farther around the sandy bay, a young Thai family relaxed on faded beach towels. The parents maintained a keen interest in their two children, delighting in their play with effortless, toothy smiles. Farther away from the water, partially shrouded in the palm tree border, an older European gentleman lay face-down on a fully horizontal sunbed. A nubile Thai girl straddled across his back, massaging his shoulders. Maddie allowed her gaze to linger, watching the man lift a hand, brushing it against the girl's thigh. Inappropriate contact, or perhaps … *contract.* She shuddered, forcing her eyes to move on, sweeping them away to the horizon.

'Pragmatism, for marriage vows …' She sighed, slowly shook her head.

Rupert flashed her his charming, dimple-cheek smile. 'Why not?' His smile ebbed away, eyes becoming sad and sincere. 'I promised *him* …'

'I know,' Maddie said quietly, halting the rhythm of a faint nod. She glanced away, her curiosity drawn to a pair of teenage travellers humping rucksacks across the beach. She watched them pick a spot and shrug off their packs. The girl removed a red and white polka-dotted bandanna, kicked away her flip-flops then peeled off her crumpled tee-shirt and faded cut-off denim shorts, revealing a bikini. She sank down onto the sand next to her lean and muscular companion.

'We need to be more flexible, in our partnership,' said Rupert softly. He studied Maddie for a moment, then sank back and closed his eyes, luxuriating in absorbing the sun's warmth. 'Set out some mutually advantageous benefits.'

'No doubt balanced in your favour …'

Rupert pushed up on one elbow, pursed his lips and tilted his sunglasses down his nose. 'Genuinely, Maddie, this isn't about *that* issue.'

Her eyes darted over to briefly meet his.

'I'm trying not to be insensitive, but it's a concern. A guy's got to … you know, have a *release.*'

Maddie studied the sand between them, the familiar sensation of prickly heat rushing up her neck. Rupert reached out, gently, carefully placing his palm on her arm.

'The sensitive stuff aside, we need each other. To share all of this …' He lifted his hand, swept it in an all-encompassing semi-circle. 'I don't do well without your companionship. And you benefit from the familiarity of *us*. It's a good balance. It's comfortable.'

'I'm not as reliant on you as you think, Rupert.'

'You sure about that?' he said softly. 'I provide stability, Maddie, have done for years.' He lowered his voice to a murmur. 'Please, just recognise my needs, is all I ask.'

Maddie shrugged a cardigan over her shoulders and drew it around her Eres one-piece swimsuit, turning away from him. Her interest drew back to the teenage travellers, making themselves comfortable on towels spread out on the sand.

'I'm just being realistic, Maddie. And honest.'

After a few seconds studying her silence, Rupert twisted round to follow her gaze, homing in on the teenage backpackers. He watched them share a bottle of beer. 'You travel through life with significant baggage, Maddie. You're not carefree, like they are.'

She bit her lip, turned sharply towards him. 'I could be ...'

He shook his head. 'No. You're locked into this life. *That* designer label swimsuit, all your fancy catwalk clothes, a handcrafted one and a half carat diamond engagement ring ... it's a life of cosseted luxury, Maddie. It's a million miles away from those two, their travellers' way of life.'

'I don't need your interpretation of *my* life, Rupert.'

'You sure about that? You can't live any other way, Maddie. It's in your DNA—'

'Rubbish! I don't revel in it like you do – the champagne lifestyle, oozing through your pores.' Maddie held up her hand, waggled her ring finger. *'This* is *your* life—'

'Which you benefit from.'

'Yes, but—'

'You want to be like them?' Rupert arched his head towards the young travellers, lying back on the beach, soaking up the sun. 'You think you can party like a teenager, live on cheap beer and sleep in sleazy hostels?'

Maddie shrugged. 'Sometimes, yes.'

'You're deluded. You envy their freedom, but you wouldn't last a week on that sort of budget. Here or at home.'

She crossed her arms across her chest. 'Of course I would.'

Rupert sniggered and shook his head. He used his middle finger to ease his sunglasses down, offering his other hand to her, palm facing down. 'Wanna bet?'

Maddie eyed his outstretched hand. She lifted her chin up to his amused, dimpled smile and glanced at her multi-coloured reflection in his shades, perched off-kilter on the end of his nose. She flicked her eyes away.

He withdrew his hand and pushed his sunglasses up, laying back, returning his clasped fingers behind his head. 'Didn't think so. No micro-budget backpacking aspirations are *ever* going to be shoehorned into an eight hundred and fifty quid pair of Jimmy Choos.'

A screech farther down the beach drew Maddie's attention away from Rupert's victorious grin. She watched the teenage girl splashing through the shallow water in the skimpy bikini, her hot-blooded male companion chasing her. He took a few more lunging strides before scooping her up, both of them tumbling into deeper water.

She sighed and reached under the sun lounger for her thick, glossy paperback.

*

Maddie planted her elbows on the teak counter and hunched over her pear-shaped margarita glass. She allowed her gaze to drift around beneath the beach bar's thatched reed roofline. She blinked at the fine shafts of light filtering through gaps in the uneven contours of the spindly bamboo walls, the sun sinking towards the distant horizon. Aquamarine colours mingled and shimmered across the tiny ripples of a near-flat calm sea.

So beautiful. And yet—

She glanced behind her at a drunken cheer from the murky depths of the bar. Rupert yanked his hands over his head, whooping and posturing, spinning a pool cue through shards of sunlit cigarette and marijuana smoke. He lost his grip, sending the cue clattering against the side of the shabby, stained-cloth pool table.

So soulless.

Maddie shook her head, turning back to slump her arms beside the margarita, her head just high enough to sip the weak concoction through a stripy straw. She sighed and reached into her bag, fished out her book.

Who does this?

She fanned through the pages without stopping at the leather bookmark.

Who is so bored on a night out that they bring a book with them?

Raucous laughter echoed across the beachfront. Maddie glanced over to see the girl from the beach with the red and white bandanna stagger into the bar, her arm draped around her male companion. She wore the same crumpled tee-shirt, jean-shorts and flip-flops. They had the same *ease* with each other. Maddie covertly flicked her eyes between her book and the young travellers weaving through the cluster of tables, noting their relaxed smiles. The girl staggered sideways, both giggling as he reached out and steadied her. Maddie flinched, kept her eyes glued to the book as the couple plonked down on nearby barstools.

The girl braced her palms flat on the bar. 'This world, has gotta stop moving.'

'You rock *my* world, Lizzy,' said her male friend.

The girl rolled her eyes, then exaggerated a long steadying intake of breath. She turned and winked at Maddie, exhaling. 'Hi, I'm Liz. What's the cocktail …?'

Maddie wrinkled her nose at the waft of alcohol. She attempted a polite smile, looking away to avoid a lingering, salivating stare from Liz's companion.

'It's a bit sickly, actually – excuse me.' Maddie eased off the bar stool, squinting through the dim pockets of light and wisps of cigarette smoke being swooshed into random, swirling cloud patterns by Rupert's spinning pool cue.

'Posh bitch,' a voice rasped behind her.

Maddie frowned and half-turned back to the bar, catching a sideways leer from the male traveller. She flinched as the opening riff to AC/DC's *Highway to Hell* blasted through the bar, distorted and juddering through battered speakers.

'YeeaaAHHHH!' Rupert wrenched the cue to his side and sank down onto one knee in a guitar hero posture. He snatched his head up and down in time with the raucous guitar rhythm. 'What an intro!' He swung his arm in a wide circle, pausing with each rotation to wrench his fingers against his imaginary electric guitar. He sidled up to a seventeen year old Thai girl who delighted in cosying into his back, mirroring Rupert's one-man rock god display, gyrating her hips behind his.

Maddie lurched, mid-step, her stomach clenching. She glanced at Rupert as she hurried past the smog of dishonour, heading for the toilets.

She pushed the bamboo cubicle door shut and sank down onto the toilet seat.

Bastard!

Maddie rubbed her eyes with her palms, hoisted her shoulder bag onto her lap and withdrew the book, leafing through the pages, scanning the text's reassuring familiarity.

Deep breath ...

Bastard!

Deep breath ...

The sound of flip-flops outside the cubicle door clack-clacked through her concentration. A pause, then: 'Hello in there, um ... *book girl.*' Liz stifled a hiccup. 'Oops, s'cuse me. Sorry about Anton – sometimes he's a prick.'

Maddie held her breath.

If I just keep quiet, maybe she'll—

'That guy, by the pool table ... your boyfriend, or husband? The rock star wannabe.'

Maddie tucked the paperback into her bag and gingerly opened the door.

'Got you a cold beer,' said the teenage traveller, smiling at her and holding a glass of amber liquid. 'To drink, or chuck over him.'

'Oh, thanks. That's very, er ... considerate of you.' Maddie stood up and reached out to accept the glass.

'It's the local brew – he's not worth the good stuff.' Liz winked and turned to walk out.

'Thank you. I'm Maddie, you're ... *Liz?*'

'Yup, that's me.' Liz offered her hand. They shook awkwardly, both having to shuffle to one side to allow another girl to enter the washroom.

'You look like you need a proper drink.'

Droplets of condensation trickled down the glass, cooling her fingers. She studied Liz's raised eyebrows and twitch of mischief flickering across her lips. Maddie found herself slowly nodding.

*

'Having fun, Rupert?' Maddie yelled above the pounding music.

Rupert turned, straightening up from his attentive stoop, hastily dropping his arm off the Thai girl's shoulder.

'Maddie, hi babe. This is—'

'A bad idea?'

Rupert's stare glazed over. He rolled his saucer-sized eyes, blinking rapidly and trying to pull focus back on Maddie. 'Noooo. Nothing … sins … sinis—'

'Sinner? Sicko? *Sinister?*'

'Erm … yeah. That one.' Rupert swayed on his feet. His head lolled back and forth, eyes twitching, flitting without focus around the bar.

Maddie held up the glass of beer. 'Too much of this, per chance? I'm going for a girly chat with Liz, over there. You're not invited.' She raised the glass to her lips and drained half the cool liquid, closing her eyes as it slipped down. 'Mmm … not bad, for a local brew.'

Splosh!

Rupert staggered back, lifting up his hands to shield his face, far too late to avoid a soaking. Maddie turned and strolled away, placing the empty glass on the bar, to collective whoops and cheers. Rupert's uncoordinated attempt to wipe the sticky liquid from his eyes caused him to lose balance. He clattered to the floor, arms flailing.

'Med-a-lion …! Come bock, meh …'

Maddie glanced over her shoulder. Rupert lay crumpled against a speaker, his woozy, lopsided grimace slowing her exit. She stopped walking, turned to stare at him, deliberating.

Liz linked her arm under her elbow. 'He'll be making no sense for hours.'

Liz steered Maddie through the tables of seated drinkers, out onto the beach. They kept walking until the music and amusement had faded behind them. 'I don't know who looked more shocked, him or you.'

'Me, probably. I'm in big trouble tomorrow.'

'Hey, tomorrow is another adventure.'

A male voice called 'Hey Liz, what's the plan …?'

Liz glanced over her shoulder at Anton. 'Gotta bounce, Ant-man, girlie talk.'

'But it's our last night together. I've got the good stuff,' he protested, holding up two bottles of imported Heineken.

'It's early, we'll catch up later.'

Three

Maddie rattled the empty shot glass down on the bar. She winced as the fiery liquid worked its way down her throat. She slouched down on the stool, flinching at the lack of back support, causing her to jerk her hands out, bracing her palms flat on the sticky bar. 'Whoa …'

'More drink!' yelled Liz. She slid their empty shot glasses across the counter and wiggled her bottle of beer, signalling to the barman.

'Too much already …'

'Drink, or be gone!'

Maddie groaned and shook her head. Liz studied her for a moment, then pointed to her diamond ring. 'Engagement?'

'Yes, but upside down. Rupert calls this holiday our sunny-moon. He couldn't get the time off work, after. Some big project he's working on.'

'So when's the wedding?'

'Six weeks' time.'

'Wow. You still up for it?'

Maddie stared at Liz. She opened her mouth to say something like *'Of course, why wouldn't I be …'* but instead a deep frown creased her forehead. She took a swig of beer, dropped her gaze to her hands, concentrating on fiddling with the bottle's label. 'I think so … I mean, it's all planned. I don't really have a choice, not this close.'

Liz regarded Maddie with a steely focus. 'You *always* have a choice, hon. You think you're tied in, but,' Liz closed her thumb and forefinger around Maddie's ring finger, lifting it off the bar, 'till death do you part … that's epic. It needs to be respected, by *both* of you. Is he gonna make that solemn promise, and keep it?'

Liz maintained her fixed stare, tracking Maddie's eyes as they tried to dart away. 'Cos based on the three and a half seconds I've known you, I gotta say,' she waggled Maddie's ring finger, 'this ain't got no fairy-tale parachute.' Liz released her grip, dropping her hand.

Maddie slumped further over the bar, avoiding eye contact. 'It's a good life with Rupert,' she mumbled. 'I'd be a fool to pass it up.'

Liz took a swig from her bottle of Singha. 'You gonna feel the same in six months' time?' She studied Maddie's troubled expression and noncommittal shrug. 'I need a wee. Then I'll walk you back to your hotel. Okay?'

Maddie nodded, focused on peeling the label off her beer bottle as Liz shuffled off the stool and tottered off.

*

Moonlight glistened on the calm sea. Barely a ripple of inch-high surf gently swooshed on the warm sand. Multi-coloured lights twinkled from the sporadic row of thinly thatched beach bars, hugging the treeline. An eclectic mix of music at different volumes competed with resonating insect sounds. Maddie's walking pace slowed to an amble.

'You okay?' Liz asked.

Maddie shrugged, scooping up sand between her toes. 'Difficult to say, after so much to drink.' She half-smiled and shuffled on, sand flicking off her sandals. 'How do you manage, travelling all the time?'

'Financially?'

Maddie nodded.

'Easy. The expensive bit is getting here. The rest is oh-so-cheap …' Liz flicked her eyes over Maddie's elegant dress, expensive jewellery and designer sandals, '… if you're prepared to rough it. I get by on twenty dollars a day.'

Maddie considered this for a moment. 'But that's about a hundred pounds a week.'

'Yep.'

'How is that possible?'

Liz flicked her roll-up stub across the beach and blew smoke above her head, then turned to scrutinise Maddie. 'You've not travelled much, have you?'

'I've been fortunate to have visited several countries, with Rupert …'

'I mean properly travelled. No glitzy five-star air-conditioned hotels with truffles on the pillow. Boots, backpack and a tight budget.'

Maddie shrugged.

'What gives with this contract Robert wants you to sign?'

'Rupert.'

Liz waved her hand. 'Whoever.'

'The agreement ... I suppose it's mostly about moral flexibility.'

'He shags around, while you're the dutiful wife?'

Maddie nodded vacantly. 'I accept any potential indiscretions. In return I enjoy a comfortable lifestyle.'

'S'pose it could work, if you wanted to dabble too. A friend of mine back home has an open relationship.'

'It's not a two-way street.'

Liz stopped walking. She turned sharply to face Maddie. *'What?'*

'It's one-way traffic. He made that very clear.'

'Figures. You gonna cope with that? No offence, but you don't seem battle-hardened.'

Maddie glanced over at a nearby beach bar. Her eyes lingered on the other drinkers. Most seemed to be older men, quietly single – *supposedly*. Tucked away on their own in shady corners or in small groups. Many of them enjoying the attention of young Thai girls. She turned away, acid spiking in her stomach.

'I did live a little, a few years ago. But now is ...' Maddie shook her head, attempted a smile, her features clouding over. 'Different.' She dawdled on for a moment, then turned to Liz, unable to hold eye contact for more than a second or two. 'How does your relationship work, with Anton?'

'*Relationship?* That's a bit heavy.'

'Aren't you flying home tomorrow?'

Liz nodded, momentarily glazing over.

'You going together, or ...'

Liz rolled her eyes and looked away. 'We're on the same plane to Bangkok, then he's on a different flight to Copenhagen.'

'Oh. What does he think about your companionship ... status?'

Liz shrugged. 'We had the normal understanding when we hooked up. When it's time, we go our separate ways.'

'That seems a little calculated.'

'It's the travellers' code – universally accepted.'

'Is he going to be okay with that?'

Liz cradled a cigarette paper into a V shape. She sprinkled in tobacco and delicately rolled it into a neat tube, taking a moment before replying. 'I guess we'll have the conversation.'

'Oh. How will that go?'

Liz's eyes began to mist over, the emotion contained by rapid blinking. She turned away briefly, then swivelled round on her heels, facing Maddie. 'When it's time … one last passionate, lingering kiss. I'll say something like: "You're so cute …" A hug, then, "Thank you. Someday, in another time and place we should look each other up, remember the good times." One final kiss, on the cheek this time, then I turn walk away.' Liz held her earnest expression for a long moment, then relaxed into a grin and winked at Maddie.

Wow, you've done that before.

'The last kiss on the cheek, representing closure – lovers becoming friends?'

'You got it.' Liz glanced at her watch and lit her roll-up. 'Still so many sober hours before I get on a plane. You sure you want to head back to the old man?'

Maddie groaned. 'No, but—'

'I'm thirsty … don't make me drink alone.' Liz alternated her gaze between Maddie and the nearest beach bar.

'I can't. I'd be in so much trouble with Rupert.'

Five minutes to the hotel room.

'You need to wise up, Maddie. Trust me, it's us girls who have the real power.'

'I'm not with you.'

'It's supply and demand – they want what we can give them.'

'You're talking about sex?'

'I'm talking about *pleasure*. Men are beholden to their balls – so who's actually in control of a relationship?'

'Us …?'

'Abso-bloody-lutely! They know this, and it frustrates the hell out of them.'

Maddie glanced down at her sandaled foot, sifting particles of sand through her toes.

Five minutes until …

'I guess … but with Rupert, there isn't that sort of hold over him.'

'Sure about that? No sucky-fucky-for-five-bucky?'

Maddie's brow crumpled into a frown. 'He's not like that. It's … complicated.'

'Is it? Come on, what about another drink? Little trouble, lots of trouble …' Liz exaggerated a shrug, opening her palms to the sky. 'What difference does it make?

'I suppose one more wouldn't hurt—'

'Attagirl!' Liz grinned, watching the corners of Maddie's mouth twitch upwards as she fought to suppress a mischievous smile. 'Come on, I'm buying.' Liz steered Maddie across the beach towards the nearest bar. 'You got a wild hen night planned?'

'Oh, pretty low-key. A movie followed by a pizza and glass of wine with some girlfriends …'

Liz rolled her eyes, nudging Maddie playfully. 'How old are you?'

'Twenty-six.'

'Twenty-frigging-six?! This is your last night in Thailand, on your pre-wedding, sunny-funny, *lack-of-honey*-moon slash life sentence, and all you have to look forward to is droopy pizza and watered-down vino?'

Maddie shrugged. 'I guess so …'

'Then what the hell are you still doing sober? Walk this way, Cinders – to oblivion and beyond!'

Four

Jody's eyelids flickered. She forced her eyes to open, barely enough to allow a mere sliver of light in before she scrunched them shut, ducking her head under her arms.

'That's one for your Facebook page,' said Barry, lowering his fancy-pants camera.

'Turn out the light,' she mumbled, crunching her knees up to her chest, bare thighs squeaking on the row of plastic seats. His hand reached out, a stubby finger nudging her shoulder, prompting her to squeal and recoil further. 'Oy, enough!'

'Last bus outta here, Jody. Big bang-bang lights await …'

'No way – too early.'

'Up, up, up!'

Jody groaned loudly, swivelling her hips and kicking her booted feet down onto the floor. She sat up, yawning and rubbing her eyes, forcing them open one at a time. 'Lights – too bright.'

Barry Johnson grinned and wafted a disposable coffee cup under her nose. 'The Vietnamese stuff's better, you've got that to look forward to. But a swig'll get you on the road. You can zone out again once we're rolling.'

Jody fumbled for the cup and lifted it up to her lips. 'What time is it?'

'Too early for bed, too late to be without a hot date.'

'Which in Barry-speak means …?'

'Two-thirty.'

'Wonderful.'

'In six hours it will be. Cold beer, comfy mattress. Setting Baz's budgie free in Bangkok.' Barry began a slow hip-thrusting rotation. She handed the coffee cup back, shaking her head at his gyrating rhythm.

'Where do you get so much energy from?'

Barry grinned. He raised the coffee cup in one hand, weighing his tobacco tin in his other palm like a set of scales. 'A little bit of this, a pinch of that and the occasional glug of grog.' He reached down and hoisted a backpack strap onto his shoulder, flicking a mop of dirty almond and gingery-blonde hair away from his eyes. 'Follow me, Jody. Your comfortable cattle-class coach awaits.'

Jody pushed unsteadily up to her feet and hooked her foot around her rucksack, dragging it out from under the row of chairs. 'Could use a hand with this ...'

Barry clicked his own rucksack's belt buckle together and grinned. 'You pack it, you gotta stack it.'

'What happened to chivalry?'

'What about that? Aussie girls just get on with it.'

'I'm not Australian.'

'Nope. Bummer.' He turned away and began to wander off towards the bus pulling into an adjacent bay, its headlights swooping past him.

Jody cursed, then knelt down and hauled the backpack onto her shoulders, grunting under its weight. Her legs twitched, almost buckling as she followed him at half-speed across the polished concrete floor, bathed in artificial fluorescent brightness. The soles of her walking boots squeaked in short, stomping steps, each one adding an extra fraction of an inch to the width of Barry's smile.

*

Rupert stood at the foot of the sumptuous queen-size bed, focused on his smartphone screen. He glanced up as the figure beneath the sheets twitched, sleep-yawned, then rolled over, pulling the covers. He shook his head, finished off the message and sent it, then placed the phone in his pocket. He scanned the palatial hotel room, a thin smile developing as he spied a welcome pack of leaflets on the desk. He rolled one into a cone-shaped loudhailer and crouched down beside the headboard.

'It's time to get up – its eight o'clock in the morning. It's time to get up – it's EIGHT O' CLOCK IN THE MORNING!'

'Arrrhhh!' Maddie rolled away from his booming voice, burying her head under the pillow. She gasped for air as spinny-room syndrome returned with a vengeance.

Rupert manoeuvred closer, repeating his wake-up call. Maddie yelped and jerked away, the motion sending her tumbling off the side of the bed, landing on the floor in a bedding bundle.

'You git!'

Rupert stepped around the bed and yanked the curtains open, flooding the room with dawn's first rays of piercing light. 'Wake up! Wake up! Wake up!'

'Rupert, please …' Maddie scrunched her face, attempting to squint through the tiniest gap in her eyelids.

'IT'S TIME TO GET UP!'

'Enough!' Maddie clamped a hand across her damp forehead, breathing hard. 'Ugh. Never again.' She eased up onto an elbow, clacking her sandpaper-dry tongue away from the roof of her mouth, wincing at the raw sensation in her throat. 'Would you mind closing the curtains, please,' she croaked, 'it's awfully bright.'

'Where the bloody hell did you get to last night?'

Maddie rolled up onto her side, glancing up at him through gummy eyelids. 'Girls' night out,' she rasped.

'With whom?' Rupert stepped forwards, looming over her, hands on his hips. A fine mist of alcohol-scented saliva drifted down on her.

'Funnily enough, with a girl called Liz. That's the point of a—'

'Sarcasm,' he muttered, stooping down to yank the thin duvet off of her, 'isn't an attractive quality in my future wife.'

'Rupert, this is unnecessary.' Maddie hunched over onto her hands and knees and pushed unsteadily up to her feet. She swayed, blinking rapidly, darting her puffy eyes around the room, trying to orientate herself.

Rupert took a step forwards to intercept her. 'This isn't acceptable behaviour—'

'Like you were setting such a good example last night?'

'Jesus, you stink!'

She blinked at him, at last finding a bleary-eyed focus on his unshaven cheeks and bloodshot eyes. 'Welcome to *my* world, Rupert. Wake up and take a long hard look in the mirror.' Maddie made to shuffle past him, but he stepped sideways, blocking her exit.

'Who were you with?'

Maddie jabbed a finger against his chest. 'Who were *you* with?'

'Mixing with the locals. Cultural integration.'

'Culture? More like *vulture!* You were draped all over her.'

Heat radiated off Rupert's chest, blood rushing to his face, flushing it red. He took a step closer. Maddie stumbled back against the wall.

'It's called being *friendly*. You could learn a lot about that.'

Maddie's shoulders slumped. She looked away from his scarlet face and bulging eyes. A bead of sweat trickled down her back. 'Rupert, please. Comments like that don't help.'

He let out a deep breath and lifted his eyes to the ceiling. 'Sorry,' he mumbled, stepping aside. He thrust his hands into his pockets. 'We're on a plane to Bangkok in three hours, you'd best go and get cleaned up. We'll talk about this later.'

*

Jody jolted awake at the bus's screeching brakes, the inertia sliding her forwards in the plastic seat, banging her knees into the backrest of the row in front. She yawned and peered up at Barry, sat staring out of the window between a gap in the thin, faded curtains.

'Are we there yet?'

He turned and grinned at her with his uneven, chipped-tooth smile, light dancing in his eyes despite the coach's gloomy interior. 'Almost. Welcome to a beautiful new day in downtown Bangkok.'

'Great. Colonial cheerfulness at … what time is it now?'

Barry twisted his wrist towards her. She squinted at the analogue display and groaned. He smiled and began to withdraw his hand.

'Hang on, I'm reading.' She peered at the red font below the plastic watch's O.T.S. brand name. 'My time, my decision. That's about right.'

He nodded. 'Couldn't resist. Best couple of bucks I've spent.'

'Aside from buying me that first beer, obviously,' she crooned.

'Yeah … and look at the trouble that got me into.' He winked at her and turned to glance back out between the gap in the curtain. Cars, trucks and buses crawled along in all three lanes, constantly being overtaken by scooters and small screeching motorbikes, nipping in and out of every conceivable gap in the traffic, no matter how impossibly small.

'Not yet, but I'm working on it,' she murmured.

*

Maddie swept her eyes up at the vast grey-steel lattice structure that supported the green tinted glass roof. She rotated her gaze down, slowly surveying the airport's vast utilitarian concourse, stifling a yawn by sipping a frothy takeaway latte. A mini-injection of caffeine with every taste – *lifesaver.*

'Come on, Maddie – keep up,' muttered Rupert.

Maddie shuffled forwards in the queue, wheeling her Samsonite suitcase up to his side. Her gaze returned skywards to the building's construction. A plane climbed overhead beyond the glass roof, undercarriage disappearing into its belly as it banked sharply.

The queue shuffled forwards. Maddie remained fixated on the plane.

Destination predetermined ...

'Madeline!' Rupert hissed, snatching her arm and dislodging the takeaway cup's lid, sloshing warm coffee over her wrist and thigh.

'Oh, great.' Maddie let go of her suitcase, placed the cup on top of it and shook droplets off her hand. She tried to wipe the dark liquid away from soaking into her dress, pausing to glare at Rupert, just in time to catch the tail end of his *serves you right* sneer. She removed a Kleenex from her shoulder bag and dabbed at her dress, trying to mop up the coffee. *No chance.*

Maddie lifted her eyes to gaze randomly around the airport concourse as she pressed the tissue into the stain. Other women stood queuing alongside their partners. Some looked preoccupied, or bored, others seemingly present yet appearing lost. But engaging in life …? Probably not.

A movement and dash of colour. Faster than the other shuffling figures, this traveller looked frantic. Liz sprinted across the concourse in a lumbering motion, her cumbersome backpack jiggling and swaying like a sporadic pendulum, flashing intermittent glimpses of her red and white polka-dotted bandanna. She skidded to a halt at the last check-in desk, a dozen queues away. Maddie's eyes narrowed. Awareness of other activity around her slowed to half-speed as she noticed three things in quick succession:

Only three passengers in front of Liz at her check-in queue.

The currency exchange booth's illuminated sign, at the far end of the concourse.

Her heart had instantly begun pounding on her chest cavity – LET ME OUT!

'I'm – going to – the – ladies,' Maddie stammered. She turned, made to hurry away, jerked to a stop by Rupert's hand shooting out to grasp her arm.

'There's toilets after check-in.'

'I can't wait.'

Rupert exhaled noisily. He released her arm and checked his watch. 'Be quick.'

Maddie nodded and yanked on the extendible suitcase handle, rolling its wheels.

'You don't need to take your case,' he said sharply.

She gestured at her coffee-stained dress. 'I need to change out of this … mess.'

Rupert glared at her. He clenched his jaw, deliberating. 'Five minutes. Go!'

Maddie turned and marched away, trailing the Samsonite behind her. She hurried through the throngs of passengers, pausing only to glance over her shoulder. Rupert stood facing away from her, preoccupied with his mobile phone. Maddie diverted from her direct route across the concourse to toss her coffee cup in the nearest litter bin.

'Liz!' Maddie weaved through the crowds, her suitcase zig-zagging wildly behind, a caffeine-induced grin fixated on her lips. Liz turned at Maddie's second shout. She beamed and threw her a hug.

'Hey Maddie, wild night!'

'I need to talk to you, in the loos – it's important!'

Liz glanced at the gap opening up in the queue as a passenger cleared the check-in desk ahead of her. 'Can it wait a few minutes—'

'No, it'll be too late – right now, please!'

Liz studied Maddie's puffy-eyed intensity for a moment, then nodded. She stepped to one side to look around the passengers in front of her and gestured to attract the attention of the check-in clerk. 'Excuse me, sorry. I need to go to the bathroom – how long do I have?'

'Five minutes, ten at the most. You'll have to hurry—'

'Great, thanks – please don't close, I'll be right back!' Liz grabbed Maddie's hand, turned to scan the concourse for the WC signs, then ran with her glamorous new friend as fast as their baggage would allow.

*

'Why can't we get a tuk-tuk?'

Barry pressed the lid back on his tobacco tin, the thin roll-up waggling between his lips as he spoke. 'Cos walking is healthier.'

'Says the man polluting his lungs.'

'The soul, Jody, is what we're exercising this morning. Bangkok is waking up. We get to save our wallets and stretch our imagination—'

'You can go walkabout later, I'm getting a ride. You're welcome to join me.'

Barry watched Jody stomp across the pavement to a tuk-tuk parked up in a side street. She gave the flimsy canopy struts a shove, rousing the young Thai driver who'd been curled up asleep on one of the bench seats.

'This is your dollar?' Barry called out, lighting his roll-up.

Jody shrugged off her backpack and shoved it into the rear seating area. 'S'pose so, tight arse.'

'Sweet. I'll reimburse you with my first royalty cheque.'

'Like I'm ever gonna see that. You coming?'

Barry chuckled, sauntered over to the tuk-tuk and offered his open hand to the driver. He removed the roll-up from his mouth with his other hand, gesturing for the driver to take a toke. 'Name's Barry.'

'Me, Scoot.'

'Scoot? Cool name. You fastest tuk-tuk in Bangkok?'

Scoot grinned. 'In Thailand! Much speed. Where you go?'

Barry flicked both his palms over and held them out to the side. 'Farang central, Scoot – the one and only Khoa San Road. My girl here needs a soft bed and a stiff … drink. So don't spare the dingo power.'

Scoot took a pull on the roll-up, then handed it back, his pupils dilating. He grinned. 'You want fast, yes?'

'Always – punch it!' Barry tossed his backpack onto the floor opposite Jody, lay a protective hand over the soft padded camera case hanging from a strap around his shoulder, and climbed into the tuk-tuk.

Jody reached out, plucked the smoking stub from Barry's fingers and took a puff, savouring the sensation. 'You gave our driver a happy smoke?'

'For sure. Keeps the price reasonable and accident damage treatable.' Barry winked at her and settled back on the bench seat opposite, trailing his arms along the backrest, a lopsided, gappy-tooth grin spreading across his unshaven face.

The uneven two-stroke rumbled into life with a metallic popping sound. Scoot twisted the throttle, catapulting the tuk-tuk out onto the main road, trailing oily smoke. He steered into an impossibly small gap between a taxi and flatbed truck spilling grain from wafer-thin sacks, amidst blaring horns and screeching brakes.

'Barry, you're a moron!' yelled Jody, clenching onto the seat slats with rigid fingers.

'When in Bangkok, babe!' he sniggered, clasping the camera case on his lap. He carefully unzipped it, his body swaying with the motion of Scoot's erratic steering. 'It's all about the ride!'

Barry whooped, lifting his bulky SLR digital camera, removing the lens cap and zooming in on Jody's wide-eyed – impact imminent – grimace. 'Smile like you mean it!' he shouted, pressing down on the shutter release button.

*

Maddie hurried past the toilet cubicles, heading for the row of sinks. She turned to face Liz, ignoring the other passengers filtering past, and took a deep unsteady breath, while simultaneously pulling strands of sweaty hair away from her eyes. 'How much to buy your traveller's life?'

'Living with my folks and a crappy admin job? You can have it for free.'

'Not that home life, *this* one.' Maddie pointed to Liz's battered backpack. 'Boots, clothes and a four-week travel itinerary – everything. My suitcase and cash in exchange. How much?'

Liz stared at Maddie. 'You calling his bluff …?'

'That, a double dare, or just a bloody-minded stupid whim – all crazy. But who cares – I'm twenty-friggin'-six years old!'

'Attagirl! You got more designer stuff in there?' Liz pointed at Maddie's Samsonite case.

'All the top brands, worth thousands! I'll swap the lot for a taste of proper travelling. You said it, Liz, I've already done the expensive bit, getting here.'

Liz glanced down at her watch, then stared at Maddie. She seemed to be mentally recalling all the important items in her backpack. 'I've got a few presents, some personal stuff. Those aside … I don't know, maybe two hundred quid?'

'Done! Swap your stuff over – I'll be back with the money in less than three minutes.'

'Eeeeek!' they screeched in unison, hugging quickly before Maddie broke off, thrust her suitcase keys into Liz's palm, then sprinted out of the bathroom as fast as her wobbly legs could carry her.

Five

The bored currency exchange clerk perked up at Maddie's flustered arrival. She processed the card payment and beamed as she counted off two hundred pounds in sterling. Maddie thanked her, grasped the debit card to yank it out of the keypad, then froze.

Idiot!

Twenty dollars a day, for thirty days is—

'Could I also have six hundred in US dollars, please?' she stammered, snatching short panting breaths while simultaneously clenching and opening her shaking, clammy hands.

Maddie burst back into the ladies washroom clutching the currency. Liz glanced up from her crouching position on the floor, hurriedly sifting through a pile of clothes, toiletries and travel paraphernalia emptied from her backpack.

'This is insane – I love it!' Liz squealed. She shoved three plastic bags of presents on top of the neatly folded clothes in Maddie's open suitcase, then began stuffing her clothes and other random items back into the rucksack.

'Two hundred pounds, as agreed!' Maddie thrust the notes into Liz's hand, then removed her shoulder bag and emptied the contents into a nearby sink. She removed everything of personal value: passport, purse, address book and mobile phone, cradling them in her twitchy hands. 'Help yourself to anything left. You're welcome to the shoulder bag too,' she said, fighting back a surreal feeling of detachment; that weird sensation of standing outside her own body, looking down. She frowned at the sound of her voice, echoing eerily around the tiled washroom.

'You want to keep anything?' asked Liz.

Maddie remained rigid, her mouth open, staring off into the distance.

'Maddie – you with me?'

She blinked rapidly. 'Yes, sorry. Of course.' She refocused on the Samsonite case, her heart pounding, hesitating as she tried to recall all the contents. 'Only my toiletries bag and swimsuit.'

'Coolio. We keep our underwear and swap everything else?'

'Agreed!' Maddie yanked open the nearest cubicle and leaned back against the door, hyperventilating.

Okay – I can do this ...

Maddie kicked off her Nicolas Kirkwood graffiti sandals, nudging them under the cubicle partition. Then she pulled her Alexander McQueen Obsession dress over her head, folding it neatly, her whole body trembling as she stooped down and passed it to Liz's waiting hands.

'Woo-hoo, cheers! Sooo soft ... two secs.'

'Wait! I spilled coffee down it, pick another dress from the suitcase—'

'No time, too much choice!'

Maddie jiggled in her French silk underwear, doing a silly flappy-arm chicken routine to combat the chilly air conditioning.

'Here!' Liz shoved her scrunched-up clothes under the partition.

Maddie held up the crumpled jean-shorts, blinking rapidly.

Can't do this!

'How you doing? Gotta hustle!'

Can't NOT do this! Okay ... this, is, reality!

Maddie wriggled her hips into Liz's faded shorts, pulled on the thick socks and hiking boots, then slipped the crumpled tee-shirt over her head. She wrenched the cubicle door open.

'Whoa!'

Maddie glanced past Liz's startled grin and stared at her own reflection in the mirror. Her cheeks puckered, oxygen sucked from her lungs.

Can't do this – can't do this – can't—

Liz leapt in front of Maddie's reflection. 'I gotta bounce, pronto!' Liz swiped her red and white polka-dotted bandanna from her head and pressed it into Maddie's hands. 'Let's hustle!'

Liz scanned the contents of the sink. She delved through the extensive make-up, then glanced at Maddie, who briefly broke away from staring in the mirror to nod. Liz scooped everything from the sink into the shoulder bag.

'Ready?' said Liz, searching for reassurance in their joint reflections.

Maddie flicked her eyes at her pale, painted-mannequin reflection. Doubt flinched in her eyes.

'Five seconds!'

Maddie gulped, dropped her gaze to the sink top. She yanked open the shoulder bag that had been hers less than five minutes previously, and rummaged through the contents. She clutched a wet wipe and hastily removed her artificial pigment, splashing cold water over her face to complete the transition. 'Okay, I'm ready—'

'Go, go, GO!'

Liz hoisted the backpack onto Maddie's shoulders, then grabbed her hand and began dragging her and the suitcase towards the washroom's exit. 'Jeez, this thing weighs a ton.'

Maddie slowed, glanced over at the row of mirrors. She gasped at her new scruffy clothes, shooting a look at Liz's reflection, elegant and sophisticated in *her* dress. 'I'm not sure about this, it's—'

'Too late!' Liz hauled Maddie out into the throng of passengers, threading through them as they legged it across the departure hall.

*

'Not exactly salubrious, is it?' Jody swept her listless eyes around the grubby room, its peeling grey paint, small double bed and shabby bedside cabinet. 'There's not even any hanging space.'

'For your clothes, or suicidal travel buddies?' said Barry with a lopsided grin.

'It's horrible.'

'It's cheap. Leaves more stash for the fun stuff.'

Jody shrugged off her rucksack and leant down to prod the mattress.

'Soon as you shut your eyes you won't care how shabby chic it is, you'll just be happy to get your head down. I'll see you later.'

'Where're you going?'

'The light's great. Gonna find some shades, snap some strangers.' Barry propped his backpack against the far wall and adjusted the shoulder strap on his camera case. 'I'll be back in a couple of hours, take you out for lunch.'

'But we've just got here—'

'Exactly. Sleep for you, stretching the soul for me. We'll both thank me for it later. Be good, and if you can't, be enlightened. See ya.' Barry lowered his head to kiss her, then ruffled her hair, dodged her grabbing hand, opened the door and left the room.

*

Maddie leant back against the structural pillar, eyes scrunched shut, focusing on taking deep, calming breaths. Behind her, Liz hurried across the concourse towards the budget check-in desk, thirty yards along from where Rupert stood, five passengers from the front of the line.

Maddie watched as he checked his watch then glanced over his shoulder, scanning the route across the concourse towards the toilets. 'Where *are* you, Maddie,' he muttered. He clasped his suitcase handle until the whites of his knuckles had bleached through his holiday tan, then yanked the case up to the couple stood in front of him. 'Damn you, Maddie. Don't you dare screw this up,' she heard him hiss through clenched teeth.

'Please, wait!' gasped Liz, running up to the check-in desk. She heaved the Samsonite suitcase onto the conveyor, just as the clerk switched off the overhead illuminated sign. 'Please ... *Alma,*' she added, spotting the airline clerk's nametag.

Alma looked Liz up and down, raised a mildly disapproving eyebrow, then sat back on her seat, punching commands into the computer keyboard. Liz shot a look behind her at the backpack lurking behind a pillar, then spun back round, grinning as she watched Alma label up the suitcase.

'Gate thirty-seven. You need to hurry.' Alma pushed Liz's passport and a boarding card across the desk.

'Yes ma'am – thank you!' Liz shot a discreet sideways glance over at Rupert, thirty feet away. She watched him scan the concourse behind her, before turning towards the front of his queue, stepping forwards in line. Liz dashed across behind him, making for the pillar where Maddie loitered.

'Close one! But hey, two hundred quid and a case full of designer booty happy. You okay?'

'Uh-huh ...'

'Walk with me to security. Got some stuff to tell you.'

Liz helped her to lift the rucksack onto her back, then linked her arm under Maddie's elbow, tugging her along at a fast walking pace. 'Be extra vigilant at night. Don't accept a drink from anyone unless you've seen its entire journey from the barman to your mouth, and never, ever, let that drink out of your sight. Okay?'

She glanced at Maddie who nodded, maintaining a rabbit-caught-in-headlights stare.

'What's your phone number?' Liz asked, rummaging through the shoulder bag, withdrawing her mobile phone.

Maddie rattled off her number, trance-like, while Liz concentrated on typing on the smartphone screen as they walked. Maddie's phone beeped to acknowledge the new message.

Liz halted by the entrance to passport control and threw her arms around Maddie's neck, hugging her tightly. 'You're a legend! Go find out what life is *really* all about – okay?'

Maddie opened her mouth. She swallowed, dry and gritty. Her arms trembled, breathing erratic. 'Can't – do – this—'

Liz stood back, clasped Maddie's hands and stared intently into her eyes. 'Yes. You. CAN. Trust in yourself – good luck!' Liz squeezed Maddie's hands, then turned and walked swiftly towards the customs official, holding out her passport and boarding card. Maddie stared after her.

I can still go back. Find Rupert, try to negotiate, and—

Maddie watched her sandals waltzing her dress away. Liz's hips gyrated awkwardly, unaccustomed to heels.

Negotiate what? False comfort with an openly adulterous husband …?

Maddie gulped in a lungful of cool, conditioned air, sweat running down from her armpits.

Is that truly what I want?

A hand touched her on the shoulder.

No!

Maddie screeched and spun round.

Anton visibly jumped back in shock, his eyes wide. 'I'm sorry – you look spookily like my friend. Really sorry to have startled you. Sorry … sorry.'

He backed away, his palms held aloft, darting his eyes around at the other passengers, some of whom had paused nearby to observe. A deep frown creased Anton's forehead as he turned away, scanning random faces in the crowd. He shot a glance back at Maddie, but she'd already turned to scurry away, weaving through the oncoming flow of human traffic.

Shit. Shit. Shit!
What am I doing?
Do I actually know …?
Rupert's not that bad. He's looked after me all this time and—

'No. You can't go back. Not yet,' she said aloud, hot blood flushing through her pores. She lowered her head, shying away from anonymous inquisitive faces, and stumbled onwards. She glanced up at the mechanical swooshing sound and slowed to a halt. Directly ahead, less than ten feet away, a set of large glass doors glided open, wafting humid, optimistic air through the climate-controlled atmosphere.

Trust in myself!

The sound of an electronic ping interrupted her inner wranglings. She checked her mobile phone, shuddering at the text message from Rupert:

Where the bloody hell are you?!

Shit. Shit. Shit.

Heart racing, palms sweating, Maddie twisted around, scanning the sea of faces at the far check-in desks. There. Left side, eleven o'clock. Average height, but carrying more surplus body weight. Rupert stood on tip-toe, peered over heads, surveying the crowds.

Shit, shit, sh—

Another message alert drew her attention back to the phone clutched in her hand. From Liz this time:

YOU CAN DO IT!
Taxis on ground floor. I stayed at Wild Orchid
Villas, near the Khoa San Road. I ignore the budget –
first and last day in a new country. Guidebook
in backpack pocket. 4 weeks perfect for Cambodia.
My route, in reverse. Be brave – you're a *real* traveller
now … GOOD LUCK!
Liz

Okay – I CAN do this—

Maddie's phone began to ring. Rupert's face jumped in bright bold colour onto the screen, launching Maddie's heart rate up another twenty beats. She wrenched her eyes across the concourse, peered out from beneath the bandanna, could see Rupert holding his hand to his ear, scanning the crowd.

Elevator, to your left ...

Maddie tilted her posture, shielding Rupert behind the backpack. She took several calming breaths, then hurried away from the sliding doors, staying parallel to the glass frontage.

Thump, thump, thump ...

Her heartbeat resonated around her head, like a fast-bouncing basketball echoing in a vast empty court. She placed a wobbly foot on the escalator's top step, lurching forwards. Safely aboard.

Don't look round. Don't look round. Don't—

Maddie's torso sank below the floor level, disappearing from Rupert's meerkat surveillance. *Thank God.* At the bottom of the escalator she followed the couple in front as they turned left, towards an identical set of automatic glass doors, swooshing open.

Last chance ...

Maddie scrunched her hands into tight fists, holding her breath as she stepped out of the cool, artificial airport atmosphere into the hot, sweaty, *what-the-hell-am-I-doing-here* Bangkok air. Her heart pounded. Right there, in the moment.

*

Barry stepped out of the gloomy corridor into a grey smog that filtered sunlight in hazy clumps over the chaotic Khoa San Road. Endless market stalls stretched out in front of dingy shops onto the tarmac, shaded beneath grubby heavy-duty canvas awnings. Above these, rectangular advertising banners had been strung across to the opposite side of the street, competing for attention with gaudy neon signs belonging to tattoo parlours, rooftop beer gardens, restaurants, hotels, beer brands and silversmiths. Anything and everything here, available twenty-four hours a day. Below the rigid signs and plastic banners, taxis, scooters, tuk-tuks and multicultural pedestrians mingled amongst vehicle exhaust smoke and steam from pork satays, sizzling on portable rectangular barbeques.

Barry lit his rollie and joined the throng. He plucked a map out of his cargo shorts and stopped to glance down, checking his route. He weaved around a parked scooter, narrowly avoiding a taxi. He waved cheerfully at the taxi's beeping horn and puffed contentedly, scrutinising the maze of options.

After a moment's deliberation, he pocketed the guide and strolled towards the sound of greater traffic intensity, of the motorised and human kind.

*

'Where you want go, lady?' asked the taxi rank supervisor, a smiling Thai woman dressed in a bright green and yellow outfit.

'Oh, right. Um …' Maddie reached for her phone and read out Liz's hotel instructions.

'Four hundred fifty Baht, okay lady? You go there.' The supervisor pointed at a bright pink taxi and its enthusiastic driver, who sprang into action, hurrying over to ease the backpack off Maddie's shoulders. She slumped into the back seat of the pink saloon and wiped her trembling palms on the denim shorts, then flattened her hands out on her thighs.

'You like football? Manchester United, Chelsea, Liverpool …' jabbered the driver in super-quick time. He shot her a toothy grin in the rear-view mirror as he steered through the traffic using his knees, simultaneously texting with one hand and re-tuning the car radio with the other.

'Football, me? No, but my fiancé likes …'

'Rooney. You like Wayne Rooney?'

Maddie met the driver's attentive eyes, darting at her in the mirror, and shook her head. 'No, I like Giggs – Ryan Giggs.'

'Ah, *Giggs!*' The taxi driver chattered away in a mixture of Thai and smatterings of English words and phrases, sprinkled liberally with names of prominent footballers. All the time he gestured with his hands while ducking and twitching his body in the seat as he weaved the car through the traffic, occasionally pausing to look at Maddie in the mirror. He tooted the horn at opportune moments, seldom placing a hand on the wheel until he needed to swerve across the traffic to join the main elevated expressway. The taxi wound its way through the tall buildings on the flyover, which basked sporadically in morning sunshine peeking through smoggy patches of polluted sky.

It's a new day. Promises of the unknown …

Maddie clutched her stomach as a jolt of bile threatened to force its way into the back of her throat. She glanced out of the window, quickly looking away again, shutting her eyes as a truck cut across in front of the taxi, inches from smashing into its side. A familiar ringtone fought for superiority over the taxi's music system. She glanced at the phone's screen. Rupert, again.

She rejected the call.

Okay, so this is surreal ... but the six hundred dollar question is – what the hell am I going to do next?

Six

'Sir ...?'

Rupert turned to face the check-in desk clerk. He lowered the phone from his ear and shook his head, exhaling hard through his nose. 'She's not answering.'

'What is the nature of your wife's problem?'

'She's a pain in the backside.'

'You wife is in pain? Does she have sickness?'

'Sick in the head,' Rupert muttered, fixated on the phone's screen, 'and she's not my wife ... *yet*.'

'Sir, we cannot hold the plane.'

'I know, I know. But I can't contact her. I need more time—'

'Sorry sir, no time. Please, you need to decide. You would like to check in, now?'

Rupert stared at her, hands on his hips, jaw clenched, inhaling in sharp snorting breaths. 'Damn you, Madeline. What the hell have you done?'

*

Shh-clitch.

That sound ... so reassuring, noble and *finite.* Barry's index finger lingered, keeping the shutter release button held down, activating the voice memo function. He murmured urgently as he relayed twenty truthful seconds of fast and fluid reactive observation, without premeditated sentence construction or censorship.

Memory Card 2. Pic 344
'Alone with vulnerability, anxious as the taxi leaves with her sensibility. Staring, statue-like at the hotel entrance, her well-travelled clothes and party-time bandanna – all authentic. Yet she does not *inhabit* this informed uniform, the clothes hang uneasily in stark contrast to her sparkly decoration. Appearing so obviously out of place here, highlighted perhaps by her underlying sense of fear ...'

Barry released his finger and lowered his bulky Nikon D2XS camera, cradling it as he shaded the screen with his palm and peered at the high definition image. 'Beauty.'

He glanced up to watch the woman break out of her trance and haul the backpack awkwardly onto her shoulders. She hesitated, then proceeded with small steps away from the quiet side street up into the multi-tiered, squishy leather sofa lobby of the Wild Orchid Villas Hotel.

Barry eased the camera behind him, let it hang beside his hip where he draped a protective arm around its bulk. He wandered on, strolling past the open-fronted hotel towards the shops and market traders at the end of the cobbled alleyway, whistling through pursed, smiling lips.

*

Maddie shielded her eyes from the sun, peering up into the hotel's entrance.

Doesn't look too bad. Nod to acknowledge the girl in the sarong with tattoos, past the cute guy in the street with the fancy camera. Remember to breathe.

Smile and breathe—

'Hi, how you? Checking in?'

Maddie nodded and shrugged the pack off her shoulders.

'You have reservation?'

'No.'

'How many nights?'

Good question. 'Um ... one to start with, then perhaps more?'

'Okay. Twenty dollar.'

The receptionist slid a form across the desk towards Maddie, placed a pen on top of it, then turned to a pretty young girl sat behind her and barked instructions in Thai. Maddie leaned over the desk and pressed the pen harder than necessary against the paper in an effort to stop her hand from shaking. Behind her on several levels of terracing, traveller types lounged on couches, eating, drinking, chatting.

'Please, follow,' said the receptionist, barely glancing at the completed form, which she swiftly separated from the cash payment and passport. Maddie picked up her backpack and followed the girl farther back into the hotel towards the narrow stairs.

'Okay for you, yes?'

Maddie glanced around the simply furnished room with a double bed and pale blue tiled floor.

Looks clean.

'Yes, very nice, thank you.'

Maddie watched the door close. She sank down on the bed and slumped forwards, resting her head into her hands. 'Maddie … priorities,' she whispered, her voice muffled behind her hands, pressed tightly into her face. 'Get back to reality, Maddie!' Louder now.

She lifted her head, pushing her hands onto her knees as she straightened up. 'Sooo … what are you going to do now? Check out, get a taxi back to the airport and – no!' she squealed, shaking her head and rotating her gaze around the room.

She unlaced Liz's boots, pulled off the thick smeggy socks, then stood and took three steps to the curtains, which she pulled back. Sunlight peeked through the glass panels in the wood frame, bathing the small balcony outside in warmth. She smiled, unlocked the door and peered outside, noting the bench on her right and toilet and shower wet room to her left.

'Okay … this is actually a nice place to read, relax and get a grip. That's what I need, some quiet time to figure stuff out. Definitely. Now, where's my book …?'

Maddie retreated back into the room and began unclipping the backpack straps, delving into its pockets and compartments. 'Oh. Not *my* things. Right. So … what have I got?'

She tipped the contents of the backpack onto the bed, sifting Liz's stuff into separate piles. She wrinkled her nose at the stale, sweaty odour from the clothes, quickly turning her attention to the other items, amongst which were two books: the *Lonely Planet Guide to Vietnam, Cambodia, Northern Thailand and Laos,* and *Survival in the Killing Fields* by Haing Ngor. Other items included a rolled-up suede travel backgammon set about the size of a relay baton, a pair of flip-flops, sunglasses, mozzie spray, leftover malaria tablets, basic first aid kit, box of tampons, two packs of condoms, a mosquito net, a part-used roll of duct tape, a Swiss Army knife, a leather-bound notebook and a pocket-size LED torch.

'That's it. This is what two hundred quid buys you … nice one, Maddie. What were you thinking?'

I must stop talking to myself.

She stood and placed her hands on her hips, bare feet pacing the room, leaving faint condensation outlines on the cool tiled floor. A nervous smile twitched across her lips. She shook her head, then broke into a giggle. 'Silly, silly girl!'

Maddie stepped out onto the balcony. Resting her hands on the balustrade, her gaze drifted down over the alleyway below. The buzzing rattle of a small scooter weaved through meandering tourists, leaving a trail of oily two-stroke smoke which lingered, mixing with the faint smell of a hot, musty sewer. Voices punctuated the lull in engine noises, multinational chatter drifting up from the alleyway: English, Thai, Dutch, German. She folded her arms and turned to face into the room, her gaze settling on the bed, flitting over the contents of Liz's pack. She stepped back into the room, drawn to her mobile phone.

'Okay, essentials.' Maddie searched through the piles of stuff again. 'All present and correct, except for … bugger. No charger.' She sank down on the edge of the bed, hesitated, then picked up the phone. It displayed a new messenger alert icon, from Liz:

Just boarded the plane, close one! Intensity (or temporary insanity?!) in the ladies toilets. Go Maddie! Whoop whoop! Sorry about unwashed clothes. Lovely ladies run a laundrette service just to the right of the hotel. Gullible Travels is a legendary bar to find a travel mate – not too many crazies. Kind of speed-dating for travellers. Wow, so much fun ahead – ENJOY!
Liz

Maddie read the message again. She finished just as the phone rang, the screen displaying Rupert's profile photograph: him stood in a London bar coveting a pint of Peroni. Her thumb hovered above the accept and reject prompts. She swiped her thumb across the screen.

'Hello Rupert,' she said in a neutral tone.

'Where the *hell* are you? Check-in closes in ten minutes!'

Churning stomach acids crept up towards the back of her throat. She scrunched her eyes shut, concentrating hard to force the queasiness back down.

"Maddie, where are—'

'I'm not coming,' she stammered, 'I've accepted your challenge.'

'Maddie, this is insane – what challenge?'

'You goaded me, said I wouldn't last a week on my own with a minuscule budget, remember?'

Silence from the phone. Smatterings of happy chatter drifted up from below the balcony.

'You can't do this – we're getting married in six weeks!'

'And depending on how the next four weeks go, we might not …'

'Don't be stupid. Why wouldn't we—'

'Because I deserve more!'

Maddie listened to his angry breathing over the background airport bustle, picturing his bulging eyes and crimson cheeks.

'Where are you?' Rupert demanded.

'A million miles away from signing *your* version of a marriage contract.'

'So what are you saying—'

'That I'll meet you to redefine our relationship, after …'

'You wouldn't dare! You need me, Madeline. You don't cope well on your own, especially not in a foreign country—'

'So guess what, I'm going to find that out for myself.'

'Please, Maddie. Tell me where you are, I'll ask them to delay the plane. We need to be on this flight home—'

'No, *we* don't. I'm taking the initiative, Rupert. I'm going to travel on my own. I need to do this, prove to myself—'

'Damn it Maddie, you have to be on that plane.'

'No, I really don't. I'm not being bound by a chauvinistic contract. Any *contract,* in fact. I need this time Rupert. It's important.'

'Getting on this fucking plane is important!' he yelled.

Maddie pulled the phone away from her ear. She stared at it for a moment, frowning. 'Not to me, it isn't,' she said firmly.

'For Christ sake, Maddie – this is bloody ridiculous!'

'When I get back, two weeks before *our* wedding, I'll be better equipped to renegotiate.'

'Renegotiate what, exactly?'

Maddie paused. 'Everything.'

Rupert's voice softened. 'Please Maddie, don't be stupid. Come back to check-in. Let's get home, we can talk about this and—'

'Rupert.'

'Yes, I'm listening …'

'Don't expect a postcard.' Maddie hung up. Then as an afterthought, she switched off the phone and tossed it onto the bed.

Seven

'Okay. Priority number one, clean clothes.'

Maddie gathered Liz's dirty laundry in her arms and stuffed the pungent items into a plastic bag she'd found in a pocket of the rucksack. She shook out a worn cotton shoulder bag, held it up for inspection. 'You'll do. Passport, purse, guidebook, reading book … oh. Not *my* book, but … okay, why not.' She shoved Liz's paperback into the shoulder bag with everything else and headed for the door, double checking she'd locked it behind her.

'Time to face a new reality,' she muttered as she headed for the stairs.

Maddie glanced at the calculator screen clutched in the elderly lady's wrinkly fingers. 'Bhat or dollar?' she asked.

'Bhat, okay.'

Maddie held up a fifty Bhat note and passed it with the bag of clothes over the wood trestle table, which sagged with piles of neatly folded clothes. She dipped her head at the old lady's three-brown-teeth smile.

Priority number one, sorted.

*

Rupert listened to the electronic ring tone, his eyes darting between his watch, the check-in clerk and the other passengers filtering across the concourse.

'Hello? I'm still at the airport. There's been a … complication.'

'What sort of complication?' the voice rasped.

Rupert hesitated, his heartbeat pulsing at the back of his throat. The check-in clerk caught his eye. She tapped her watch, shook her head and flicked her hands out flat, palms down – indicating *finito*.

'Something … significant.'

*

Maddie studied the Lonely Planet guide, tracing Liz's handwritten route and notes sketched on the map page. The accompanying doodles comprised train tracks, bus and aeroplane symbols that linked together in a dot-to-dot of places Liz had visited. Distance or time notes between points had been scrawled next to key locations. Cambodia, Vietnam, Laos …

'Hi, mind if I grab this seat?'

Maddie flinched, glancing over towards the English voice, her cheeks reddening. 'Of course.' She shuffled along on the sofa, swung her bag onto the floor.

'Thanks. I'm Victoria. You sound English.'

'Oh. Yes … I'm Maddie. English, yes. You?'

'For too long. I'm doing my best to shift the accent – that's travelling, right?'

'I guess …'

'So, Maddie. Are you going to Gullible Travels tonight?'

'*Gullible* Travels?'

'Yeah, I know, odd play on words. The owner reckons it suits this place.'

'Bangkok?'

Victoria nodded, held a bottle of beer to her lips, gulping back a mouthful. 'Specifically the Khao San Road. He's a local guy. American G.I. dad, Thai mother – from the Vietnam war. He calls himself *Gung Ho Joe*, Joe-Ho for short. I know, I know, it's out there. Gullible Travels is sort of … *notorious* around here.'

'Notorious for what?'

Victoria raised an eyebrow, rummaging in her shoulder bag for a packet of cigarettes. She offered them to Maddie.

'No, thank you, I don't.'

Victoria nodded, lit up and drew back smoke, luxuriating in the nicotine sensation. 'Come along tonight and see for yourself. It'll be fun.'

Maddie shrugged. 'Maybe. Are you travelling on your own?'

'I wasn't, until a few days ago. Ellis moved on.'

'Oh, sorry to hear that.'

Victoria took another swig of beer, raising her corner lip, pouting. 'Don't be. It was time, y'know.'

'So how long are you here for?'

'In Bangkok? Depends how long it takes to get hooked up.'

'With another guy?'

Victoria shrugged. 'Guy, girl or small group. I don't travel well on my own. So I will be there tonight. You fancy it?'

'Err ... sure, okay. What time?'

'Meet me here at nine. We'll walk there together.' Victoria leaned over the table and stubbed out her cigarette, leaving it smouldering in the ashtray. She stood up, surveying the clusters of travellers lounging on sofas. She winked at Maddie and picked up her bottle of beer, heading for a group of girls huddled together on the far side of the lobby. Maddie watched Victoria pick her way through the other hotel guests, occasionally nodding and pausing to exchange a few words with some of them.

*

'Good price, lady. Velly good price. You buy, yes?'

'Is it the same as quality as Apple? It doesn't look the same—'

'Same-same – best in Bangkok!' The young Thai girl slipped the phone charger out of its cellophane packet and inserted the small plug into Maddie's iPhone. She held out the mains power end of the charger and led Maddie behind the market stall. 'Look, see ...' The girl plugged the lead into a cracked socket held together with duct tape. 'Working, yes? Look, see.'

Maddie crouched down and squinted at the phone's screen. 'Okay, yes. How much?'

'Good price, lady. For you, twenty dollar.'

'Twenty dollars seems—'

'Excessive, even for Bangkok. Five would still be cheeky, but she's a cute kid.'

Maddie turned towards the Australian accent behind her. She shielded her eyes from the sun, squinting behind her fingers, just able to make out the features of the camera guy from outside the hotel. He looked to be around five foot eight, slim with scruffy gingery-blonde hair. 'Haggle like you mean it,' he said, his green eyes twinkling with constant energy. 'I'm Barry, this is my girlfriend, Jody.'

'Oh, right. I'm Maddie.'

Barry nodded, dropping his eyes. 'Nice iPhone. Is it the latest version?'

'It was, a few weeks ago.'

'Cool. Hey, you fancy winning me two hundred Bhat? Jody here swears you're some sort of celeb. I reckon she's talking out of her English arse – so tell me, have you ever appeared in a magazine? Fashion, gossip ... *glamour?*' Barry exaggerated a cheek-crunching playful wink. Jody dug him in the ribs. He laughed and draped his arm over her shoulder.

'Just kidding, about the glamour mag. Although ...' He waggled his ring finger. 'Readers' wives – it's never too late.' Barry grinned, then quickly backed away as Maddie blushed. 'I'm just horsing around. Seriously, you're far too classy for the low end stuff. Jody's convinced you're famous.'

'Um ... not famous, no. I had a well-known boyfriend a few years ago, got photographed with him in some gossip magazines. It was—'

'I knew it!' squealed Jody, untangling from beneath Barry's arm to punch him playfully on the shoulder. She held a palm out. 'Pay up, mister!'

Maddie dropped her gaze to the pavement.

'Famous lady – I take photo?' The Thai girl grinned, wide and toothy, clamping herself to Maddie's side, wrapping her small arms around her waist.

'Take the girl's photo first, Barry. Then it's my turn. I want this on film.'

Barry glanced at Maddie. He shrugged apologetically and slipped the bulky camera off his shoulder. He removed the lens cap and hunched over the viewfinder. 'Okay ladies, say ... *clazy-clazy-celebrity.*' Barry adjusted his stance as he rattled off several shots, then popped his head over the viewfinder, catching Maddie's eye. 'This might sound a bit weird, just something I do – to capture the moment.' He ducked behind the camera, fired off another shot, then held the shutter down, speaking in a fast, seamless murmur.

Memory Card 2. Pic 368
'The famous *it* girl, daughter of an English earl. Former gossip magazine pin-up struggles to keep her chin up. Once a darling of the British establishment with her legions of fans, she attempts to strike a hard bargain for an authentic fake phone-charger brand. This will most likely break within the next forty-eight hours, around the time her love affair with Bangkok inevitably sours. Fame and fakery, folks, is a

dodgy mix, if only she'd not posed all those years ago for some dodgy magazine pics …'

Maddie frowned, releasing her arm from the girl's shoulder. She glanced at Jody, who shrugged, faux regretfully – *he does that.*

'No break, mister! Velly good quality, best for iPhone!' The girl broke away from Maddie and darted over to Barry, clutching her small fingers around his hands, easing his camera down low enough for her to peer at the screen. 'I almost as pretty.'

'Prettier!' said Barry, grinning at her.

'You take again?' The girl pulled a cellphone from her back pocket, thrust it towards Barry.

'Sure.'

The girl repositioned herself next to Maddie.

Shh-clitch.

'Okay, famous lady. Five dollar,' said the girl, grinning and holding out her hand.

Maddie extracted a twenty dollar note from her purse. 'Do you have change?'

The girl snatched the note and disappeared behind the market stall.

'That's the last you'll see of her, or your twenty,' said Barry, chuckling.

'My turn. You don't mind, do you,' said Jody, shuffling up to Maddie's side and draping an arm over her shoulder. 'Come on Barry, one more.'

'Oh, I'm not really worth photographing. I'm nobody, now …' Maddie tried to ease away, but Jody leaned in closer.

'Nobody is a *nobody*,' said Barry, pulling a small bundle of Thai currency from his pocket. He peeled off several notes. 'Here, paid in full,' he said, offering the cash to Jody, who snatched the notes from him and fanned them out under her chin. Barry stepped back, his camera poised.

'Okay, say … *nobody*.' Barry squeezed the shutter release, capturing Jody's victorious wide-eyed pout above the currency and Maddie's tight-lipped politeness.

Is there no escape from my past?

'Cheers. I knew I recognised you.'

'Here lady, fifteen dollar. Okay?' The girl thrust the money into Maddie's hands, allowing her the perfect excuse to step away from Jody.

'Nice business, with you,' said the girl, hugging Maddie.

'Thanks for indulging us. Enjoy Thailand,' said Barry, tugging on Jody's hand.

Maddie watched Barry steer Jody away through the other market stalls and crowds of travellers. Just before Maddie dropped her eyes away, Barry and Jody paused to cross a road, allowing him to rotate a little further than necessary as he checked for traffic. He flicked his gaze back at her, smiling as they made eye contact. He winked cheekily – *gotcha.*

She looked away quickly, turning to wander off in the opposite direction.

*

Maddie unlocked her room and stepped into the relative cool, cramps spiking deep within her stomach as she scanned the unfamiliar traveller's life spread out on the bed.

What am I really doing here?

She placed the shoulder bag on the far side of the bed, swept the remaining contents of Liz's backpack onto the floor and sank down onto the mattress. She untied the walking boots, eased them off and lay back, closing her eyes.

Why do you have to be such an arse, Rupert?

*

'You take me here, yes?'

The taxi driver peered at Rupert's smartphone, scrutinising the address contained in the message. 'Yes. Five hundred Baht, okay?'

Rupert nodded, withdrew the phone. He used his foot to shove the wheeled Samsonite suitcase towards the back of the taxi, prompting the driver to dutifully leap out of his seat and heave it into the boot.

'Damn you Maddie. Why go all independent on me now?' Rupert muttered as he climbed into the back seat, sank down into the worn fabric and closed his eyes. 'You've properly screwed things up.'

*

'I also do wedding photography. That's a real art, let me tell you … but right now, it's all about the book.'

Barry watched the middle-aged Brit sitting at the café's adjacent table examine the camera, feeling its weight. He closed one eye, offered the other to the viewfinder, twisting the bulky lens in and out.

'And the title of the book is *Shutter* …'

'Stutter.'

'*Shutter Stutter.* Catchy, I like it. So it's a coffee table picture book?'

Barry nodded. 'But with a by-line below the title: *The camera never lies, cries or sighs.* It's an original concept. I capture striking images and fuse them with twenty seconds of instantaneous reactive and instinctive context.'

The man pulled a suitably impressed face. 'Isn't this a bit chunky, by modern standards?'

'You get what you pay for, chief. I don't like the newer, smaller units. I like to hold the camera's weight, *feel* the gravity of my responsibility.'

The Brit chuckled. 'Sounds like you take your art pretty seriously.' He passed the camera back to Barry.

'Totally. One shutter squeeze can immortalise an everyday hero, or antagonise a nation. I capture the truth, always.'

'No Photoshop exceptions?'

'Never. That's not how I roll.'

The Brit nodded, glancing skywards as a hand touched him on the shoulder. 'I'm ready. Shall we go …?' said his wife, smiling at Barry.

The Brit shuffled to his feet and offered his hand. 'Great talking to you. Good luck with the book, it sounds intriguing. Hang onto this one, love, he'll be filthy rich one day.'

Jody draped her arm over Barry's shoulder, pulling him close. 'He's already rich – he's got me.'

Barry eased away from Jody and stood up, clasping the Brit's hand. 'Cheers. I enjoyed sharing time.' Barry watched the middle-aged couple meander away through the restaurant. He turned to Jody. 'Nice guy.'

'Yeah, for an old timer.'

Barry regarded Jody with a mischievous sparkle in his eye. 'We're all heading that way, Jody. Everyone's worn the nappies—'

'On different timelines?'

'You got it.' He flicked his gaze past her.

'You want to back up any files, send them home before we move on?'

Barry remained still, maintaining an unblinking expression as he watched the couple meander down the street. Jody leaned in close, whispering in his ear. 'Because I thought, before we go out, you might want to plug your memory card into my hard drive slot, and upload some … *pixels.*'

Barry snapped his head around. 'Let's go, times a-wastin'!' He sprung up from his seat, tugged on Jody's hand and hustled her towards the street. They left a trail of wobbling chairs and screeching laughter in their wake.

Eight

Something, at the far recess of her mind … a distant light flicking through her subconscious, rousing awareness, gradually firing up recollections. She tried to push the sensation away, sink back to sleep. Almost succeeding.

Louder now: *Knock, knock, knock!*

A pause, then a muffled, insistent voice. 'Maddie? It's Victoria – we met earlier. Are you okay? We're going to Gullible Travels, remember? It's gonna be a great evening, you'll regret not coming …'

Maddie stumbled out of bed. She scrunched her eyes tightly shut, then forced them open a fraction as she prised the door open.

'Oh, hi. Sorry, did I wake you?' Victoria eased the door back and breezed into the room. 'We need to get you ready.'

'Ready for what …?' Maddie yawned and scrunched her hair.

'The first night of the rest of your life.' Victoria surveyed the contents of the room.

'Oh, right. Thing is, thanks for thinking of me, but I put Liz – *my* clothes in for a wash. So I'm going to have to pass. Sorry.'

'Come on, it'll be fun. First cocktail is free.'

'But I've literally got nothing to wear. Everything is in the—'

Victoria grinned and rummaged in her shoulder bag. She held up a pristine white tee-shirt with two four-inch diameter heart shape emblems side by side, at breast height. The left heart contained the horizontal red, white and blue bands of the Thai national flag, within which a triangular stickwoman held hands with her male counterpart opposite, contained within an American stars and stripes motif in the right heart shape. Written centrally in the gap above the emblems, a bold US Army typeface proclaimed: *Joe-Ho's*. Mirroring this text in the gap below the heart-shaped flags: *Gullible Travels.*

Maddie rubbed her eyes and squinted at the tee-shirt. 'That's an interesting design …'

'Wait till you meet the man behind it all.' Victoria tossed the tee-shirt to Maddie and turned her back. 'Slip it on, we'll get going.'

'This is sounding suspiciously like an Ibiza bar promotion evening.'

Maddie sat down on the bed, leaned back against the wall and folded her arms. She watched Victoria half-turn, study her briefly, before stepping over and perching on the edge of the bed. 'Okay, I'll fess up. It *is* a promotional evening. And yes, I'm earning commission, which I desperately need. And I mean really, *really* need. Please, Maggie, help me out here. It'll be—'

'Maddie.'

'What?'

'I'm Maddie.'

'Oh, sorry. How about it, help me out … please? Just come along for one drink, which'll be free.'

'I'm pretty tired, I'd rather get some more rest and—'

'Resting is for retired people on a slippery slope to the *big* sleep. Or married couples who've lost their passion for life.' Victoria glanced at Maddie's left hand, raising her eyebrows. 'You're not telling me you're *happily* married …?'

Maddie shrunk back against the headboard, arms unfolding, fingers fiddling with her ring. 'I'm engaged.'

Victoria shrugged, indicating *what's the difference?* 'I don't see a committed fiancé anywhere close by.' She leant down, checking under the bed. 'He's not under there. Maybe he's hiding in here …?' She slid the bedside cabinet's top drawer open, peered inside. 'Nope.'

'Okay, fair point, but I want to be on my own right now …'

'Come on Maddie, level with me. Your fiancé has gone AWOL. So what, he's an arsehole – screw him! Get out there, plot your revenge. I'll help you, if you'll support another fallen comrade.'

Maddie's cheeks twitched, her face relaxing into a smile. 'Fallen comrade? Where did you get your sales patter?'

'Past jobs – estate agents, charity fundraiser, accident compensation call centre. Is it working?'

Maddie sighed and reached for the Gullible Travels tee-shirt. 'Give me five minutes, okay?'

'You've got ninety seconds. I'll be outside the door.'

*

Maddie followed Victoria into the lobby. A dozen assorted travellers watched them enter.

'Okay, let's go have some fun!' Victoria yelled, responding to the lacklustre reception from the ensemble. 'Great, we've got a German contingent,' she muttered to Maddie, before beaming at the group and throwing her hands into the air. 'Okay guys and gals. Get ready to juice up and chill down into slo-mo – it's off to Joe-Ho's we go ... happy, happy, happy!'

Maddie observed Victoria virtually skip down the steps, hands held out, gathering her brood into following her with a theatrical sweeping motion. Maddie tagged on behind two fresh-faced boys, barely twenty, both with smooth haircuts, earlobe piercings and *all about us* chest-puffing bravado.

For the hundredth time – what the hell am I doing here?!

*

Rupert stepped out of the taxi into the bustling nonchalance of the Khao San Road. He paid the driver, retrieved his suitcase and stared up at the flashing neon signs, becoming more prominent now as dusk cloaked the grey skyline with a darker, broody palette.

He checked his phone, reminding himself of his instructions, then picked his way through the human traffic, heading across the flow of pedestrians to a narrow alley between a clothing parasol and a rickety trestle crammed full of mobile phone accessories. Both stalls touted their wares beneath a white sign with red and blue lettering, advertising a sterling silver shop.

Rupert walked with slow, muscle-cramping steps, sweating more than the cool evening temperature would normally encourage. His eyes darted left, right, over his shoulder, twitchy fingers tightening around the Samsonite's extendible handle, the wheels juddering across the road's textured flagstones. Around him, the narrow sides of the alley closed in, getting progressively darker the farther away he shuffled from the normality of the street.

*

The flashing red, white and blue two-hearts neon insignia for Gullible

Travels out-dazzled all the other signs on the Khao San Road – bigger, brighter, with more vibrant psychedelic colours. Below its enticing magnetism, a constant stream of scooters weaved their way through the bustling crowd, leaving trails of exhaust fumes swirling at ankle level, eerily illuminated by flashes of red brake lights in the dusky night. This fresh intermittent pollution overlaid the competing aromas of alcohol breath, fatty pork skewers sizzling on miniature barbeques, body odour, stale vegetables and potent *pour hommes et femmes* perfume, constantly mixed together with the motion of human legs, out on the prowl.

'Never underestimate the adventures waiting inside Gullible Travels! Let's hang loose and party hard!' Victoria yelled, whooping and punching the air.

She led the group beneath the flashing neon sign, between two twenty-foot high, ten-foot long fibreglass hiking boots. One boot had been painted in the American stars and stripes, the other in the Thai national flag colours, matching Maddie's tee-shirt emblems. The tongue of each boot lolled lazily back over the toe, forming the counter to an open-top booth. In the left boot, a Thai girl danced provocatively, wearing skimpy cut-off khaki shorts and signature two-heart design bikini top. To her right, a slim Western guy gyrated enthusiastically, displaying his abs beneath a cropped US Marine combat top and Army cap, which hosted the Gullible Travels insignia.

Victoria paused by the tall, purple-gloss entrance doors beyond the huge boots. She turned to face the group, making eye contact one by one, then raised her hands to the sky and plunged them down, crumpling her body into a low squat, signalling the purple doors to open. The group became saturated with the sound of Tina Turner belting out *Simply the Best,* with enough volume and accompanying blast from a giant wind machine to sway some of them back half a step, plastering involuntary grins across their wide-eyed faces. Multi-coloured flashing floor squares with signature heart shapes lit in sequence underfoot, their red, white and blue glows projecting heart images sporadically on the chest-height swirling smoke, interspersed with pulsating red, white and blue laser strobes emanating from deep within the club. The entire building throbbed with a bone-rattling acoustic bass and Tina's soulful lyrics.

Maddie's hair swept back in the blast of air, puffing her cheeks, forcing an involuntary grin as she swayed back. She held out a hand to prevent the person in front from stepping backwards onto her, then cautiously followed the other travellers into the carnivorous interior. Maddie filtered past Victoria, still crouched on the floor, her hair dancing on the rush of air, arms outstretched, palms upturned in a *welcome to this not-so-humble establishment* greeting.

'You okay down there?' Maddie asked, stooping down to peer at Victoria, who cocked an eyebrow.

'My knees can't handle much more of this.'

Maddie scooped her hands under Victoria's arms, helping her up.

'Did they like the grand entrance?'

'I think so … is it always like this?'

'Oh, yeah. "This is big-banging-*kok*, babe," as Joe-Ho would say.' Victoria swept her hand out in a grandiose gesture. 'It can be overwhelming, all this extravagance. But I absolutely love it.'

Maddie followed Victoria further into the stroboscopic, flashing-floor wind tunnel. She half-turned, aware of the entrance doors closing behind her, coinciding with the strength of the breeze subsiding. The multi-coloured floor slowed its sporadic blinking, now matching their walking speed, the squares changing colour under each footstep. Red. White. Blue.

'Drinks!' yelled Victoria over Tina Turner's vocals, now blending into a vibrant contemporary dance remix, played at a marginally quieter, teeth-tingling volume. The narrow corridor opened out to a reception area, fifty feet square. Neon pink up-lighting bathed the floor in a soft glow, illuminating the smiling faces of the bar staff, three quarters of their height consumed within sunken floor booths. Victoria stooped down and collected two azure-blue cocktail glasses off the knee-high bar. She straightened up to hand one to Maddie, waving a hand in front of her face to break her fixated ground-level stare.

'Lilliputian bar staff?'

'Yeah, kind of a quirky theme, isn't it?'

'I guess … feels a bit weird – uncomfortable.'

'That's the idea, I think. Cocktails laced with irony.'

Maddie sipped the cool blue peppermint flavour liquid through a curly straw. 'Unusual flavour. It tastes—'

'Potent. Yeah, they call it Blue Rinse.'

Maddie stifled a cough, wincing as she forced herself to swallow. She glanced around at the other travellers, mingling by several other identical sunken bar areas. Victoria followed her gaze. 'It's a curious mix of voyeurism and social commentary on the perception of an East meets West superiority complex, don't you think?'

'Is that Joe-Ho's intellectual marketing concept, regurgitated into your sales patter?'

Victoria sniggered. 'Perhaps. Have fun, I've got to mingle. I'll keep an eye out for you.'

Victoria scanned around the room, nodded at Maddie, then sauntered off towards her next target. Maddie watched her approach a group of young male travellers, all sporting slicked back hair and carefully shaped wispy beards, oozing testosterone-fuelled confidence.

You'd be right at home, Rupert.

'You're new here,' said a polite, slightly nasal English voice.

Maddie turned to face the man. 'That obvious?'

'There's a look, that first-timers adopt. Sort of a glazed sheen of disbelief and mild shock that a Thai owner can belittle his compatriots so blatantly.'

'Or is he belittling us? We're paying customers, after all.'

He grinned, perfect white teeth glowing in the UV light filters. 'Could be … I'm Darwin.'

'Of course you are. I'm Maddie.'

'Madeline, by birth …?' Another flash of impossibly white teeth, the focal point of his deeply tanned parchment-like complexion. 'So …' Darwin began, easing his head in closer, as if to confide something of staggering importance.

His twinkling eyes, cheeky smile and amiable body language were cruelly curtailed by the bar plunging into darkness. An instant later several multi-coloured laser holograms of Elvis Presley in his classic white jewelled suit appeared around the room. Glitter began falling from the ceiling, its sparkling freefall vividly illuminated with flashes of UV light, casting a shroud of dreamlike anticipation throughout the clientele.

Dum dum daaa … Dum DUM, DAAA!

The opening chords of *Eve of the War* from the musical version of *The War of the Worlds* pounded through chest cavities and echoed inside near-perforated eardrums. Beyond the edge of the bar area, dry ice smoke crept eerily out from floor level, its pink pigment gradually darkening to devilish blood-red. Piercing white spotlights projected ghostly skeletal shadows onto a large projector screen on the far wall.

Maddie glanced at Darwin. He looked mildly amused and oddly nonplussed. At least he'd stepped back, no longer crowding her.

'It's time …' a soft, Thai-accented voice whispered, becoming louder and deeper. 'It's time … it's time for Gullible Travels speed-mating – big-banging Bang*kok* style!'

Smoke filtered away and spotlights pulsed intermittent beams, revealing more of the large multi-tiered amphitheatre-inspired space. Music faded out, as everyone turned to watch a figure rise up from the floor, illuminated by powerful spotlights. He had short spiky hair, coloured with an inch-wide red line over each ear and a two inch-wide blue band from his forehead to the nape of his neck. Below the two-hearts Gullible Travels tee-shirt he wore faded jeans and pristine white sneakers. Arms stretched high above his head, he yelled into his headset microphone. 'Heeeeere's … Joe-Ho!'

Cheering and canned laughter erupted, echoing around the multi-speaker system, prompting accompanying wolf whistles and whoops from the assembled travellers.

'Tonight, giants of the world, we search for Gullible travel mates – big-banging Bang*kok* style!' The random spotlights settled, picking out miniature tables and chairs randomly placed on tiers of different height terracing around the club. Each table had been set up with a miniature table tennis net and two bats, which had 'Yes' written in neon green US Army-style lettering on one side, and 'No' in red on the reverse.

'New game, no blame. Banging-Bang*kok* style.' Joe-Ho crouched into a pseudo-Usain Bolt lightning posture. His outstretched hand pointed a smartphone towards the nearest couple seated at a tiny table. 'Gullible Travellers …' shouted Joe-Ho, his words echoing around the club. He sporadically pointed at random tables, lit up under flashes of spotlight beams as he delivered his staccato instructions. 'Download our travel mate app, and – start – your – questions!'

Joe-Ho pressed a command on his mobile phone. A whirling spotlight beam pulsated around the miniature table tennis desks, at each location highlighting a male traveller on one side of the table's low net. They hunched awkwardly on the tiny chairs, facing towards a girl, crouched down opposite. On the screen, the drivers leapt into their vintage race cars, wheels spinning away, chaotically weaving across the track to avoid the other cars, all vying for position. Joe-Ho raised his arms, grinning, then dropped them to his side. 'Go, go, GO!'

Maddie flinched at the hand laid on her shoulder. She spun round, stepped back and swept her arm out, brushing the hand aside.

'Whoa, relax – you're up ...' said Victoria, rubbing her forearm, pointing at a table high up on a far tier.

'Sorry, some of these guys can be ... persistent.'

'I hear you. Up there, at those shrunken tables, the world's finest blaggers, freeloaders and ten-second-lovers await. But knowing that, makes it fun. Go investigate, find yourself someone ...'

'You're not painting an attractive picture.'

'Yeah, well, I'm on the rebound.'

Maddie watched Victoria saunter over to the nearest table, where she sat down opposite a guy with dreadlocks, muscular arms and a ready smile.

'He nice. You go there,' said an accented voice beside Maddie, belonging to a pretty Thai girl. She hooked her arm under Maddie's elbow and led her towards a vacant miniature chair opposite a teenage guy with acne, windswept gelled hair and a tight tee-shirt.

'Hi. I'm—' Maddie began.

'Uh-huh. You're new to this? Yup, thought so. The guys do the asking. Rules, see. How old are you?'

'Oh. I'm ... *older* than you.'

'For sure.'

She wriggled to get comfy on the tiny chair, holding eye contact with him, the silence building. 'I'm Maddie. What's your—'

'I ask the questions.'

Maddie eased back, straightening her back. She folded her arms and tilted her head, observing him.

'How old are you?' he asked again.

'Too old for this bullshit.' She pushed up from the chair and turned to walk away.

'Wait. You're married – the ring. So why are you here?'

Maddie stopped, glanced back at him. 'Escaping from those sort of questions.'

'I'm Rod. I'm eighteen – nineteen next month. Finishing off my gap year. Sorry if I seemed abrupt, I thought girls liked the confident types.'

Maddie examined him for a few moments, then rolled her eyes, relaxed her shoulders and sat back down. 'Confident doesn't mean arrogant,' she said, toying with the table tennis bat. 'I'm twenty-six.

I'm here ... actually, I'm here because of this engagement ring. It was given to me by someone I was once very fond of. It's now six hours since I left him at Bangkok Airport after deciding I needed to prove that I'm worthy of more from a marriage than being suffocated by insensitive hypocrisy. So I'm going to travel for a month, see if I can manage alone.'

'Oh. I thought you were here to have some fun.'

*

Shh-clitch.

Memory Card 2. Pic 377
'The uncomfortable awkwardness of his body language is key, why doesn't the young buck now desperately backpedalling take stock, really *see?* He's miscalculated, underestimated her self-conscious ambiguous persona – does her distaste at his immature directness suggest he might be hiding a massive boner? And yet, he seems to have encouraged her to pull back from the brink of finality, forcing her to re-evaluate, to question: what is this wannabe's *true reality?* What will be the result of her rejection of his curiosity, will it open up the opportunity for her to look inside, explore her own *honesty?*'

*

Maddie glanced over at Barry, his expensive camera dangling from its strap as he ambled away, Jody clamped to his side.
Is that the guy from the market?
'Maddie ...?'
'Sorry, this place, is ... mesmerising.'
Rod picked up his table tennis bat, slowly twirled the *Yes* and *No* sides. 'Ready to vote?'
'Oh, right. Already?'
'That's the idea of speed-travel-mating, Banging-kok style.'
She picked up her bat, flicking her wrist between each side.
'*Banging-kok* style. Is he for real?' she mumbled, absently.
'Joe-Ho? Oh yeah. He's a legend. Sooo ... what's it going to be?'
Rod flicked his eyes down and twirled the bat to display a luminous green *Yes*. Maddie briefly met his gaze.

'Ah, thing is Rod, I'm not really in the market for—'

'Gullible Travellers, make your choice ... NOW!' yelled Joe-Ho, centre stage under a bright spotlight, his arms stretched skywards. Individual beams of light targeted each table, illuminating the couples under an eerie effervescent glow.

Maddie mouthed 'sorry' at Rod as she held up her *No* rejection. She stood awkwardly, shaking cramp out of her legs, catching his crestfallen expression. She shrugged, then paused, as if considering saying something else. Instead she attempted a smile, then stepped down from the tiered clusters of couples.

'Oh, no. No, no, nooooo! No escape for pretty lady!' Joe-Ho beamed and clasped Maddie's hand, scampering with her across to the opposite side of the dance floor. 'Plenty more gentlemen. Not all same-same. But first, you need drink. Better then, much better ...'

Nine

Maddie poured a glug of Chang beer into her mouth and savoured the cooling sensation as it worked its way down her throat. 'Joe-Ho's right, much better now,' she mumbled.

'Who's right about what?' said a coarse, East London-accented voice.

Maddie lifted her focus from the half-empty bottle in her hand to the guy who'd just plonked himself down opposite her. He folded scrawny tattooed arms across his chest, hands propping up tiny biceps. A wispy, patchy excuse for a beard clung to his sallow cheeks. Long greasy hair poked out from below his stars and stripes bandanna.

Is he for real?

'You're American … with *that* accent?'

'Sure am, honey.'

She nodded, cast her eyes around the other tables. 'This anything like dating at home?'

'Same-same.'

'Banging-*kok* style? God help you.'

'You don't seem to be in a very *interested* place, right now.'

Maddie took a slug of beer. 'Nope.'

He stood up and walked away. 'Beaver basher,' he muttered as he left.

Touchy.

Maddie gazed around at the other tables. A girl of around twenty-five with blonde spiky highlights and eyebrow piercings had moved her chair to the same side as her male companion, an ordinary-looking guy in his late thirties. She held her mobile phone at arm's length, filming their conversation, smooching shoulder to shoulder with him, all touchy-feely body language and animated hand gestures. Maddie shifted her gaze on. Two guys leaned across another small table, their mouths clamped together, eyes tightly shut. Above them, at the top of the last tier, Victoria sat opposite Darwin, sharing a cigarette.

'Hello. Hope you don't mind me asking … but is this seat taken?'

Maddie glanced up at the figure towering over her. She took in his expensive-looking Velcro-strap walking sandals, ripped jeans and fashionable patterned shirt, with the sleeves rolled up and two buttons open at the collar, below a strong jawline and piercing blue eyes.

'Oh, er … sure, please take it. The other guy left. I think I scared him off.'

'Actually I thought I'd sit down, here with you. If that's okay?'

'Right. Okay … I'll try to be civil.'

He pulled a slightly quizzical expression which creased his cheeks. 'I'm Charlie,' he said, offering his hand across the table as he crouched down and squeezed his tall frame into the restrictions of the tiny chair.

Maddie shook hands, straightening up to make eye contact. 'Hi Charlie, I'm Maddie. You sound like a Brit?'

'Partly. Swedish mother, American dad. I've been living in Oxford for the last five years, studying. It's a confusing, unauthentic accent.'

'Wow. I'll bet there's an interesting story, how your folks met.'

'Yes, but I won't bore you with it. Forgive me, but you don't seem to be having much fun. Did a friend talk you into coming this evening?'

'That's either very perceptive, or slightly stalker-ish.'

'People intrigue me, I enjoy playing detective. Some, like you, have amusing mannerisms.'

'How so?'

'You dispatched your last speed-mate swiftly. I wonder, what did you say to him?'

'Oh. I think I may have been a tiny bit dismissive. Lack of sleep and alcohol are a bad mix. The most inappropriate stuff just pops out.'

'It happens.'

'Uh-huh, so it seems. What are you studying in Oxford?'

'Engineering, specifically water purification. I'm on a fact-finding tour of Asia.'

'Not a sex tourist? Bugger – you see, this is what happens. It's why Rupert doesn't like me drinking …'

'Rupert is your husband?'

'Fiancé. I think.'

'You don't sound too sure.'

'No. It sort of depends on—' Maddie waved her hand in the air, twirling her wrist, '—stuff.'

'I see.'

They held eye contact for a moment before Joe-Ho's voice interrupted, booming through the surround-sound speakers. 'Gullible Travel mates – it's time to decide!'

Charlie toyed with a smile as he picked up the table tennis bat in front of him and flicked his eyes up to meet Maddie's. 'At the risk of revealing my hand too early, please be advised ...' he rotated the bat to display a *Yes*, 'that I take rejection well.'

Charlie watched Maddie slowly rotate the handle of her bat between her fingers, flicking back and forth between each response.

A smile flickered across Maddie's lips. 'It's been a random, unexpected sort of day, so ... let's see what the travel gods decide.' She stood the top edge of the bat on the table, and teased the handle between her finger and thumb, flicking the different colour luminous fonts. Left, then right.

Charlie's eyes twinkled in the spotlight as he hunched over the table, scrutinising the bat's alternating motion. 'Tell me, Maddie. If it's a yes ... is your fiancé a big bloke?'

She shrugged. 'Maybe you'll get to find out, maybe you won't – this is actually quite intriguing.'

'Your curiosity about the possible outcome has surprised you ...?'

Maddie held his gaze. 'I think it has, yes.' She flicked her fingers and released the bat, letting it spin. It rotated several times, then wobbled and clattered down on the table. She dropped her eyes from Charlie's to examine the single word displayed. 'Now isn't that interesting ...'

*

Rupert hunched forwards on the tiny wooden chair and wrung his hands together, checking his watch again. Somewhere from the depths of the building a deep powerful bass boomed, resonating through the walls and the floor with a distant, dull throb. He glanced up as the reinforced steel checker plate door swung open, bathing the sparse windowless room with a soft, warm-white pigment.

'Mister Rupert, naughty bear. Please enter,' Joe-Ho's voice called out.

Rupert swallowed. He squeezed his hands together, then leant forwards and stood up, grimacing at the pain in his knees. He tipped the suitcase onto its wheels and trailed it towards the open door, his stomach lurching as if in a freefall skydive – without the luxury of a parachute.

*

'He's gorgeous,' whispered Victoria, sinking down into the chair opposite Maddie.

'I hadn't noticed.'

'Liar. Why'd you turn him down?'

'Oh, it would just get complicated. I'm not really sure about my, um … availability, right now. Can I get you another drink?'

'Sure.' Victoria slurped the remainder of the cocktail and tapped her glass on Maddie's empty beer bottle. 'I'll have a Chang.' She glanced up and scowled at Barry, loitering ten feet away, his camera poised.

Shh-clitch.

Memory Card 2. Pic 447

'The green-eyed monster prowls, oozing jealousy and mistrust, her cold eyes targeting like a heat-seeking missile, primed with ambiguous lust. For now this interest in *him* is not replicated, his preferred prey isn't interested in getting X-rated. That smooth-talking chancer has ideas way above his station, his exaggerated adoration is misplaced in this liberal Asian nation. The subject is uncomfortable with unwanted attention, she senses unfulfilled and ambiguous sexual tension. This newbie hasn't yet built up her travel armour, time will tell if the pretty boy is a decent bloke, or a snake pit charmer ...'

'Where are you heading?' asked Charlie, sliding a bottle of beer across the table in front of Maddie. He squatted down beside her, ignoring Victoria.

Maddie glanced away from the nearby camera lens and Barry's lopsided grin. She glanced at Victoria with an apologetic expression and edged her chair away from Charlie. 'Generally, in life?' she replied.

'If you like. But I was referring to the next few days. What's your itinerary?'

Maddie eyed the fresh bottle of beer, stealing a glance back at Barry's roving camera.

'No plan as such. By this time …' she checked her watch and made a mental calculation, 'I'd be on a plane home, thinking about sinking into my sofa with a soothing cup of Earl Grey. But my day hasn't exactly panned out that way. Instead, I'm contemplating heading across the border to Cambodia.'

'Interesting choice. Thailand might be an easier start to your travelling experience,' Victoria noted, a sour edge to her voice.

'A friend suggested Cambodia.' Maddie reached out for the bottle of Chang. She noted the missing top and instead picked at the damp label, absently scanning the dance floor for the exit.

'If you're serious about Cambodia, there's a bus leaving tomorrow. A few of us are booked on. It'll take us to the border, then on to Battambang.'

Maddie teased up a corner of the label, peeling it back in one unbroken piece. She paused to stifle a yawn. 'Excuse me. Yesterday was a heavy night. Sorry, I'm going to head on.'

'Good idea.' Victoria beamed, lifting her arms to offer Maddie a quick hug, in the process edging a little closer to Charlie as Maddie withdrew.

'I'll walk with you, I'm heading the same way,' said Charlie, knocking back the remainder of his drink.

*

Rupert stared through a large smoked glass viewing panel, high up above the miniature tables and chairs scattered around the perimeter of the dance floor, thirty feet below. He watched traveller types mingle. Drinking, chatting, flirting. To his left, Joe-Ho sat back behind a large mahogany desk, his feet resting on the leather inlay, hands linked behind his head.

'Naughty Rupert-the-bear is not on that aeroplane. He is standing in my office. Why is that?' said Joe-Ho in a conversational tone.

Rupert turned to face him. He released the suitcase handle and held out his hands, opening his mouth to respond, but an unseen voice cut him off, speaking clearly and undistorted over a conference call speaker on the corner of Joe-Ho's desk.

'Because he's either very scared, or supremely confident,' said the crisp, distinctly British voice.

Joe-Ho tilted his head at Rupert. 'He both – something gone very wrong. He look confident of being scared.' Joe-Ho swept his feet off the desk and strolled over to Rupert, standing beside him and surveying the mingling travellers below.

'Losing your fiancée, Rupert, is indeed significant.'

Rupert waited for the voice on the speaker to continue, but he heard only a faint constant static to counter the muted background chatter and music beyond the glass. He cleared his throat, tried to maintain an even tone as he projected his voice towards the desk. 'I don't know what happened. We were there together, in the check-in queue. She spilt coffee over her dress, went off to the toilets to change and … never came back.'

'Was the coffee spill genuine?'

'Yes, I jolted her arm. It was my fault.'

'Sure about that? Could it have been premeditated?'

'Of course not. She wouldn't—'

'Make a business decision?'

Rupert stared at the speaker-phone. 'Something must have happened. Maddie is … predictable.'

'It sounds premeditated. Like she sold out, to a competitor.'

'She wouldn't – couldn't know. Besides, she works, has money—'

'That kind of dollars?' said Joe-Ho. Rupert turned back to face him. 'Why else she disappear?' Joe-Ho studied him with an amiable expression.

'Sit down, Rupert,' said the voice over the speaker, 'and gather your thoughts. Then tell us everything – omit nothing and do not attempt to lie. We're reasonable businessmen, but we only ask nicely once.'

*

'I'll be okay, thanks,' said Maddie, quickening her walking pace as she glanced back at Charlie, jogging up to her side.

'Are you really heading to Cambodia?' he asked, catching his breath.

'That's the thing about taking up a challenge. I'd be short-changing myself if I didn't follow it through.'

'Perhaps we could hang out, buddy up. For safety,' he added.

'Yours, or mine …?'

Charlie's mouth formed an enigmatic smile. They walked on, side by side. Charlie buried his hands in his pockets, darting her an occasional appreciative glance.

*

'That's everything?'

Rupert leant his elbows on Joe-Ho's desk, rubbed his eyes and nodded. 'Yes. Maddie knows I have an appreciation for other girls when I've had a few beers. But my wallet had disappeared, so I was in a filthy mood the next morning. Maybe that's what pushed her over the edge.'

'You farangs, you think Thai girls are stupid? They got business sense,' said Joe-Ho, without turning from staring down through the smoked glass at his thriving nightclub.

The conference speaker buzzed with static. 'You've failed to uphold our arrangement, Rupert. There's an outstanding debt to settle. So my suggestion to you is this: find your fiancée. Retrieve the missing item. Get on a plane home, then we'll consider the debt repaid, without any additional penalty. If you're not on a plane in twelve hours with said item, our debt collector *will* find your fiancée. When he does, your life, and hers, will become extremely uncomfortable. Do you understand?'

Rupert slumped over the desk and dropped his head into his hands. 'Yes,' he managed to utter, scrunching his eyes tightly shut.

*

'I saw you taking photographs of *that* girl, the B-list has-been celebrity princess.'

Barry looked up from scrolling through images on his camera's screen. He tilted his head at Jody and surveyed her expression, the corners of his mouth twitching mischievously. 'I took lots of photos tonight. It's what I do.'

'You like her.'

'I like people. They intrigue me, from an artistic perspective.'

'Bullshit.'

Jody watched Barry shrug then take a swig of beer, finishing the bottle.

'What's *that* look supposed to mean?'

'It means it's time for another beer. You want one?'

Jody pursed her lips, folded her arms. He stared at her for a few seconds, then chuckled and shook his head as he strolled off towards the bar, his camera dangling from its shoulder strap.

'Don't stress, sister. Did you see the smokin' guy she hooked up with?' said Victoria, sidling up beside her.

Jody nodded. 'He'll soon realise she's a snooty cow.'

'And when he does, others will be ready to pounce.' Victoria winked, provoking a cackle from Jody.

By the bar, Barry looked over his shoulder at the two girls. He swung round, lifting his camera up to his eye in a smooth, seamless motion, quickly focusing in on them.

Shh-clitch.

Memory Card 2. Pic 448

'Vultures circle nearby, their unfortunate prey unaware as they squawk their dire plans to make her cry. Run away, demure little bird, find the inner confidence not to fly with the herd.'

*

'You lucky. I good guy, here in Thailand. London, very different …' Joe-Ho tutted and shook his head. 'Not reasonable men. Profit, much to lose. For me, no supply problem. There little risk, what I care? But I like you, Rupert. You not running, you standing. Try to make right. But man they will send …'

Joe-Ho stared at Rupert for a long moment, then slowly shook his head. 'He like that movie shark. Duuun dun. Duuun dun … dun, dun, dun, dun, dun … haaarrrgggrrrhhhh!' He leapt around the desk, grabbed Rupert's leg with both hands and clawed his fingertips into the pressure points around the kneecap, jolting him upright.

'Arrhh!'

Joe-Ho released Rupert's leg and perched next to him on the edge of the desk. 'I hope wife-in-waiting still in Thailand, got what London want. If not, is very bad news. For two of you …'

Ten

'This is me.' Maddie began to speed up as she and Charlie approached the Wild Orchid Villas Hotel.

You say, "me too," and I'm seeking reinforcements ...

'Ah, I'm just down the road.'

'Cool. I guess I'll see you around,' she said over her shoulder as he dropped back.

'Hey, maybe on the bus tomorrow?'

'Oh, right. Yeah, maybe ... thing is, Charlie, I'm in a weird place right now – emotionally. I wouldn't want you to misunderstand my ... availability.'

Charlie stopped walking. He chuckled. 'Hey, no problem. Sleep well, travel safe.' He smiled and turned and strolled away, back the way they'd come.

Maddie began to climb the steps into the reception lobby, pausing to half-turn and watch him depart. She instinctively rubbed her thumb on the underside of her engagement ring, an image of Rupert jumping into her mind; younger, more relaxed, happier.

So different, back then ...

The memory of Rupert mutated into Stefan, seven years previously. Fresh-faced, optimistic, roguish. Barely twenty-four years young, before ... Maddie shuddered. She glanced briefly back at Charlie, then scurried up the remaining steps, into the depths of the hotel.

*

'Three miles away ... backpacker central. Not your style, Maddie, not your style at all. Unless your mobile's been stolen.'

Rupert pocketed his smartphone, picked up his suitcase and hurried across the lobby's marble floor, leaving the cool air conditioning behind. He paused on the kerb outside to slip on his sunglasses, shielding the glare from the rising sun, then scanned the near-deserted street. He checked his watch and crossed to the opposite side of the road, peering down a row of parked cars. He marched past each one, halting by a taxi, scrunching his hand into a fist to hammer on the rear window.

The startled driver leapt up, squinting at Rupert, who thrust his phone through the open window. 'You take me here?'

'Okay, okay. We go.' The driver opened the door and hurried around to open the boot, heaving Rupert's suitcase inside.

'Meter, yes?' said Rupert, tapping the electronic box mounted on the dashboard as he climbed into the passenger seat.

'Yes, okay. No problem,' the man replied. He swiftly settled into the driving seat and pressed a button on the black box to zero the neon figures.

Rupert held his phone up next to the meter, the screen facing the driver. 'Here, okay?' he said, pointing to the flashing location icon on the electronic street map.

'Yes, yes.' The driver slipped the taxi into gear and accelerated away.

*

Maddie stepped into the dim corridor and closed the door to her room, checking she'd locked it. She shielded a yawn with her hand and glanced down to check her watch through sleepy-sore eyes, groaning. *Far too early.*

The schoolgirl-age Thai receptionist looked up from the glow of her tablet's screen and beamed, easing one side of her headphones away from an ear. 'Okay, lady?'

Maddie nodded, pressing her cheek against her flat palms and shaking her head, by way of explanation. She made her way past the desk towards one of the comfy sofas on the far side of the lobby, in the process filtering past a handful of wasted-looking travellers slouched around a low table stacked with dozens of empty beer bottles and an overflowing ashtray. Maddie sank down onto a vacant couch, resting her shoulder bag next to her. She pulled out Liz's paperback and fanned the pages.

Outside the lobby a clunking diesel minibus rumbled to a stop, its brakes squeaking. The engine spluttered and died. A door creaked open, then slammed shut with a muted *thwack*. Footsteps shuffled up into the lobby behind Maddie, past the all-night party table, seeking out the young receptionist. Maddie zoned out the fast exchange in Thai between the receptionist and the minibus driver in favour of the drunken group's English murmurings and occasional tittering. The background voices began to merge and dissipate as her eyes grew heavy, sleep beckoning …

The minibus driver perched on the reception desk and lit a cigarette, checking his watch. Maddie sank further into the couch, her arm draped over the shoulder bag, limbs relaxing, consumed by the soft leather. She drifted further from Bangkok, away from Rupert, leaving the humidity and reality behind ...

*

Rupert stepped out of the taxi and collected his suitcase from the driver, handing him three dollars – just over the metered amount. He glanced up at the tiered entrance lobby and began to climb the steps.

'You want go to Cambodia?' the minibus driver asked, slipping off his perch on the edge of the reception desk, pointing to Rupert's suitcase.

'No, thank you. I'm looking for a friend.'

'Okay.' The minibus driver sucked on his cigarette and withdrew.

*

The minibus driver passed Maddie, slumped on her side, hidden behind the couch's backrest, her eyes wide open. She took a slow calming breath, listened to the footsteps passing by. Other Western voices drifted into her woozy awareness.

'How many hours … ten or twelve?'

'Twelve, although it depends on the driver's right foot and how many other vehicles he manages to avoid slamming into.'

Maddie listened intently, until … again – *his* voice, instantly recognisable.

'I'm looking for a friend of mine, Madeline Bryce.'

Maddie snuck a look up to her left, around the side of the couch.

'Morning Gabby, you on the bus too?'

Maddie glanced right, towards Victoria. She caught her eye, sprung a finger up to her lips before Victoria could call out her name. She frowned and threaded her way between two tables, easing herself down onto the sofa beside Maddie, her back to Rupert, who stood at the reception desk behind them.

'What's with the secrecy?' Victoria whispered.

Maddie leaned in and cupped her hands around Victoria's ear. 'Up there, at reception, is my ex. He can't know I'm here …'

Victoria shifted around slightly, enough to steal a look up at Rupert.

'Will you take me to her room? I need to make sure she's alright,' Rupert explained to the receptionist.

Victoria looked back at Maddie. 'But I thought—'

'Me too. I don't know how he found me, but I need to be on my own right now. Will you help me, please?'

Victoria's expression changed from sleepy indifference to wide-awake intrigue. She glanced back up the steps. 'The receptionist is taking him to your room.'

Shit.

Maddie propped herself up. 'I've got my essentials here. He won't recognise any of the clothes or other stuff …' She glanced down at the street, pointing. 'Is that the minibus to Cambodia?'

'Yes. Some of the passengers are loading up.'

'Okay. I'll get my passport when Rupert's looking at my room. Can you nip up and grab my stuff when he comes back down?'

Victoria nodded, pocketed the key and glanced over her shoulder. 'Go now. Wait on the main road, around the corner by the 7-Eleven. I'll make sure we stop to let you on.'

'Thank you,' said Maddie, scampering up the steps to the vacant reception desk.

*

'You're sure this is Madeline Bryce's room?'

'Room eleven, yes. But she not here.'

Rupert stepped into the room, scanned the unfamiliar backpack and boots. 'This isn't hers, she must be in another room. You have a signing-in book, a list of guests?'

The girl nodded and led Rupert out of the room. He followed her through the corridor and down the main staircase, brushing past a hotel guest, making her way up to the first floor.

Rupert loomed over the reception desk, watching the girl search through the pigeon holes, opening different colour passports, shaking her head, replacing them methodically. He glanced sideways, flicked his eyes over the same attractive girl from the stairwell. She looked away, hoisting her backpack higher on her shoulders. She maintained the same sedate, untroubled pace down the steps until she reached the street below.

Rupert rested his hands on his fleshy hips and gritted his teeth, exhaling through his nose as he looked back at the receptionist. 'She has to be here somewhere. I tracked her mobile phone, look, see it's … here.' He held the screen between him and the hotel manager, showing a navigation map and flashing flag icon.

Below him, in the street, the minibus clattered into life and pulled away from the hotel entrance. He remained fixated on the phone, his eyes bulging. 'She's moving – bollocks!' Rupert spun around, his eyes scanning the lobby, darting back to stare at the phone. 'Outside!'

He grabbed his suitcase and rushed down the steps into the street, fixated on the screen. A scooter buzzed past, swerving to avoid hitting him. The rider tooted his horn as he sped off. Rupert sprinted down the alley to the main junction, dragging the Samsonite case.

*

'Get in!' yelled Victoria, flinging the sliding door open. Maddie squeezed into the packed minibus, helped by several pairs of hands. Victoria turned to face the driver. 'Go, go, GO!' The van lurched forwards, accelerating away from the convenience store on the corner of the main road, quickly filtering into the traffic amidst honking horns and erratic, zig-zagging, wasp-like scooters.

Memory Card 3. Pic 008
'Stowing away, launching into an adventurous fray. Grabbing life by the balls, scaling the confines of her relationship's walls. Leaving behind the well-trodden tourist trail, the hope that a traveller's life is better than one merely *existing,* behind a veil. Her fiancé, a few frantic steps behind – in hot pursuit, perhaps her backpack will transform into an emotional parachute? A leap of faith into the travel abyss, will it all end in tears, or a near-miss? A lunge of desperate optimism is a brave move, you go for it ritzy-chick, find your own journey's groove.'

Maddie scowled at the camera lens, her glare disrupted by Victoria's hand pressing her shoulders below the window.

'Down! He might be following us.' Victoria peered at the back window. 'There! He's flagging down a taxi. What is he, some kind of control freak?' she said, her voice an octave or two higher than normal.

'Sort of,' came Maddie's muffled reply from floor level, 'I don't understand how he found me—'

'You got a mobile phone?' asked a male voice.

Maddie shifted onto her side, looked up towards the back of the van. Charlie poked his head between a gap in the seats.

'Yes.'

'Is it switched on?'

'Um ...' Maddie pulled her shoulder bag out from under her. She shifted into a sitting position and rummaged through it, retrieving the phone. 'Yup. I left it on charge overnight, switched it on early this morning. Should I turn it off?'

'Definitely. Remove the SIM card to make doubly sure. He's probably used a find-my-phone website and tracked you to the hotel.'

'How is that possible?'

'You didn't set it up?'

'No, of course not!'

'Is your phone passcode protected?'

'No. I never saw the need.'

'Then it's easy enough for someone else to access your phone and register it on the tracking website—'

'But I didn't agree to that!' Maddie gritted her teeth and leaned back against the side of the van, jolting with its motion as she focused on the phone, shutting it down. 'Rupert, you're a jealous git,' she muttered.

Shh-clitch.

Memory Card 3. Pic 009
'Concealment confusion, but unplugging from technology may lead to seclusion. Ripping the heart out of being online, how will she cope without her social media shrine? Uncertainty how Facebook friends will cope without her, be mindful gossip girl, that the world doesn't pass by in an indifferent social media blur.'

'Oy! Give a girl a break, will ya?' Maddie's glare bored into the dimple-cheeked, stubbly face behind the lens.

Barry peeked over the top of his camera, grinning. 'Hey, just trying to capture a moment—'

'Yeah, I got that. Just not right now, at this precise, uncomfortable, moment!'

Barry lowered the camera and winked at her, withdrawing. Jody wagged her finger at him, quietly tutting.

'You okay?' Victoria asked Maddie, snatching a sideways look at Charlie.

Maddie ran her fingers through her hair, wiping a sheen of moisture off her forehead. She nodded and stowed the phone and SIM card in her bag. She turned to face forwards, her heart racing, chest aching.

Jesus Christ, Rupert!

Maddie's tummy lurched as the minibus's suspension swayed to the right, creaking and groaning as they made a sweeping, tyre-squealing left turn. She peeped over the bottom of the windowsill at pedestrians ambling behind railings on the Phra Pin-Klao Bridge.

'Stay low,' hissed Victoria, pushing Maddie's head back down. 'His taxi's coming up fast, honking its horn. I don't think he's seen us … we'll know in a few seconds. Looks like he's going … straight. There he goes – close one. You must have turned the phone off just in time.'

'Really?'

'Uh-huh. His taxi's heading off on the main drag. Same bloke asking questions at the hotel – bit overweight, face like a city banker.'

'I bet he's seething,' said Maddie, pushing awkwardly up to a crouch, glancing around at the other passengers. She attempted a sheepish smile to acknowledge anyone who met her eyes. 'Cambodia, here I come …' she muttered, to several muted whoops and stilted hand-clapping from a few of the other passengers.

Eleven

Memory Card 3. Pic 012
    'Urban living, Thai style. Black spaghetti power lines dangle, strung out like weeping willows in a burdened telegraph-post tangle. Dotted beneath on the potholed scree and tarmac, children of school age lay mud bricks beside an old wood shack. These power and communication dreadlocks suggest hope and progression, but will these kids really be able to build a future out here, on the edge of civilisation? That, my friends, is the West's perpetual, unanswered guilty question.'

    Barry lowered his camera onto his lap and turned away from the rear window. He slumped back in the seat, absently panning around his fellow travellers. His gaze rested on Maddie, squeezed in next to Victoria in the front row. She shifted her eyes away, darting past the side windows.
    'What are you listening to?' asked Maddie.
    Victoria paused her MP3 player and tugged an earphone out. 'Bit of Chicane. Old stuff, but it fits somehow, being on the road.'
    Maddie nodded and gazed out of the side window, watching a muddy river zip by beneath a small provincial bridge. 'I prefer to watch music videos. Feels strange, being disconnected.'
    'I'd be totally lost. Necessary, for you though – being pursued. How long are you going to torment him?'
    Maddie frowned. She leaned back to refocus on Victoria, seated in uncomfortably close proximity. 'I'm not with you.'
    'It's a punishment, right? I mean, you still want all that don't you – the lifestyle?' Victoria tapped her earlobe to emphasise her point. 'They look expensive. Were they a present from hubby?'
    Maddie touched her ear, fiddled with the pearl and diamond cluster. *What was the occasion ... a birthday, Christmas, perhaps?*

'Rupert was very generous, and attentive in the early days. After ...' Maddie's expression glazed over. She smiled a sad smile. 'When we first got together.'

Maddie placed both hands in her lap and massaged her thumb into her opposite palm. Victoria placed her hand on Maddie's shoulder. 'They all start out being charming, even in my world. My last one was a loveable rogue. You know the type. So he had to go.'

'How did you end it?'

'Packed my stuff, left a note and walked a hundred yards to the nearest hostel.'

'You bump into him again?'

'Oh yeah, but that's the great thing about travelling in a hot climate, sunglasses are your forcefield. They save a lot of awkward eye contact.'

'It sounds so easy ...'

'It wasn't, still isn't,' Victoria said quietly, 'but show no weakness, that's my motto. Never let them see that you gave a shit.' Victoria flicked her gaze away from Maddie, replaced her earphones and sat back, closing her eyes.

Maddie folded her arms and turned to face forwards, staring past the back of the driver's head, through the windscreen. She watched rain drops form, smeared to the sides of the glass by the wipers slowly dragging across the screen, too slow and worn to cope with the increasing intensity.

*

'So you fail, to find wife. She off, having good time,' said Joe-Ho's crackly voice over the intercom system outside in the narrow alley. 'You know not where?'

Rupert ran his fingers through his saturated hair then wiped his wet hands on his sopping shirt, which clung to his belly. He shivered as a waft of cool air gusted past. 'No. I set a location alarm on one of those phone-tracking websites. It woke me this morning – she must have switched her phone on. But when I got to the hotel, the signal disappeared.'

'She know you coming.' Joe-Ho sighed, his breathing rattling in an elongated yawn through the plastic speaker housing.

'So what happens now?' Rupert clenched his arms around his chest to contain a shiver as the rain increased intensity.

'You speak to London, they decide. You go in, same place.'

A buzzer sounded, clunking the door an inch away from the catch. Rupert hesitated, then pushed it open and stepped inside.

*

'So what made you change your mind about Cambodia?'

Maddie gazed out through the windscreen, watching the chaotic intensity of scooters, cars and bicycles. All those people, with somewhere to go. They had a purpose.

'Maddie …?'

She jerked in her seat, spun round, her eyes searching the minibus for the voice's source. Charlie made eye contact with her.

'Me?'

'I think you're the only Maddie on board.' He scanned around the rest of the travellers. 'Yup, you're an original.'

'Sorry, what was the question?'

'I didn't think you were getting the bus. Guess the taxi in hot pursuit persuaded you?'

'Um …' Maddie glanced away, paused, then shuffled her body around to fully face him. 'That was my fiancé – possibly now an ex. We had a misunderstanding.'

'Sounds terminal.'

Maddie's gaze twitched away, her eyes glazing over. 'Maybe not. I just need some head space ... to reflect.' She looked back at him. 'What's your story? Last night you said you're on a research trip.'

'My story is nowhere near as interesting as yours. But yes, I'm looking into volunteering on some village regeneration projects, to give them clean drinking water. To cut down on typhoid, among other diseases.'

'How long are you travelling for?'

'A few months. I want to see for myself where the help is really needed, cut out the corruption when the money starts to roll in.'

'Is it that much of a problem?'

'You never heard of Pol Pot, back in the Seventies …?'

Maddie returned a blank look.

'The killing fields – mass genocide and starvation of the Cambodian people?'

'No, I ...' Maddie frowned. She rummaged inside her shoulder bag, pulled out Liz's book: *Survival in the Killing Fields.* 'I've just started reading about it.'

'Oh, wow. May I see ...?' Charlie weighed the book in his hand, flicking through the pages. He turned it over to read the blurb. 'I was hoping to pick up a copy of this. The writer starred in the movie, with Sam Waterstone and John Malkovich. Incredible story. Perhaps I could borrow this, after you've read it?' Charlie passed the book back, watching its journey back to Maddie's hand.

'Oh, sure. Soon as I'm done with it.' Maddie turned to face forwards, cradling the book in her hands as she reread the description on the back cover.

Barry glanced up from sprinkling tobacco into a Rizla. He glanced sideways at Charlie, perched attentively on the edge of his seat, still looking at Maddie. 'Sick fucker. Never brought to account, survived until 1998—'

'Heart attack, wasn't it?' Charlie cut in, ignoring Barry's unblinking scrutiny.

Maddie shifted in her seat, turning around. She alternated her focus between Charlie and Barry.

'That's one theory. Another is that he took a cocktail of anti-malarial pills and tranquilisers to avoid an investigation by the United Nations. Valium and chloroquine makes for a lethal combination.'

'Oooh, look at you, Google-geek,' said Jody, switching her focus between Barry, Charlie and Maddie.

'Just being aware of my environment. It's background research, for my book,' Barry replied quietly, dropping his eyes back to his cigarette rolling.

'What was his infamous catchphrase? "If you live it's no gain, if you die, it's—"'

'"To destroy you is no loss, to preserve you is no gain," that's the quote,' said Barry. Glowering at Charlie, he clamped his fingers around his tobacco tin, snapping the lid shut, his knuckles white and bony.

'Easy, baby, relax ...' Jody whispered, laying her hands carefully over Barry's. Then, projecting her acidic tone from the back of the minibus, she asked 'So, Maddie. What lies ahead?'

'A bit of quiet time, to gather my thoughts,' Maddie replied, turning away.

'What then?'

The minibus trundled on, passing dusty, narrow side roads between rough-faced concrete shopfronts. Maddie dropped her eyes back to the book, began reading.

'I said, what *lies* next?'

Maddie twisted around just enough to glare at Jody. 'I told you, some quiet time.' She held Jody's icy stare. Charlie flicked his eyes between the two girls, then at Barry, who toyed with a wry smile.

Barry tucked his freshly prepared roll-up behind his ear. 'Has anyone heard my theory about Bangkok?' He glanced at Jody before he panned around the minibus, seeking out anyone showing signs of interest. 'It's a simple analogy to do with food. Take my dinner last night, for example … red snapper. A big, beautiful, colourful fish. Strong possibilities for a decent meal, you might think. Add the seasoning: lime, garlic and chilli. But, and this is key, the lime was sliced and laid on top. Garlic, raw, also sliced, as a decorative topping. Chilli sauce – most likely from a supermarket – in a dipping dish on the side. A promising meal spoilt by superficial flavours. That's Bangkok's tourist district – backpacker-ville. It's a reasonable starting point to get acquainted with Southeast Asian culture, it offers exotic, yet diluted possibilities. It's tainted by a mere sprinkling of authenticity. Now imagine that same red snapper – or even a lesser fish – served somewhere other than Bangkok, away from the tourist scene. This time it's been marinated in lime, crushed garlic and freshly diced chillies. The chef has allowed the flesh to soak up these sumptuous flavours over several long, *genuine,* hours. Now the same seemingly similar eating experience is so much richer. Flavours dance on the taste buds. This culinary experience is infused with an authentic taste of Thailand, yet emanated from the same raw ingredients. It's the quest for all real travellers – to seek out the truth from their surroundings.'

Barry glanced around the minibus at any remaining mildly intrigued faces. Jody had already plugged her headphones in and stared out of the window. Maddie appeared to be reading her book. Charlie exaggerated a bored yawn.

Barry dropped his eyes to fiddle with his camera, harmony restored.

*

Rupert stood by the same smoked glass observation window looking down at the dance floor, now flooded with bright lighting and even brighter clothed Thai men and women, aged from sixteen to north of eighty years old. They stood on rubber mats, arranged in perpendicular lines, all replicating – to varying degrees of success – the yoga postures being demonstrated by a highly flexible and sprightly sixty year old woman.

'You interrupt my karma, Yogi Bear.'

Rupert turned towards Joe-Ho's voice, emanating from behind the office's side door.

'She not be happy.'

'Who?' asked Rupert, frowning at the sight of a bright green, walking, talking, pot-bellied figure of Joe-Ho's height, dressed in an alien-design morph suit. The green alien strolled over to join him beside the glass.

'The queen Swami. She punish me for missing class, if she know who I am …'

'You do yoga, dressed like that?'

'I have fearsome reputation, Rupert Sullivan, outside of here.'

'But not dressed as a little green man.'

'No.' Joe-Ho shook his head, his black alien eyes and thin black line of a mouth remaining expressionless. 'Polyester and spandex make me any normal person, down there.'

'Err, yeah … I suppose so.'

'You unconvinced.'

'I'm sleep deprived.'

'And deprived of a wife. Also, property of others. London, not happy.'

'No ... have you spoken to them?'

'Only now,' said the alien, motioning with a green thumb over his shoulder, prompting the speaker-phone to crackle into life.

'Mister Sullivan, we are extremely disappointed.'

Rupert glanced at Joe-Ho, who remained facing the glass, now flexing his green limbs, replicating the postures of the yoga class.

'I'm sorry, I—'

'This disruption is unfortunate, but not irretrievable. You are to go back to your hotel. You will contact your employer and explain that you've been unavoidably detained in Thailand due to a medical issue. You will then wait for the arrival of our associate, Mr Fender. Together you will locate your wayward fiancée and return together to the United Kingdom, bringing with you what is ours. If you fail to wait for Fender, he will track Madeline down on his own, and recover your debt. He will then focus on finding you. He will not rest until he's repatriated both of you, one body part at a time. Do you understand the severity of your failure to comply?'

Rupert glanced across at the lunging, downward dog posturing green alien beside him, then turned towards the speaker-phone. 'I understand,' he squeaked, his body trembling.

*

The minibus driver slid the side door open, smiling as he surveyed the weary travellers. He motioned for them to step out.

'Chanthaburi,' said Victoria in answer to Maddie's enquiring expression, 'one stop away from the border town of Ban Pakard, where we'll cross into Pailin. After that is Battambang.'

'In Cambodia?'

'You betcha.'

Maddie shuffled across the seat and eased herself upright as she stepped out, stretching and yawning. The other travellers followed, tired aching muscles almost tumbling them out of the door into the fading sunlight, their colourful mixtures of Western and Thai tourist clothing brightening the dusty grey path. The driver opened the rear doors and began passing backpacks to waiting hands.

Maddie shrugged Liz's rucksack onto her back and wriggled to adjust to its weight. *That's odd.*

'Oh shit!' Maddie shrugged off the straps, lowered the pack and unclipped the main section, slipping her hands inside. Her shoulders slumped.

Virtually empty.

'You okay?' asked Charlie, stepping up to her side.

'The clothes … I've left them with the laundry lady, outside the hotel.'

'Hey, I won't wear any either if that makes you feel better,' said Barry, puffing his rollie into life. 'Or we could trade. Your Victoria's Secrets for my board shorts and vest. What d'ya reckon?'

Maddie ignored him and followed the slow procession around the side of the building to a tiled veranda beneath a road bridge, fifteen feet above them.

'Don't worry, we're in Thailand. Everything is cheap, cheap, cheap. You won't have any problems finding something,' said Jody, waltzing past. Maddie glared at her. Directly ahead, a muddy, lazy flowing river meandered past a wood picket fence lined with pot plants bordering the veranda, which contained a random collection of tables and chairs.

'Welcome to our house,' said a woman to their right, stepping out from a set of patio doors onto the terrace. 'I am Huey. Please come, for refreshments ...'

Barry held back on the far side of the veranda beneath the bridge, smoking, watching some of the travellers head inside. Others mingled by the fence overlooking the river. Barry squinted upstream into the setting sun, then rotated to look behind him, his gaze following the arch of the bridge across the water. Its elongated arch span mirrored above the road, where bunches of cables sagged between concrete columns in an opposing curve. He reached for his camera.

'You pay now?' the driver asked Maddie, his eyes beaming, matching his happy smile. Maddie glanced at Victoria, shooting her a *how much?* expression.

'We all paid ten dollars to get to the border. We'll split the cost of taxis on the Cambodian side, tomorrow.'

Maddie nodded her thanks and paid the driver, nodding to acknowledge his palms pressed together and bowed-head gesture.

'Local buses are cheaper, but it's much more comfortable this way – one seat each is a real luxury.' Victoria stepped up to the reception desk and handed her passport to Huey, who glanced up at Maddie.

'You are one more, in group?'

'Oh, yes. Late addition. Do you have another single room? Or perhaps a twin, we can share,' Victoria turned to Maddie, 'if you're okay with that? We could split the cost – it's normal practice,' she added.

'Of course. That would be great, thank you.'

Huey searched through her bookings diary. 'One night?'

'Yes.'

'No more single. Double, share, okay?'

Victoria glanced at Maddie who nodded. 'Yes, that's fine.' She watched Maddie hand over her passport. 'Saves having to fend off your shadow …'

Maddie turned to follow Victoria's gaze to Charlie, leaning against the fence outside, surveying the sun setting over the river. 'Ah … yes, he's—'

'Fit, gorgeous – melt in the mouth delicious?'

'I was going to say, attentive.'

Victoria picked up the room key from the desk. 'We'll see. Got your stuff?'

'Yup, all set.' Maddie followed Victoria up the concrete stairs. She stole a look back at the veranda just before the view disappeared. Charlie half-turned, caught her eye and held her gaze. Maddie looked away quickly and scurried upwards, hot on Victoria's heels.

Shh-clitch.

Memory Card 3. Pic 018
'Jousting to feast at dusk, no doubt will commence soon, he stands beneath the setting sun, hopeful that she'll see him and swoon. Presenting himself in the best available light, missing only his mighty charger, is this whiter than white, phony knight. A new day dawns in twelve hours' time, how long will it take her to work out that he's a piece of slime? His dream of a nocturnal conquest rests with her emotional state of mind, dream on fella, dream on … do you really think she's *that* naïve and blind?'

'Something amuses you …?' Charlie folded his arms and shot Barry a quizzical look.

Barry lowered his camera and chuckled. 'Buddy, you always amuse me.'

Jody slipped her arm around Barry's waist, cuddled in and steered him towards the guest house entrance. Barry shrugged the camera strap over his shoulder and pulled Jody closer as he sauntered away. 'Don't leave me out here with the phony testosterone,' he whispered huskily, causing her to snigger. Barry waggled his little finger at Charlie, who shook his head and turned away to face the river, visibly bristling as he heard Jody screech with laughter behind him.

Twelve

Immaculately polished black brogues strolled into the departure terminal without pausing beneath any of the numerous flight information screens. The shiny leather shoes threaded their way across the busy concourse, sidestepping anxious and excited holiday-makers, walking past rows of check-in desks, heading straight for baggage security and passport control.

Rachel Brown, the duty security officer, watched the suited figure avoid the segmented queuing system, approaching her from the roped-off side of the metal detector. She straightened, taking a moment to assess him. Tall and lean, yet solidly built. Probably six-two and thirteen stone. Sandy coloured hair, wire-framed glasses, clean shaven with piercing blue-grey eyes. *Early fifties?* Yet he carried himself with the poise of a younger man – springy on his feet, almost as if in constant state of readiness.

The man slowed his cadence, lifted a hand and snared his security pass in a thumb and finger from where it dangled on a web cord hanging between the vee of his jacket. He held up the photo card ID in clear sight and waited patiently while Rachel examined every detail, comparing it to her morning briefing sheet. Satisfied, she scanned the security pass barcode with her company-issue smartphone and confirmed his clearance grade on the screen. 'Thank you sir, please proceed.'

He nodded once and coasted around the side of the metal detector, walking briskly yet seemingly unhurried. Rachel shifted on her feet to sneak a glance at his profile as he exited the area.

'He a spook?'

Rachel glanced over at Gareth, her male colleague. 'Got to be, with that clearance level.'

'They throw some cash at these guys, don't they. His suit's got to be more than my monthly salary.'

'More, probably, given your expanding waistline,' she smirked, refocusing to peer over Gareth's shoulder at the luggage X-ray images on the screen in front of him.

*

Victoria sat back in the wicker chair and flicked her wet hair over its high back. She nodded at Jody as she raised a bottle of cold Chang to her lips and savoured the cooling sensation as she swallowed. 'You can't beat this after a long day on the road.'

'Sure can't.' Jody leant forward to chink her bottle of beer against Victoria's.

'What route are you guys planning?'

'The usual. After Battambang – Siem Reap and Angkor Wat, then Phnom Penh. That's when things could get a bit … lonely.'

'Oh. You heading off in different directions?'

Jody nodded. 'I'm heading down to Ho Chi Minh City after Phnom Penh, then up the Vietnamese coast to Halong Bay. I'll fly home from Hanoi. But Barry's already done that route, only he crossed the border into northern Laos, travelled down through Luang Prabang and Vang Vieng.'

'Ah. Tricky.'

'Yup.'

'What's his plans, after Phnom Penh?'

'Says he's flying out to Peru, ending up in Argentina. Flying back to Australia from Buenos Aires.'

'South America? That's a disjointed trip, via Asia. That's literally halfway around the world.'

'I know, I keep telling him. But he's going to a wedding in Argentina. Figures while he's out that way he'll check out Machu Picchu. He's already got his ticket.'

'Must be a close friend getting married.'

'His brother. Barry's the best man.'

'You don't fancy going with him …?'

Jody fiddled with her mobile phone. She shrugged, without looking up.

'Oh. He's not—'

'No, not yet. But I'm pretty set on my route, I wouldn't change it anyway,' she said quietly.

Victoria nodded slowly, watching Jody's eyes glisten. 'C'est la vie.'

Jody attempted a smile and looked up at Victoria. 'Maybe, maybe not,' she murmured, her gaze tracking up over Victoria's shoulder, her expression brightening at the sound of flip-flops clacking across the marble floor.

'Started already, I see. Want another?' Barry called out from across the lobby, pointing at the beer bottle clasped in Jody's hand.

'Sure.' Jody drained the remaining beer. She leaned forwards, whispering to Victoria. 'Where's miss-prissy-pouty-mouth?'

'Maddie? In the shower. She volunteered to let me go first.'

'Naïve of her.'

Victoria shrugged. She opened her bag, pulled out a packet of cigarettes. 'She's okay, just unaccustomed to budget travelling.'

Jody smirked.

'If I didn't know better, I'd say you two girls were bitchin' around the bushy-tailed newbie.' Barry handed Jody a fresh bottle of Chang and stood over them, preparing a roll-up.

'You're not drinking?' said Jody, glancing up at him.

'Gonna enjoy a smoke first.' Barry shot her a dimpled-cheek grin as he placed the roll-up between his lips.

'Happy baccy?' said Victoria.

'I'm always happy with a bit of baccy … see ya in a tick. I'm gonna watch the river.'

Jody watched him pad across the tiles and step outside onto the terrace.

'How long you guys been together?' asked Victoria, lighting her cigarette.

'Eight or nine days …'

'Really? You seemed way more familiar than that.'

'Yeah … he's an easy guy to get along with. Got some quirks though.'

'Haven't they all. Doesn't he drink?'

'Not all the time, depends on his mood. Sometimes he likes a smoke instead. Says it balances him out.'

Victoria's eyes narrowed as she took a drag on her cigarette, surveying Jody as she exhaled.

'What about you and Charlie? I noticed your … appreciation of him.'

Victoria flicked her eyes away from Jody, her features tightening into a puckered frown. She shrugged. 'He *is* a dish …'

'I think he likes you.'
'Maybe. Don't think I'm the only one.'
'She's no competition. For you, I mean.'
'We'll see …'

*

Barry turned away from the river and puffed the joint into life, blowing smoke luxuriously from his nose as he refocused past the glowing tip onto Jody and Victoria's table, beyond the sliding doors inside the open-plan lobby. He watched their silent reaction as a pair of tanned legs belonging to Charlie appeared at the top of the stairs and the rest of him descended into view. Both girls turned to greet him. Jody motioned with her spare hand, offering Charlie a spare seat at their table, while Victoria tossed her head to one side, running her fingers through her hair, teasing several strands into a loop.

Barry grinned and raised his camera.

Memory Card 3. Pic 027
'The pretty boy struts in, posturing and preening, this pea*cock* ruffles feathers, enjoys teasing. The spoken-for-magpie checks him out, with her carefully timed pout. His interest however lies elsewhere, with the newbie, but he doesn't stand a prayer. He demonstrates all the charisma of an oil slick, in his clandestine pursuit of this particular posh chick. Little do his gaggle of admirers know he has a target in sight, but is the girl in question aware, will she put up a fight? His pursuit of her is bound to end in tears, best accept failure, chuck, line up those consolation beers.'

Barry eased back from the viewfinder and took another drag on the joint, his gaze once again drawn in close to its glowing embers.

*

The suited gentleman removed his jacket, folded it neatly and laid it carefully in the overhead locker. He settled into his business class seat and removed a set of expensive wireless headphones from his bag, then tabbed through a set of menus on his smartphone. The text to speech conversion software commenced its narration:

'Subject: Rupert Sullivan, civilian. Born, March second, 1985, in Surrey, United Kingdom ...'

He shut his eyes and relaxed back into the seat, listening intently, barely noticing the jet engine hum building in intensity as the plane powered down the runway.

Thirteen

Maddie stepped out of the shower, wrapped a towel around her and pressed her ear to the bathroom door.

Silence.

She eased the door open and peered into the empty room. Victoria's clothes and possessions lay scattered over the bed.

Not the tidiest of roommates.

Maddie swept a corner clear of co-traveller debris and perched on the bed. She hunched over, elbows resting on her knees, fingers fiddling with her engagement ring. 'The question is, little one … do I take you off for a while?'

She studied the way the light danced in the angular contours, how the intricate rainbow patterns glinted in the polished prism. With a sigh she stopped her examination and sat up straight, twisting her back to ease out muscular tension, rewarded with a burst of cracking deep in her spine. She groaned and rotated the other way, repeating the sound effects. 'Should have kept up with my yoga.'

She stood up and hoisted the backpack onto the corner of the bed, emptying the contents onto her side. She scanned the meagre offerings, hands on hips, cursing the loss of Liz's clothes.

*

Memory Card 3. Pic 044
'Strolling across the bridge, meandering in the night, heading downtown towards the sparkling gold-chain-like light. The illumination dangling in trees and beneath ornate poles, like a frozen waterfall, raising smiles and stirring our souls. A slower and relaxed mood here after the sun has set, so why do I sense underlying tension from a predatorily dual-nationality threat?'

Charlie glared at Barry. He turned to face Maddie. 'It's almost like we're moving from an era of black and white to full blown

Technicolor, all in one short walk across the bridge,' he said, trying to catch her eye.

'A bridge-of-bullshit too far,' Barry called out.

Charlie rolled his eyes, watching Maddie's reaction. She turned to look at Barry, hesitated, then nodded, slowing her walk to take in the lights and colours. 'Just as bright as Bangkok but minus its manic flashiness. Subtle by comparison,' Maddie murmured, glancing away as she noticed Charlie's scrutiny.

'See, I knew you'd get into my red snapper theory.' Barry crouched nearby, camera poised, squeezing the shutter, capturing another shot.

The group left the single file pavement behind, able to spread out in the quiet side street. Maddie glanced over her shoulder, flicked her eyes past Jody, pausing briefly on Barry, his camera pressed to his cheek as he reeled off more murmured descriptions. Jody glared at her, encouraging Maddie to hastily look away.

'Oh wow, check out the Buddha bling!' shouted Barry. He ran down the dim road past the group, heading towards a vibrant glow on the opposite side of the street, his flip-flops resonating on the concrete. *Clack-clack, clack-clack, clack-clack ...*

Hundreds of red and gold lampshades hung from under the shop's canopy, extending out from the shopfront over the pavement. Rows of different sized pointed-hat gold Buddhas stood to attention in one corner, surrounded by neat stacks of colourful boxes of sweets, treats and knick-knacks, all bathed in slightly different shades of harsh white fluorescent lighting.

Victoria stared at Barry, dancing beneath the canopy's red, gold and amber sheen. 'Is he okay?'

'He gets a bit hyper sometimes,' Jody replied, watching Barry spin and pump his hands in the air, holding his camera high above his head.

'That looks like some good stuff he's been smoking.'

'Yeah ... actually, he says it calms him down.'

'Really?'

Jody nodded, watching Barry strike a matador posture: hips back, chest puffed out, hands held out at an angle, his hands grasping an imaginary cape which he swooshed and twirled in front of the group. Jody jogged up to Barry's side, cupped her hand and whispered in his ear. He sniggered, relaxed his stance and flung his arms out, hugging her.

'That's what you get from a nation of convicts.'

Maddie turned from studying Barry towards Charlie, who had his arms folded on his chest, his chin held up, defiantly. 'Looks like he's having fun,' she remarked.

'He's making a dick of himself,' Charlie snorted. He stretched his hands out, cracking his knuckles.

'Ooh, don't … sends shivers up my spine,' said Victoria, slipping her hand over Charlie's fingers. He flinched, glanced apologetically at Maddie and tried to pull back from Victoria, but she slipped her arm around his waist. 'It's okay, he doesn't like you either,' she said playfully.

'Who?'

'The Aussie.'

'Oh, I don't doubt that.' Charlie eased away from her.

'Is anyone eating straightaway?' asked Maddie, scanning the edge of a collection of market stalls. 'I might just do a bit of clothes shopping first—'

'Love those red-hot chillies!' yelled Barry. Pulling Jody with him, he dashed away from the illuminated shopfront, leading her towards the food stalls.

*

Maddie lay on the double bed, staring up at the ceiling. Beside her, Victoria twitched, turning over to face her, snoring lightly, venting spicy beer fumes and muttering snippets of incomprehensible sentences. Maddie twitched her nose, stifled a sneeze and rolled over, shuffling away from her room-mate towards the edge of the bed.

She scrunched her eyes shut, willing sleep to come, again asking herself the perpetual, unanswerable question.

What the hell am I doing here …?

*

'Cambodia, are you ready?!' Barry yelled out of the window, his words muffled, buffeted by the airstream rushing past the speeding minibus. He let out a screeching *'Woo-hoo!'* then pulled his head back inside, running both hands through his scalp, taming his wild hairstyle. The driver glanced over his shoulder and shot Barry a nicotine-stained toothy grin.

'Hey sweetie, you gonna try and calm it down a bit?'

Barry turned to grin at Jody. He reached up to cradle her head in his hands, pulling her close for a long, firm kiss. 'I'm the king of the jungle, baby.'

'I know … how about taking some photos, balance things out.'

'Sure thing.' Barry unzipped his camera case, deliberating over his selection of lenses.

'How are you this morning?' said a soft Irish voice beside Maddie. She turned away from staring out of the window towards a lady in her late sixties with glasses, a pale complexion and wearing camping-store travel clothes.

'I'm well, thank you. Sorry, I don't think we've properly met. I was a bit distracted, yesterday.'

'Understandably, from what I gather. I'm Rose. Lively crowd we're travelling with.

Nice mix of age and personalities.'

'Yes. I haven't had a chance to get to know many of them yet, but I've been made very welcome.'

'Exciting for you, taking off on your own. Such a courageous decision.'

'Mmm … thanks. I still have my doubts, but—'

'You're still here.'

'Guess so. Are you going over the border?'

'Only as far as Siem Reap. I'm not on a big trip, like some of the others.'

'Oh, what's happening there?'

'Aside from the temples at Angkor Wat – which I'm told are quite magical – I'm doing a stint volunteering at the children's hospital.'

'You're a doctor?'

'I was, I retired a few years ago. My kids are off doing their own thing. Husband left me last year – for a girl two years older than my youngest daughter. I needed a distraction.'

'Wow. Sounds like you're the courageous one.'

Rose shook her head softly, her gaze drifting away from Maddie. 'No, just pragmatic. My home life was …' Rose hesitated, scrunching up her face behind her glasses. 'I suppose the best description is stagnant.' She looked back at Maddie, half-shrugged, then shifted her glazed, faraway expression back to the window.

Maddie studied her for a moment, then checked herself and sat back in her seat, busying herself with reading her book.

At the back of the minibus, Barry edged forwards. 'Hey man, do you mind if I take your photo?'

The man in front to Barry's left twisted his torso around. 'Me? You'll break the lens,' he said, draping a muscular tanned arm over the seat back.

'No chance. Don't get spooked – when I take a picture I normally record twenty seconds of—'

'I know, heard you yesterday. Ever been slapped?'

Barry grinned, swept his eyes around the bus. 'Always a first time. You a former boxer?'

'Yeah, few years ago. That obvious?'

'Shall we see …?' Barry eased back, lifted the camera to his face and clicked the shutter, holding it down.

Shh-clitch.

Memory Card 3. Pic 064
'Worldly-wise streetfighter, a nomadic Buddhist blighter. He seeks enlightenment and travel karma, without twelve rounds of punch-drunk drama. Wise beyond his years on this planet, he's lived a life on his wits thanks to a chin made out of granite. Avoiding the pursuit of material wealth, this hustling honey-magnet has held onto his mental health. A brawler in his teens and twenties, nowadays a gooey charisma fondue, watching the pennies. The coolest dude I've met so far, beers are on me while we chew the fat in the next bar.'

Barry lowered his camera.

'That's it?' said the man in a neutral tone, maintaining a steely gaze, nothing in his expression hinting at any kind of emotional response.

'That's my twenty seconds of gibberish and your nanosecond of celluloid immortality. Pretty painless, eh? Name's Barry.' He offered his hand and cheek-dimpled, crooked smile.

'Sandy.'

'Nickname or by birth?'

'Does it matter?'

Victoria swivelled around in her seat next to Sandy, a flicker of amusement on her lips.

'Nope, but I'll bet there's a long and exciting story there, either way,' said Barry.

Sandy's rugged face creased into a deeply rutted, missing-tooth grin. 'It's a double-digit grog story, young 'un.'

'You're on.' Barry released Sandy's hand, turning his attention to Victoria. 'Mind if I take your photo, with the old bruiser?'

'You don't want me on my own?'

Barry smirked and shook his head. 'No offence, but you're more interesting to me as a couple. For the contrast.'

'Oh.'

Barry lifted his camera and fiddled with the settings. Jody unplugged her earphones, and leaned forwards, addressing Victoria. 'Don't take any of his bullshit to heart, it's his creative *up his own arse-tistic* side.'

'Right.'

'Yeah, I don't see the world like other people.' Barry flicked his eyes between Victoria and Sandy. 'Try facing each other so I've got you both in profile. Yup, that's great. A bit closer ... fantastic. Now imagine you've just woken up and just laid sober eyes on last night's drunken shag.'

Shh-clitch.

Memory Card 3. Pic 065
'Bazza's fantasy snapshots, designed to encourage laughter, so here's a pair of mismatched travellers looking sheepish, *the morning after*. No need for my normal spiel of verbal crap, congrats Sandy and Victoria for this post-coital snap. Beauty and the beast, on a bus in Cambodia, heading east. But that description ain't quite right, now it's getting light. Booty and the priest, more like, take a closer look Sandy – you ended up scoring the village trike.'

Barry sniggered, yanking the camera away sharply. Victoria swung her open palm, narrowly missing snatching his hand. Barry shielded the screen, whooping with laughter at the image. 'Yeah – rock n' roll!'

'Cheeky bastard! Let me see ...' Victoria knelt up on her seat, reaching for the camera. Jody jabbed Barry in the ribs and wrapped her fingers around his hands, rotating the camera's screen towards Victoria, who stared at the photograph, tight-lipped. She glared at Barry, then turned to Sandy, her head slanted slightly to one side, an eyebrow arched. 'You look pleasantly surprised, and I'm not as appalled as I should be, having scored me a coffin dodger. Maybe we should, you know … consider hooking up.'

Sandy held Victoria's gaze, his poker face unyielding. Barry stopped laughing. He stared at Victoria, open mouthed, alternating his stare between her and Sandy. Victoria searched Sandy's eyes, his gaze trance-like.

'You're kidding …?' Barry murmured.

Victoria slowly shook her head. She edged towards Sandy, lowering her chin to move in for a kiss … turning away sharply just before their lips touched to lurch over the backrest, scrunching her knuckles into Barry's tee-shirt at the neckline, forcing him back into the vinyl seat, her nose inches from his. 'Bet you wish you had *that* picture, eh, you uncouth fuckwit-wallaby-wanker.'

The minibus trundled on, only the driver's tinny music audible. All attention on board focused intently on the back seat. Barry finally broke the silence, sniggering at Victoria's clenched-jaw death stare. He licked his lips and winked at her. 'Fuck me, Vicky, you nearly had me – that's Oscar-worthy!' He inched forwards, his nose almost touching hers, lips twitching into a lopsided grin. 'You ever been in show business? Appeared in any adult movies …?'

Victoria pulled back from Barry. 'You'll never know, arsehole.' She shot Sandy a *maybe next time* pout as she turned to face forwards.

Sandy caught Barry's eye, raised half an eyebrow then sat back with amusement twitching across his furrowed jowls, leaving Barry sniggering behind him like Muttley from the *Wacky Races* cartoon series.

Fourteen

'These border crossings are notorious.'

Maddie looked up from her book and glanced across at the source of the comment, a woman in her late forties. She had faded thin ribbons braided into her curly brown shoulder-length hair, and wore sandals with a wraparound printed floral skirt beneath a well-travelled ivory cotton shirt.

'Notorious for what ... *drugs?*' replied a Chinese girl who sat between Maddie and the woman. She wore a plain white sleeveless blouse, the fabric cut high enough to show a grey tattoo of a wispy dandelion on her shoulder, its stalk flexing as if reacting to a gentle breeze. An inscription in elegant, swooping black font followed the contour above the stalk. On the top right of the fluffy flower, a quarter of the seeds had dissipated, inked floating randomly away.

'Corrupt officials and a cartel of tuk-tuk drivers scamming the tourists, demanding extortionate fares. Fortunately we're heading south, to Pailin. It should be relatively painless. I came through in '89 ... very different back then.'

'Is there a reason you've come back now?' said Maddie.

'Yes. Why after so long?' asked the Chinese girl.

'The best and worst motivation in the world ...'

'For love?'

'For a *first* love.'

The Chinese girl nodded, her gaze drawn across the row of seats to Maddie, who dropped her eyes back to her book, aware of the rush of blood reddening her skin. 'I am Kao,' she said, pressing her palms together in a prayer greeting.

'I'm Maddie. Sorry, I didn't mean to snoop on your conversation.'

'Hey, not at all,' said the older woman. 'I'm Gabby.'

Maddie lowered her book and shook both their hands, maintaining eye contact. 'You may have gathered from my slightly ... um, hurried entrance yesterday that I'm travelling just to see if I can. If it's not too rude to ask, what about you two?'

Gabby sat back and ran her fingers through her long hair, smiling at a secret memory. She lowered her eyes, prompting Kao to go first. Kao leaned forwards, flicked her eyes around the minibus, then whispered 'I broke up with boyfriend. My parents send me away, to discover my new heart. I am practising English and repairing.'

Maddie nodded then shook her head with admiration. She switched her gaze to Gabby.

'Same-same, right …?' Gabby shrugged, withdrawing a silver inscribed tobacco tin from her shoulder bag. She opened it and began preparing a roll-up. 'Twenty-seven years … I wanted to come back, find out before it's too late. I was a student, first year at university ... I was impressionable, passionate. He was my lecturer.'

Kao gasped and spun round to face Gabby, wide eyed.

'I know … improper, perhaps. Clichéd, definitely. But this guy … completely unique and *so* sexy. He had that *phwoar* factor. I couldn't resist him.'

'What happened?' asked Kao.

'Everything …'

Maddie and Kao stared at Gabby, waiting for her glazed expression to refocus.

'Do you think this is it?' said Victoria, craning her neck around the travellers in front of her to look out of the windscreen. The minibus began to slow, turning into a lay-by beside a simple brick building and faded red and white striped barrier. The driver turned the engine off and twisted around to the expectant faces.

'Kampuchea!' he said with a toothy grin.

'To be continued!' said Gabby, grinning at Kao and Maddie as she hurriedly finished off constructing her ciggie.

The weary travellers climbed out of the minibus. They chatted excitedly, stretched and collected their packs.

'You, go there,' said the driver, a palm held open as he dropped his fist into it, replicating the passport rubber-stamp routine. 'Then, you go there. Same-same.' He pointed across a dusty stretch of open ground to another barrier, over two hundred yards away. He dropped his fist into his palm again. 'Okay?'

Barry raised his camera, twisted the lens, bringing Jody and the foremost border crossing into focus, his finger hovering over the shutter button.

'No! No picture!' shouted a border guard rushing out from behind the building, his Kalashnikov rifle swinging on its shoulder strap.

'Whoa, okay buddy. No picture.' Barry stepped back and replaced the lens cap, tucking the camera back into its padded bag, slung off his shoulder.

'Passport – you go,' said the guard, pointing at the building beside the barrier.

'You're in charge, chief,' said Barry, smiling easily at the border guard as he strolled to the front of the group. Jody jogged to catch him up. She latched her arm around his, leaned in to whisper in his ear.

'Easy babe, slow deep breaths …'

Barry chuckled, shot her a look. 'It's cool, all part of the game.'

Jody steered Barry up to the border control hut. They handed their passports through the hatch to another guard.

'Fifteen hundred Baht, easy border crossing. You pay now.'

Barry glanced over at the young Thai guy wearing shades and jewellery who bounded up to them, staying behind the barrier. Barry turned back to the guard inside the hut, watched him flick through their passports, locating the Thai entry visa. Jody squeezed Barry's arm. 'The guy over there, he wants money for the crossing,' she whispered.

'It's cool, no stress,' Barry replied softly, smiling at her anxious expression.

Thunk-thunk. The guard stamped both passports and handed them back. Barry nodded his thanks and led Jody away. They began to walk around the barrier into no man's land.

'Easy border crossing, fifteen hundred Baht …'

'We're good thanks buddy, no problem,' said Barry, leading Jody at a casual walking pace.

'*Is* a problem. You pay, for visa.'

'What's your name?' said Barry, stopping.

'Yamo-nak.'

'Cool name! Nice to meet you, Yamo-nak.' Barry offered his hand. Yamo-nak stepped closer to Barry, accepted his handshake, smiling.

'You go on, Jody, I'll meet you on the Cambodian side.'

'You sure? The guide book said we don't need to—'

'We don't, I'm just being sociable. Go with the others, I'll meet you over there.' Barry winked at her, then he turned to Yamo-nak. 'You like to smoke?'

'Is he okay?' asked Victoria.

Jody looked back at Barry, stood by the Thai border with the two guards and Yamo-nak. 'He does this – befriends random folk. Reckons a smile and a smoke can diffuse most situations.'

They watched as Barry accepted something from Yamo-nak, passing an unseen item back. Barry swung his backpack up off the ground and shrugged the straps over his shoulders. He waved goodbye to the guards and began ambling towards the Cambodian border control.

'They've not shot him yet. That's positive, I think.' Jody turned away from no man's land and shuffled forwards in the queue, as Gabby accepted her documents from the customs official in the kiosk and moved away.

Maddie stepped up to the open window and slid her passport and twenty dollar fee across the desk.

'That's for a three-month visa.'

Maddie turned to face Charlie, stood behind her shielding his eyes from the sun.

'Yes ...'

'That what you want?'

'Think so. Although it does feel a bit uncertain.'

'That's a good thing.'

'Mmm ...' Maddie glanced towards the sound of an approaching flip-flop metronome. Barry shrugged the pack off his shoulders and swept Jody up in a bear hug, making her screech. 'I made it back alive. So where's my reward?'

'Right here, baby.' Jody wriggled around in his arms and pressed her lips against his. When they parted she drew back, studying his pupils. 'You okay?'

'Always. We had a laugh.' He released her and glanced at the rest of the group. 'Let's go crazy in Cambodia!'

*

Memory Card 3. Pic 067
'Homes built on stilted flood defence foundations, without help or intervention from the United Nations. Our elevation on the causeway road, looking across, yet *down* on this type of bricks-and-mortar abode. Developing world pragmatism, versus the Western-world kudos of a penthouse prism. These scandalous double standards should fill us with

shame, but instead we in the West just shrug, and say *we're not to blame*. Built to survive the rainy season, these simple homes rise above capitalist materialism. Forty years on from the famine and genocide, these amazing people hold their heads high with their Cambodian pride.'

Barry eased back from the open window. He carefully wiped dust from the camera lens with a soft cloth, then stared out at the vast expanse of lush, green rice paddies zipping by. The relentless flatness occasionally interrupted by sporadic isolated clusters of single and two-storey buildings. 'The fragility of life, eh ...' he murmured, flinching at Jody's hand on his shoulder. He turned slowly, raising his eyebrows.

'Alright?' she asked, her eyes searching his.

He nodded vacantly, gently squeezed her hand. He turned back to the window to absorb the heat and dusty aroma of natural vegetation, increasingly interspersed with exhaust fumes, mixing with wafts of decaying household rubbish and open sanitation drains that signified a growing density of dwellings and population. Barry continued to stare, a deep, uneasy quiet enveloping him. His camera stayed perched on his knee, always ready, spontaneously and guiltily so.

*

'Hotel?' asked the driver as he steered the minibus to a stop at the side of the road, leaving the engine idling. He turned to peer at the travellers, memorising the accommodation they called out.

'Tomato Guesthouse.'

'Golden Land.'

'Ganesha.'

'Banan.'

'Royal Hotel.'

The driver nodded and clunked the minibus into gear, pulling out behind a scooter carrying two adults and two children, one of whom clutched a cage containing a live chicken.

'Guess you don't have anything sorted yet?' asked Gabby.

Maddie looked over and shook her head.

'The Ganesha is a really sweet little place. We could see if they have a spare room, if you like?'

'That would be great, thanks.'

'Alternatively, there's other places to try – all walkable,' Charlie pitched in.

Maddie shifted her gaze away from Gabby, out of the dusty window where dozens of overloaded scooters buzzed by. A familiar suffocating, acidic sensation began to creep into the back of her throat, chilling her stomach. She closed her eyes, took slow deep breaths.

Gabby nudged Kao, who looked up from her guidebook. She watched Maddie squeeze her hands into fists, slowly releasing them and stretching her fingers, repeating in time with her slow, deliberate breaths.

Kao reached out, placed her hand lightly on Maddie's shoulder. 'We help you ...'

Maddie opened her eyes with a start, her fists still clenched. She shrank back from Kao's touch. 'Will be okay.' Maddie nodded, her red puffy eyes darting away as she began to hyperventilate.

'Stop – please stop!' yelled Gabby.

The brakes squealed the minibus to a halt at a busy crossroad, amidst beeping horns and rasping motorcycle engines. Kao crouched beside Maddie, allowing Gabby to squeeze in behind her and yank the sliding door open.

'Okay?' asked the driver, hurrying out of his seat.

'Our friend, not well. We walk to Ganesha.'

'I drive …?'

'No, thank you. Walk is okay.'

'Okay. Bags, yes?' The driver jogged to the back and began rummaging through the luggage. Gabby climbed out of the minibus and turned to address the group.

'We're gonna take off, guys – need to stretch our legs, get some air. Maybe see some of you later at the Riverside Bar?' Gabby nodded at the murmur of agreement and helped Kao to guide Maddie out of the van, escorting her to the selection of backpacks piled up in the road.

'Which one's yours, Maddie?' asked Gabby, heaving her own pack onto her shoulders.

Charlie stepped out of the minibus, hands on his hips, loitering. 'I'll walk with you.'

'It's okay, really. Maybe we'll see you tonight for that drink,' said Gabby.

Inside the minibus, Barry swivelled around in his seat, craning his neck to watch.

'But you may need—'

'Protection, *here?* Thanks for your concern, but please don't worry.'

The driver slammed the rear doors shut and scampered around to climb back in the front.

The minibus pulled away, leaving Gabby, Kao and Maddie at the side of the road. The faces inside disappeared in a cloud of dust and exhaust fumes. Maddie slumped down onto her pack, her head over her knees, hands trembling. 'Thank you, that was horrible,' she mumbled.

'It's been a tough twenty-four hours. Probably just caught you up.'

Maddie nodded. She pursed her lips, controlling her breathing. 'Everything closed in. Too hot, too fast, too—'

'Shh … no need to explain.' Gabby turned to Kao. 'Which hotel are you staying at?'

'Tomato Guesthouse.'

'Cute name. Okay, let's see how close they are on the map. We'll drop you off on the way.'

'I should check my phone, see what's going on with Rupert. He's—'

Gabby stooped down in front of Maddie, rested a hand on her shoulder. 'Take a moment, it's been a long, stressful day. Think about how much better you'll feel after a shower and some food with a cold drink. Okay?'

Maddie lifted her head and nodded. Gabby and Kao offered their hands, helping her up. She swept dust off her lap, took a deep breath and heaved the backpack onto her shoulders. 'Thanks, I'm all set.'

*

Rupert darted his eyes around the familiar hotel lobby, seeking the source of a squeaking sound. A middle-aged English couple wearing matching quick-dry beige trousers and plain white cotton tee-shirts transited across the white marble floor, their rubber-soled walking shoes departing through the glass door. He dropped his eyes back to the mobile phone resting on his knee, scanning down the list of emails.

'You're looking tired, Rupert Sullivan.'

Rupert flinched, glancing up at the immaculately suited gent. His tall lean frame loomed over the couch, face honed verging on gaunt. Yet his unblinking eyes remained bright and alert behind his spectacles, scrutinising him.

'I expect our mutual acquaintances have told you my name's Fender. A matter of personal baggage.'

'Oh, right.'

'Indeed. Do you mind?' Fender gestured towards the empty space beside Rupert.

'Please, go ahead.' Rupert swallowed, inched over towards the couch armrest, watching Fender pinch his trousers above the knee and elegantly lower himself. He relaxed against the backrest, uncomfortably close.

'So, Rupert ... your fiancée, Madeline. Wedding jitters or a calculated decision to break away from your influence?'

Rupert eased away from Fender's unyielding gaze. 'I wish I knew. She appears to have gone off the rails and—'

'Coffee?'

Rupert blinked. He looked up from fidgeting with his fingers in sweaty palms. 'Oh, okay. Yes, thanks.'

'Excellent. You relax here and apply the grey matter. Over a refreshing hot drink, you're going to tell me everything you don't even realise you know. Beginning with Madeline's state of mind leading up to her – from what I understand – voluntary leave of absence. Yes?'

Rupert nodded, shifting his gaze down into his lap.

'Good man. Exclude nothing, however trivial or seemingly irrelevant. Before we get to that, do you take milk and sugar in your coffee – one broken leg or two ...?'

Fifteen

Maddie rinsed shampoo from her scalp, a time-consuming process under the fine jets of lukewarm water. She wiped moisture from her scrunched-up eyes, opened them and spent a moment watching the bubbles gather around her feet on the tiled floor.

'Still think you know what you're doing?' she mumbled, aware of how hollow and distant her voice sounded in the enclosed shower room.

Maddie finished rinsing off, towelled herself dry, then stepped into the small neat bedroom, the painted floorboards creaking under her bare feet. She dressed quickly, her eyes drifting around the sparse décor.

Life on the road. I must try to embrace the simplicity ...

*

'Better?' asked Gabby from her seat at a wicker table on the tiled terrace.

'Much, thank you.' Maddie glanced around the open-sided restaurant area. 'This place is really sweet.'

'Isn't it? It was recommended in a traveller's blog. Are you hungry? The menu looks lovely.'

Maddie sat down, clutching her rumbling tummy. 'Excuse me. I didn't think I was, but actually ...'

'Creeps up, doesn't it. Kao went off to find a friend who's in town, she's meeting us later.' Gabby slid a menu across the table. She watched Maddie open it and scan down the options, her engagement ring twinkling in the afternoon light. 'Some interesting characters today,' said Gabby, shifting her eyes away from the angular rainbow patterns tickling across the glossy menu.

'Mmm ... some were more interested than others. On the minibus, you were telling Kao about the purpose of your trip. The guy you once knew ... your teacher?'

'My lecturer. Oh yeah, he could *teach*, let me tell you …' Gabby pushed back in her seat, suppressing a shiver with a muted smile.

'You mentioned an age difference?'

'Uh-huh. He's fifteen years older. I know what you're thinking, he's going to be old, wrinkly and unattractive, but,' she shook her head and broke into a wide grin, 'he's still got it.'

'Older men can be just as sexy.'

'More so.'

'Do you have plans to meet him here, in Battambang?'

'No. He's at Siem Reap – the next major city. I'll see him in a few days.' Gabby leant forwards, glancing around the empty restaurant, holding onto an impish smile. 'I'm enjoying the anticipation.'

'How was it left, back in the day?'

'Oh, badly. Young impressionable student – older, wiser tutor. It got intense, but I never regretted our love affair. It's been twenty-seven years ... so much life has gone by, and yet so little has changed, inside.'

'What if it doesn't work out?'

Gabby hunched further forwards in her seat, light dancing in her eyes. 'These feelings, they've been buried deep for so long, I *have* to let it play. If the reality doesn't match the anticipation, at least I'll finally know.'

'Hence the reason for not rushing to get there?'

'Exactly. I'm savouring the build-up, because these lovely moments – the tingly tummy excitement – they disappear so quickly.' Gabby beamed, her relaxed, shiny-eye smile radiating honesty and warmth.

Maddie dropped her head to study the menu. She stole a look back at Gabby. 'I wish I had your optimistic outlook. I struggle, sometimes …'

'So did I, at your age. You learn over time to trust your instinct.'

'Does it still hurt as much, if things don't work out?'

Gabby nodded. 'It always stings.'

Maddie turned away, blinking rapidly. Gabby pulled several tufts of thin paper napkins from the dispenser on the table and pressed them into her hand. 'But it gets easier to let go, forgive yourself,' she said gently with a squeeze.

'Such an idiot.'

'No, you're not. I can give you some space, if …' Gabby shuffled her seat back.

Maddie shook her head. 'My relationship ... isn't straightforward. Rupert has looked out for me, over the years. But recently, he's changed. I changed, after ...' Maddie dabbed the paper napkin against her puffy eyes.

'Hello, you would like to order?' asked the Cambodian waitress.

Maddie looked up, scrunched the napkin into her palm and pointed to a description on the menu. 'Could I have the vegetarian curry, please.'

'Two, and a pitcher of beer, thank you,' said Gabby, nodding encouragingly at Maddie.

'I don't know where to start.'

'What about when you began to change, after ...'

Maddie nodded slowly, concentrating on suppressing the spikes of poisonous bile gurgling in her stomach. 'It's not a fun story.'

'They never are,' Gabby replied gently, sitting back, ready to listen patiently.

*

Fender relaxed into the soft leather cushions and pressed his fingertips together, resting his chin on his thumbs. He watched Rupert swallow the last of his coffee and place the china cup on the low coffee table.

'Aside from the argument the night before, and your sharp tongue the next morning, there were no other issues between you?'

Rupert shook his head.

'No one else involved, no other money problems or strong reservations about the wedding?'

'Not that I'm aware of.'

'You think Maddie was reluctant to get married?'

Rupert glanced away. 'Not until the last two days.'

'Alright.' Fender reached forwards and held out the palm of his hand. 'I'd like your mobile phone.'

'I don't think that's—'

Fender's expression stiffened. He levelled his scrutiny on Rupert's restless eyes and moved his hand closer. 'Now, please.'

Rupert reached inside his pocket, placed the smartphone in Fender's rigid palm.

'Good chap. Would you like another coffee?'

He nodded. Fender's features softened. He stood up, pocketing the phone and strolled away. Rupert turned to watch him brush past a suited Cambodian man. The phone passed discreetly between them, disappearing beneath the man's jacket in a smooth, barely noticeable sleight of hand.

Rupert clenched his teeth, forced down a tickly dry swallow, then bolted for the hotel's front door.

*

'It's greener than I expected … the taxi ride in,' said Jody. She cast her eyes along the row of two- and three-storey terraced shops from the wide pavement on the opposite side of the busy road. 'I suppose I thought it'd be similar to Africa. You know, dusty and barren.'

'Yeah, looks vibrant and promising. Finally Kampuchea has started to shed its destructive history,' Barry replied, carefully wiping dust off his camera.

Jody shielded her eyes from the bright sunshine as she scanned along the balconies, most adorned with bright, colourful electrical brand names, boldly advertising commercial produce. She dropped her gaze back to Barry, absorbing his cheerful expression.

'How long do you think we'll be here?'

'Couple of days, maybe three. Depends … you know how it goes.' He turned to grin at her as they walked on.

'And after you've done your thing, will you meet me in Phnom Penh?'

'Sure. When are you seeing your friend?'

'A week from tomorrow.'

Barry slowed his walk, glanced at her. 'Going to be tight. The temples at Angkor, they deserve a decent chunk of time. You're missing out, big time—'

'I need to meet Penny. Come with me, we'll double back to Angkor together. It'll be more fun.'

Barry slowed to a shuffle. He shook his head. 'We've been through this, Jody. It'll burn too much time. I need a quality stint at Angkor, then Tuol Sleng before my flight out. You know how important that part of the journey is to me—'

'Yes, but—'

Barry shook his head, looked away from her. 'I can't risk missing that flight. It'll impact on my other plans. I made promises.'

'So did I, Barry. I changed my plans on the understanding that I needed to meet Penny, remember?'

He turned, bristling. 'Hey, I didn't force you into hanging with me. I've accommodated you too—'

'*Accommodated* me?' Jody halted, raised her hands to her hips. 'You're not the easiest travel companion, mister. Up and down like a tripping clown on a bungie.'

Barry held her intense stare for a moment. 'Which is why you like me. "At least you're not boring," you said.'

'Okay smartarse, maybe not boring, but definitely unpredictable and unmanageable!'

He began to snigger. 'Ha! Now we're getting to the truth. Your Jedi mind tricks are failing you. Not able to control me, eh? Ain't that the truth.'

'You're such a wanker,' she shouted, turning away from him.

Barry watched her stomp away. 'C'mon Jody, where's your sense of humour?' He broke into a laugh, clutching his belly as he jigged from one foot to the other. She continued walking away, raised her right hand above her shoulder, clenching her fist and flicking him the finger.

*

THWACK!

The thick pane of glass wobbled, pulsing in its frame as Rupert slammed into it. His body hung there, squished, cartoon-like against the glass, then slid down to the floor. He slumped awkwardly, his head lolling to one side, cheek resting on the cool marble, his peripheral vision distorted and at an odd angle.

A pair of polished leather brogues tip-tapped their way towards him, the sound amplified through the floor into his throbbing temple. Smart, neatly creased black trousers lifted and twitched rhythmically above the shining leather, looming into focus. Fender eased to a halt and sank down to a squat beside Rupert's head. He surveyed Rupert's cruciform sprawl next to the glass entrance door.

'That looked nasty,' he said in a cheery tone, dangling a set of keys in front of Rupert's face. 'I thought it prudent, in the interest of our personal security. There's no telling what sort of untrustworthy city bankers there are out there.'

Fender swung the keys into his palm, straightened up and unlocked the entrance door. 'A few dollars tucked into the right hands is a small price to pay to preserve our privacy. Now, shall we begin our conversation again? The one that starts with you promising to tell me the truth, the whole truth and nothing but the *there-are-no-second-chances-or-I'll-break-every-bone-in-your-considerable-size-effing-body* truth …?'

Fender squatted back down and angled his head to connect with Rupert's side-on, blinking stare. 'Agreed?'

Rupert cringed in pain as he nodded minutely.

'Excellent. I'll be over there, when you're ready.' Fender pointed across the lobby at the same couch and coffee table. 'I wouldn't recommend trying to leg it again. If I have to hurry after you and crease my suit, I'll be very, *very,* tetchy.'

*

Maddie wandered along the wide leafy pavement between the grassy segments lined with trees. To her left, thirty yards below the rainy season high-water mark, the wide, muddy brown river ebbed gently past. On her right, mopeds and scooters zipped by like a swarm of mosquitoes, outnumbering cars five to one, tormenting the other vehicles with their unpredictable manoeuvres.

Maddie glanced over at Gabby ambling along beside her. 'How did it go with your friend?'

'Matthew? Good, thank you. We've arranged to meet in five days, as the sun rises over Angkor Wat.'

'Wow, sounds romantic.'

'Yup, should be pretty magical.'

Maddie caught Gabby's faraway gaze and whimsical twitching smile. They walked on in silence, past the white stone benches surrounded by neat sections of thick tufty grass. Maddie breathed in the warm evening air, flinching as a motorbike screeched by, its small capacity engine revving hard, leaving a lingering waft of oily two-stroke exhaust fumes in its wake. *NeeeeeeeEEEERRRRRRR!*

Maddie tracked the bike as it sped past, the rider hunching low on the seat, his chest leaning over bent arms. Her nose twitched, threatening to develop into a sneeze. She pinched her nostrils, shuddering, rolling her shoulders to encourage the cool, prickly sensation to disperse. Her heart rate jolted up forty beats.

Was it really seven years ago ...?

His angular, dimpled-cheek smile. Brooding, hypnotic dark brown eyes partially hidden beneath a mop of black hair, colour matching sporadic patches of uneven stubble. Bold features that hinted at a taut, lean muscular frame. The sort of coiled strength that comes from long hours of practice, not the faintest hint of office-tummy puffiness. The edgy excitement as she swung her leg over the seat, wrapped her arms around him – man and machine, immortal. Lifting her feet onto the pegs, the engine barking, background rushing by as they accelerated hard, the breeze sweeping her hair back behind the crash helmet. Clutching his chest tighter as they leaned into a bend together, the throttle opening wider, engine roaring, heart soaring as he searched for the higher gear, propelling them onwards, even faster ...

'You okay?'

Heart pounding, feeling its echo deep inside the back of his ribcage. Clinging on, tighter. Faster and tighter, and—

'Maddie?' Gabby lay her hand on Maddie's shoulder, squeezing gently. She jumped, shot Gabby a startled glare, which quickly dispersed into pale, hollow-eyed vacancy.

'What is it?' Gabby asked.

Maddie stared through Gabby, her glazed eyes unresponsive for ten, twenty seconds. Finally she shook her head, blinking rapidly.

'Someone ... a long time ago,' she whispered, barely audible. 'He was ... we *were* ...' She shook her head. 'I lost him.' Maddie dropped her eyes to the pavement. 'Do you mind if we walk over there instead, by the river?'

'Of course.' Gabby followed Maddie away from the road, walking silently by her side.

Sixteen

The buzz of conversation and pulsating dance mixes resonated through lusty limbs, mingling in close skin-tingling proximity on the Riverside Bar veranda. Clusters of different nationality travellers stood drinking, socialising, enjoying nocturnal networking amidst enthusiastic chatter, laughter and good humour.

'Where's your girlfriend?' asked Kao, glancing up from the camera's high definition screen.

Barry shrugged, eased his hands around his camera to accept it back from Kao's small fingers. 'Threw a hissy fit.'

'Oh, is okay?'

'She'll get over it. You guys want another beer? Gonna get some grog on, cut loose.'

'No, we okay.'

Barry nodded. He withdrew, weaving his way through the crowd.

'He funny,' said Kao, returning her focus to the group.

Victoria pulled a face, shot a look at Charlie. 'He's a brash beach-bum. There's something edgy and dangerous beneath that mask of creativity, y'know?'

'He talented. Good eye for – how you say, small events?'

'Detail.'

'Yes. He notice things, like interesting people.'

'Where's Maddie?' Charlie asked, looking at Gabby.

'Gone to the ladies.'

Charlie nodded, took a swig of his beer, casually asked 'She okay?'

'Settling in nicely,' replied Gabby. 'How's the research going?'

'Oh, yeah … okay thanks. Progressing in line with my expectations.'

Victoria opened a new packet of cigarettes, offered them around. 'What happened to the others?'

Gabby nodded her thanks to Victoria as she accepted a cigarette. 'Sandy is around somewhere, think he went to do some shopping. Rod said he'll be here later and Barney is over there talking to the girl with the blonde hair and flowery dress.'

'Who's Barney?'

'The kooky German guy trying to sleep his way around Asia.'

'Aren't we all,' Victoria mumbled, jigging to the music vibe. She flicked her eyes at Charlie, delicately sipping the cocktail through a straw with pursed lips.

*

Barry sank his elbows behind him onto the bar and glanced across the long expanse of unvarnished teak, scanning the animated faces of other drinkers, busy chatting and trapping.

'Arrrh! No more fossil music!' yelled the guy next to him in a German accent. His hands clasped against his ears as the first few bars of a remixed version of Madonna's *Material Girl* blended in over a contemporary dance tune, reverberating through hissing speakers.

'Yeah, man, something this century!' Barry yelled, to the delight of the German. He turned towards the veranda, something sparkly catching his eye. He pushed up off his heels, homing in on the shiny earring, making its way across the back of the dance floor. Barry grinned, absorbing Madonna's sultry lyrics as they merged into a synthetic remix.

'Hey, Madge! Yeah, you – material girl!'

Maddie frowned, scanning the sea of gyrating bodies, her eyes darting past unfamiliar faces.

'Over here – Britpop princess!'

Maddie's searching gaze found Barry's wide-eyed lopsided enthusiasm. 'You want a drink?' he yelled, delighting in the cheer and collective "YES!" shouted by his fellow revellers.

Maddie shook her head, moving onwards, squeezing by two more people before Barry shouted again. 'Hey, *Madge*. Don't be getting all sensible – I don't like drinking alone!'

Maddie hesitated, shot Barry another look as she eased through a gap behind a couple kissing. She watched his arms reach skywards, hands opening and closing, punching the air in time with the music. 'Coz I am a material guy, and I'm living in a materialistic-bullshit world …'

Maddie abruptly turned and headed over to him. 'Where's your girlfriend?'

'Sulking! What ya drinkin'?' he yelled over the music.

Maddie stole a look behind her shoulder at the minibus group. Victoria stood leaning in close to Charlie, Kao was chatting to an Italian-looking guy much older than her, and Gabby raised her bottle of water in acknowledgement. Maddie returned Gabby's smile, then refocused on Barry. 'I'll have a beer, thanks,' she said, observing his energetic on-the-spot dance moves.

'Reminds me of my folks' music collection,' he said. He leaned over the bar to signal for another drink, frowning at the lack of anyone to serve him, then turned back to her. 'Could be a while, have mine. I've not touched it.'

He thrust a cold bottle of Chang into Maddie's hand. She hesitated, eyeing the missing top.

Barry raised an eyebrow, nodding earnestly. 'Good point. I wouldn't trust a guy like me either. It's the gobby ones you've got to watch, right?' He plucked the bottle from her hand, held it above his open mouth and poured in a glug of beer. He swallowed and wiped away stray droplets from his chin, then handed it back to her. 'There you go. If it's contaminated, we'll both be trollied. It was good advice, whoever gave it,' he said, his cheerfulness momentarily clouding over. 'Immerse yourself in the experience, but be careful who you trust.'

Maddie held eye contact with him for a moment, then broke away. She lifted the bottle to her lips and took a sip. 'Thanks for the drink, and the advice. You don't seem to follow it yourself.'

'Me? Nah, different for blokes. My life's too short to be cautious – I just rock up with a smile and hope for the best. There's not as many shitty people in the world as everyone says. Besides, I'd rather come a cropper occasionally than carry around the fear of mistrust. That's too big a burden to keep unpacking.' Barry glanced away. He spun around towards the bar and whistled – short and piercing, catching the attention of an Australian teenager appearing from a side door. 'Hey, bud – two Changs please. Have one yourself.'

Barry settled up and handed one of the fresh beers to Maddie, swapping it for the part-drunk bottle in her hand.

'Sorted. No Rohypnol stress.'

'That's unnecessary, but—'

'Reassuring?'

'Yes, strangely. Cheers.' She tapped the neck of her beer bottle against his.

'Don't let me trick you. I'm still a knob, according to Jody.'

'Oh, where is she?'

Barry shrugged. He looked away at the dance floor. 'We always knew we'd be heading in different directions when we got to Battambang. She didn't like being reminded of the conversation.'

'Sorry to hear that.'

'That's travelling … I've got a timetable, this time around.'

'How long have you been together?'

'Not long enough for me to deviate.'

Maddie took a sip of beer, narrowly avoiding the bottle being jostled away from her mouth by a thick-set guy pushing into a gap beside her.

'Whoa, easy chief,' said Barry, shooting the guy a mild warning glare. He reached out a protective arm and guided Maddie away.

'S'alright mate, chill,' slurred the guy in a British accent, his eyes twitching into focus as Barry leaned in close.

'Sure thing, chief. Just mind my friend, yeah?' Barry's hand closed around the guy's elbow, taut fingers pinching the pressure point.

'Fuck man, easy!'

Barry eased his body in front of Maddie, shielding her as he squeezed harder on the guy's elbow.

'Yeeeeaaarrrhhh!'

'Have a pleasant evening.' Barry released his grip. He turned to smile at Maddie. 'This way.'

Maddie followed Barry away from the bar. She flicked her eyes up at the British guy, stood rubbing his elbow with an angry, puzzled expression.

'Don't worry about him, it's just the booze.' Barry led Maddie towards the veranda, steering her to the periphery overlooking the river, where patrons mingled with more space and less bar-room volume.

'So what happens now, with you and Jody – do you toss a coin or something?'

'To decide who follows who?'

Maddie nodded.

Barry looked away, pulled a face. He withdrew his tobacco tin from his cargo pants pocket, carefully pinching the stringy leafy curls into a cigarette paper, focusing intently on the process. 'This was always going to happen. We're both tied into separate itineraries. There's no decisions, just different paths.' He glanced up at her. 'Tell me about your travel plans.' He gently licked along the length of the fragile paper.

'There never were any plans. Just a stupid impulse …'

'Hey, that's as it should be. You're out here, doing it – living and breathing the journey.'

She watched him place the roll-up between his lips, then pause thoughtfully before he lit it with a disposable lighter. 'Unless you quit. Then, yeah, that would be a bit daft.' Barry puffed the ciggie alight, inhaling and squeezing his eyelids shut. He shivered in pleasure as the sensation kicked in. He opened his eyes and offered her the roll-up.

'No, thank you.'

He studied her for a moment before pulling his hand back, tapping ash into the lid of his tobacco tin before taking another draw. 'But you used to, right?'

Maddie looked away, darted her eyes around the bar, unable to see the minibus group. 'How can you tell?'

'Flicker of taste, in your eyes. You sure …?' He offered the joint again.

Maddie slowly shook her head. 'I'll stick to the beer.'

'Cool, me too after this. It's one of those nights.'

'One of those *cheating* nights?'

Barry turned towards the voice. He smiled easily at Jody who stood behind Maddie, her arms folded, eyes cold. Maddie spun round, took a step back. Barry took a swig of beer, finishing the bottle. He smirked. 'I hadn't figured it that way, but knowing me as you do, Jody, you shouldn't pre-judge my—'

'You're an arsehole.'

'I certainly have an arsehole.' Barry studied Jody through the end of his glowing roll-up, it's intermittent glow briefly shrouding her in a red sheen. 'But as to being one—'

A flicker of interest diverted his gaze, breaking his contemplation. He took half a step back, his eyes bright and attentive. 'Hold it right there, don't move a muscle.' Barry yanked his camera up from where it dangled on its strap by his waist. 'That's such a cool shot. Captures your mood perfectly.' He leant back to squint through the viewfinder.

'You fucking arsehole!' Jody swung her right palm, hard and fast at his face.

Barry swayed his head back, rotating his elbow up to block the incoming blow, shielding his camera. Jody yelped as her wrist struck his forearm. 'Whoa, easy Jody!'

She screeched, gritted her teeth and staggered back, simultaneously swinging her left fist, off-balance now. He ducked her wild blow, which instead connected with a nearby male traveller, whacking him in the ear. Barry shrugged the strap off his shoulder and thrust the camera into Maddie's hands, bundling her away from Jody. 'Look after this, will ya – go and get the aristocratic water-diviner. Might need a hand here …'

Barry kicked off his flip-flops and leapt between Jody and the owner of the whacked ear – an Italian guy in his mid-twenties, four inches taller than Barry. The Italian clutched the side of his head, arm muscles taut, veins bulging. He squared up to Barry, the remains of his drink soaking into his Ralph Lauren shirt. The Italian spat abuse in his native dialect, his chest puffed out, arms straight by his side, posturing and thrusting his chest at Barry, jostling him like a prima donna football player. Jody whirled her flailing helicopter arms at him, raining down blows – some on Barry, some on the Italian – whose nostrils flared, also letting loose on Barry with a barrage of his own punches.

'Nice one, Jody!' Barry yelped, hunched down, arms clamped protectively over his head. He mentally counted to three, then sprung up, shoving the Italian hard while yanking his right hand forwards, spinning him around. Barry kicked the back of the Italian's calves, collapsing him to the floor, then wrapped his forearm under the guy's stubbly chin while pressing his left palm against his neck, pinching his windpipe.

The Italian gasped, tried to wrench away, but Barry squeezed tighter. He ducked his head down to shield them both from Jody's relentless attack, causing her to overbalance and tumble to the floor.

He searched the faces of the Italian's angry friends, his eyes connecting with a black haired, pock-faced character, who appeared to be more concerned and less aggressive than the others. 'Just a misunderstanding, okay?' Barry yelled.

'Okay – you let go, yes?' said pock-face.

Barry released his arms, shoved the Italian away from him and stepped back, his hands hanging loose by his side. He flexed up on the balls of his feet, his gaze unblinking as the Italian turned towards him, pain creasing his pretty-boy features. Barry watched his opponent glance around the faces of the other travellers, then nod curtly at Barry, merging back into the crowd seeking solace with his friends.

Barry lowered his gaze to the floor, retrieved his flip-flops, then took three steps and picked up his jettisoned ciggie. He rummaged in his pocket for the lighter, lit up and took a slow drag, blowing smoke from the side of his mouth. He panned around the other travellers in the bar, offering them a lopsided, apologetic smile. 'Round one to the commonwealth criminal,' he said, his snigger dispersing as his gaze rested on Charlie, crouched down beside Jody. 'You calmed down?' he said, meeting her murderous glare.

'Busted my hand – you're such a wanker!'

'Hey, you hit me, remember.'

'You deserved it!' shouted Jody, yanking her hand away from Charlie's examination.

'For what, being sociable?'

Jody gritted her teeth, fought back angry tears. Barry sighed, stifled a laugh and turned away, picking his way through the dispersing crowd, heading for the bar.

*

'You're a very lucky chappie, Rupert. This is the latest model, very sophisticated – all the bells and whistles.'

Fender pulled Rupert's trouser leg down over the probation ankle bracelet and straightened up from his kneeling position beside the double bed. He fished his smartphone out of his pocket and began tabbing through several command screens.

'The primary battery is good for six weeks. A multi-network SIM card recalls real time GPS positioning, which is linked to a separate satellite tracking system for complete coverage, anywhere in the world – accurate to within half a metre. But the feature I particularly like is the location tracking alarm, with variable distance profiles. It's the function that really bites, so to speak, thanks to the built-in Taser, which is activated either by you straying from a pre-set location, or manually by me. So if you decide to do another runner, the Taser will zap you. If you tamper with the ankle bracelet in any way, it will zap you. And if you irritate me, *I* will zap you. In summary, if you do anything to invite my displeasure, it's going to hurt.' Fender enabled the last command prompt on his smartphone and glanced up. 'Understood?'

Rupert stared at him, nodding, a weary slump in his shoulders.

'Smashing. You're fully commissioned. Breakfast at eight?'

Rupert dropped his head into his hands and mumbled something inaudible.

'Good chap. I'll see you in the morning, pleasantly rested. Or, alternatively, I'll get woken by an alarm in the early hours advising me that you've tried to abscond. In which case, I'll find you lying paralysed in the hallway, five metres from here. It's your choice.'

Fender withdrew from the room, closing the door gently behind him. 'Sleep well, Rupert. Big day tomorrow.'

*

Barry swung his bare feet up onto the bed, lay back and hooked his hands behind his head. He glanced over to his left as Jody exited the bathroom, cradling her right arm on a bag of ice. 'You'd better hope it's not broken. Healthcare in this part of the world is costly,' he said.

'Is that supposed to make me feel better?'

'I've done nothing wrong.'

'You were flirting with that posh cow!' Jody winced in pain. She adjusted the ice to a new position.

'You ever considered anger management therapy?'

'Piss off!'

Barry grinned. 'It's getting closer to that point, Jody, where I just might.'

She stared at him. A long silence descended.

'Charlie doesn't think it's broken.'

Barry glanced up from studying his camera screen.

'He said it's most likely bruising.' Jody met his gaze. 'Charlie did a great job of fixing me up.'

'He strikes me as that type. Patch 'em up, rather than scrap it out.'

'He had lovely hands.'

Barry laughed. 'After a few days together, you're already pulling the jealousy angle. Have you learned nothing about your travel mate?' He placed his camera in its padded bag on the bedside cabinet and lay back, eyes shut, hands behind his head. The corners of his mouth twitched mischievously.

'You're going to sleep? You're pathetic.'

'I'm only pathetic on Fridays. The rest of the week I'm a pretty reasonable guy,' Barry mumbled, his voice trailing off. He allowed his body to relax into the mattress, leaving Jody staring at him, slack jawed.

Seventeen

'Welcome to Smokin' Pot restaurant, I am Banock. It is said that we Cambodians eat anything with four legs, except table and chairs. Today we will make two tasty dishes – rice noodle soup and fish curry.'

Banock looked around the table at the six travellers and nodded to each of them. 'Late night, eh, my friends? Too much happiness …?' he chuckled, waving them to follow him away from the corner restaurant, out onto the street. 'We go to the market for fresh, really fresh ingredients, okay?'

'Good camera,' said Barney, the curly haired, twenty-three year old German as they followed Banock through the quiet side street.

Maddie glanced over at him, hunching the camera strap further over her shoulder, repositioning it. 'I'm looking after it, for … a friend.'

'Ja, ja. I see, yesterday. I laugh loud – puffing Matilda.' Barney mimicked Barry's double-arm choke hold then jiggled his cigarette to the corner of his mouth, replicating Barry's mannerisms in such a robotic and comical manner that Maddie had to stifle a giggle.

'You mean Barry?' Maddie asked, noticing Charlie glance over his shoulder at her.

'Ja, his English girl is crazy, no? I buy him beer, try to happy him up.'

'Did it work?'

'No! We smoke, small bit. Then, who cares?' Barney exaggerated a palms-upturned shrug, a broad grin stretching across his cheeks, almost to the point of a grimace. Barney shot Maddie a conspiratorial glance and leant in towards her. 'In her eyes, the crazy one … I see much darkness.'

Barney shook his limbs in a theatrical, eyeball-wobbling full-body shudder. He stopped and pulled back, winking at her, laughing as he trotted away. She watched him skip up to Kao and engage her in witty conversation.

Maddie shook her head and draped her hand around the camera to stop it knocking into her leg as she followed the trainee-chef convoy behind Banock, into the busy market.

*

'Boy oh boy, what a night.' Barry rolled over, stretched and opened his eyes. 'Jody … you in the dunney?'

He listened for a reply. *Silence.* He sat up and swung his legs over the edge of the bed, padding across the cool tile floor. Before he got to the bathroom door, he stopped and turned to scan the contents of the room. On his side of the bed, clothes lay scattered on the floor around his rucksack. On Jody's side, nothing. No neat stack of clothes. No rucksack. No Jody.

Barry poked his head into the bathroom to make sure. Nope, no girl's toiletries bag. He pulled on a pair of board shorts, speared his flip-flops between his toes and grabbed a tee-shirt, yanking it over his head as he stepped into the corridor and pulled the door shut behind him.

'Hi. My girlfriend, Jody. Have you seen her, please?' he asked the girl on reception.

'Today, one hour before. She go.'

'Did she say where?'

'Bus, to Phnom Penh.'

'From here, or the bus station?' he asked, pointing first to the floor, then switching his gesture to indicate outside the hotel lobby.

'Bus bring her. At ten-clock. Go to Phnom Penh.'

He sighed and dropped his head, swearing softly. Then he slowly straightened. 'Okay, thank you.'

Barry sank back against the door of the hotel bedroom and stared at the empty corner where Jody's stuff should have been. 'Nice one, *mate.*' He stepped away from the door, retrieved his mobile phone form the side table and scrolled through his messages.

From: Jody
I can't stand goodbyes, especially on bad terms.
You clearly don't want to travel with me anymore,
so I guess this is *Leah Hari*. It was fun, while it lasted.
I hope you find what you're looking for.

Jody

Barry deposited the phone into his pocket and lifted his camera bag up onto the bed. He searched through the compartments, carefully setting out assorted size lenses, spare batteries and a notebook. He stared at the empty bag. 'Great. Cheers Jody – just peachy.'

Clutching his hands on his head, he pushed the bathroom door open with his foot and hoofed it shut behind him.

*

Maddie placed the camera carefully in her shoulder bag and laid it down in the corner of the open shopfront. She smiled at the other budding cooks and surveyed the selection of different-height tables pushed together in the centre of the shop. On top of each sat a single-burner camping gas stove, deep-sided wok and neatly laid out ingredients. Banock stood at the far end of the cluster of tables, hands on his hips, grinning at his apprentices.

'Stoves on, yes? We begin in three, two, one … cook! Into the pot: oil, garlic, onion, chilli paste. Stir – fast, fast, fast!'

Maddie grabbed the line of small dishes one by one, pouring and stirring them into the sizzling wok, ducking back from the billowing smoke and potent spicy cooking fumes. Behind her, unseen hands reached down and carefully plucked the camera out of her shoulder bag. The figure stepped back from the shopfront and threaded tanned, hairy legs between bamboo tables and chairs, opening up the perfect wide-angle shot.

Shh-clitch.

Memory Card 3. Pic 086
'Cookery sorcery, Cambodian-style farang gourmet forgery. Our intrepid travellers learn the art of creating food farts, from a young Yoda master, with a big heart. An intoxicating gastronomic steam room of exotic smelling spices, guaranteed to purge the pores of impure thoughts and vices …'

Barry lowered his camera, offering the trainee chefs a weak smile. 'Morning, travel mates …' He turned to Maddie. 'Cheers for looking after me camera.'

Maddie shot him a concerned look. 'Oh, no problem. Are you—'

'No burning – stir, stir, stir!' yelled Banock, his hands on his head in mock panic as he ran around the cluster of gas stoves.

Maddie spun away from Barry to tend her wok, keeping her head down, focused on stirring the ingredients around the pan. She added the diced fish, chopped chillies and red pepper before stealing a quick glance up, in time to witness Barry amble away.

'He not happy-snappy,' said Barney.

'What happened?' asked Sandy, peering at Barney through the collective woks' cooking fumes.

'You didn't see last night …?'

'What?'

'Jealous Jody.'

'Of who?'

Barney pointed his spatula at Maddie, who didn't notice, too focused on vigorously tossing sizzling ingredients around her pan. Barney placed his thumb and finger in his mouth, whistling at Barry, prompting him to stop and wander back towards them.

'Sorry for being moody, everyone. I'm skipping town, heading for Phnom Penh – there's a bus in twenty minutes. Maybe I'll see you again. Remember, always capture life.' Barry lifted his camera, freeze-framing the group's mixture of expressions.

Memory Card 3. Pic 087
'A collective adios, to the Aussie pain-in-the-ass. Peering through a cooking haze, they stare back in an inquisitive daze. Their opinion of the man behind the lens, unlikely to be someone they'd accept as Facebook friends. So farewell all you travel folk, the condemned man's off to score himself some action in the big smoke …'

Barry chuckled as he lowered the camera. 'Focus on the food – fools! Don't let a waster like me distract you.' He turned away from Smokin' Pot's open shopfront kitchen and strode purposely away.

'That's it, gone – just like that?' Maddie muttered, tending her wok.

'He *was* a strange one,' said Charlie, suppressing a smile.

'Or possibly, honourable,' suggested Gabby, raising her eyebrow in response to Maddie's enquiring glance.

Around the group, woks spluttered and hissed, encouraging more vigorous spatula action. Banock cast his eyes over his students and began to work his way around the tables, peering into each pan, nodding his head and turning down the heat setting. 'Good. Sixty more seconds, then we feast!'

*

Banock surveyed everyone sitting quietly, sampling their own-cooked meals. Background street sounds filtered into earshot. A moped droned past on an adjacent road, music tinkled from a nearby jewellery shop, a misfiring lorry clunked to a halt down the street, several hire bicycles rattled and squeaked past, drowning out a distant, fast-talking Cambodian discussion.

Maddie sat back from the table and lay her spoon in the empty bowl, resting her hands on her tummy. 'That. Was. Delicious.'

'You leave any plastic, on plate?' smiled Banock.

Maddie licked her lips and shook her head. 'Nope. Thank you Banock, I needed that.'

He tipped his head to acknowledge her, then asked 'The man with the camera, he is one of your group?'

'We're all individuals on the bus, so not really a group,' said Charlie, glancing up from his mobile phone when no one else volunteered a reply.

'It is a mysterious murder movie, ja? We each were bus customers, but some disappear. Until only one is remaining …' Barney leant forwards in his seat, scanned around the table in slow motion, his mouth open, eyes wide. 'Two gone already, never returning. Who is next?' He picked up his spoon, slowly drew it across under his neck then screeched, miming blood spurting from his jugular. He slumped down on the seat, his body jerking sporadically.

Banock slapped Barney playfully on the shoulder. 'This is the end of your Cambodian cooking experience. You have survived your own food. Please, enjoy the rest of your day – you are most welcome here. Thank you for learning.'

Barney, still slumped back in his seat, began clapping under the table, quickly accompanied by the rest of the group. Maddie lifted her bag up onto her lap, delved inside and pulled out Liz's book about surviving in the killing fields. She toyed with the pages, fanning them through her hands.

'That's a remarkable story,' said Gabby, pushing up to her feet.

'A friend gave it to me,' Maddie replied quickly.

'It's necessary, I think, to read it while you're here.' Gabby stepped away from the table.

'In Battambang?'

'In Cambodia, and in life, generally.'

Maddie nodded, noting the flicker of a troubled emotion dulling Gabby's eyes. 'I'll catch you later,' she said, drifting away.

'You gonna stay here and read for a while?' asked Victoria, smiling past Maddie to make eye contact with Charlie, perched on his seat opposite.

'I think I might, yes. Bit of quiet time …'

'Cool. Catch you later?'

Maddie nodded, shifting in her seat as she noticed Charlie still sat down, focused on scribbling in a notebook.

'That is good – for Westerners to understand,' said Banock, gazing at the book cradled in Maddie's hands. He held her enquiring expression, his eyes calm, serious. He sat down next to her, opened a bottle of water, took a gulp.

'Were you affected?' she asked.

'*Everyone* was affected,' he said solemnly.

*

'Aggggrrrrhhhh!' Maddie scrunched her face in agony, buried in the pillow. Wiry fingers kneaded, squeezed and pressed sore muscles, the pressure consistently firm until each brief ten-second respite. Then the hands repositioned, fingertips digging in deeper for another burst of muscle-pummelling discomfort.

'What. The. *Hell*. Did. You. Tell. Them?' gasped Victoria, spluttering her words out between manipulations.

'They ask, medium or strong. I say maximum man-power massage. Good, ja?'

'Jesus!' yelled Victoria, panting between each knuckle-clenching wave of pain. On the next couch along, behind a curtain screen, Maddie tensed, her eyes clenched shut, mouth open, catching short, sharp snorting breaths. 'Sure. They. Can't. See? Aaaarrrrhh!'

Their combined wheezing and stuttering mutterings settled into a consistent pattern of grunts and squeals, until finally the pain eased and warm palms pressed down flat onto their shoulders, radiating heat.

'Bloody hell …' Maddie muttered, breathless.

'Good exercise, ja?'

'Barney – fuck off,' said Victoria in a muffled voice.

He laughed, deep and guttural. 'More pain for the English. My great grandfather, he be proud.'

'Don't joke about that shit.'

'All finish,' said a velvety soft voice belonging to Suki, the Cambodian owner.

Maddie allowed her body to sink into the padded bench, her shallow raspy breaths slowing, gradually becoming deeper, less painful.

'I thought you said this place was called Healing Hands. Felt more like pummelling knuckles. I don't think I'll ever be able to move again.' Victoria flopped her legs over the treatment couch, levering her body upright. 'I'm ruined … Barney, you're a knob.'

'Ja. But tomorrow, you will be wonderful, feeling me.'

'Please …'

Victoria stood behind the curtain and peeled off the cotton massage pyjamas, wincing as she lifted the smock above her head to change back into her shorts and tee-shirt.

'I'd like to punch whoever recommended this place, but I don't think I have the strength.'

'Me too …' muttered Maddie, in a subdued voice. She swept the curtain partition aside and dragged in a sharp breath as a stabbing pain shot across her shoulder. She flinched, shielding her eyes from the low sunlight flooding in from the street, mercifully cooler than the fiery heat of the day.

'Ah culnm,' she said to Suki, passing her five US dollars, respectfully dipping her head and pressing her palms together under her chin.

'I need a drink,' said Victoria, joining Maddie on the pavement outside.

'Did you tip your masseuse?'

'Oh yeah. I gave him a few pointers …'

'I meant, money.'

Victoria shook her head and pulled her sunglasses over her eyes. 'I'll deposit something into the local economy shortly – in the nearest bar.'

Maddie watched Victoria saunter rigidly away.

'Good fun, ja?'

'Definitely an experience.'

'Tomorrow, you thank me. Blind massage is best.' Barney looked left and right, waved both hands up and down in opposition, then settled on his outstretched right hand. 'Bye.' He smirked and marched off, stiff-limbed, to his left.

Maddie watched him leave. She shook her head, then reached down to rub her thumbs along the top of each thigh, smarting. She shook each leg, then hobbled off down the street, following Victoria's distant footsteps.

Eighteen

Barry plugged his headphones into his MP3 player and selected the shuffle function. He watched the bus station fall away behind him, the ancient engine rattling through the seat's thin fabric as it strained to accelerate, jolting the passengers as the driver clunked up through the gears.

'Warp factor ten, Mister Sulu,' he muttered, jiggling and twitching in time with AC/DC's *Shot Down in Flames*.

He winked at the Cambodian lady opposite who had a live duck sat in a straw bag beside her feet. He drew a flat palm across his neck, raised his eyebrows, silently asking: *Is the duck for the chop?* He noted her affirmative nod, then dropped his gaze to the duck, and gravely shook his head. The duck blinked back at him, bobbing its head forwards as the minibus braked heavily, the side door sliding open.

Barry looked over at the ten year old boy perched in the open doorway clutching a fistful of Cambodian currency, jabbering at a couple standing by the side of the road. The man turned to the woman, exchanged a few words. She called out, haggling with the boy over the price. The deal done, the couple stepped into the bus, the man handing the boy several Riel notes. Barry watched them settle in a seat, then retrieved his mobile phone from a pocket and began to construct a text message.

> To: Jody
> I'm coming to find you in Phnom Penh. Where you bunking down? Save a cold one for me, I'll be in the capital in a few Cambodian hours.
> Baz
> PS. I hope your hand doesn't hate me.
> PPS. My head has forgiven you.

*

'Hey, how was your massage?' Charlie called out from a side street, jogging up to intercept Maddie.

'Oh, um … quite intensive. Did you manage to catch up with your folks?'

'I did. Pretty good Wi-Fi signal, actually. Skype really is amazing.'

'Mmm.'

They walked on in silence, Maddie with a slow painful shuffle, Charlie forcing himself to slow to half his normal pace.

'Can I buy you a drink? You look like you could do with some pampering.'

'Pampering? That *was* the idea of the massage. But yeah, that would be nice. Thank you.'

Charlie grinned. He glanced directly ahead, aware of Victoria, fifty yards in front. 'Great, I know the perfect place.' He steered Maddie down a side street, heading for the river.

At the bar, Charlie filled two glasses from the jug of frothy beer and took a sip. 'Less than a dollar a glass, and it's pretty good – cold too. Cheers.' He raised his glass. 'To the open road, full of adventure and discovery.'

Maddie lifted her glass, catching his unblinking gaze. 'Ouch.' She cringed in pain and rubbed her wrist.

'That bad?'

'The German, he told them we all wanted maximum pressure. I heard him laughing at us. Or maybe he was crying in agony, I couldn't tell.'

'So the masseuses are blind?'

Maddie nodded. 'It's a charity. They're really good at finding the pressure points. A bit too good.' She rubbed her elbow, flexed her fingers and rotated her wrist.

'I guess the body is a map and they navigate their way by touch.'

'Yep. The pain aside, it's actually pretty impressive.' She lifted her glass, took a long drink. 'You didn't fancy it?'

Charlie took a hurried chug of beer and shrugged. 'Maybe next time.'

She nodded and glanced away, down towards the river. She watched a fisherman standing on a wide, low-sided punt. He held aloft a neatly gathered weighted net, then swayed his hips left and right, swooping his hands out wide to cast it over the water. Maddie watched the net fall gracefully over the surface in a perfect circular shape. The fisherman allowed the net to sink for a few seconds, then pulled on a central line, helped to haul it back aboard by his young assistant. 'Wow, that's some skill,' she said, watching the well-practised routine.

'No doubt passed on through the generations. How's your book going?'

'Oh, good thanks.' Maddie turned away from the fishermen. 'I'm a few chapters in. It's setting up the political situation in Cambodia. The author's describing his normal life as a doctor, before the Khmer Rouge regime.'

Charlie dropped his eyes, fiddling with his glass. 'Some tough reading ahead,' he said quietly. Maddie watched him trace his finger across condensation droplets on the beer jug.

'What's your plan for travelling, after here?' she asked after a while.

'I was going to ask you the same question. Tomorrow some of us are cycling out to the killing caves at Phnom Sampeau. The day after I'm on a bus to Siem Reap to look around the temples at Angkor.'

'And after that?'

'Possibly up to Laos via northern Cambodia, I haven't planned that far ahead. The temples are the main tourist event for me. Angkor Wat is supposedly the eighth wonder of the world.'

'Yeah, I read that in the Lonely Planet guide. Apparently a sequence from the film *Tomb Raider* was shot there.'

He chuckled. 'How old is that movie – and it's still their sales pitch. I guess that's the draw a Hollywood blockbuster has.'

'I'm sure it'll still be fantastic.'

'We'll see. What about you? I understand you hadn't planned on being in Cambodia at all.'

Maddie's cheeks creased into a smile. Her eyes shone, radiating energy. Charlie shifted on his chair, fixated on her face. 'No … it's surreal. And weirdly, the more strange it gets, the more I feel settled. Can't figure it out.'

'So no firm travel plans?'

'I don't even know what tomorrow holds in store. That might actually be the bit I'm enjoying the most. Although I have to confess, it's still pretty scary.'

'They do say doing something that scares us every day is good for the soul.'

'I'll test the theory and let you know.'

'I look forward to that.'

Maddie glanced up, caught the penetrating expression in his eyes. She swept her glass off the table, finished the beer, then stifled a yawn. 'Thank you, this was really nice. But it's time to take these tired aching bones off to rest.' She stood up, groaning as she stretched. 'That German lad needs strangling. Thanks for the drink, Charlie.'

'You can't leave me to finish the rest of the jug on my own,' he said, pulling a bogus sad face.

'That, Charlie, is inevitable. Enjoy.'

'What about the caves tomorrow – there's a few of us going.'

'Maybe ...' she called over her shoulder, already hobbling away.

*

Fender looked up from behind the English newspaper. 'Good morning, Rupert. I assume you slept well, didn't sleepwalk out of the hotel and get hit with the Taser.'

Rupert slid into the seat opposite Fender and clonked his elbows on the table top. 'Is all this really necessary?'

Fender took a moment to finish reading an article, then carefully folded the newspaper and laid it on the table beside his cup of coffee. 'There's some elements to your predicament that I'm not fully aware of, yet. So until I feel fully enlightened, yes, all this is obligatory. But the ankle bracelet is fairly unobtrusive – you're comfortable, yes?'

Rupert shrugged, reaching across the table to pour himself a coffee.

'Excellent. Now, take a look at this,' Fender passed Rupert a menu, 'and fuel up. We've a long day ahead.'

*

Tap, tap, tap ...

Maddie stirred, rotating her head towards the door. She stared at it, blinking. 'Hello?'

'Maddie? It is Kao. A few of us go to caves. You come too?'

'Um ... sure.' Maddie slid out of bed, opened the door.

Kao grinned at her. 'You sleep for twelve hours!'

Maddie frowned, tilted her head to squint at Kao's digital watch.

'How you feel?' Kao rubbed her thumbs on her thighs, jostling her hands back and forth, grinning.

'The massage? Oh, actually …' Maddie jiggled her shoulders, tentatively smiled, then stretched her hands above her head. 'I feel pretty good. Wow, that's amazing, I don't feel sore.'

'Very good! Breakfast, ten minutes. Okay?'

'Perfect. I'll see you there.'

*

'How much?' asked Maddie, peering at the row of bicycles.

'One dollar each, for the whole day,' said Charlie. He flicked the side-stand down on a traditional lady's shopping bike with a low crossbar, a rack over the rear wheel and a large wicker basket in front of the handlebars.

'You're kidding?'

Charlie shook his head and pointed to the rear wheel. 'It's even got a dynamo, for the front light.'

'Wow, retro. I haven't been on a bicycle for years.'

'It's like making love, you never forget,' murmured Charlie, watching Maddie's neck glow with a red pigment.

'Which gets better with age, like a good wine … so I'm told,' added Sandy, wheeling his bike away from the neat row outside the shop. He shot Gabby a mischievous glance as she cycled past, returning his wink.

Kao looked over her shoulder from the lead bike. 'Ready?'

Maddie stepped through her bike's frame and gripped the handlebars. 'You sure this is a good idea?' She squeezed and released the slack brake levers. 'There doesn't seem to be any rules at the junctions and my brakes feel a bit woolly.'

'There are no *rules*, just Westerners' staying alive procedures,' said Sandy. 'Number one: look left, right, backwards, forwards, all at the same time. Procedure two: keep pedalling, no matter what. The faster you ride, the safer you are. And three: never, ever, expect anyone else to give way. He who is biggest, squishes everyone else. So in the words of Peter Fonda from *Easy Rider*, "Ride hard, or stay home!" Let's pull out.'

Sandy pedalled out into the deserted side road, whooping like a submarine dive alarm. 'Wuuuup! Wuuuup!'

Maddie tacked on to the back of the group, her eyes darting left and right as they approached the first turning. Her fingers tightened around the sloppy brake levers, trailing her heels on the dusty road in an effort to help slow the bike.

'Shit! Shit! Shit! Slow, slow, sloooow …!' Maddie's bike squeaked to a halt behind Charlie. He shot her a concerned look over his shoulder.

'Okay?'

'Um …'

'Here's a gap. Ready … pedal, pedal, pedal!' yelled Charlie. Maddie took a deep breath, stood up off the seat and pedalled hard, shooting out between three scooters sporadically scattered across the road.

'Okay, okay, okay, that's good. Safely across. Turn coming up …' said Maddie, speed talking, coaxing herself through the manoeuvre. She caught a glance from Charlie. 'This is crazy!'

'Wait till the main road, it gets better.'

'Better, how—'

'More exciting! There's the next gap, between the red scooter and the pick-up truck. Go, go, go!' he shouted, accelerating away from her.

Maddie gritted her teeth, pushed her body up over the handlebars and forced down on the pedals. 'Bloody hell!' she yelled, pedalling fast and breathing hard as she cycled up to Charlie's back wheel.

He glanced over his shoulder at her. 'Hey, well done. We're a proper convoy. I'll pull out, let you go past on the inside to shield you from vehicles overtaking.'

'I'm okay here thanks, getting the hang of it.' A nervous smile twitched across Maddie's lips, growing into a fully-fledged grin. 'Woo-hoo!'

*

Rupert stepped out of the lift and slouched his way across the lobby, his Samsonite case skidding behind him on the polished marble. He hunched the straps of his small day-pack off his shoulder and deposited it beside the couch, where Fender stood waiting.

'I almost didn't recognise you,' Rupert mumbled, casting his eye over Fender's lightweight canvas boots, cargo pants with deep pockets, short-sleeve travel shirt and sand-coloured Tilly hat. Beside him, a compact backpack rested against the couch.

Fender surveyed Rupert for a moment, then dropped his eyes to the suitcase. 'Check it into reception as left luggage.' He began to walk towards the reception desk. Behind him, Rupert hesitated for a second too long. Fender turned to study his reaction, locking onto Rupert's twitching eyes like a Death Star tractor beam.

'What?'

'Follow me,' said Fender curtly. He led Rupert to a corner of the lobby. 'Let's find out *exactly* what it is London want. Open it,' he instructed, prodding the suitcase with his boot.

Rupert bristled. 'It's my holiday stuff, it's expensive. I wouldn't want to leave it in a random hotel somewhere and—'

Fender swung his hand down onto Rupert's wrist, squeezing hard. Rupert yelped. His hand fell limply away from the extendible suitcase handle. Fender grabbed the case and hauled it up onto the couch. He held out his right hand, hooked his left thumb behind his belt, his fingers laying over the chunky buckle. 'Keys.'

Rupert flinched, glanced at the lobby entrance door and began to shake his head.

Fender pressed the front of his belt buckle. *Click.*

'Oomph!'

Fender watched Rupert's lock-jawed muted gasp. He reached out in time to guide Rupert's crumpling body down onto the couch, beside the suitcase. Fender ignored Rupert's wide-eyed whimpering and searched through his pockets, withdrawing a set of small keys. He used them to unlock the suitcase and methodically searched through the contents.

'Hurts, doesn't it?' Fender murmured. 'In addition to the proximity settings on your ankle bracelet, I have a manual trigger for the Taser. Now, tell me Rupert ... how much do you know about this particular suitcase?'

Rupert tried to open his mouth to speak, but could manage only a series of whimpers. Fender carefully checked through each item of clothing, then discarded them, forming a pile on the floor. 'On initial examination the contents appear to be clean. However ...' Fender looked down at the pile of clothes, then focused back on the case, '... the weight ratio seems a little off.'

He closed the lid and lifted up the empty case. 'Possibly by an unaccounted kilo or two. Which means either it's made out of an unusual Samsonite grade of granite, or—' Fender crouched down, his fingertips tracing every inch of the suitcase's construction, scrutinising it, inside and out.

Rupert let out a low squeal, glaring at Fender, unable to move a muscle. Fender stopped his search. He eased his fingertips back a centimetre, peered closely at the plastic around the carry handle. 'The craftsmanship is excellent. They've matched the bungs almost seamlessly. It's time to be truthful, Rupert. Blink once for no, twice for yes. Did you know about the case's special construction?'

Rupert squealed and shook his head, an inch either way.

'Stubbornness? Oh dear. You want another hit of Taser?'

Rupert stared at Fender's index finger, hovering over his belt buckle.

One blink.

'Good. We understand each other. So you knew your fiancée's suitcase was identical to this one?'

Rupert hesitated, looked away from Fender, who pulled a lock knife from his pocket.

'Please understand, Rupert, your testicles and this blade will have a *very* close shave unless you're absolutely, completely straight with me. So, once again—'

Two blinks.

'You knew both cases had the same inner and outer double skin construction?'

Two blinks.

'Which contains … cocaine?'

One blink.

'*Heroin?*'

Rupert managed a tiny proper nod, the effects of the Taser wearing off enough for him to partially open his mouth and dribble, mumbling, 'Same.'

'Quantity?'

'One n' alf ilo.'

'High purity?'

'Es.'

'In each one?'

Rupert jolted a nod, able to move his neck two inches now.

'So each case has an approximate street value of one and a half million US dollars, roughly a million pounds sterling.' Fender stared down at Rupert. 'You're in Thailand, Rupert Sullivan. A country with some of the harshest drug trafficking laws in the world, including the death penalty. You and your fiancée are walking around with suitcases vacuum-packed with high-purity Class A narcotics, with a combined street value of three million dollars. Tell me, are you completely insane?'

'Desperate … times,' Rupert spluttered.

'Desperate indeed.' Fender slowly folded the blade away, pocketed the knife and crouched down, hunching forwards on the balls of his feet. He levelled a steely glare.

'You can think of me as a debt collector, Rupert. Sometimes, this means finding people for my clients, other times I recover valuable items. I don't normally concern myself with why my clients want these things returned, or people found. I concentrate on providing an efficient and confidential retrieval service. In doing so, I never expose myself to unnecessary risk. So you, Rupert, are going to pay in advance for another seven days, then you are going to deposit that suitcase in your room, for collection later. This means the trail stops *dead,* with you. When we find Madeline, and have recovered the other case, you can negotiate with your London creditors as to what happens next. I hope for your sake they're feeling suitably charitable. Otherwise, you and your wife-to-be are truly in a deep, deep world of hurt.'

Nineteen

Maddie relaxed her state-of-constant-readiness grip on the spongy brake levers and flexed the tension out of her fingers. She took several deep breaths and allowed herself a quick glance around her as she pedalled along. The pace of traffic on the main road out of Battambang had slowed marginally to a continuous conveyor belt of vehicles, rather than the multi-directional chaos of the town centre.

She cycled past low-lying paddy fields and makeshift roadside petrol stations. The smaller fuel stops sold clear one-litre glass bottles containing varying shades of cloudy, amber-brown liquid stacked on rickety tables. Bigger service stations consisted of an oil drum filled with fuel with a hand pump and hose dispenser under a parasol. Occasional market stalls dotted the road, serving cold drinks from battered polystyrene cool boxes with home-built wooden seats, shaded under ice cream insignia parasols. Other stalls offered cooked rodents on sticks, displayed above a smoking barbecue.

The bicycle convoy meandered on in the stifling heat, skirting the edge of the potholed tarmac road. The frequency of lone palm trees increased the farther away from town they cycled, vying for space amidst the growing density of lush vegetation. Trucks and motorbikes weaved their way past towing trailers stacked high with produce, regularly overtaken by scooters carrying up to four passengers, often zipping by on both sides of the road.

'Water stop, pulling in ...' Charlie called out over his shoulder.

The procession slowed, brakes squeaking, wheels and baskets rattled over the loose scree as they peeled off to the side of the tarmac onto a compacted mud verge. Maddie squeezed her brakes early, freewheeling to a controlled halt behind Charlie.

'Getting my stopping distances sorted now – result.' Maddie eased off the saddle and propped the bike up against a fence surrounding a plastic table and chairs. She slipped under the parasol beside Kao, her cheeks glowing. 'Thank goodness for the shade. Its scorcheo out there.'

'Mad frogs and English ladies go out in the midday sun,' said Sandy. 'There's only two things to drink on a day like this. Bottled water or fresh coconut milk.'

He stood up respectfully to greet the café owner, a cheerful Cambodian lady in her mid-forties. Sandy removed his sunglasses and smiled, exchanging a few Cambodian phrases with her. 'Everyone, this is Chanlina.' The group all smiled and nodded. Sandy sat back down into his seat. 'Call out your drinks order, folks.'

Chanlina scribbled on her notepad and glanced across at Sandy, darting her eyes away quickly when he met her gaze.

'I think we're around halfway,' said Charlie, spreading a pamphlet map on the table.

Sandy unfolded an old pair of scratched reading glasses, perched them on the end of his nose and studied the map. 'Yup. We've been going an hour, so that's about right. I was chatting to the owners of our guest house about the killing caves. This is almost unbelievable, but the Cambodian government has had to restrict access to some areas due to tourists taking souvenirs.'

'What sort of souvenirs?' asked Kao.

Sandy glanced around the table, his eyes misting over. 'Remains of the victims.'

'Seriously?' said Gabby.

Sandy nodded gravely. 'Bones, skulls … macabre memorabilia.'

Silence descended around the table, interrupted only by the occasional exceptionally noisy scooter buzzing by or an ancient truck graunching and groaning, its engine clinging on to life.

Charlie folded up the map and removed it to allow Chanlina to place the first fresh green coconut on the edge of the table. She picked up a machete.

Whack, whack, whack! Chanlina expertly sliced three diagonal cuts in the top, rotating the coconut one hundred and twenty degrees between each swing of the machete, using the edge of the blade to prise out a perfectly cut triangular bung. She removed a new straw from its plastic sleeve and placed it in the hole, then slid the coconut across the table to Kao. Chanlina repeated her expert chopping strokes, deftly cutting an upside down pyramid section out of the top of each coconut. Maddie watched the blade swipe through the air, each blow forming a consistent slice on the green flesh, perilously close to Chanlina's fingers. She looked away and shuddered, wringing her hands together in her lap, an uneasy sensation spiking in her palms, transiting through her limbs like a taut guitar string being sadistically plucked.

*

Fender studied the entrance to The Wild Orchid Villas Hotel. 'This is the place?'

Rupert nodded. He hobbled up the steps behind Fender, his joints still stiff from the Taser shock.

'Good morning. I'm looking for my daughter, Madeline Bryce. I believe she stayed with you recently.' Fender opened a small notebook with Maddie's name written in it and placed it on the desk. Then he held up Rupert's smartphone which displayed a photograph of Maddie. Two fifty-Baht notes poked out from beneath the notebook.

The receptionist studied the phone and discreetly palmed the currency. 'Yes. She been here. I check.' She opened the hotel registration book, leafing through the pages until her finger rested under Maddie's details.

'I believe she left yesterday, on a bus to Cambodia. I need to know who else was with her. The bus company told me there were twelve travellers. Do you know how many stayed here, at this hotel?' Fender withdrew a bundle of folded bank notes from his pocket. 'I would be very grateful if you can tell me their names ...' He peeled off five one-dollar bills and tucked them under the corner of the registration book.

The receptionist flicked her eyes around the lobby, then studied the list of names again, cross-checking with a separate receipt book containing numbered stubs of bus tickets, handwritten with the date and passenger room numbers. She copied several names onto Fender's notebook and passed it to him. He glanced at the list of names and nodded. 'The other five passengers, do you know who they are?'

She shook her head. 'You need ask them.'

'Okay. Can I look at this?' Fender rotated the registration book to face him and flicked back a page, using his phone to photograph the relevant names, making sure the passport numbers were in sharp focus. 'Thank you,' he said, pocketing his phone and notebook. The receptionist smiled, sliding her hand clutching the money under the desk.

Fender pressed his palms together under his chin and nodded once, then turned to Rupert. 'It's likely some of the group are doing a circular route, taking in the main attractions. My bet for their first major destination would be the Cambodian capital, Phnom Penh, or the temples of Angkor at Siem Reap. I'll relay this intel up the line, see what we get back. In the meantime, I've had confirmation that she crossed the border at Pailin.'

'Confirmation from whom?'

Fender glanced at Rupert. 'Sources.'

*

Maddie glanced hurriedly left and right, following Sandy's bicycle through a lull in oncoming traffic, pedalling across the main road and into the small, winding lane. She allowed her shoulders to relax, slowing now in keeping with the sedate pace of the inhabitants milling around the periphery of the road. Overgrown trees, banana plants and bushy greenery dangled, encroaching over the narrow strip of tarmac. Music played from a roadside shack, clear and undistorted. People tended to their properties, chatting, washing clothes, hanging them on lines strung between single-storey wood buildings. Scooters zipped past, pulling out from random hidden paths, some staying on the opposite side of the road, others hurtling directly towards them, haphazardly dodging the group at the last moment.

Ahead, through a near-tunnel of overhanging foliage, a green algae and vegetation-clad rock face rose majestically, tall and imposing in the stifling, penetrating heat. Children ran to the roadside, waving and smiling at the cyclists. 'Sous-dey!' they called out, grinning at the pale-skin visitors.

'Hello!' Maddie smiled, lifting a hand to wave, quickly dropping it back onto the handlebars to rescue a front-wheel wobble.

Sandy eased to a stop beside a small official-looking payment shack. He stepped off his bicycle and rested it against the fence. 'We can leave our bikes here, they'll look after them while we walk up to the caves,' he said, removing his wallet from a pocket as he approached the kiosk.

'How are your legs?' asked Kao, leaning against the fence at a forty-five degree angle, stretching her calf muscles.

'Still there, I think.' Maddie removed a bottle of water from her basket and took a long drink. She passed the bottle to Kao then looked up at the steep twisting path clinging to the side of the rock.

Kao took a mouthful of water and rolled her eyes. 'Medium next time!' she declared, pulling a face as she rubbed her sore muscles.

*

Rupert watched the other vehicles fall away behind them as the taxi weaved its way through the suburban traffic, far less intimidating and congested than Bangkok.

'I'm intrigued, Rupert. What possessed you to take that ridiculous level of risk?'

Rupert turned from the window to face Fender who had his phone balanced on his knee, fingertip-typing a message.

'It's complicated.'

'Then give me a summary.'

Rupert took a moment, sat back further into the seat. 'Turns out I'm not so good investing my own money.'

'Cards and roulette?'

'A bit. That and bad stocks, underperforming shares – with borrowed funds. Trying to buy myself out of trouble. But the market turned against me.'

'Did she know?'

'No. Maddie's had enough to deal with.'

'She didn't know about the Samsonite specials?'

'No, of course not.'

'Deniability – if you got caught?'

Rupert shrugged, shifted his eyes away.

'Still a huge risk, not to mention a tad inconsiderate.'

'Maddie's married to her designer clothes and comfortable lifestyle.'

Fender looked up from his phone. He studied Rupert's expression. 'How much are you in for – what might you lose, if you don't complete your delivery trip?'

Rupert swallowed hard. He looked down at the foot well. 'Everything and … *everything*.'

'Is the right answer.' Fender leaned in towards Rupert. 'Because if we don't locate Madeline and that other Samsonite case …'

Rupert glanced up, briefly holding Fender's hard stare before nodding vacantly and sweeping his gaze back out of the window. 'I know,' he muttered, his voice strained and barely audible.

Twenty

Barry stepped out of the minibus into the heat and energetic bustle of Phnom Penh. A dozen Cambodian drivers ranging in age from late teens to early sixties pressed forwards, all vying for his custom.

'Tuk-tuk … tuk-tuk …' they proclaimed, a constant mismatched chorus of sales patter.

'Hiya guys, no thanks. No. Ort the! Ort the!' Barry filtered through the throng of bodies to the back of the minibus and retrieved his backpack, pressing a ten Baht note into the driver's hand. 'Leah hari,' Barry said cheerfully, winking and pressing his palms into a prayer gesture before weaving his way through the crowded market stalls.

He headed for the far side of the street where the concentration of bodies thinned out, allowing him to find a quiet corner to rest his pack against a building. He glanced back at the thronging market, shook his head and chuckled to himself as he opened his tobacco box and began rolling a cigarette. 'Barry me old mate,' he muttered, 'this girl had better be worth it.'

*

Maddie rested her hands on her knees, doubled up at the edge of the steep path, waiting for her sporadic breathing to settle down.

'You okay?' said Charlie, stepping up to her side.

She nodded, accepted the water bottle he offered, taking a swig. 'This heat … there's no air.'

'No. Getting here was easier than this,' he agreed.

'Yeah. Who'd have thought I'd miss a bicycle.'

'Or stilettos.'

She shot him a quizzical look, gauging his expression.

'I read a magazine article, some time ago. You remind me of … well, it's just that you seemed similar to—'

'*The Bryce is Trite?*'

He nodded.

'Not the kindest of headlines.'

'That was you?'

'According to the gossip columnists. Their photographers caught me after a boozy night out, trying to climb into a taxi in the early hours. You've seen the image a thousand times – smudged eyeliner, creased party clothes, laying in the gutter. Not their finest hour, or mine.' She handed the bottle back to him. 'Cheers.'

Maddie straightened up and continued plodding up the relentless steep slope. Charlie unscrewed the bottle's lid, wiped the top and took a long drink, watching her bottom wiggle as she traversed the next corner and disappeared from view.

*

Barry panned slowly around at the hotel lobby. Smoked glass windows, shiny soft leather seats, a long black marble bar top. Plush and elegant decor. He shrugged the pack off his back, propped it up against the side of the bar and climbed onto a stool, glancing over at the figure on his left, a lopsided grin lighting up his face. 'Bit classy, ain't it?'

Jody rested her hand between the two cocktail glasses stood on the bar in front of her and slid one towards him. 'But I'm worth it, right?'

Barry picked up the glass, tossed the straw onto the bar and took a gulp. He gargled, then swallowed the cool liquid, crunching on a fragment of ice cube.

'Filtered water ice. It *is* a classy joint.'

Jody picked up her own glass and swivelled around on the stool, pursing her lips as she sipped the muddy liquid through the straw. 'Glad you came,' she said in a neutral tone, replacing the glass on the bar.

'Guess we'll soon find out …'

She slowly rolled her lips, licking the remnants of the cocktail. 'Recognise the taste?'

'Sex on the beach?'

She pouted, licking along the length of the straw. 'Only if you're a really, *really* bad boy.'

Barry swept the glass up to his mouth, drained the remaining contents in one mouthful and picked up his pack. 'You can always rely on an Aussie to be a problem child.' He reached around her and plucked her room key off the bar, sauntering past, heading deeper into the hotel.

'Did somebody miss me?' she called after him, a smile twitching on her lips.

'Come and find out, before I go it alone,' he replied, pressing the lift call button.

Jody collected her mobile phone from the bar top, slipped off the stool and strolled over to him. 'So, mister man. Who's going to apologise first?' She twirled a curl into her hair.

'Let's just cut to the fun bit.' He pulled her close, kissing her firmly on the lips.

'You boys, so predictable.'

Barry led her into the open lift. 'I surprise myself, sometimes.'

Jody pressed her body against him. He cocked an eyebrow and dropped his chin down to kiss her again, discreetly checking his watch as the doors closed behind them.

*

Maddie lowered herself carefully into the hammock and gazed out over the endless shades of green and brown patchwork terrain, far below. The fields were bordered with straight roads over which a dusty vehicle haze hovered, smudging the crisp boundaries. She flapped her tee-shirt, lifting her chin to maximise the cooling effect as she ducked back under the shade offered by the woven leaf roof above the hammock.

'I've got a local guide to show us around,' said Sandy, from the periphery of the group. He wiped beads of sweat from his forehead with a handkerchief, stepping aside to reveal an eleven year old boy with tightly cropped black hair, wearing shabby leather-strap sandals and a red wraparound monk's sash.

'I am Malik. Hello. Follow, please …'

Maddie wriggled out of the hammock and eased her feet onto the ground. She stretching her arms out and twitched forwards.

'Need some help?' Charlie offered his hand.

Maddie grasped it and hauled herself up. 'Thanks, was getting a bit too comfy.'

'Yeah, looks cosy. Good for a snooze, later.'

Maddie released his hand, cast her eyes away from his and scurried ahead of him to catch up with Gabby and Kao.

'We'll take a circular route around the top, finishing at the caves,' Sandy said to the group, nodding at Malik to lead on.

'How are you doing?' asked Gabby, pausing to allow Maddie to catch up to her side.

'Okay, I think. You?'

'Good. Your shadow seems … keen, today.'

Maddie glanced over her shoulder at Charlie, a little way behind. 'You think so?'

'Oh yeah.' Gabby winked and squeezed Maddie's arm as she leaned in. 'He needs a cold shower – or chemical castration.'

'Wow, make great photo,' said Kao, peering through the group gathered at the top of a long flight of concrete steps descending into a deep, vast cavern. A thick stone handrail – carved to look like a snake's body – sat on top of foot-square balustrades and descended with the steps, sitting up and fanning out at the cavern's floor into a tall, wide tail. High above the steps, the cave dripped with moist spiky green and brown stalactites.

Maddie followed the group down into the coolness of the cave, her eyes drawn upwards to marvel at the draping rock formations, pitted alcoves and patches of mossy clumps. From the last step at the bottom of the cavern, the floor levelled out for thirty feet, then sloped down to a lower tier, where the enclosed roof opened up to reveal tall rocky outcrops. The foliage, small trees and bushes at the base of the crags basked in warm sunlight. The group meandered around the plateau between the overcast gloom beneath the rock canopy and sunlight flooding into the gorge, all their eyes fixated skywards, feet mingling in silence, allowing the high-pitched insect sounds to resonate and dominate.

'This Panang-san-pon – *bat cave,*' said Malik, holding his hands aloft, gesturing to the cavern's rocky ceiling.

'Bats …?' said Charlie, shrinking back.

'Don't worry. Like wayward women, they only come out at night,' said Sandy, patting him on the shoulder, chuckling.

Charlie shrugged Sandy's hand away and edged out of the shade, into the warmth and lush greenery adorning the gorge. He wandered towards more steps at the far end, his sweating palms clutched behind his back.

Maddie stood on a patch of higher ground, panning around the village, which clustered around the periphery of the cliffs far below. Grey, terracotta and pacific-blue rooftops peeked out from overhanging trees and bushes, dotted ad hoc – some clustered together, others spread out with more land between them. Adults worked in the clearings, washing, sawing, tinkering with machinery. Children played in the dirt, skipping or chasing each other, their muted squeals just about audible.

'It's hard to imagine what it must have been like, back in the late Seventies …' said Maddie.

'We're about to find out,' replied Sandy in a grim tone. He exchanged a sad look with her, then looked over at Malik and nodded.

'We go,' said Malik. He took the group down a series of steps of irregular gradients into a clearing between rocky sides, replicating a shallow flat-bottomed volcano crater. He led them across the shiny compacted mud basin to the far corner, where he stopped and turned, waiting for everyone to catch up.

'Here are killing caves. Please be respecting, to the spirits.' Malik stepped into a narrow rocky entrance, leading the shuffling, stooping, human caterpillar through a tunnel no more than two people wide and barely tall enough to remain upright. They filtered down the slope past alcoves lit with flickering candles that dripped hot wax onto miniature pyramid mounds of multi-coloured waxy blobs. The naked flames wavered eerily, casting fragmented shadows across the craggy walls that constantly changed size and orientation, confusing rocky boundaries with the passing waft of each visitor.

The rocky tunnel descended farther, its uneven compacted mud floor requiring cautious, stuttering footsteps and outstretched arms to prevent bumping into the person in front. The group wound its way deeper into the claustrophobic gloom, eyes darting warily, lungs heavy in the dank, chilly tunnel. A cloak of darkness descended as candlelight faded around the final curve in the path. Their progress slowed to baby steps, fingers grasping loose clothing of the person ahead, willing the distant glow from the next hidden flame to reach out and find them, bringing its paltry psychological warmth and dim consolatory light into view.

'Bloody hell.' Sandy paused, jostling the rest of the group behind him, bunching them together in a heart-pounding halt. He stepped to his left, allowing just enough space for all of the group to crowd up, the flickering elliptical light from a dozen candles dotted around recesses in the rock reassuring, but barely so. A single chain barrier had been strung across the tunnel sides to protect them from a black void beyond.

Maddie huddled within the group, like a penguin cuddling up, vying for shelter from an arctic breeze. She peered through gaps between their heads, holding her breath as she stared into the candlelight, the consistency of the numerous flames fluctuating, wobbling, shuddering in the turbulence of their arrival. Elongated shadows flickered across the floor, stretching deeper into the recess behind the chain. Their eyes gradually adjusted enough within the gloom to make out where the floor dropped away, plunging over the edge of the cliff into an abyss.

A gasp spluttered from within the group. 'Is that a hip bone – *Jesus!*'

Incredulous eyes searched the heavy shadows. Pulses quickened, stomachs twinged with bile. Limbs shuddered, breathing hastened, chests thumped, souls strained against the bodies' boundaries, itching to escape.

'There's more … further in. I can see a tiny skull,' said Charlie.

Gabby turned away, her hand clamped across her face, hyperventilating.

Sandy forced down a dry, painful swallow, then began to read the dimly lit sign, paraphrasing for everyone else's benefit. 'The Khmer Rouge would drag their victims down here … academic types, anyone with an education. To save money on bullets, they'd strike them with machetes, or simply throw them off the cliff to their deaths. There was no mercy for anyone, of any age.' Sandy turned away, wiped his eyes and shuffled carefully past the others, heading back up the tunnel.

Maddie watched him depart. She edged forwards, only to falter and sway back with the *rat-a-tat-tat* pulse of a series of stark white explosions of light.

'What the—'

The final burst of light lingered for a split-second, ruining night vision, plunging the cave and the group into darkness. The fleeting, sporadic illumination revealed more horrors through Maddie's squinting eyelids, many more bones lay scattered in the deeper recesses and alcoves.

'Who the hell was – Christ!' she whimpered, her voice breaking.

'Sorry everyone, I didn't think.'

Maddie hurried away from Charlie's hollow voice, leaving it lingering ghoulishly in the suffocating depths of the cave. She raced upwards, her hand clutching another, following the meandering candlelight together, the flames flickering erratically as they rushed past. She virtually sprinted out of the cold claustrophobic confines of the tunnel, raising her hands to shield her face from the glare of piercing light outside, gradually creeping back, the sun creating long shadows.

Maddie withered away from its last glowering shimmer, startled yet grateful for its brilliance, warmth and reassurance. She took several deep gulping breaths, one hand still gripping Kao's hot, shaking palm, her other hand resting on her hip. She angled her head back, expanding her chest with lungfuls of warm, sticky air, blinking back the moisture gathering in her eyes.

'Are you both okay?'

Maddie glanced over at Sandy's soft, gravelly voice. She blinked away her emotion, then looked into Kao's puffy eyes and released the grip on her hand. Maddie nodded, reaching out to hug Kao, who'd begun sobbing relentlessly.

'Please … take my handkerchief.' Maddie eased back to allow Sandy pass the white cotton cloth to Kao. Her gaze briefly flickered over to meet his, then she dabbed her eyes and melted away to find her own space. Maddie turned, drawn to movement at the cave's entrance. Charlie stepped out into the sunshine, his compact camera dangling on a strap around his wrist.

'Okay, okay – I'm sorry. I didn't think. I realise now that was a bit inappropriate—'

'A *bit* inappropriate? Tell that to the families of … you fucking insensitive cowboy!' Sandy shook his head in disgust, trance-like, staring at Charlie for several seconds before he wrenched his eyes away.

Charlie shot Maddie a sheepish, apologetic glance. She shuffled away from him, clutching a hand across her mouth, seeking out a quiet space in this most tragic place.

Twenty-One

Barry sat down on the bed and watched the bathroom door close.

'I'm anticipating an energetic welcome,' said Jody in a muffled voice.

'You can count on it.'

Barry scanned the room and reached across the bed, peering at the bedside cabinet. 'There you are, my beauties.' He swiped a clear plastic 35mm film container off the melamine surface and peered at the two memory cards inside, then deposited the film container in his camera case's side pocket.

'Okay Bazza,' he murmured, rolling off the side of the bed, 'light the blue touch paper, and …' He unzipped a section on his backpack and removed a handwritten envelope, which he propped up against the lamp on the bedside cabinet. '… Scoot off to a safe distance.'

He removed his flip-flops, hoisted the backpack onto his shoulders and picked up the camera case. He padded silently out of the room, taking care to close the door softly behind him.

*

'Figured out where you're heading next?' asked Gabby, handing Maddie a bottle of beer.

'I've been reading about the temples of Angkor.'

'Hey, good for you. The spirits are calling you to the open road, eh?' Gabby clinked her bottle against Maddie's.

'That and more – I've been reading more about Cambodia's recent history. It's horrific, but the resilience of the people is inspiring. It's incredible optimism, against all the odds …' Maddie felt her throat tighten, a bubble of nausea fizzing beneath her collarbone. She sloshed beer into her mouth, forced it down, coughing. She lifted a hand to shield her mouth. 'Tell me more about this guy – how long now, until you meet?' she said, her voice distorted behind her palm.

'Thirty-two hours and forty-nine minutes. But who's counting …'

'Wow, that's so exciting! What's the first thing you're going to say to him?'

'I'm not going to say anything. We'll watch the sunrise together, look into each other's eyes and—'

'Boom – get on it!' yelled Barney, slamming his hand down on the table. Maddie and Gabby jumped, recoiling from Barney's hysterical laughter. 'You two, kiss – smooch, yes?'

'Sod off Barney! Scared the shit out of me,' Maddie yelled, her hands gripping the edge of the table.

'Tomorrow, you go to Siem Reap?' he asked in an interested voice, crouching down between them, resting his chin on the table top.

'Maybe. Hopefully not on the same bus as you,' replied Gabby, with a trace of mild amusement.

'But alas, it is in the gods' laps—' Barney jumped up, twirled around in mid-air, landing with his back to the table. He poked out his bottom, half-turned and dazzled them with a wacky grin. 'And the gods can kiss my arse!' He screeched and leapt away, hopping on alternate legs to the far side of the bar.

Maddie watched him depart. She took a slug of beer. 'Why do we bother with them?'

'Men?'

Maddie nodded.

'Because for eighty per cent of the time, the right one can make a lonely heart sing.'

'You think?'

'I know.' Gabby reached out and squeezed Maddie's hand.

'That's still a twenty per cent pain in the arse.' Maddie sighed, removed her bandanna and ran her fingers through her hair. 'Do you have plans, after meeting up with ...'

'Matthew? No. I booked a one-way ticket, wanted to truly step into the unknown. We may see the sun rising over Angkor Wat and feel no connection, no urge to be together. And if that's how it is, that's okay. It'll still be nice to catch up. An hour, a day, a week … there's no time limit set. Sometimes things need to play out, y'know.'

Maddie caught the faraway glaze in Gabby's eyes, lost for a moment in her internal speculation of what might happen. 'That's a lovely, carefree way to view the future.'

Gabby shrugged, refocusing, back in the moment. 'We dig our own channels, in our little corners of the world, to encourage the water to bring life, hoping it'll trickle in a preferred direction. But ultimately that liquid will always find its own path. Sometimes in the channel we've diligently prepared, other times not.'

'So just go with the flow?'

'For now.' Gabby grinned and finished her drink. She pulled focus back onto Maddie. 'Talking of drips – Charlie is an interesting, slightly ambiguous prospect.'

Maddie paused, mid-drink. She lowered the beer bottle, studied Gabby's inquisitive expression. 'For who?'

'You've not noticed his interest in you?'

The embryo of a smile twitched on Maddie's lips. She glanced around the bar, leaned forwards and lowered her voice. 'He's a nice enough guy. Intelligent and well mannered. Today excluded, obviously.'

'Good looking too.'

'Yes, okay, he's attractive. But I think Victoria has a thing for him.'

'Of course she does. But why's that a problem?'

'Um … because she'd be upset. And she's been good to me.'

'She's a big girl. Don't sacrifice your own happiness for the feelings of someone you don't know. If she were a long term friend, then of course, step back. But out here, in the world of the traveller, we're acting under a different set of rules. I'm not saying be an unfeeling bitch and elbow her out of the way. It's about having faith, the confidence to let go and embrace the spontaneity of the moments ahead. So if he makes a play for you, and you're open to that, then don't be afraid to go with it. If it's a mutual attraction between two *available* parties, then that's one of life's beautiful moments.'

*

Rupert peered across the table, watching Fender make notes. He paused to sip his coffee before looking up at Rupert. 'Twelve-seater minibus, all seats pre-paid prior to departure. Unlike the jam-packed public bus on a cheaper tourist route, this was a one seat per person comfort special. Which means we could be looking at eleven or twelve other travellers, depending if Maddie signed up in advance, or jumped on board that morning. I have five names from the Wild Orchid Villas. They are: Victoria Stevens, British. Barnaby Vogel, German. Kao

Yeung, Chinese. Rodney Sharp, British, and Gabby Evans, Welsh. I've made some other enquiries, but can't verify who else was on board because they all bought their tickets elsewhere at different times, without records being available. I've prepared a file on each of the five and have mobile phone numbers for three of them.'

'How is that possible?'

Fender levelled his unblinking gaze on Rupert, who shifted in his seat. 'High roaming charges on their home networks mean travellers often buy cheap pre-paid SIMs, which in Southeast Asia require mandatory registration.'

'Let me guess, validated by a passport number?'

'Yes, for foreign nationals. Six years ago the Thai telecoms regulator standardised registration for Thailand, Laos, Cambodia and Myanmar – formally Burma – into a single data pool. A little incentive deposited in the right pocket and voila, a name and passport number from a hotel register is cross-matched, producing three local SIM numbers. Which, when collated with other useful data,' Fender held up a several sheets of A4 paper, 'produces a wealth of useful intel, which the receptionist kindly printed off for me.' He passed the bundle of files to Rupert.

'No doubt in exchange for hard currency?'

'Correct. Take a look – one of the three phones is currently switched off, the other two are located ... here.' Fender used a thumb and finger to enlarge the satellite map's scale on his smartphone. 'Battambang, and Phnom Sampeau, both in Cambodia.'

'I didn't think it was possible to track a phone number that's not been registered on a location-finding website ...'

'It's not, ordinarily. But the network providers do have logs of cell-site location information – CSLI, as the industry refers to it. These can sometimes be utilised, for the appropriate consideration.'

'You mean bribe.'

Fender peered over his glasses at Rupert. 'Money talks, Rupert. Literally. Or in this case, it provides a historical record of CSLI radio wave *pings* from the phone's SIM to signal masts, which can be triangulated to estimate a rough location.'

He sat back, stretched his arms above his head and linked his fingers, resting them on the back of his neck. 'The Cambodian border opens at nine-thirty tomorrow morning. From there it's a ninety minute drive to Battambang, sixty if the taxi driver accepts my inducement. Get some rest, tomorrow is going to be an important day.'

*

Maddie eased the pack off her shoulders and glanced around the bus station. A few shops hugged the perimeter of the dusty, oil-stained concrete, unpopulated and distinctly sleepy looking at this time in the morning. Several old coaches stood in their allocated bays, their drivers sleeping along the back seat or stood chatting outside a shop front, clasping a steaming cup of coffee.

Victoria sat down on her pack and checked her watch. 'Could have had an extra thirty minutes in bed.'

'I have been early before, still I miss my bus. It is the way of Cambodia,' said Kao, shielding her eyes from the rising sun peeking over the far buildings.

'Yeah … it's messed up.'

'I wonder who else is leaving today?' said Maddie.

Victoria glanced up from behind the flame flickering under the end of her cigarette. She snapped the Zippo's lid shut, puffed the tobacco into life and scrutinised Maddie through the smoke. 'Don't worry, he'll be on the bus.'

Maddie looked over at her. 'Who?'

'Charlie. He told me, *last night*.'

Maddie studied Victoria's cheek-sucking pout, then turned at the sound of approaching footsteps. Gabby plonked a plastic carrier bag on the ground and sank down onto her backpack. 'Water and snacks, for the journey. There's a toilet over there too. Not the most hygienic, but if you close your eyes and hold your nose it's no different to a city centre public loo.'

'That clean? Wow, progress,' said Victoria, flicking ash.

The distant rumble of an old diesel engine drew their attention to the bus station's entrance. Smoke billowed as the bus accelerated and changed gear, clunking with an elongated metallic graunching sound.

Kao stood up, peering at the sign on the front. 'Can anyone see, where going?'

'Phnom Penh,' said Maddie, craning her neck up, then relaxing back onto her makeshift perch.

'It for me! Good luck, in future,' said Kao, reaching down to hug Maddie, then Gabby and Victoria. She collected her rucksack and followed the bus to its parking spot. 'Have fun, travel happy!' she called out, turning to wave at them, grinning.

'Such a lovely girl,' said Maddie, following Kao's progress skipping towards the bus.

'Where's she heading?' asked Victoria.

'Oh, she's on an epic trip. From Phnom Penh she's catching a boat south into Vietnam, heading for Ho Chi Minh City. Then she's getting the coast train north, home to China to go back to university,' said Gabby.

The low rasping of a small motorbike engine sped across the grimy concrete, racing a second bike which pulled out and buzzed past the first, accelerating with maximum sound and minimum speed. It slowed at the last minute, squealing non-existent brake pads grating against bare metal. Barney leapt off the pillion seat of the tiny machine wearing his hefty backpack. 'Whoop, whoop!' he yelled, holding his hand up to high-five the young Cambodian rider.

Barney turned to face the other bike, rapidly decelerating behind him. He formed the letter 'L' with a thumb and finger and held it against his forehead. 'Loooooosssssser!' he shouted, prancing and spinning around on the spot.

Charlie climbed off from behind the second bike's rider, red faced. He wobbled on his feet under the weight of the backpack, glanced sheepishly over at the group and turned to pay his fare, taking a moment to compose himself.

'Great. Evil friggin' Kin-weasel and Steady Eddy, the cuddly teddy …' Victoria muttered, shooting Maddie a playful look.

Barney dumped his pack by Victoria's feet and swept into a low bow, lifting her hand in his, wetting his lips with his tongue, then puckering them firmly onto the back of her wrist.

'Oh, yuk!' Victoria squealed, yanking her hand away and wiping it on her shorts.

Barney lunged one leg forwards, flexing down to the ground. He sprung back up and swapped legs, repeating the scissor action, his hands propped on his hips, head rolling around. 'Morning English minions! Keeping fit for zee temples, ya!'

'Hey Barney, you need to change your dealer – those happy-happy ingredients, they're too hardcore for this early in the morning. Have a normal smoke,' said Victoria, holding out a packet of cigarettes.

'Ah, cancer drugs. Wonderbra!'

Maddie watched Barney jump upright, spin round and robotically moonwalk backwards to collect the cigarette from Victoria's outstretched hand. 'Good gear last night, Barney?' she asked, watching as he tossed his lighter into the air, spun around three hundred and sixty degrees, caught it, and flicked it into a flame in one smooth motion.

'Very ... simulating,' he said.

'You mean, stimulating?'

'Nooooo ... think around it.' He tapped the side of his head with his cigarette hand, which swirled smoke around him.

The low growl of an old engine rumbled off the main road, drawing the group's attention. An ancient bus with faded paint and peeling chrome lacquer bumpers revved hard as it built speed towards them, smoke trailing in its wake. The engine faltered for a second as one wheel crunched down a pothole, before resuming its uneven rhythmic clatter, pausing briefly to allow cogs to graunch into the next gear with a teeth-grinding screech.

'Gotta love this first class executive travel,' Victoria muttered, raising a hand and gesturing for Barney to help pull her up.

Maddie climbed up the narrow steps past the driver and glanced down the rows of passengers already on the coach. She began to make her way towards a spare seat midway along, pausing to smile at Sandy who'd sat down next to Rose. 'Hi, I didn't know you were both heading to Siam Reap,' she said.

'Rose was already booked on, last-minute decision for me,' said Sandy, pulling himself upright and reaching out to encompass her in a gentle hug. 'Great to see you.'

Maddie pulled back before he released her. She sat down on the seat behind them. Rose knelt up and turned to face her. 'How's everything going?'

'Good, I think. The Cambodian people are really friendly and the kids are fantastic – so enthusiastic.'

'I know, aren't they wonderful? I can't wait to start work at the hospital.'

'How long will you be there?'

'A few months, depending how it goes.' Rose turned to glance over her shoulder at Charlie, stood in the walkway beside Maddie's seat.

'Do you mind if I—'

Maddie looked up at him. 'Not at all.'

'Thanks. I'm escaping from our mad German companion.'

'Oh, yeah. I noticed he's a bit wired.'

Charlie pushed his bag onto the floor between his knees and swivelled round to face her. 'Sorry again, about the camera, in the caves – wasn't thinking.'

'Oh, that. Forget it. No harm done.'

'Cool, thanks. Thought I'd blown it,' he added quietly.

Maddie looked away from Charlie's enquiring eyes to stare out of the window. The bus engine turned over, firing in a bone-shaking, full throttle roar. In front of them, Sandy chuckled, glanced around at the other travellers. 'Yeah, give it some beans, man!'

Maddie watched through the window as they pulled away from the depot, obscured through the smog of dust and thick, oily exhaust smoke.

'Do you know how long the bus journey is?' asked Charlie.

Maddie rolled her eyes and turned to face him. 'I think around eight hours?'

'Cool. Lots of time to catch up with what's been going on with you.'

'Oh, yeah. And, um … other stuff – music, for example. Bit early for conversation – I'm not really a morning person. Gonna plug in, catch up on sleep. Do you mind?' Maddie reached into her bag, rummaged for her headphones.

'Is that such a good idea, switching your phone on?'

'Oh, it's fine. I know Rupert, he'll have given up and gone home ages ago. He won't allow me to continue being an irritation.' Maddie tilted the phone screen away from Charlie and tried to switch it on. The blank screen stared stubbornly back at her.

Great. Best Bangkok phone charger. Quality purchase.

She pretended to be listening, jiggling her head to the rhythm of an uplifting song and snuck a sideways glance at Charlie.

Illusion that music is on. Check.

Maddie laid the phone face-down beside her.

Overly inquisitive but intriguing travel guy, silenced. Check.

Twenty-Two

'We've got updated locations. One phone is heading south east, the other two, north west. The north west phones are located within the same triangulation zone. Both sets of signals are travelling at speeds which vary from twenty-five to seventy kilometres per hour, calculated between different signal masts.' Fender looked up from his iPad and checked his watch. 'If Maddie's still travelling with some of the original minibus group, she's most likely caught an early morning bus, which these speeds and directions of travel support. So which way is she heading ... north, or south?'

Fender unfolded a map of Cambodia. 'Heading north on the main road to Sisophon leads to a junction: west from there is the popular route to the Thai border near Poipet. Alternatively, east is towards Siem Reap and the temples of Angkor. Whereas the other phone's route south from Battambang leads to the capital, Phnom Penh.'

'Maddie doesn't do budget travel. She likes her luxury boutique hotels,' said Rupert, looking over at Fender.

'The most obvious route from Sisophon, given where they entered Cambodia, is to head east to Siem Reap. The temples at Angkor are a big tourist draw. If we were to follow the bigger more luxurious hotel theory, the other route, south to the capital Phnom Penh is also a strong contender. So it's a straight choice between north or south. However, she could still be in Battambang, whilst the others travel on. We currently only have three phones from the original twelve travellers to monitor. What if she's with some other members of the group whose phone numbers we don't have?'

'Which leaves us a bit stuck,' said Rupert.

'Maybe, maybe not.'

'What about ringing each number, asking if they're with Maddie?'

'We don't know her situation, or state of mind. There's a risk that if she doesn't want to be found, she'll separate from the group – if in fact she's still travelling with any of them. Our initial play is to get across the border, maintaining a track on all three phones. When we get to Battambang, it's decision time.'

*

Maddie reached into her bag and lifted out Liz's paperback, *Survival in the Killing Fields.* She wriggled to get comfy, rotated away from Charlie's gaze and found her page, marked with her redundant airline ticket. She dropped her eyes and immersed herself in the text.

Through the window outside the bus, the miles fell away in glorious, uninterrupted tranquillity.

*

Fender counted out three ten-dollar bills and handed them to the taxi driver, nodding at the chap's enthusiastic bowed-head prayer gesture. He led Rupert away from the taxi, towards the Thai border crossing. 'Are you carrying anything else I should know about?'

Rupert frowned, shook his head as he studied Fender's expression. 'No. That was because I *had* to.'

'Was it your first time?'

'Yes, of course – I'm not a drugs trafficker.'

'Once is all it takes.'

They drew to a halt at the small Thai customs building. Fender nodded at the guard and handed his passport through the hatch, watching him make obligatory checks. He accepted his stamped passport and moved aside for Rupert to approach the kiosk.

'You're not going to ask them if Maddie's crossed here?'

'No need. I've already confirmed that Maddie came through with the minibus group, three days ago.'

'So you have names of the rest of her group now?'

A small smile creased Fender's lips. 'Bravo, Rupert, welcome to the programme. Late last night, I had more intel. Six new names to investigate. If we're lucky, some of them will have purchased local pre-paid SIMs, in which case there'll soon be more mobile numbers to light up our placement map.'

Rupert pocketed his passport and followed Fender around the faded red and white barrier. 'Doesn't that complicate things? More people to follow, I mean. What if they all split up?'

'It could, in the short term. But once we're closing in on Maddie's locale, it means we're less likely to miss the one person she may have hooked up with, who doesn't have a phone we can track.'

'But if she takes off on her own, we're screwed.'

'Potentially. But we'll still have the list of travellers and their last known locations to assist us. So we check and discount them, one by one.'

'How do you get hold of all this information?'

'Your creditors have associates. They have contacts, open to financial persuasion.'

'Government contacts?'

Fender shot Rupert a devious look. 'Everyone has a price.'

*

Maddie stepped down from the bus onto the dusty gravel car park and wandered over to Gabby and Victoria.

'Food stop and comfort break,' said Charlie, latching onto her side.

'Yes, I thought it might be.'

'How's the book going?'

Maddie slowed her walk, pausing before answering. 'I'm only a third of the way in, but it's building into a compulsory read.'

'Excellent. Do you fancy a bite to eat? My shout.'

'No, thank you. I've misplaced my appetite.' Maddie walked on to catch up with the other girls, Charlie still trotting along at her side. She stepped away from him and leant in towards Gabby. 'Do you know where the ladies are?'

Gabby pointed to a path down the side of a corrugated tin roofed building. 'Past the kitchen, hang a left. Loos are just there. Have you got toilet paper?'

Maddie shook her head. Gabby opened her bag, passed Maddie a packet of Kleenex. 'Thanks.' Maddie strolled off on the path. She glanced to her side at Charlie, shadowing her.

Great.

Maddie followed Gabby's directions behind the building, heading for a door with peeling varnish and 'WC' letters marked with chalk beside a crude sketch of a stick woman wearing a triangular skirt.

'I think I can manage from here,' she said to Charlie, a curt edge to her voice.

'Oh, right, sorry. I didn't mean to … I'm heading over there,' he said, pointing to the door with a stick man.

'That *is* a relief.' Maddie shoved the door open, shaking her head, muttering, 'You men, always same-same.'

*

'Of all the taxis in all the fleapits in all of the Asian world …'

Fender poked his head through the open door and stared at Rupert, sat on the back seat. 'Funny, I never took you for someone with a sense of humour, Rupert. The heat getting to you?'

'Just trying to lighten the mood, bond with my captor.'

'Don't. Attachments formed in a crisis are rarely sustainable.'

'Can't blame me for trying to increase the odds of a positive outcome.'

'Based on your current predicament, there's not a fluffy bunny in an alligator pen's chance of that.'

Fender slid onto the seat beside Rupert, pulled the door shut and patted him on the knee. Rupert returned a confused, apprehensive look. 'Just engaging in banter with my hostage,' said Fender, handing Rupert a clump of printed pages. 'Worth a perusal – background info on the six missing travellers.'

'Oh, right. Any more surprises?'

'Take a look.'

The taxi accelerated away from the Cambodian border. Fender checked his watch. 'We've got about an hour. I've just had confirmation of mobile phone numbers associated with four out of the six new names and the location of the last signal masts their SIMs communicated with. Read them out, I'll find them on the screen.'

Rupert shuffled through the wodge of paper. 'You got all this from border control?'

'Indirectly, for a small consideration. London has useful friends.'

'Money talks, eh?'

'Always.'

*

Rupert looked up at the paint peeling from the hotel's wood shutters, then dropped his gaze to the electronic device held in Fender's palm, about the size of a handheld VHF radio.

'That looks expensive.'

'Not as much as you'd think.'

'What is it?'

'A type of mini Stingray. Unlike its bigger brother, which mimics a cellphone mast to pinpoint a phone's location, this device listens for a cellphone's signal ping, communicating with the nearest mast. This one's called a Wolfhound. There are other versions – Jugular, for example.'

'Catchy names.'

'Indeed.' Fender glanced down at the screen. 'Signal's getting stronger … this way.'

Rupert trotted up to Fender's side. They headed for a run-down looking hotel doorway.

'So what's the plan, wait until he gets back and …' Rupert caught Fender's reproachful expression. 'What?'

'Rodney Sharp. Born January 5th, 1998. He's eighteen years old.' Fender offered up his watch up for Rupert to see. 'It's ten-fifteen in the morning. No eighteen year old on a gap year travelling around Asia is going to be out of bed at this hour by choice.'

'Okay, I take your point. So we knock on his door and—'

Fender opened his wallet and withdrew a five dollar bill. 'Hard currency generally opens doors far easier than a shoulder barge.'

The lightweight wood door rattled in its frame, Fender's clenched-fist *rat-a-tat-tat* echoing around the corridor. He stepped back, allowing the receptionist to unlock the door and ease it open. Inside the room, movement stirred beneath a thin cotton sheet. A pimply, spotty face twitched on the grubby pillow next to a mane of soft black hair spilling out from under the covers, her face nuzzling into his neck.

'I hope she's legal, sonny.'

The sleeping boy's eyelids sprung open. His head jerked up, startled pupils staring at the open door. The receptionist flicked his eyes inside the room, then scurried away, armed with a set of hotel master keys in one hand, a five dollar bill in the other. Fender stepped into the room, followed by Rupert, a few tentative steps behind. 'Morning Rod … you look a little jaded. It is Rod, isn't it, rather than—'

'Who the hell are you?' Rod shrank back against the headboard. His young female companion jumped up, clutching the sheet around her chest, trembling. Rod yelped, dropping his hands to shield his naked groin. 'What do you want?'

Fender pressed his finger to his lips, then gently eased the door back into its frame, leaving it slightly ajar. He turned to face the girl, pulling out his wallet. 'How much?'

'Five – dollars.'

Fender glanced at Rupert. 'Seems to be the going rate for irregular requests. Here's ten dollars. Collect your clothes, enjoy your day.' Fender lay the money on the edge of the bed, pinched his shirt, then jerked his thumb over his shoulder. The girl nodded.

'Turn around.' Fender said to Rupert, rotating on his heels to face the door.

'Why?'

'To be respectful.'

'But she's a prostitute.'

'Yes, I know,' he snapped, glaring back at Rupert, before softening his tone. 'She's also a teenager – someone's daughter.' Fender held his first finger up, then pointed it at his belt buckle. 'You don't want me to ask a second time.'

Rupert shuddered and turned around.

'Good boy.'

The girl slipped between them. 'Khawp jqi. Saba-dee.' She pulled the door open and scurried away.

Fender took a step forwards, closed the door and twisted the locking catch half a turn. He turned to face Rod, cowering at the far side of the bed, his hands covering his manhood.

'Mister Rodney Sharp, 14 Sykes Lane, Uxbridge, United Kingdom. All I need from you is a brief look at your mobile phone and some information about a fellow traveller, Madeline Bryce – Maddie, to her friends. I believe you shared a minibus with her from Bangkok, across the border into Cambodia.'

Fender held up Rupert's mobile phone, displaying a picture of Maddie for Rod to examine. 'She's in imminent danger. Do you understand the context of the word *imminent?*'

'You want to find her, pronto.'

'Correct. So, take a look and—'

'She jumped onto the minibus after we left the hotel, in Bangkok. She was being chased by a taxi, with that guy in the back.' Rod pointed a shaking finger at Rupert.

'Excellent. How long was she on the bus?'

'All the way here.'

'To Battambang?'

Rod nodded.

'Do you happen to know where she is now, or who she's with?'

He shook his head. 'I think she was catching another bus this morning. I should have been on it too. But—'

'You got side-tracked.'

'Er, yeah.'

'Okay, Rod. You can put some clothes on while I take a look at your mobile phone.'

'I don't have one.'

Fender raised his eyebrows, retrieved his own smartphone from a pocket and tabbed through several commands. He glanced up at the erratic ringtone emanating from the far side of the room. At Fender's instruction, Rupert stepped around the bed and delved through a pile of clothes, plucking a smartphone out from under a pair of grubby underpants. Rupert dangled the phone between a thumb and finger and passed it to Fender. Rod's eyes darted nervously between them. He sank further back against the headboard, pasty faced.

'Passcode?'

'Five, one, three, seven,' he croaked. 'How'd you get my new number?'

Fender scanned through the recent call logs, text messages and contacts list on Rod's phone. He completed his inspection and tossed the phone onto the bed. Rod reached out, clutching it. 'Get dressed, we're nearly done – it's unnerving talking to a naked teenager.'

Rod crept off the bed, crouched down and scrabbled through the pile of clothes, pulling on a pair of board shorts and a grungy tee-shirt.

'A few more minutes of your time, Rodney, then we'll leave you to indulge in the rest of your day.' Fender pointed his phone at Rod, selected the camera function and began video recording. 'Mister Sharp, please purge your brain cell. I'd like some information relating to the other travellers on that minibus. Firstly, a description of each of them. Then some answers to my questions, such as: did Madeline like or dislike any of the others in particular? Who did she hang out with over the last few days? That sort of harmless stuff.'

A little while later, Fender pulled the hotel bedroom door shut and strolled along the flaky-paint corridor. Rupert trotted along dutifully by his side.

'He looked petrified.'

'A happy-herb pizza, a beer or three, he'll get over it.'

'What next?'

'It's time for a coffee. We'll collate what we have, then make a decision.'

'About heading north or south?'

'That, and other things,' Fender replied, shooting Rupert an ominous look.

*

The bus creaked and groaned on its handbrake, the bodywork vibrating as the engine shuddered and died. Maddie opened her eyes, blinking slowly. She turned her head to glance out of the window at the assortment of other buses parked up, from which multinational travellers spilled out, milling around outside.

'You've been asleep for the last three hours,' said Charlie, standing to reclaim his bag.

'Really …? Must be your scintillating conversation.' Maddie yawned as she stretched. She looked up at Charlie, caught his puzzled expression. 'What?'

'Nothing. We're here, in Siam Reap. The holy temples await, your majesty.'

Maddie watched him waltz away down the coach. She pushed up in her seat and shuffled into the aisle.

'How are you doing?' asked Rose, perched on the seat in front.

'Good, thanks. Caught up on some rest.'

'Ah-hah. I thought you'd want to stay awake, participate in some scintillating conversation.'

Maddie smiled, leaned towards her. 'What do you think sent me off into such a deep sleep?' She flexed her eyebrows and headed off down the bus towards the door, leaving Rose smiling behind her.

*

'It's the usual eclectic, random mix,' mused Fender. 'Twelve travellers on the bus, now confirmed, plus Maddie. Exclude her and our young friend Rodney leaves eleven. Of these, we have six who we know are still in play because we're tracking their phones. Six phones, minus one, currently static here in Battambang. That leaves five. Two are currently still heading south towards the capital, Phnom Penh, with three near the Angkor temple complex at Siam Reap. If your fiancée's intention is to head home, the capital is favourite. If, however, she's getting into the budget travel scene, she's most likely been drawn to the temples at Angkor.'

Fender leaned back in his chair, scanning the neatly laid out files on the table in front of them. 'So let's look at who we know is heading in each direction. First off, Kao Yeung. Female, Chinese. Next, Melanie Bannister, American. It's possible they are travelling together, but unlikely given that they arrived in Southeast Asia from different countries of origin. Also, Melanie has a pre-paid bus transfer to Kampot. On the bus north, three mobile signals: Barnaby, Victoria, and Charles.'

'Is it time to toss a coin?'

'Not necessarily. Who's Maddie most likely to travel with?' Fender studied the paper files spread out across the table. 'Two girls of different nationalities heading south to the capital, both fairly close to Maddie's age. Or, a mixture of genders and greater age ranges in the other group, heading north. My instinct would be the northern bus. If she's hooked up with a guy, he's most likely on that route—'

'Maddie's taking a break as a negotiation tactic, she's not going after other guys!'

'Perhaps, but you're her fiancé – your pride wouldn't allow you to think dispassionately. You need to distance yourself from emotional attachment for a moment and apply calculated logic.'

'Still the same reasoning from me. I know Maddie.'

Fender studied Rupert. 'Explain.'

'Maddie is ... *cautious*. Vis-à-vis other men.'

Fender's eyes narrowed. He watched Rupert intently. 'The reason being?'

Rupert broke eye contact. He looked away across the adjacent tables in the small café and slowly shook his head. Fender eased back from the table, dropped his hands into his lap, a few inches from his belt buckle.

'Tell me …'

Twenty-Three

'Hey, Gabby. How many hours to go now?'

'Thirteen hours, fifty-two minutes.'

'Exciting!'

'I know! It's so close now that I can almost taste his first kiss … sooo exhilarating. I'm getting a tuk-tuk to meet him there early tomorrow morning. Do you want to catch a ride into the temple complex with me?'

'Are you sure? It's your special day …'

'Actually, I'm getting a tiny bit nervous. If he doesn't show, it would be nice to have a friendly face close by. Would you be willing to hang around for half an hour, just in case?'

'Of course, I'd be honoured! It's so romantic.'

'Or foolhardy. At my age you'd think I'd know better than to pin my hopes on an old flame. But I have to find out.'

'Taking a chance *is* living. Boredom suffocates the soul,' agreed Maddie, her features frozen in a wistful expression.

'Interesting …who'd you get that philosophy from?'

Maddie flicked her eyes at Gabby, held her gaze. 'You,' she said quietly. 'Thanks for the offer of a ride tomorrow morning, I'll be there.'

*

Maddie opened the bedroom door and peered out into the corridor. Charlie, Victoria and Barney stood waiting, all wearing a change of clothes.

'We're heading into town for some food, would you like to come?' asked Victoria.

'Oh, um … thanks for thinking of me, but I think I'm going to grab something local, get an early night—'

'After the amount you slept on the coach?' Charlie rolled his bottom lip, sullenly.

'No worries, we'll see you in the morning,' said Victoria, already turning to leave.

'This princess, not needing beautiful sleep. Come, party with us peasants.' Barney offered his open hands theatrically, swooping down into a low bow.

'Thanks guys, but my alarm's set for four-thirty, to catch the sunrise—'

'*Four-thirty*. Are you nuts?' Victoria pushed her hand under Charlie's arm, tugging him away. 'We'll catch you there, later tomorrow.'

Barney watched Victoria lead Charlie away. He pulled a puffer fish face at Charlie's forlorn glance over his shoulder, then turned to face Maddie, his head cocked to one side, looking her up and down. 'If mind is changed, lovely boy Charlie is bedded in twelve, okay?' Barney held both his arms out, offering a comical double thumbs-up, then he skipped off down the corridor, sporadically spinning around, screeching and slapping the walls like a court jester on an amphetamine and LSD cocktail.

Maddie watched him pinball down the hallway, shaking her head, breaking into an amused frown. She stepped back and closed the door, making sure to lock it.

*

Maddie zipped up her fleece, wrapped her arms around her chest and peered through the darkness beyond the hotel's dimly lit façade.

This is certainly different from a normal Wednesday morning ...

She blinked back to reality at the whirling rattle and popping sound of an approaching tuk-tuk, its single motorbike headlight dimming as it slowed to a stop beside her.

'Morning!' whispered Gabby, grinning at her from the back seat.

Maddie stepped into the carriage, straight into a welcome hug. 'This is Dal,' said Gabby, giving the driver a thumbs-up sign as he turned to look over his shoulder. Dal nodded, smiling at Maddie, then revved the engine and steered the tuk-tuk out into the street. 'It's nearly time!' Gabby squealed over the noisy engine, passing headlights dancing in her glistening eyes.

'Are you nervous?'

'Hell, yes!' Gabby lay a hand over her heart. 'It's going crazy, beating a zillion miles an hour. I feel just like a teenager – tingly stomach cramps, sweaty palms.'

'It's a good sign,' said Maddie, mirroring Gabby's infectious grin.

The tuk-tuk pulled out of a side street, joining the main three-lane road, jostling for position with other motorcycles, coaches and taxis. The increase in speed forced a cooling breeze through the carriage.

'I can't wait to see him, find out what's been going on in his life …'

Maddie nodded, drinking in the muggy, early morning air. She glanced left and right, squinting through the passing headlights which illuminated everyday life on the street. People were sleeping rough on the pavement, the lucky ones laid out in hammocks strung up between lamp posts and garden fences. An old lady scrabbled around in the gutter, searching with her fingertips, her milky eyes staring off to one side. The tuk-tuk whizzed on past, Maddie's hair flailing, buffeting her face in the airstream whenever she turned to catch a longer look at life in downtown Siem Reap. She watched street food trailers being wheeled across the pavement – fragile-looking glass cabinets on trolleys beside a single gas burner stove. Several were already lit, large pans sizzling over bluey-yellow flames. On the road, the traffic steadily increased intensity. More vehicles, more urgency, more chaos.

'We must be close to the entrance now,' said Gabby, an excited twang to her voice.

Maddie nodded, her eyes sweeping across each side of the road. They passed a billboard advertising a free cello concert, a fundraiser for the children's hospital. In a side street, more hammocks had been strung out between power line poles, streetlight columns and fences, precariously attached to anything static. Children slept on car bonnets, their heads laid back against the windscreen. A mother sat on an upturned wooden fruit box beside a camping gas stove, peeling vegetables which she dropped into the pot while her kids slept on a blanket next to her. Countless people in dire poverty, yet apparently *coping* with remarkable resourcefulness. Maddie watched it all, mesmerised.

The tuk-tuk slowed, easing to a crawl behind a tourist bus that belched thick acrid smoke. Seeing a gap, Dal pressed the horn, pulled out and accelerated, the tuk-tuk's small engine squealing. Cutting back in from the outside lane as it filtered off right, they crawled along again, tight on the bumper of a taxi in front. Another few hundred feet and the taxi banked left, allowing the tuk-tuk to push on, until a few minutes later it peeled off the main road, slowing under the guidance of a female security guard waving them up to the entrance gate to the Angkor temple complex.

Dal turned and grinned at Gabby. 'You pay, there. I wait, okay?' Dal gestured towards the rugby scrum of coaches, taxis, tuk-tuks and mopeds parked up opposite the payment booths.

'Nearly time – so excited now!' Gabby hurried over to the nearest ticket kiosk to join the queue. Maddie followed her, pausing to study the sign displaying entrance costs.

'What's your plan? Are you just here for today, or longer?' asked Maddie, scampering up to Gabby's side.

'Good point, I'd not even thought of that … maybe just the day. See what happens, in,' Gabby checked her watch, 'about twenty-three minutes!'

Maddie nodded and turned back to look at the ticket information, the remains of a smile creasing her lips. 'I heard the others chatting about the temples and I've been reading up about them. The general consensus was to spread a visit over three days. I'll work out what I do next after that.'

'Sounds like a plan.'

Maddie followed Gabby up to the ticket counter and counted out eighty US dollars.

'Come on, the sun will be up soon!' Maddie accepted Gabby's outstretched hand and ran with her towards the waiting tuk-tuks, heading towards Dal. They climbed aboard, Gabby squeezed Maddie's hand. 'Right here, right now!'

Dal manoeuvred away from the waiting area and nipped in behind a long line of tuk-tuks, all chugging slowly along the long tree-lined road, the darkness gradually diluting as night gave way to dusk. Maddie leaned outside the carriage, peering along the motorcade. 'It goes on forever.'

Gabby checked her watch. 'Fifteen minutes – sooo close!' She glanced to her right, the first hint of hazy dark-blue diluting the black, glimmering over the horizon. 'Nearly sunrise, hope we make it …'

Maddie ducked her head out again. 'The queue is picking up speed, we'll be okay.' She turned to smile reassuringly at Gabby, matching her grin.

*

Maddie sank back against a tree trunk and gazed out over the lake. It formed part of a vast moat around the imposing stone towers and rugged perimeter wall guarding the entrance to Angkor Wat. She checked her watch: 5:36am. *Nearly time.*

Twenty yards away, not far from the elevated stone walkway that led across the water to the temple entrance, sat Gabby. She perched on the low wall bordering the water, waiting. Maddie watched her stretch out her hands, fingers spreading over the rounded edge of the wall, arms straight, pushing her back upright. Barely a wisp of breeze teased across the water surface, only the faintest oil painting orange-peel texture distorting the reflection of the nine stone steps meeting the lake's far shore. Above the steps, the perimeter stonework rose, robust and proud, protecting the temples inner grounds. To the right of the third pine cone-shaped tower peeked a warm yellow glow, spreading a bright radiance that shimmered across the water, a pink tinge transcending the yellow, gaining in intensity, blooming into a deeper, darker red.

Maddie turned to her left at the sound of a squeaky wheel. The troublesome bearing calmed its protest as sandaled feet stopped pedalling, freewheeling the bike to a standstill. The wiry man stepped over the low crossbar and leaned the bike onto its stand. He knelt down and locked the back wheel, then stood up and turned towards the east. He stood there for a moment, perhaps preparing himself. Then he turned and scanned the handful of people sat on the lake's perimeter wall. *There.* His footsteps scuffed on the dusty stone promenade.

Maddie grinned at the breaking dawn, adjusting her gaze to Gabby, who turned away from the magnetic spell cast by the palate of pastel colours oozing across the sky, bathing the greyscale stone perimeter in bright, warm, sunlit tones. She watched Gabby drop her gaze across the water, the dark tiers of the tower's reflections ebbing now in tandem with the rising sun, pulling her focus back to the approaching footsteps. Gabby smiled and turned, her eyes meeting his as he stopped, a few yards away. She gazed into the depths of his dark brown eyes, his mop of hair long and greying, pulled back in a loose ponytail. Rutted laughter lines scored his face, deepening as his smile grew, matching hers.

He eased himself down onto the step beside Gabby, holding his unblinking gaze. His hand reached out for hers, their fingers entwining. She nodded lightly, then cast her gaze back out over the water, watching the kaleidoscope of rich sunrise colours stretch farther out over the lake, illuminating the walled temple, red ripples texturing the patchy cloud overhead.

Maddie grinned, wallowing in a warm fuzzy sensation as she observed their joint profiles. Gabby tilted her head, resting it against his shoulder. Maddie allowed her smile to dissipate slowly. She rolled her head away, watching the light spreading long shadows, a warm breeze rippling the lake's surface, shimmering the towers into a distorted reflection as the sun broke away above the treeline, majestically spreading its tentacles of light, warmth and optimism.

*

That hypnotic vibration of the motorbike's powerful engine, the four-stroke throb resonating up through the seat, tingling into her stomach, agitating with prickly stabs and a plummeting-roller-coaster sensation. He rocks the bike forwards, jolting off its stand. Her arms, slipping around his waist, snuggling up to his muscular shoulders as he revs the throttle, smoothing the engine, the exhaust roar pulsating through her hands and feet. He releases the clutch, the bike surging forwards, her heart soaring ...

'Maddie?' Gabby stooped down and gently shook her shoulder.
Jerking against him as he changed gear, surging forwards again—
'Whoa!' Maddie's body tensed. She jolted awake, eyes wide, pulling focus, her senses gathering information, placing her in a recognisable place and time. She stared up at Gabby, darting her eyes between her and the tall, bohemian yet distinguished-looking figure stood beside her.

'You've been asleep for over an hour. This is Matthew.'

'Nice to meet you,' he said, offering his hand.

Maddie nodded and briefly squeezed his palm, mumbling a greeting.

'We're going to find Dal, take a ride to get some breakfast. Would you like to join us?'

'Oh, that's very kind, but I'm okay, thanks. I'll get something later.'

'I feel bad about leaving you on your own, especially as you were here to look out for me.'

'That's okay. I'm enjoying being here, it's peaceful.'

'Have you been to the temples before?' asked Matthew in a deep, unhurried tone.

Maddie shook her head.

'She's got a three day pass,' said Gabby.

'Then you can't start your visit here, at Angkor Wat. It would spoil the experience. Have you got the map they gave you?'

'I think so …' Maddie rummaged in her shoulder bag, found the ticket and guidebook pamphlet, which she handed to him.

'Okay, so you need to get out to see furthest temples of Preah Khan and Neak Poan first. I can mark up a route for you, if you like?'

'That would be great, thanks.'

Matthew produced a pen and crouched down, resting the map on his knee. 'Tomorrow you can work your way back to Ta Prohm and Sra Srang, finishing with Angkor Wat and Bayon, on the last day. That will give you the best perspective of the temple complex.' He lifted his head from the map and looked up at Gabby. 'We're spending the day together …?'

'Kinda hoping so.'

'Perfect.' He turned back to Maddie. 'If you're happy to do the tour on your own, why not take my bicycle? It's the best way to see everything and means you can mooch around at your own pace.'

'Would that be okay?'

'Certainly. It'll be a long cycle ride out to Preah Khan – around twenty-four kilometres – but it'll be quiet. It will also prepare you gradually for the crowds on the last day.' Matthew flicked up the bike's stand and wheeled it over to Maddie. 'Hang onto it for a while …' He glanced over at Gabby. 'We've got some catching up to do.'

'That sounds wonderful, thank you.'

'We might see you later in town, for dinner?' said Gabby.

'Sounds good. But don't worry about me if you two get … distracted.' Maddie grinned. She strummed the bike's bell as she pedalled off onto the perimeter tarmac road, leaving Gabby and Matthew standing holding hands.

'Watch out for the first left hand turn at the corner of the lake, and the big junction at the main entrance road – it's a free for all!' Matthew called out.

'Cheers!' Maddie shouted over her shoulder. 'I'm going for the grand temple tour …'

*

Fender sat back from the paper files spread out on the table and folded his arms, studying Rupert. 'So based on Madeline's history, particularly her … reservations towards men, that leaves us with the two girls, heading south to the capital.'

'That would be my suggestion.'

'I'm not completely convinced. But I understand your reasoning, given your unique insight into her psyche. Regardless, it's logical and advantageous for us.'

'It is?'

'Yes. I don't see a valid reason that will keep her in Phnom Penh for long. The other travellers will disperse quickly once in the city. It'll be difficult to track them efficiently, or her there. Siem Reap holds the central attraction of the temples. Most guidebooks suggest three days is a decent time to see the complex and there is only one entrance. So every traveller will have to funnel through that same gateway, twice a day. This means we'd have some time in hand, to backtrack there if necessary. Whereas once they leave the bus station in Phnom Penh, they could end up anywhere, it's a travel hub. So we pay a taxi driver handsomely to get us to the capital as fast as possible, then locate, interview and discount those travellers from our list. By my reckoning, if we leave now we might only be four hours behind the bus arrival time.'

'Makes sense.'

'Excellent. Let's mobilise. It's time to make a random taxi driver very happy.'

Twenty-Four

Maddie glanced down the line of cars, tuk-tuks, minibuses and coaches crawling towards her, all being overtaken by gnarling scooters beeping and weaving across onto her side of the road, encouraging her to hug the tarmac near the verge to let them zip safely by. The queue of opposing vehicles stretched back in a hazy, metal caterpillar far into the distance.

She lifted her gaze beyond the traffic, marvelling at the vast lake-size moat around Angkor Wat. The gentle breeze was now rippling the water, further distorting the reflection of the perimeter wall which sparkled under the rising sun. To her right beside the road, children gathered in small groups, the girls wearing pretty flowery dresses, boys in shorts and European football club shirts. Some shyly observed her, others were bolder, running over, shouting hello and waving. Maddie grinned and waved back, pinging the bell as she cycled past. Through gaps the trees, she glimpsed market stalls and canvas-canopied restaurants with colourful tablecloths and enthusiastic hosts, beckoning tourists over to sample their menu.

'Uh oh – suicide squad …' Maddie slowed her pedalling, keeping a watchful eye on the cluster of scooters zooming towards her. They scattered out from the junction in a chaotic multi-directional two-wheeled dogfight. She glanced over her shoulder, wobbling over onto the mud verge, letting a scooter whirl past. She flinched, clenching her teeth, began pedalling faster, recalling Sandy's advice. Her eyes darted from side to side as she aimed for gaps between scooters, motor cycles, tuk-tuks, other visiting cyclists – anything with wheels. She ploughed onwards, turning hard left at a junction straight into traffic chaos, reminiscent of a climactic *Star Wars* movie battle scene – two-wheeled TIE fighters screaming past in every conceivable direction but the conventional one.

'Shhhhiiiiittttttttt! Left turn, left, left … and pedal, pedal, PEDAL!' Maddie clenched her fingers around the plastic grips, her feet chopping up and down, knees aching as she pumped the crank faster and faster, until she'd finally negotiated the multi-directional carnage.

She risked a quick glance over her shoulder, adrenalin draining from tired limbs as she reduced pressure on the pedals, freewheeling, her breathing calming down, fingers relaxing their death grip. She reached out with her thumb to strum the bell lever in a victorious celebration.

Tring, tring! Tring, tring! Tring, tring!

'Woo-hoo! That was insane!'

*

Two wheels revolving in unison, spokes thrumming, a thin, dark shadow of the bike frame on the tarmac, consistently progressing, level and uniform. Maddie looked up from her grey outline and began to make a gradual turn, aware of the sun tracking across her shoulder, warming her back. She glanced down again, the shadow overtaking her, stretching forwards, the triangular frame soon absorbed into one straight line beneath the saddle width and her hunched outline over the front wheel.

A scooter overtook her, the metallic buzzing exhaust interrupting her mid-daydream, causing her to wobble. She wrinkled her nose at the two-stroke fumes drifting behind her and continued riding, the scooter's racket fading with every swooshing rotation of her pedals. She took a deep satisfied breath, pollution free once more. Only the long tree-lined road and her shadow accompanying her for long glorious uninterrupted periods, other traffic mercifully rare this far into the park.

Perched comfortably on the saddle, sitting tall, head held up high, Maddie couldn't suppress a constant grin. No unnecessary rules, reasons, expectations …

A little later, she steered off the road, freewheeling onto the rutted verge beside the edge of the forest. She leaned the bike against a tree, locked it and took a long drink of tepid water from the bottle stored in the basket. The tree-lined path led towards a flagstone walkway two hundred yards away, beyond which an uneven, decaying roofline stretched away from a grand pillared entrance, enticing her in.

She pulled a sarong from her bag and wrapped it around her waist, tucking in the loose end, smoothing the folds over her knees. Next, she opened the tourist map Matthew had marked up for her, and scanned the photographs and text for a description of the Preah Khan temple.

Square statue figures stood shoulder to shoulder, parallel to the treeline behind. Occasional tourists gathered in groups of two or three, some studying the carved stone characters, others taking photographs or roaming amidst the ancient structures. Maddie stepped up onto the walkway, bordered on both sides with twelve-inch high chamfered kerb stones.

Directly ahead, the imposing entrance loomed, guarded by two twelve-foot high headless warriors. One soldier rested the tip of a sword on the ground between his feet, his hands clasped around the handle. The other figure's arms bent forwards at right angles, a forearm missing on one side, a hand and whatever weapon he'd originally wielded lost from his other elbow.

Maddie paused to crane her neck up at the intricate carvings set deep into the stone beneath the entrance apex. Two bow-wielding archers opposed each other, standing proudly on their chariots. Around them, horses pranced, fighting figures and animal heads merging in a scene of battle mayhem, eroded by weather and time.

She ducked her head and stepped into the cool dark entrance. She shuffled farther into the gloom to allow light from side windows and courtyards beyond to filter in, revealing lighter greys and creamy beige walls, which rose into a stone-clad triangular peak, twenty feet above. Ahead, one stone-framed doorway stretched on to the next opening, which in turn led to the next, the repeating corridors replicating a seemingly unending hall of mirrors.

Maddie stepped out of the cold stone sanctum into glorious sunshine. She shielded her eyes and squinted, pausing to slide her sunglasses down, drinking in the sun's warmth. She roamed through the dilapidated east entrance, beyond which a boulder-strewn jigsaw had been spread randomly over the grass courtyard. She turned to look up at the partially collapsed roof, then scanned the ground, trying to picture where the missing irregular-shaped blocks belonged.

Shh-clitch.

Memory Card 3. Pic 111
'Standing amongst the wreckage in an unfamiliar place from another time, she surveys the damage, this curious girl, not yet in her prime. Irreparable, perhaps, or is there an opportunity to better herself, rebuild so as to avoid being left on the shelf? Does she have the courage to

start somewhere else, anywhere, and begin again – only time and tenacity can determine the outcome – but if not now, when ...?'

Maddie shifted her gaze from the rickety roofline, about to turn away when she frowned, drawn to an intricate carving. Recessed into the wall beside an ornately shaped window surround, a woman had been sculpted. She stood three feet high, looking out as if watching over the collapsed building debris. Maddie drew closer, gently tracing her fingertips over the intricate stone carving, marvelling at its smooth texture and detailed engraving. She dropped her hand to her side and meandered on, past a Spanish family sitting on a giant egg-shaped rock embedded in the ground and a lone photographer, his features partially obscured behind a stone window aperture, only a glimpse of a flat tartan cap.

Maddie drifted on, time slowing, mirroring her meanderings. She padded along the narrow wooden boards that formed a long pedestrian walkway, elevated on supports a few feet above the muddy quagmire below.

Something hummed past her head, causing her to instinctively duck away from the high-pitched fluttering sound, accompanied by tiny reverberating air movements. She carefully straightened up from her semi-crouch, panning around the tangled vines and thorny bushes that poked out above the muddy swamp. Another high-pitched miniature helicopter thrummed past, pausing to hover for a moment in front of her hand, bringing with it hundreds of other double-winged, black and yellow dragonflies. Maddie stood for a moment, mesmerised, surrounded by a cloud of the delicate creatures drifting around her. They were transiting across the path and congregating in lively groups in the middle of the marshland, above the twisted vines and tentacle-like trailing plants. She reached into her bag for her mobile phone, holding it out, her finger poised on the inactive shutter button.

Careful ...

She frowned at the blank screen, drew her hand closer, her thumb hovering over the power switch.

This isn't simply switching my phone on to take a photograph.

Maddie replaced the dormant phone in her bag and ambled on across the wood plank causeway, passing through more congregations of fluttering dragonflies. At the end of the walkway, a grassy path rose up an embankment to a crest overlooking a square lake, bordered with banks of stone steps, which gradually dropped down to the water's edge. In the middle of the water stood an ornate miniature temple. The tower stood proudly on a round stone base, the remains of a naga serpent's head rising up beside a wallowing horse, marking the centrepiece. Four smaller ponds bordered the main lake, one at each corner. Only a few other visitors mingled around the perimeter, making minimal sound, shrouding the grounds in a shawl of peaceful serenity.

Maddie selected a secluded spot beside the water's edge and sat down on the steps, elbows on her knees, fingers entwined. She glanced down at her bag, separated her hands and reached for her mobile phone.

Shh-clitch.

Memory Card 3. Pic 119
'A difficult decision, swapping liberty for convention, comfort and familiarity, risking stagnating, drowning in complacency. Or, instead, stay on this uncertain and rickety path searching for self-discovery and truth, forever developing and growing inwards, holding onto a glorious and everlasting youth.'

Maddie turned at the sound of his voice. She shielded the sun with her mobile phone, squinting at the figure being obscured by shards of light twinkling behind his shoulder. Barry adjusted position, shielding the glare, grinning at her from behind his camera lens as recognition clouded her features. He dropped his head back behind the viewfinder and rattled off several more shots.

'You ...?'

'The one and only. You couldn't look more shocked if your fiancé suddenly appeared with a bottle of champagne and a heart-wrenching apology.'

'Yeah, imagine the odds ... what are you doing here? I thought you'd gone to Phnom Penh.'

'I did. Needed to reclaim my memories.' He swung his hip, flicked the strap on his camera case around in front of his groin and opened the lid, retrieving a plastic 35mm film pot. He rattled the memory cards inside it.

'You went all the way there, then came back? That's nuts.'

'Some might say ... okay if I sit down?'

Maddie shrugged, waved her hand in his direction. Barry carefully packed his camera into the padded bag, lowered it between them and sat down. 'This represents a demarcation between my space and yours, offers me some protection. I don't want you getting any ideas.' He grinned at her pout, placed his tobacco tin on the step between his legs and leaned forwards to prepare a roll-up. 'I saw you at Preah Khan. You're doing this in the right order.'

'Gabby's old flame recommended a route.'

Barry nodded. 'Makes sense. How you finding the cycling?'

'Peaceful.'

He cocked his eyebrow at her and chuckled. 'Until I encroached on your harmony?'

She turned away, looked out over the lake. 'You came back to see this place, capture it on film?'

Barry placed the roll-up in his mouth and lit the end, puffing it into life. 'Yup. I need it, for the book. It's also a sort of pilgrimage, coming here.'

Maddie turned back to face him, raised her eyebrows.

'It's a beer time story. You here on your own?'

'I left Gabby and her fella at Angkor Wat. I'm going to meet up with the others later.'

'Cool. How was the sunrise?'

She smiled. 'Pretty special. Especially magical for Gabby, meeting up with Matthew.'

'Yeah, I bet. You asked why I doubled back, there's your answer. Those few special moments of … clarity. They're important.'

'How does Jody figure in your being here?'

'Ah … Jody chose a different path. A friend arrives, her travel mate departs. Same-same.'

Maddie watched Barry luxuriating in the ritual of smoking. 'Those things will kill you.'

He nodded, his eyelids narrowing briefly. He relaxed back as he exhaled, a plume of smoke dispersing over the water. 'Most likely. But I shoulda gone a long time ago, before the *baccy* stuff started. But fear not, it'll be beautiful spanking life for as long as it lasts.'

'Another beer time story?'

'Is there any other kind?' He cocked his head to one side, studying her. 'Your story, for example … is not a single-cup-of-coffee kinda deal either, is it?'

Maddie held his gaze for a long moment, then broke off and reached out, plucking the rollie from his fingers. She took a hit, then tilted her head back to blow smoke over her head. 'It's normal tobacco.'

'You sound surprisingly disappointed.'

'In you, or that it wasn't something stronger?'

'Now that *is* the question, isn't it? I'm not always stoned.'

'And I'm not always sober …' Maddie handed the cigarette back.

'That would be worth seeing, Princess Madge, trollied.' He chuckled, took a final draw on the roll-up and stubbed the end out on the upturned tobacco tin lid. She watched him carefully tip the ash into the tin and deposit the butt inside before snapping the lid shut.

'That's very considerate.'

He shrugged. 'I'm quite happy to pollute my own lungs, but I like to leave everything else as I found it.'

'How admirable.'

He shot her a raised eyebrow. 'You Brits enjoy your sarcasm.'

'It keeps everyone else on their toes.'

'It keeps you lonely.' He winked at her.

She stood up, made a show of dusting ash off her sarong and began walking up the steps. 'Have a nice afternoon.'

'That's it, conversation over …?'

'What were you expecting, me to roll over with my legs dangling in mid-air?' she called over her shoulder.

'It's not my favoured position, but I could be persuaded.'

'Dream on, buster,' she muttered, heading for the wooden walkway, leaving Barry sniggering.

*

Memory Card 3. Pic 133
'Transportation alienation. Pinching a lost cause, without realising times like these should make one stop to reflect, hit life's pause. Scuppered by an inch of flat rubber, should this travel buddy stay to help, or walk on, and snub her …?'

'Could you be any *less* helpful?' Maddie released her thumb and finger from the flat tyre and turned towards him, tight-lipped, her eyes narrow.

'Hold that pout – perfect!' Barry clicked off two more frames before he lowered the camera. 'Ah c'mon, it's a great shot – upper class princess, stranded in the depths of the Angkor temple complex. Her survival determined by the integrity of the Australian degene*rate* ... will she allow him to come to her rescue in exchange for a dinner date?'

'Piss off!'

'Oooh yeah, there it is! Even the warmth of the late afternoon sun, can't enthuse Madge with a sense of frolic and fun ...'

Barry's voice tailed off as he watched her lurch back on the ground, clutch her hands to her face and squeal, her breathing making a distorted groaning sound from behind her fingers.

'Sorry ... *Darth*. Would you like some help?'

She mumbled a reply.

'Say again?'

'How can you be so bloody insensitive? Do you have some sort of disorder that makes you—'

'Yep.'

'*What?*' Maddie separated her fingers, peered out at him.

'It's a form of attention deficit hyperactivity disorder, mixed with some other stuff I can't pronounce. I try to keep it in check, mostly succeed. But sometimes, I get a bit ... hyper.'

Maddie lowered her hands and stared at him.

'The photography helps, gives me something to focus on. So does the occasional beer. Smoking the special *happy-happy* blend is especially helpful.'

'Oh. I see.'

'Yep. There it is.'

'So in effect, you self-medicate?'

'Sure, works for me. You don't wanna see what that Ritalin crap does to people. It steals their souls.' Barry gestured to her bike. 'We can get your tyre fixed out by the main entrance.'

'That's twelve miles away!'

'Yeah, it's a hike. Probably take about four or five hours to walk ...'

'But it'll be dark soon – don't they shut the park?'

'They do that alright. Suppose I could give you a backie. We could tow your bike.'

'Would that work?'

'Sure. Get you as far as Ta Prohm, about halfway.'

Maddie frowned. 'Is that where you rented your bike from?'

'Nope. That's me, till tomorrow.'

'You're not leaving the temples tonight?'

He shook his head. 'I want to capture some dusk and dawn shots. I read about the tree roots at Ta Prohm, they've literally consumed the stonework. Mother Nature reclaiming what's hers. That's where I want to be, at sunrise.'

'So you're camping out, overnight?'

'I sure am.'

'On your own? I mean, are there others staying there too?'

'Possibly, but I doubt it. It's no stress. You can take my bike from Ta Prohm, get you back to civilisation. We'll swap them over in the morning.' Barry packed his camera away and strolled over to an adjacent tree where he'd parked his identical classic shopper bicycle. 'Or, you can walk your bike out. Up to you.' He placed his camera case in the front basket, tied the strap around the handlebars and wheeled the bike over to her. 'What's your preference?'

Maddie pushed up to her feet, brushing twigs off her bottom. 'I'll accept your offer of help, thank you.'

Barry nodded and sat back on his saddle, pointing the bike towards the road. 'Climb aboard the rack, hold your bike's handlebars across your lap and lift your feet up. We'll drag your bike along on its back wheel, okay?'

He turned to look over his shoulder at her lack of movement. 'What's up – you okay?'

'I don't think I can do this …'

'It's easy. Just jump on behind me and—'

'You don't understand, it's—'

'A beer time story?'

'Yes.'

'Okay, two choices. You can tell me the story first, then climb aboard, or you pedal and I'll jump on the back instead. You can tell me on the way.'

'That would take some time.'

'Hey, I've seen how fast you ride. Half that speed with my weight – trust me, there's time for your entire life story.'

'I can't ride pillion.'

Barry sighed. He climbed off the bike and flicked out the side-stand. 'No bother, on you get.' He straddled the rack, his feet planted on the ground either side of the rear wheel. 'Time's a-wastin'.'

Maddie climbed through the frame, flicked up the stand and pushed back onto the saddle, barely able to balance the bike on her tiptoes. 'Seat's a bit high.'

'You'll be okay. Go for it.'

Barry looped his arm under her bike's handlebars and held them across his thighs. Maddie began pedalling. He scooted his feet along the ground until they had enough momentum for him to lift them up, balancing the edge of his flip-flops on the rear wheel nuts. 'Okay?' he asked, grasping the saddle spigot with his free hand as they wobbled off the path onto the tarmac road.

'Think so, it's hard going – you're a heffalump!'

'Just keep pedalling. More speed equals a smoother ride—'

'No sexual innuendo!'

'Just offering some friendly advice ... there you go, that's a decent speed.'

'You okay on the back?'

'All good. This'd make a great photo, eh?'

They cycled on in silence, their grey shadow constant and unflinching on the tarmac.

'So ... about that beer time story,' said Barry, turning his head to one side to avoid her hair flailing into his eyes.

'Yours or mine?'

'The pillion problem. Was it a motorbike?'

Maddie cycled on. She focused on watching the front wheel cut through the lines of tree shadows stretching across the road. The low sun casted elongated projections of their outlines, sunlight peeping and glinting through the tops of the trees, sinking lower towards the horizon. A minute passed. Two more ... Eventually she sighed. 'My first proper boyfriend, Stefan ... he used to give me a lift.'

'You hated it?'

Maddie shook her head. 'No. I loved it,' she said quietly, 'the sensation of speed, the freedom. I used to feel so ... *alive.*'

The distant putt-putt trundle of a tired old engine grew louder, resonating through the treeline.

'Is that behind us?'

Barry half-turned to glance over his shoulder, causing the bike to wobble with his shifting body weight.

'Whoa, easy—'

'We're okay. Yup, he's already pulling out, we're good.'

'Thanks.' Maddie kept close to the trees on her right, allowing a motorbike towing a converted tuk-tuk trailer to overtake. The three tourists in the back waved. The engine's high-pitched squeal left the bicycle engulfed in a trail of wispy fumes.

'I love the smell of two-stroke in the evening,' said Barry, mimicking an American accent. He sneezed, causing the bike to wobble again. Once their balance had returned, he asked gently 'Were you on the back when the motorbike crashed?'

The bike quivered again. Maddie tweaked the steering, lining the handlebars up straight. She cycled on for another minute before answering. 'No. Stefan was alone, on a country road … a car pulled out. He had no time to react – ironic, considering he raced motorbikes for a living.'

'When did it happen?'

'Seven years ago. I've never been on the back of a motorbike since.'

'I'm sorry … that must have been tough.'

Maddie nodded, her breathing uneven, eyes misty. She blinked rapidly, pushed her legs down harder on the pedals.

'There's East Mebon. We're about halfway to Ta Prohm,' he said, as they passed a partially hidden wall of blackened, green stones, shielded behind the trees.

'Okay, thanks,' she murmured. She focused on squeezing her legs down even harder, blanking out the burning muscular sensation in her legs in an attempt to manage her pain.

Twenty-Five

'Madge? How are your legs doing?'

She frowned, breaking out of her catatonic stare, glancing away from the dusky grey tarmac. 'Madge?'

'Your new nickname. Like it?'

'What – *why* ...?'

'Why not? Means we're getting to be mates.'

'That takes more than an hour of saddle sore.'

Barry sniggered, blowing puffs of warm air onto the nape of her neck. 'You've been in the zone, working pretty hard.'

'Yeah, needed to ...'

'It's helped, we're nearly there, look. See the lake on the left? That's Sras Srang, the royal bathing pool.'

The vast expanse of still, dark flatness lay dormant and eerie beyond the smattering of trees lining the waterfront. Ahead, beyond the far shore where silhouette statues guarded the vast ablutions pool, the sun gradually slipped below the horizon. On the road, dusk had banished their constant, trailing shadow. Barry reached down beside the rear wheel and released the dynamo clip, pinging the small charging wheel onto the tyre's sidewall.

'Whoa, easy ...' The bike weaved across the road as Maddie wrestled the handlebars to regain steerage.

'*He* said let there be light ... and behold, there was light.' Barry peered around her shoulder to check out the cylindrical glow illuminating the road ahead. 'Better?'

'Uh, yeah. Thanks. Not that bright though, is it?'

'You'll have more headlights soon, from the traffic heading out.'

Maddie cycled on in silence for a while.

'Take this left.'

'The path?'

'Yup, it's the place I've been told about. You can leave me and your bike here and carry on to the entrance.'

'What time do they shut the gates?'

'I think the complex shuts at six-thirty. Don't know if there's gates as such, but so long as there are people still leaving, you'll be fine.'

Maddie steered the bike off the tarmac onto the rutted track, the dynamo-powered light dimming and juddering on the uneven ground.

'Just there. See those ruins, beyond where the path crosses the stream? A hundred yards further.'

Maddie nodded and pedalled for another half a minute, then slowed to a gradual stop. Barry assisted by trailing his feet on the ground. 'Yeouch, gonna be stiff tomorrow,' he said, standing up and laying Maddie's bike on the ground. He stretched his aching muscles, watching Maddie remain straddling the tubular frame, casting her eyes over the outline of a twin tier stone-clad building. It had been built to incorporate two six-foot high by three-foot wide window sections, each side of a crumbling column entrance beneath a deteriorating stone block roof.

'You're staying in *there* tonight?'

'Sure am.' Barry reached around Maddie and removed several small nylon bundles and a hessian bag from the basket, then crouched down next to her bike. 'Do you want the rest of the water?' he asked, peering up at her through the gloom.

'No, I'm okay thanks.'

'Cool. It's a hike to the nearest food shack and I don't want to draw attention to being here. See those headlights? That's the road. Turn right, go about quarter of a mile, then take the first major right. Follow the main drag back to the moat surrounding Angkor Wat, and tag onto the flow of traffic all the way out. Very straightforward. Okay?'

Maddie followed his outstretched hand pointing at the sporadic flashes of headlights beyond the distant treeline. 'Okay, thanks.' She watched him switch on a small torch and prop her bike up, gathering the bags and water bottle off the ground, placing everything in the other bike's front basket. 'What about in the morning – swapping the bicycles over?'

'I'll meet you at the entrance to Ta Prohm at ten. I should have got your tyre fixed by then.'

'Oh, okay. Thanks.'

Barry began wheeling the bike with the flat tyre towards the building. Maddie gazed at his beam of illumination, dancing on the path. She turned to look behind her at the distant pinpricks of light, then hastily swung back round towards Barry's jigging torchlight.

'Hey ... wait up,' she called. She stepped out from the bike frame, fast walking beside it towards Barry, having to squint in the faint light from the bike's dynamo.

Barry's torch arched around, spotlighting her pushing the bike towards him. 'You okay?'

'Of course, no problem. It's just ... I'm not sure I'll make the entrance in time. So I wondered ... could I hang out here?'

'With me? No.'

Maddie held a hand in front of her, attempting to block the beam of light from his head-torch. 'Oh. That's not very chivalrous.'

'That's Aussies for ya. We're uncultured crooks.'

Barry panned the torch around, held it under his chin, lighting up an elongated grin and shadowy eye sockets. 'Just kidding – look, big smile!' He swung the torch onto the ground at her feet, chuckling as she stepped over to join him.

'Not funny, Bozzer.'

'Bozzer?'

'Yeah. Bullshitting-bulldozer-Barry from Oz. Sums up your personality perfectly.'

He chuckled. 'Okay, Madeline, up-her-own-arse material girl. From now on, you shall forever be Madge. This way, pop princess ...'

Bozzer turned his head, aiming the torchlight ahead, picking out their route over to the building entrance's rickety steps. 'We'll carry the bikes inside, away from sight. Here, take the torch. I'll take mine in first.' He lifted his bike up the steps between the slanting columns, stepping over fallen stone blocks, carefully working his way through the building to the inner courtyard.

'What was this place?'

'Somewhere for the worshippers to rest, perhaps. Or for house for servants, away from the grandeur of the main temples.'

'How do you know about it?'

'I read a blog about a guy who stayed here a few years ago. He bought a day ticket and camped for a week. I scoped it out on the way in this morning.'

Maddie shivered. She slipped on her fleece and zipped it up.

'Are you hungry? I've got some scran we can share.'

Bozzer sat down on the flagstone terrace and rooted through the selection of bags. Maddie watched him set a compact aluminium pot on the ground. He separated its deep dish lid and removed a cup-size gas canister and a compact single-burner stove, which he screwed together and lit. He produced a small bag of rice which he poured into the pan with a good soaking of water.

'No spare liquid to rinse it, so it won't be your normal cordon bleu. But it'll do.'

*

Kao held the chopsticks halfway between the bowl and her partially open mouth. She alternated her eyes between Fender, Rupert and the photograph on the smartphone, laying on the table in front of her.

'Your wife?' she said slowly, lowering the chopsticks.

'Not quite. His fiancée,' said Fender, his open palms touching the top of the chair opposite her. 'May I?'

Kao nodded, her eyes flitting around the busy noodle bar.

'Thank you. This won't take long.' Fender slid the chair out from under the table and sat down. 'Maddie left her fiancé at the airport, in Bangkok. He's worried about her safety. Will you help us to find her?'

Kao looked at the photo again, then lifted her gaze to stare directly into Rupert's eyes. 'She a nice person.'

Fender didn't let him reply. 'Yes, she is. Rupert owes her an apology.'

'How you find me?'

Fender clasped his hands on the table and smiled thinly. 'It's what I do. How upsetting were the killing caves, near Battambang?'

'Very sad.'

He nodded, his features solemn. 'Yes. That period of Cambodian history was extremely distasteful.'

Kao nodded. She dropped her gaze from his.

'Is Maddie here in Phnom Penh?'

'No. Last place I see her, at bus station in Battambang. Going to Siem Reap, with others.'

'Okay, good. Can you name any of the group? In particular, anyone else she seemed friendly with?'

'She with Victoria and Gabby. Charlie like her. Think she liked the Australian boy too, made her smile. But he gone, be with girlfriend.' Kao shifted her eyes away, a clump of chicken noodles falling off the end of the chopsticks, plopping into the bowl.

'Please, eat while it's hot. Thank you for your help.' Fender retrieved the phone from the table. He stood up and strolled away.

'I hope you have fun, travelling,' said Rupert before he followed Fender out of the noodle bar into the dusky humidity of Street 460, in the heart of Phnom Penh's uniform grid layout.

'What's next?'

'Back on the road, dear boy.'

Rupert's shoulder's slumped. 'Now?'

'The sun rises over Angkor Wat in less than twelve hours. If you want to hold onto your future wife, and your testicles, we need to be there.'

'What about getting some sleep?'

'Sleeping's for wimps. You can get all the shut-eye you need once we've located that suitcase. In the meantime, make do in the back of the taxi.'

'With these roads, are you kidding?'

'You think I'd waste my time on frivolity? Saddle up, Tonto, wagons roll.'

*

'Fork or spoon?' said Bozzer, the beam of light from his head-torch filtering through pockets of steam billowing from the pan.

'Fork, please.'

Bozzer lifted his head and looked over.

'Whoa, easy with the spotlight.'

'I can't switch off my dazzling personality.'

Maddie groaned and peered into the saucepan. Bozzer reached up and balanced the head-torch on a stone window sill behind them, adjusting the angle to illuminate the cooking pot.

'What did you say is in there?'

'Rice, obviously. A few edible animals I found in the forest, some seasoning, and the secret ingredient.'

'Edible animals?' she glared at him, her fork poised.

'Yeah, you can pick those bits out if you're a vegetarian. I think they're all dead ...' Bozzer dipped his spoon into the pot, stirred the contents then loaded up his spoon, lifting it to his lips, blowing the steam away. He shovelled the rice into his mouth, chewing and puffing vapour. 'Nothing wriggling – bonus.'

Maddie glared at him through the gloom, away from the torchlight.

'Okay, okay. Not the death stare, please. It's rice with chopped-up pork satays, bought from a market stall. I had some for breakfast on the way in, saved the rest. Bit of soy sauce and some happy herbs to give the rice a little extra zing. It's actually not bad.'

'Extra zing?'

'Yup.' Bozzer dug his spoon in again and took another mouthful. 'Oh yeah, that's pretty good. Hey, you don't want any, that's cool – more for me.'

Maddie flicked her eyes between the pot and Bozzer, deflecting his incoming spoon with a fork side-swipe. 'Patience. Ladies first.' She scooped a forkful of rice *a la Bozzer* into her mouth. 'Ugh, hot!' she yelped, her mouth hanging open, puffing like a steam engine.

'Ha ha – patience!'

Maddie chewed fast, blowing vapour, her hand scrabbling around on the floor.

'Here,' he said, passing her a bottle containing a quarter litre of water.

Maddie glugged back several mouthfuls. 'Thanks.' She scooped her fork back into the pot. 'Actually, this isn't bad.'

'Why so surprised?'

Maddie shrugged, glancing over at him. 'Most men can't cook.' She analysed his features. 'So what really happened between you and Jody?'

'Our companionship had carried us as far as the journey allowed … it goes that way sometimes.'

'How long have you been on the road?'

'Before Jody, couple of months.'

'Where have you been?'

'Kind of a circular route. I flew into Saigon, took the train up the east coast of Vietnam to Hoi An, dropping off here and there, ending up in Hanoi. Overland across the border into northern Laos, worked my way south, taking in Luang Prabang, Vang Vieng and Vientiane. Then across the border into Thailand at Nong Khai. Got the bus to Bangkok, then here.'

'Wow, quite a trip. When did you meet Jody?'

'At the legendary Vang Vieng. We hooked up tubing down the Nam Song River.'

'Tubing? What's that, some sort of weird traveller's ritual?'

He laughed. 'Sort of. You rent an inflated truck tyre inner-tube. The locals have a great business, they transport a load of us with tubes a few miles upstream. There's maybe four or five riverside bars to stop at on the way down the river. You float past in your tube, pulling in where you fancy a beer or two. It's calmed down a lot – a few years ago it was crazy-party central. Zip wires, high diving boards, exotic drink mixes and drug cocktails ... it used to be *really* wild.'

'But not anymore?'

'No. Too many people died.'

Maddie stopped eating. 'You're kidding?'

'Nope. Two or three tourists a year, more towards the end. The current is really fast in the rainy season, and at other times there was shallow water under some of the zip wires, if you dropped too early. No lifeguards of course, and limited medical expertise. That's in addition to being on the water and overdoing the hooch and happy herbs ... drowning was quite common. Recipe for calamity, big time, and no good for tourism. So the government shut down half the bars, cleaned up those that remained and clamped down on the circus antics. It's a mellow deal now.'

Maddie gazed at him through the cooling steam. A flicker of unease creased his brow, dispersing as he lifted his eyes to briefly meet hers. 'How's the grub?'

'Good, thank you. Better now it's not scalding hot.' She stole another look at him, studying his shadowy features.

'Enquire away.'

'About what?'

'Whatever it is that you're itching to ask.'

Maddie tapped her fork on the edge of the pot. 'Okay ... I thought I noticed something – a look of regret, or uneasiness perhaps. Did *you* lose someone?'

He finished chewing and tilted his head slightly to one side, studying her. 'You're very perceptive.'

'That surprises you?'

'I guess so.' He reached for the water bottle, took a swig. 'My grandfather, among others ...'

'Oh.'

'You thought I'd say a mate, or girlfriend.'

She met his gaze and nodded.

'He died young. He's had this ... influence on my life, on this trip. Even though I never knew him.'

'So this *is* a pilgrimage?'

'In a way. Gramps worked for a news agency. He was sent here, to Cambodia. Back in the mid-Seventies.'

'During the time of the Khmer Rouge?'

Bozzer nodded, a solemn expression momentarily darkening his features. 'Ugh, snap out of it, Baz!' He slapped himself on the cheek, winced, then rubbed his chin. 'Ignore me, being morose. Eat up. Put some calories back into your legs, you'll need them tomorrow.'

'For what?' she said sharply.

'To chauffeur me, dumbo. Two bikes, one with a flattie. Remember?'

'Tomorrow it's your turn to pedal your own lazy arse.'

'I woulda done today, if you'd been up to it,' he said softly. Maddie looked away from him and peered into the pot, scooping up another forkful of rice. 'But I think you secretly enjoyed being in control.'

She glanced up, mid-mouthful, the sides of her mouth twitching into a smile. 'Doesn't every girl?'

Twenty-Six

'What was that …?'

Maddie wielded the torch beam above her head, picking out spindly shadows from dangling tree branches.

'Bats.'

'No way.'

'Yup. They feed at dusk, it's when all the mozzies and bugs come out. Target-rich environment.'

'Great,' she said, stifling a giggle.

Bozzer frowned. 'You okay?'

'Oh yeah, peachy. I'm trapped in an ancient Cambodian temple with a batty bloke – who has a strange accent – whilst I'm *taking a break* from my fiancé, without the first clue what I'm going to do tomorrow morning. Any morning, in fact. Other than that it's all gorgeous in my mad, sad, world. Silly girl. Hey, Jody, she messed up, letting you go. Did you have a big argument? It's a bit spooky here. Forests are like that. I feel sleepy. Can you make my bed now? Maddie bed time …'

Only the soft flapping of wings overhead punctuated the silence. Bozzer rolled his head left, the cool building stonework pressing into his ear. He blinked, refocusing on her, slumped back against the wall beside him. The torch lay on the ground, shining away from her fingers. Maddie's head lolled to one side. She breathed lightly, emitting sporadic miniature snores. He grinned, shaking off the woolly numbness engulfing him, dulling his senses. 'Bedtime, that'd be an idea.' He eased up to his feet, picked up the torch and shone a beam at the nearby ground, searching for the hessian bag.

Bozzer surveyed the hammock under torchlight, checking he'd securely tied the cords between the two trees and that the mosquito net stretched out above fully covered it. Maddie groaned at his gentle shaking, her heavy eyelids barely flickering open. She shied away from the light dancing on the ground and slowly rotated her stiff neck. 'What, doing?' she mumbled, losing the battle to keep her eyes open.

'Bedtime. Come on Princess Madge, your sumptuous boudoir awaits.'

'Sleep here,' she mumbled.

'No, no, nooo ... that cold stone floor that will sap your body heat. Come on, up you get.' Bozzer grasped Maddie's hands and lifted her limp arms, hauling her rag-doll body upright. 'Need to get a mozzie net over you, keep out the creepy crawlies.'

She grunted as he stooped down and draped her torso over his shoulders in a fireman's lift. 'Lesson learned, Madge. Happy-happy herbs, not so good for posh totty. Steps coming up, ready?'

'Steps were not an Australian band, they were British, okay mister,' she slurred.

Barry sniggered and carried her down the steps.

'Whoooooaaaaa, flying ... where's the batty-bat-face-man taking meee ...?'

Barry stumbled across the rutted ground towards the hammock. 'Madge, I need you awake for one minute, that's all. Then sleep time, okay?'

'Sleepies, now. Yes, lovely. Bye.'

'*No*. Stay awake for sixty seconds, then you can pass out.' Barry eased her off his shoulders, planting her feet by the base of the hammock's string netting.

'Sixty seconds is all I get? What does a girl have to do ...'

'*Maddie* – focus. Here's the hammock.'

'Okay. I'm with you. Where are we?' She reached down to feel the netting. 'Room for one. Where you at?'

'We're going to top and tail.'

Maddie giggled. She flopped over the unstable hammock. He grabbed her just before her body collapsed.

'Maddie, we need to coordinate. Lower yourself in, bum first, then legs follow. Ready? One ...' Barry rushed around the tree to stand on the opposite side of her. Maddie swayed on her feet, her body quivering. 'Two ...' He grabbed her arms to support her from toppling over. 'Three.' Bozzer stretched the netting open with one hand as he lowered her arms, her bottom resting in the hammock.

He swept her legs up and guided her head back, watching her body flop down, timing sitting back into the netting himself to coordinate with her. The ropes creaked, netting tightening as they lay there, heads at opposite ends, swaying back and forth. He wriggled to adjust his weight, letting the hammock settle.

'Did we survive?' she mumbled from the other end.

'We did. Sleep well.' Bozzer reached out to pull the sides of the mosquito netting over them, then stretched his hands behind his head and stared up at the stars, glimpsing a new moon, peeking through clouds. 'Hmm … this'll do.'

The hammock settled to a gentle rocking motion. Bozzer watched the night sky for a few minutes, listening to her light snoring. Amusement twitched across his lips as he scanned the bright concentration of stars, untainted by light pollution. With a satisfied sigh he allowed his heavy eyelids to close, his side pressed against her warm body.

*

Bozzer twitched awake at the vibration against his thigh. His phone pulsed the lone church bell bonging intro to AC/DC's *Hell's Bells*. He twisted around enough to sink his hand into the offending pocket and silence the alarm.

'It's four-thirty, Madge, time to get up,' he whispered, sliding his feet onto the floor. He carefully shifted his weight as he stood up, reaching out to balance the hammock and prevent it tipping. 'Going to water a tree.'

He listened for her response. *Nothing.* He leaned over her face, his cheek tickling from her light, regular breathing. Satisfied, he padded away, his torchlight skipping across the rutted ground.

Once he was back, Bozzer rocked the hammock. 'Madge – popcorn princess … time for your morning toe-sucking.'

'You'd better bloody not,' she muttered, slurring her words. She reached out in slow motion to rub her eyes. 'It's still dark.'

'Yup. Stealth mission. Goin' looking for the spirit people.'

'Off you trot, then.'

'The temples open soon – we can't be seen camping here. You need to get your lazy arse up and come with me. Right now.'

'Spoilsport.'

'C'mon, legs first. Ready?'

'Nooo …'

Bozzer grasped her ankles and lifted them out of the netting, swinging her legs onto the ground.

'Whoa, *okay* mister. Less physical contact equals a happier camper. Ouch ... my head is pounding. I'm thirsty and I need a wee.' She groaned and slumped forwards, resting her elbows onto her thighs, dropping her head into her palms. 'Hangover from hell ...'

'Yeah, happy herbs can do that. They don't suit everyone.'

Maddie snapped her eyes fully open and stared at the outline of his face. *'Happy herbs* – as in, marijuana?!'

'The very same.'

'You effing bastard!'

'Hey, I hadn't planned on a dinner guest. Would you rather I let you starve?'

'No, but you didn't have to put them in—'

'You assume that I'd be able to sleep outside, in this place, without a little deeply-sleepy-happiness?'

She shook her head beneath her hands, muttering to herself.

'Embrace the experience. You tried something new, slept well and didn't have to pay for a hotel. What's to complain about?'

Maddie lowered her hands, her expression darkening. 'You drugged me!'

'Not intentionally. I thought everyone in Asia understood the true meaning of happy. Happy shakes. Happy pizza. Happy—'

'Ending?'

He sniggered. 'See, there you go – sense of humour restored. It's no biggie, right? Tell me, who else has visited Angkor and stayed overnight in a temple? It's a story to tell your grandchildren, that *one* time you really lived a life—'

Maddie pushed off the unsteady hammock, jerking upright. 'You fucking drugged me!' She stepped up close to his outline, her hands clenched into fists.

'Whoa, take it easy! You knew what was in the cooking pot before your first mouthful, because I *told* you. You could have declined. So take a step back, have a serious word with yourself and calm the hell down.'

Maddie's stomach contracted, her jaw clenching as she squeezed bursts of air from her nose, making a wheezing snorting sound. Bozzer stood rigid, facing her down. He studied her posture and grainy tension in her face. 'What happened, in the past, to make you react this way?' he asked gently.

She shook head vigorously. 'No.'

'Yes …' he soothed, 'what happened? Did someone misplace your trust—'

'No – you can't ask that.'

'Did they, Maddie?'

She started to shake. Her muscles cramped up as she blinked rapidly, drew rasping inhalations, panting out snuffled exhalations. 'No. No – I can't—'

'It's okay. Tell me what happened,' he whispered, his voice calm, reassuring.

Maddie's shaking intensified, her entire body shuddering as she tried to gasp enough oxygen.

'It's okay. You're safe. Nothing can harm you …' Bozzer knelt down, gingerly touched her hand, eased his fingers under her palm, cradling it. 'It's okay. Let it go—'

'You – don't under – stand …' she gasped.

'Maddie, I'm gonna give you a hug. Okay?'

She sank down, her body crumpling, curling up into a ball, trembling uncontrollably. Bozzer manoeuvred around the hammock and knelt beside her, carefully draping his arms lightly over her quivering shoulders.

'Shhh …' Bozzer lifted his head to glance up at the sky. Bright stars began to fade as the first deep navy blue tinge peeked over the horizon, blending seamlessly with the lowest visible edge of the skyline. 'How you doing?' he whispered, lifting his arm off her shoulders.

She shifted up to a kneeling position, her face red and tearstained.

'White flag.' He pressed a Kleenex into her palm.

'Thanks,' she whispered.

'Do you think you're ready to make a move? I'd really like to get into the temples before the sun comes up.'

A slight nod, then a trembling sigh. She wiped her eyes, blew her nose. Bozzer stood up, waiting for her to join him. 'Come on, grab a seat over here. I need five minutes to pack up and we'll be off. Okay?'

She nodded, following him to the wall where she sat down and slumped forwards. Bozzer untied the hammock and scrunched it up, stuffing the material into the drawstring bag. He collected the stove and cooking equipment, packed everything into the bicycle basket and returned to her side. 'All set. We'll push the bikes back to the road. It's only a few hundred yards to Ta Prohm, so no need to pedal until later.'

Maddie nodded. They carried the bikes down the uneven entrance steps and wheeled them along the path. Ahead, the charcoal-bluey-green-orange-grey glow of dawn began lifting the inky black tones. This gradually defined their surroundings, guiding them towards the tarmac. Spokes whirled past worn brake pads, the side wall thrumming regularly past a twitching buckle in the wheel.

'I'm sorry,' she said after a minute of silent walking. 'I shouldn't have let you see me like that.'

'Guess I contributed, unwittingly. So I'm partly at fault,' he said, glancing over at her. They walked on, the misshaped wheel ticking. 'Want to talk about it? Might help.'

She shook her head without looking at him. 'Another time.'

'Sure?'

The front wheels bumped up onto the tarmac road. 'Some things … are best left in the darkness, where they belong.' Maddie glanced at him. 'Which way?'

'Left. See the wall opposite us? That's the outer perimeter of Ta Prohm. We'll be there in a few minutes.'

'What then?'

'Then, Madge, you are going to witness some of the most amazing photography of Ta Prohm ever captured by an Aussie …'

She smirked, her cheekbones lifting. 'That good, huh?'

'Someday, maybe. This place we're going to is dramatic. The trees have taken over. Their roots are massive, they've overrun the buildings. Makes it one of the most picturesque and unusual temples in Angkor. Built in eleven hundred and something AD, by this king dude, who dedicated it to his mother, the goddess of wisdom. Mother Nature, however, didn't take that on the chin. She's reclaimed the land from man, stealthily, over hundreds of years. These giant tree roots are literally strangling the place, engulfing the stone building blocks, pulling them back into the ground. Seriously, it'll make for a mental photo shoot.'

'Just as long as I stay behind the lens.'

Bozzer glanced over at her puffy, recently-been-trying-not-to-cry face and sombre, lethargic eyes. 'No worries, sweet as a biscuit. But when you see this place, you'll understand my enthusiasm.'

She looked over at him, her attempt at a half-smile rapidly dispersing. 'I doubt it, but thanks for trying.'

Twenty-Seven

'We've got a strong signal approaching, keep a sharp lookout.' Fender lifted his head from the dim glow of the Wolfhound's screen and peered through the taxi's side window. 'My guess would be a bicycle, or tuk-tuk.'

'Which traveller?' yawned Rupert.

'Victoria. You got her ID photo ready?'

Rupert flicked through the paper files on his lap, picked out the relevant paperwork. 'Yes.'

'Excellent. Signal's getting stronger, should be passing through the ticket checkpoint imminently. She could be with some of the others.'

Rupert rubbed his eyes and turned to watch the approaching vehicles, the majority of which were a mix of tuk-tuks, scooters and bicycles.

'There – on a bicycle. She's with a guy—'

'That's the Hybrid. The German's behind them. He's said something, they're conversing. Which means—'

'They know each other.'

'Exactly. Moving off now, no sign of Maddie. Keep watching. If they came in together, she won't be far behind.'

*

The darkness crept towards them with every dim judder of flickering, ebbing torchlight. The light finally died, plunging them into blackness.

'Bozzer?'

'Yup.'

'Your torch—'

'I switched it off.'

'Why? Isn't it creepy enough?'

'Shhh. Don't look.'

She turned towards the sound of a low pitched electronic whine.

'Look at what—'

Whumpf-PING!

A twin one-two burst of sterile white light pulsated from Bozzer's camera, bouncing off the perimeter wall and stone entrance arch, fleetingly illuminating everything in a fifty-foot arc before dispersing, sucked back into the darkness marginally slower than it had arrived.

Memory Card 3. Pic 138
'Ta-da-de-da-dum – Prohm! Green algae-like moss spilling out of the stone cracks, suffocating the wood frame as if splintered by an axe. The shin-height naga body along the path, marking a runway up to the entrance at the end of a flight path. The imposing tower above gaping like a giant open-mouth invitation, drawing us deeper into the devil's cauldron.'

'Oy! Thanks for the warning!' Maddie clutched her face, obscurity returning, blacker and more comprehensive than before.
'I did say not to look. Shut your eyes, it'll help preserve your night vision. Here, take my hand, I'll lead you into the courtyard.'
'No way, chum.'
'Madge ... *Maddie.* Trust me.'
'Not sure I can.'
'Try. We're not all monsters,' he said, quietly.
Bozzer slipped his hand into hers, gently tugging it forwards. 'Two steps, left foot first. Ready – step up. And again. Clear now for a little way ... we're going through the entrance. There are intricate stone carvings on the wall, a shapely woman carrying a water jug on her head, elephants, warriors and ... here we are. On the edge of the inner courtyard. Stay there, I'm just ahead of you. Keep one eye open, one shut. It'll be less invasive on your vision when the flash goes off – if you want to look. Ready?'
'Okay. Go for it.'
Whumpf-PING!

Memory Card 3. Pic 139
'Nature snatches back, her giant velociraptor claws lunging down from the sky to pillage the stony plaque. Rough textured hardwood limbs, like a sinewy ligament, knotted talons wrapping around the building and crushing it into a finite predicament. Hooks buried in the earth, incarcerating the stone wall in a vice-like grip, whilst laughing in mirth ...'

'Your narrative is very floral and thoughtful, for a bloke.'

Bozzer picked his way up onto a pile of scattered boulders, gaining height. He lined up the viewfinder to incorporate the backdrop of the first yellow glow of sunrise, peeking above the wall.

'Not so much *Shutter Stutter* as animated elegance.'

'A compliment … *really?*'

'Surprising, but true.'

'You're warming to me.'

'No.'

'Interesting. Here's one for you, ready?'

Whumpf-PING!

Memory Card 3. Pic 140

'A sting in the serpent's tail – uplifted and fanned out, embossed with multiple faces in braille. One such, upside down, a mixture of a cuddly lion and doll's face, painted on a clown. Others menacing, not carefree, the many shades of multiple moods, but this one right now, distinctly scary.'

'Thanks for that.'

'De nada.'

'This place is almost as weird as you are.'

'Almost. Mother Nature on the rampage – she sure does have a dark side … it's pure devilment, consuming man's best work like this. Constricting, strangling his enchanting worship. In no hurry, either, taking a few hundred years to fuck with his faith.'

'You do talk some crap.'

'It's a gift. Be prepared to be illuminated again, Princess—'

Whumpf-PING!

Another twin burst of flash bathed the courtyard in twisted tree trunk, snake-pit shaped light and peripheral shadows.

Memory Card 3. Pic 141

'Elephant trunk tree, stretching tall and straight into the sky with glee. The snout protruding from the ground, thirty feet circumference around. Reaching tall and proud, towards the nearest cloud. No branch offshoots – dependable, solid and unmoveable, these prehistoric roots.'

'How many years do you think it took for the trees to take over?' she asked, scrutinising the snapshot image captured in her memory.

'Several hundred, give or take a quarter-century.'

Whumpf-PING!

Memory Card 3. Pic 142

'Eight hundred years of decay, a cascading, slithering search for prey. Serpents intertwined at the trunk, headless, blind drunk. Perched across the tiered roof, bodies twisted, knotted, a chaotic horror spoof. Basking in first light, the snake bodies mash together, like solid veins, leaching from the soil forever.'

'Jesus, that's creepy.'

'Or is it ... fragile.' Bozzer picked his way carefully into a stone corridor, just a bit too wide to touch his outstretched hands against each wall. 'Check this out.'

Maddie crept in behind him, preparing herself for the explosion of light in the enclosed space.

Memory Card 3. Pic 143

'The escaping tree-man seen from behind a stone doorway, his upside down 'Y' legs like frozen clay. An arse crease between the boughs, a man climbing, escaping – as far as his master allows. Immortalised in space and time, crushing smaller Lilliputians under the urgency of his frantic climb.'

'He's not the only one desperate to escape.'

Bozzer chuckled. 'You know where the door is.' He brushed lightly past her as he climbed over part of the tree trunk, heading back out into the courtyard. It was easier to see the way now, in the soft glow of dawn.

Memory Card 3. Pic 144

'The brain tree. Its twisted spinal cortex rising, an umbrella of multi-directional veins searching, analysing. Silhouetted, not dissimilar to Kao's fragile dandelion tattoo, arteries feeding a vast cluster of skull-shaped capillaries, twinkling in the sunlit dew. The spinal column clings to crumbling stone blocks, crushing to dust with networks of tentacles criss-crossing every gap in the rocks.'

Bozzer lowered his camera. 'You know, we're in a very exclusive group. Only a handful of people in our lifetime have had the privilege of seeing Ta Prohm from this perspective. It's simply magical—'

'Don't you mean post-hallucinogenic-*radical?* Liz warned me about this sort of thing. I let my guard drop and—'

'More accusations. Are you angling for an apology, again? I'd have seasoned your tucker with arsenic if I'd known about my uninvited dinner guest—'

'Just pointing out, you're different.'

'And you, Madge, are—' Bozzer lifted his camera to capture another shot.

Whumpf-PING!

Memory Card 3. Pic 145
'Sunrise, sun life. Darkness evaporates, spindly shadows track across the stone walls, urging this blinkered girl to forget about society's rules and grab life by the balls. Light should breathe optimism and contentment, lifting the burden of resentment. But insomniac dreamers must find their own way to evolve, allow themselves the space for their mistrust to dissolve. Or else, inside they will remain dead and dingy, lazy and forever whingy.'

'I'm *what?*'

'Polygonal.' He turned and winked at her bemused expression. 'Look it up ... who's Liz?'

'Another traveller. We met the evening before I was supposed to fly home, with Rupert.'

'I bet she's more fun than you are.'

'Everyone is more fun than me, according to you.'

'You got her phone number?'

'You're such an arsehole.'

He sniggered. 'I prefer charismatic. And yet, I intrigue you.'

'Dream on, buster.' Maddie folded her arms and turned away from him, drawn to the outline of the sun peeking through a doorway, casting scrawny, elongated tree-root shadows across the courtyard. She clutched her stomach as it suddenly grumbled, loud and churning. 'S'cuse me.'

'You hungry?' Bozzer turned at her silence, studying her silhouette in the inky blue light. 'There's a group of cafés, back at Sras Srang lake. I'll buy you breakfast, to make up for the hallucinogenic dinner. We should be able to get your puncture fixed there.'

She glanced over at him. 'You think so?'

'I reckon. Saw some pit stops on the way in. Good business out here, captive market.'

'Have you finished photographing?'

'For the next hour or so. I'll get some more shots later, with human subjects. It'll give a sense of scale and contrast. Since you won't let me take your photograph, I'm stuck until the normal *happy* people get here.'

'So that's a yes, to being done with the camera?'

'That's a yes to let's get your bike fixed, and send you on your way.'

'Bored of me, so soon?'

'Oh, I'm way beyond boredom.' Bozzer led her back through the dawn colours peeking over the walled enclosure to Ta Prohm's dramatic dilapidated entrance, where they collected the bicycles. 'Same again, or do you think you can handle sitting on the back?' said Bozzer.

She watched him wheel the punctured bike up to her side. 'I don't think I can do pillion …'

'Okay, pedal away.' Bozzer climbed onto the panier rack and clutched the other bike's handlebars across his thighs. Maddie stood up on the pedals and began to pull away with minimal wobbling.

'Nice. I think you ride better after a taste of happiness.'

'Button it, Bozzer.'

He sniggered, waving to a pillion rider on a tourist scooter, as it buzzed past. 'Faster, magical Madge, faster! Take me to the munchies.'

Twenty-Eight

Fender glanced down at his watch, then continued scanning the constant flow of traffic through the admission checkpoint. 'We'll give it another thirty minutes. After that, we'll track down Victoria, have a little chat.'

'What if Maddie isn't with them?'

'She can't be far away. We'll find her.'

'What's going to happen then, if—'

Fender turned slowly, fixed Rupert with an unblinking stare. 'In that event, it'll be time to cash in my insurance policy.'

*

Maddie pushed her plate to one side, sat back and rested her hands on her belly.

'Feel better?'

She nodded. 'Thank you, I needed that.'

'No wucking furries.' Bozzer glanced over Maddie's shoulder. 'Looks like our man has repaired your bike …'

Maddie turned to see a ten year old Cambodian boy stood perched on the pedals in the gap between the saddle and handlebars, cycling towards them. His mop of chestnut brown hair flopped rhythmically with each lunging motion, his arms lifting and dropping as the wheels bounced over the furrowed path. They watched the boy jam the brakes on, the pads squealing as they reluctantly locked against the rims, skidding the bike to a dusty stop. The boy dropped his foot and kicked the side-stand. He beamed and ran up to their table, holding his hand out. 'Five dollar!'

'*Five* dollars? You, my little hustler are pulling my dingley-danglies. We agreed two.' Bozzer held up his fingers in a v-sign.

'No, no – morning. Cost more!'

'Overtime, *really?*' Bozzer tutted and shook his head. He reached into his pocket. 'What's your name?'

'Me, Prong Ron. Five dollar!'

Bozzer peeled off two one-dollar bills from a small fold of notes and passed them over the table, holding firmly onto one end. 'Okay, Prong Ron. You know ping pong?' Bozzer mimed a table tennis action, tossing an imaginary ball into the air, then used his open palm to imitate a slicing spin trick-shot. Prong Ron pulled a confused face. 'That's you, *ping pong.*'

'No ping pong – Prong Ron – you pay, mister!'

Maddie shot Bozzer a *what-the-heck-are-you-on* expression. He caught her stern look. 'Hey, just being friendly … two dollars, yes?' Prong Ron yanked on the dollar bills, Bozzer playfully tugged them back.

'Five!'

'Here, this makes three dollars,' said Maddie, offering him another dollar bill. Prong Ron's eyes widened. He giggled, reached out his other hand and gently took her dollar. Bozzer released the two notes and watched Prong Ron hastily dip his head and press the money between his palms in a prayer gesture before running away, his hands held aloft, whooping and clutching the payment.

'Cheeky bugger. You've spoilt him.'

'It's an extra seventy pence. Here, allow me.' She placed two dollars on the table in front on him.

'Peachy.' Bozzer squinted at the menu, mentally calculating the bill. He added some more notes to hers, then shuffled out from the plastic table. 'Right, pommy princess – baby-sitting duties concluded. I'm heading back to Angkor Thom and The Bayon, see if I can snap some wacky tourists around the temples.' Bozzer slung his camera case strap over his shoulder and mimicked Prong Ron's thank you prayer gesture. 'Madge, it's been … unexpected.' He turned away from her.

She watched him walk off towards his bicycle, jiggling her fingers on the table, a hundred possible responses left tingling on her tongue.

*

Fender stared at the Wolfhound's illuminated screen. 'Judging by the signal strength and consistency, Victoria is on foot, probably heading towards Angkor Wat. She's the most likely candidate for Maddie to have been in contact with. So we'll intercept her next.'

Rupert nodded. 'Makes sense.'

Fender indicated to the tuk-tuk driver to pull in beside the causeway to Angkor Wat. He passed the driver five dollars and held up his first finger. 'Wait here, one hour. Okay?'

'Okay. I wait, there,' replied the driver, pointing to an ice cream van in the congested car park.

Fender nodded and climbed out of the tuk-tuk. 'Let's go,' he said to Rupert. 'Time is short.'

Rupert scanned left to right across the temples perimeter wall as he jogged up to Fender's side. 'This place is vast.'

'Built in the twelfth century, dedicated to the Hindu god Vishnu. Later modified into a Buddhist shrine. The temple complex spans almost two million square metres.'

'You been here before?'

'No. I read the guide book, did you?'

Rupert shook his head.

'Perhaps you should have.' Fender weaved his way through the throngs of tourists milling around the steps leading up to the imposing narrow entrance. The multi-tiered stone rooflines culminated in the peaked cylindrical tower above them. Fender bounded up two steps at a time, leaving Rupert puffing hard behind him, trying to keep up.

*

'Wait!' Maddie hunched her body over the handlebars, pedalling harder, focusing on the back of his bike, trying not to look down at the speed of the ground whizzing by beneath her.

'Oy, Bozzer!' she yelled.

He stopped pedalling and glanced over his shoulder. 'Hey, material girl. How's it going? I haven't seen you for *sooo* long.'

'I've been trying to catch up, you inconsiderate pothead!'

'Hey, it's medicinal magic hocus-pocus.'

'Whatever.' Maddie coasted up alongside him, red faced and sweaty. Bozzer looked
    her over, tip to toe.

'Wow, something must be important.' He winked at her. 'Or, alternatively, some*one*.

Such a quandary ...'

'I needed to tell you – Jody's a lucky girl, to have escaped from your evil colonial charms. Race you to the next temple – see if your nicotine-contaminated lungs can handle it.' She stood up on the pedals and powered her legs down, accelerating away from him.

'What the—'

Maddie dropped into a low stoop over the handlebars, her legs spinning faster and faster.

'Playing that game, eh?' Bozzer stood up off the saddle and forced his feet down on the pedals. 'Wait up, posh-pom-hoity-toity!'

Maddie pushed through the dull ache in her quads, chopping her legs down like two pistons working flat out in perfect unison. She peered down the road with tunnel vision, homing in on the east gate to Angkor Thom.

'Bollocks,' Bozzer muttered between wheezes, shaking his head at the widening gap.

Maddie brought her bike to a halt at the gate then glugged down half a litre of water, eyeing his breathless approach. She screwed the top back on the bottle and wiped her mouth with the back of her hand. 'Tyre's fixed.'

'Yeah, I noticed,' he panted, squeaking the bike to a stop. 'Bloody kid, put supercharged compressed air in there.' He rested his bike on its stand, accepted the water bottle from her and ignored her artfully raised eyebrow.

'Something you need to say ...?' she asked, lightly.

'Such as?' he spluttered, gulping down the water.

'"You're actually quite fast on a bike, Maddie."'

'Sure. You're ... actually ... quite ... daft.' He sank down onto the ground, laid back with his knees pointing skywards. 'It's too early in the morning for a pissing contest.'

'You boys, no stamina. Don't have a heart attack, my CPR isn't up to date.'

He propped up on his elbows, shaking his head. 'Hand me my camera – need to capture this gloating.'

Maddie reached into his bike's basket, handed the camera case to him.

'Cheers. Victory pose, if you please: arms folded, one foot on a pedal, tilt those hips and ... pout.' Bozzer clicked the shutter, sank his head back on the ground and laid his arms out by his side. 'Perfect.'

'What, no drivelling slutty-smutty observation?'

'Too knackered.'

'My turn, then – loser shot.' Maddie lifted the camera from his hand, stepped back and adjusted the lens, bringing him into sharp focus. 'So to record as well, do I press the shutter once, twice, or—'

Bozzer rolled his eyes. 'Have a heart, man down – ruptured ego …'

'There's no humility in victory. It'll be good for the book blurb to see the Aussie author suffering for his art. So much more interesting than a sterile studio portrait.'

Bozzer smirked and took another swig of water. 'Once the shutter makes its aperture opening sound, keep the button held down and say what you need to. Then release it when you're done. I normally aim for—'

'Twenty seconds of flowery bullshit. Yes, I know.'

Shh-clitch.

Memory Card 3. Pic 146
'Deflated drongo. The man from down under, gasping to recover. Beaten by his ego, and a pommy cycling ho. Will his damaged pride ever repair, or will he end up in despair? The author of *Shutter Stutter* lies where he belongs, exhausted and breathless, in the gutter. His unwritten book of pictures and words, could well end up being a huge steaming turd.'

Maddie released the shutter button. Bozzer lifted his head and middle finger simultaneously, grinning at her. 'Thanks for the vote of confidence, it means so much.' He dug his hand into his pocket, removed his tobacco tin and rolled onto his side, propping up onto an elbow. 'Ciggie break for the condemned man. Then we'll negotiate rates for resuming the grand tour – most definitely at a slower speed.'

*

Victoria slipped her hand over Charlie's shoulder and held her mobile phone at arm's length. He flinched as she squeezed in tighter to him and pressed the screen.

'Fantastic, great shot.' Victoria showed him the picture of her grinning face and his quizzical expression in the foreground, with the Angkor Wat towers behind them. She slid her arm off his shoulders, left it hanging loose around his waist and lifted her eyes up to his.

Charlie looked down, meeting her gaze. Her eyelashes flickered, arm tightening around him as she eased her chin up, her lips closing in …

'Hold that pose – you're such a lovely couple. Would you like me to take a shot for you?'

They turned simultaneously to look at Fender. He was smiling warmly, his fingers forming a square, framing an imaginary photograph.

Victoria glanced at Charlie, who shrugged. 'Oh, okay. Thanks.' She handed Fender her phone and cuddled back into Charlie.

'Perfect.' Fender took a step back and held the phone up, close to his face. 'And say … Madeline Bryce.' Fender captured their confused, wary expressions. 'She got on the same minibus as you, from Bangkok to Battambang.'

Victoria glanced at Rupert, loitering a few feet behind Fender. 'Can't help you.' She held out her hand. 'I'd like my phone back.' Victoria took a step towards Fender, who turned and tossed the phone to Rupert.

'Of course. But first, a few questions about Maddie.'

Charlie eased away from Victoria, flicking his eyes between Fender and Rupert.

'I wouldn't recommend doing anything rash. All I want is to locate her, make sure she's safe.' Fender gestured behind him at Rupert, busy checking Victoria's phone. 'This is Maddie's fiancé. He wasn't very … inclusive of her needs. So she took some time out, to think things through. But Maddie isn't particularly streetwise. I need reassurance that she isn't mixing with the wrong crowd.'

Charlie took a step towards Rupert, holding out his hand. 'My friend would like her phone back. Now.'

Fender side-stepped, blocking his approach. 'I wouldn't, buddy.'

'You might not, old timer, but—' Charlie pulled a clenched fist back and swung it at Fender, fast and low, aiming for his stomach. Fender deflected the blow easily, flexing his hips and swatting the fist away while simultaneously using his left hand to yank down Charlie's shoulder. Fender jerked his knee up hard into his groin, collapsing him onto the ground.

'Ahhrr!' Charlie writhed in a foetal position on the grass, sucking in short rasping breaths, his face contorted in eye-watering agony.

Fender crouched down, used his palm to press Charlie's cheek into the dirt.

'Word of advice, mucker. Never underestimate anyone, no matter how old and incapable they might appear. Now, when did you last see Maddie?'

'She was with us, but we haven't seen her for two days,' said Victoria, sounding scared.

Fender glanced up. 'Go on.'

'She went to bed early, got a tuk-tuk to Angkor Wat for the sunrise, yesterday morning.'

'On her own, or—'

'With Gabby, another traveller, who was meeting an old boyfriend. Maddie went along to keep her company, in case it didn't work out. We were supposed to meet her there later, for breakfast. But we didn't get up early enough.'

'Where's Maddie staying?'

'Somewhere in the tourist part of town.'

Fender eased off the pressure on Charlie's face. 'Has Gabby got a mobile phone?'

Victoria shrugged.

'Don't know,' said Charlie, spitting out particles of dirt.

'So the question is, where did Maddie go?'

'She was talking about getting a three day pass.'

'Excellent.' Fender glanced over at Rupert, still fixated with Victoria's phone. 'Anything?'

'She's got Maddie's number in here, but there's no text messages or phone calls logged between them.'

'What about the German, Barnaby?' Fender directed his question at Charlie and Victoria.

'Barney? What about him …'

Fender released his grip on Charlie. 'Does Maddie like him?'

Charlie pushed up onto his side, rubbing dirt off his cheek, brushing dust out of his hair. 'No, I don't think so. Barney's weird.'

'Weird, how?'

'He's eccentric, that's all. An extrovert,' said Victoria.

'Is there anyone else you think Maddie might be with?'

Charlie and Victoria looked at each other and shook their heads. 'The only other person would have been Barry. But his girlfriend didn't like Maddie. Anyway, they've moved on to Phnom Penh,' said Victoria.

Fender glanced at Rupert, who shrugged. He jerked his head over at Victoria. Rupert stepped forwards and handed her the mobile phone.

'Here's my contact details,' said Fender. 'You see Maddie, please call me.' He handed Victoria a business card and a fifty dollar bill. 'For your time. I'll double it if you contact me with details of her location.'

Fender flitted his gaze between them, making sure they understood, then he turned and walked away. Rupert dutifully fell in at his side, matching his purposeful stride.

Twenty-Nine

Maddie swallowed a mouthful of water and handed the bottle to Bozzer. He took a long drink then sank back onto his elbows, slouching against the stone steps, stretching his legs down towards the edge of the lake. 'Imagine having all this as your own private bathroom. Be a bit excessive.'

'And not especially secluded.'

'No ... swimming twenty lengths before breakfast would take a month.'

'But it is tranquil. I like it.'

They sat there for a while, taking in the view.

'So, tour guide extraordinaire, what's the plan?' she asked.

'I'm off to score some steroids so I can keep up with you. After that, mingle with the minions at Angkor Wat to complete the tourist *thang*. I'm meeting up with Barney and the others in Siem Reap later, for dinner.'

'Isn't Barney a bit odd?'

'Yeah, but he makes me laugh. He's heading off east tomorrow, so we're gonna hang out. Maybe score some happy ... memories.'

Maddie watched him shift his eyes away. '*Memories* ... really?'

'What?'

'Nothing. You boys ...' She looked out over the secluded lake and sighed. 'Is Angkor Wat going to be rammed with tourists?'

'Oh yeah, guaranteed. Didn't you notice the build-up for the sunrise, with Gabby? It'll be even worse at this time of day.'

'So nothing like the tree temple.'

'Ta Prohm? Nah, that was solitary, and ... significant.'

They sat quietly for a few minutes, watching the sun shining over the vast serenity of the bathing lake.

'How many copies of this book do you need to sell, to cover your expenses?'

'I'd be happy to sell one, to make it official, y'know. But, I suppose, four months travelling, Southeast Asia and South America ... all in, maybe five thousand copies.'

'After that you're in profit?'

He sat up and considered her with a mild frown and single half-raised eyebrow, a quirky smile twitching at the corner of his mouth as he swept a hand out across the lake's expanse. 'Look where we are – I'm already in credit.'

'That's a nice way to look at it.'

Bozzer yawned and stood up, stretching his arms above his head. 'It's the *only* way to look at it.' She turned to watch him walk towards the bikes, propped up against a tree. 'Time to move on, magnificent Madge. The minions await …'

*

Fender handed the correct amount of change to the man behind the van's serving hatch and passed Cambodia's answer to a Magnum chocolate ice cream to Rupert. He unwrapped his own and took a bite.

'This is surreal. Seeing you eat that, like just another tourist.'

Fender cast his eyes over Rupert. 'Have I not worked hard enough pursuing your AWOL fiancée and her Samsonite contraband to have earned a regular tourist treat?'

'Maybe, but it's still weird. I'm starting to think you might actually be a normal guy, under all that ruthless efficiency.'

'It's what I do. This is—'

'Just another day at the office?'

'Ordinarily … but today happens to be slightly different.'

Rupert studied Fender's expression. 'You're celebrating something?'

'I am.'

'Joe-Ho's released me from the debt?'

'Sadly not. Why would he? This is business.'

'Something else then ... your birthday?'

'Correct. It will be, tomorrow.'

'Really?'

'Yes.'

'Let me guess – forty-five?'

'Flattery will not buy you any concessions.'

'Steady, that looked like the beginning of a wry smile.'

'No. You were mistaken.'

'So how old are you?'

'Tomorrow, Rupert, will be my fifty-fifth birthday.'

'Wow, life has been kind. We should celebrate.'

Fender held up the ice cream. 'I am.'

'You're a day early.'

'I'm taking small pleasures as they present themselves. Tomorrow may not bring the time or opportunity to mark the occasion.'

'So this is it? No Skype call home, meal out later with a few beers?'

'I'm working.'

'All the time?'

Fender headed off a melting chocolate and ice cream landslide with his mouth. He savoured the taste as if he'd not had a sweet treat for a year. 'Interesting that you berate me, Rupert. Are you not currently lacking normality? I doubt Maddie will be the same girl she was, when we find her.'

Rupert swallowed, blinking rapidly, his chest tightening. 'Meaning … you're about to get nasty?'

'Meaning, when your future wife finds out about your predicament, and *hers,* is she really going to stand beside you while you face up to your catastrophic situation?'

'Maddie is—'

'Madeline has already taken the first lunge away from you. Get used to reality, Rupert. It's called being a singleton, with substantial baggage.'

Rupert shrugged and looked away.

Fender added, 'Best hope we find her today, while I'm still in a good mood. We might be able to sort this mess out in a civilised manner.'

'Meaning the rest of the time you're a calculated and ruthless enforcer?'

'There's a debt to recover. I've been employed to clean it up.'

'By any means necessary?'

'I've built my reputation on positive outcomes.'

'So what happens when we find Maddie?'

Fender took another precisely targeted bite of the ice cream's chocolate coating. He enjoyed the sensation for a moment before replying. 'Maddie intentionally distanced herself from you, the rules you were about to inflict on her. Once we've dealt with the Samsonite issue, she gets to decide what she wants to do next. With, or without you.'

'What happens to me?'

Fender paused in his ice cream demolition. 'You think I have instructions to punish you?'

'Haven't you?'

A thin wry smile momentarily creased Fender's lips. 'I generally deal with debt recovery, rather than liability eradication.'

'So what happens if Maddie doesn't have the other suitcase?'

Fender narrowed his eyes a millimetre. 'Why wouldn't she?'

'I'm examining the hypothetical risk.'

'To you, or her?'

'Both of us.'

Fender sucked the remnants of ice cream off the wooden stick and pressed the curved end into Rupert's chest. 'You'd better hope she does still have it, Rupert. For *both* your sakes.'

*

Memory Card 3. Pic 188

'Ant invasion, curious hordes disrespectful of the gravity of occasion. They scurry amongst the ancient iconic temples of Angkor, seeking selfies with the subtlety and respectful observation of a leaking supertanker. Filming, snapping, posing in an effort to illustrate their grasp of culture, instead immortalising their portrait as one of many self-absorbed social media vultures. Individuality is gone, only this remains. Men have diluted their ability to better themselves, despite lessons learned over generations failing to embed in their greedy little brains.'

'Wow. Quite the anarchist, aren't you?'

Bozzer released the shutter button and lowered his camera, his narrow field of vision widening across the full panorama of the Angkor temple boundaries. 'I do sometimes wonder where it comes from. There's something a bit unsettling about all this, don't you think?'

Maddie followed his gaze, looking down from their perch high up on the central stone tower, over the grassy sections below where clusters of colourfully dressed tourists mingled.

'I'd ask what you've been on, to come up with such an avant-garde description, but I'm still partially, unintentionally, on your wavelength. It is odd, seeing this holy place overrun like this. Particularly surreal, knowing there's a massive car park beyond the moat.'

'Yeah ... kinda peaceful up here, though.'

She nodded, scanning the horizon, the distant treeline filtering the blue and yellowy tinted sky. 'How long does it take to build something like this?'

'Quite a few years, without a JCB.'

She giggled, shot him a disapproving look, then relaxed back into a reflective gaze over the temple's perimeter. 'Some commitment.'

He turned to face her. 'I've been trying to figure this place out. It's no fortress, built to protect against an attack from enemies, like an English medieval castle. It has a sense of harmony ... like it's a sanctuary. It's here to celebrate life, rather than defend against an invasion and impending death. The strength in this place comes from within.'

'Sounds like a life lesson is in there somewhere.'

'For sure.' Bozzer opened his tobacco tin and began to roll a cigarette. 'We'll make a move back in a bit, join the masses. If that's cool?'

'Sounds good. I wonder how Gabby's getting along with her guy.'

'Perhaps you'll see her later.'

'Maybe. Where are you meeting the others?'

'At a restaurant called Le Tigre de Papier. Some big cheese celebrity chef is supposed to have cooked there once. Your buddy Charlie, and his shadow – vindictive Victoria – will probably be there too.'

Maddie frowned. She turned away from the ebbing sun and pastel-coloured panorama to study his expression.

'What?'

'Charlie's not my friend.'

'Someone should probably tell him that, cos he's well into you. It irks the shit out of Victoria, which is kinda amusing.'

Maddie shook her head. 'People are funny.'

'And travellers are especially peculiar.'

'I'll drink to that.'

Bozzer gave her a sideways glance, lighting his cigarette. He lifted his gaze to look out over the multi-tiered turrets of Angkor Wat and the uneven profile of the pitched-roof terraced buildings linking them, forming an imposing boundary wall. The moat beyond shimmered, reflecting the sunset's dying embers of red, yellow and azure, as the last of the sun's golden crescent dropped below the trees and disappeared.

*

'This is nuts.' Maddie stood beside her bicycle, surveying the queue of red brake lights stretching out along the side of Angkor Wat's vast moat. Tuk-tuks, coaches and taxis crawled along the tarmac road, being overtaken by scooters and bicycles, accompanied by tooting horns, ancient rattling engines and smoky fumes.

'Ceremonious structures built for worship meets the convenience of the combustion engine … society has indeed progressed.' Bozzer pressed the shutter, bathing the traffic chaos in a flash of light. He shook his head as he lowered the camera. 'You ready to chance it?'

'There's a cold beer waiting, right?'

'There surely is, if we survive the next hour.' He pushed up onto the saddle and looked left and right, waiting for a gap. Then with a ping from his bike bell, he pushed off, his feet spinning past the lingering red-tinged fumes that swirled lazily at knee height. Bozzer glanced over his shoulder, saw the yellow glow from Maddie's front light behind him. He was just able to make out her face, her cheeks glowing, framing her smile perfectly.

*

'You sure about this theory?'

'It's based on strong intel.'

Rupert leaned back against the taxi and folded his arms, studying Fender's surveillance of the long line of vehicles crawling out of the entrance. Their yellow-tinged headlamps and red brake lights illuminated exhaust smoke that lingered at low level, creating eerie tree-branch shadows. The grey tentacles reached out from the darkness, stretching across the road like a fidgeting octopus.

'But this amount of people, it would be easy to miss her. Street lighting would have been helpful—'

'What's the matter Rupert, already forgotten what your fiancée looks like?'

'Of course not.'

'Then switch on and focus. Your future prosperity depends on finding her, and that suitcase.'

Rupert clenched his jaw and squeezed his arms against his chest. He scanned each vehicle as it edged past them. Scooters and bicycles made faster progress, zipping into gaps, weaving across the road, the contours of their riders' faces quickly dissolving in the changeable light.

'Remember, tuk-tuks and bicycles are most likely. But check everything.'

'Will do.' Rupert looked up at a modern coach, tall and imposing above them. He scanned along the row of faces, then dropped his eyes back to the road, frowning as the dim flicker of a bicycle light disappeared behind the coach's bulk. A scooter buzzed past, over-revving in a low gear, the passenger wedged behind a Cambodian rider. Another bicycle passed behind the side screen of a tuk-tuk, reappearing briefly in the gap behind the coach, now crawling past them. The headlight from another overtaking scooter cast a beam of light across the cyclist's face, briefly illuminating a red bandanna and fluttering blonde hair … The departing scooter's headlight flickered past her shadowy profile, disappearing behind the coach. Rupert flinched, his posture springing upright.

'What is it?' said Fender, still closely observing the passing traffic, but tracking Rupert out of the corner of his eye.

'I think I saw something.' The coach accelerated forwards to close the gap in front, overrunning. It jerked to a stop millimetres from the tuk-tuk ahead, with a screech and hiss of air brakes. The cyclist pedalled on, the changing shadows obscuring Rupert's line of sight.

'Did you see her?' barked Fender.

Rupert scanned the red glow of brake lights snaking away from them, bicycle spokes churning past the low-lying fumes. 'No. The light … playing tricks. Damn. This is impossible.'

'Nothing is impossible.'

'Maybe we should come back in the morning, in daylight—'

'That might be too late. Keep looking!'

Rupert snapped his gaze away from the blips of disappearing bicycle lights and refocused on each passing vehicle. He tried to summon up a freeze-frame snapshot of the red-bandanna girl. But she slipped away, teasing his powers of recognition.

Thirty

'Room nineteen please,' said Maddie, smiling at the young girl of about twelve sat behind the counter. The girl reached into a row of pigeon holes behind her and withdrew a handwritten note.

> Hi Maddie,
> Hope you're okay! I'm staying with Matthew tonight. (Tuesday) Not sure what I'm doing after that, can only say at the moment that it's going well.(!) Matthew will collect his bike at some point, maybe in a day or so. Could you lock it up outside and leave the padlock key with reception please. If I don't see you before one of us moves on, good luck and keep in touch!
> Gabby

Maddie finished reading and pocketed the notepaper. 'Do you have the key please?'

The young girl smiled sadly and shook her head. 'Sorry, room gone. Very full.'

'Oh. All the rooms?'

'Yes. Because of celebration. For three days. We have bag.' The girl poked her head though a row of hanging beads draped over a doorway behind her and called out. After a moment, a sleepy man in his early thirties appeared. They exchanged a few words and he withdrew, reappearing with Maddie's backpack.

'Very sorry. For Cambodia day, we have many people. We think you not come back.'

'Okay, I understand. So I need to pay, for yesterday?'

'No, please. Your friend. She has given already.'

'Oh, right. Thank you.' Maddie hoisted the backpack onto her shoulders, helped by the girl's father. 'Can you recommend another hotel?'

The man shrugged. He pulled a sympathetic expression. 'I am sorry. For next three days, many people visit. But try, lots of trying.'

Maddie nodded and withdrew. She stepped out onto the dimly lit pavement and glanced left and right, deliberating which way to turn.

*

Rupert poured the remaining beer into his glass and signalled with the empty bottle to a Cambodian waiter for another. 'You still think Victoria will lead us to her?'

'I do. She's a social butterfly and our best option right now. We observe her tonight, then return to the temples tomorrow. If she meets up with anyone else in the group, she's most probably going to tell them about us – our interest in Maddie.'

'Why?'

'Because of all types of people, travellers particularly love to gossip. It's often boring, being on the road – juicy titbits are social currency. So we observe. Anyone she meets with who looks concerned or suddenly takes off after she's spoken to them, we follow. One of them will lead us straight to your future wife. If she still wants you.'

Fender maintained a discreet surveillance of the restaurant opposite, through the constant stream of tourists transiting the narrow street. He watched Barney wander through the open air seating to sit down at a table with Victoria and Charlie.

The waiter arrived to replace Rupert's beer. He nodded his thanks and topped up his glass, then chinked it against Fender's sparkling water. 'Happy advance birthday. I hope your frivolity extends past midnight. I like the marginally more relaxed side of your robotic personality.'

'Pace yourself and you might yet find out – this could be a long night.'

Rupert shrugged and glugged back a mouthful of beer. 'I'm on holiday ... besides, doesn't the condemned man get granted his last wish?'

'Not on my dime – take it easy.'

Rupert glanced away from Fender's piercing stare and looked out into the street. Opposite them, Charlie signalled to a waiter, handing him several notes from his wallet. He stood up, exchanged pleasantries with Barney then departed with Victoria.

'The German doesn't look like he's in a hurry to do anything.'

'No. Anything Victoria and Charlie might have told him about their encounter with us this afternoon hasn't troubled him. Okay, we follow Victoria and Charlie tonight. Tomorrow morning we'll be back at the entrance to the temples before sunrise.' Fender reached into his wallet and laid a five dollar bill on the table, then stood up. They joined the other tourists mingling in the street, meandering through the evening throng, in no particular hurry whatsoever.

*

Bozzer strolled across the road, a thumb and finger in his mouth as he let rip with a piercing whistle. He held his palms out at the neon strobe lights and bright Western-inspired gaudiness, rolling his eyes at Barney. 'Hey, Hanz Rolo – what's wrong with the Cambodian part of town?'

Barney screeched and leapt around the table, running into the street to body-check Bozzer into a man-hug.

'You want a beer?'

'Ja, always is drinking time.'

Bozzer caught the waiter's eye, winking at him as he held up Barney's empty bottle, waggling two fingers. 'So, you get lucky, Hanz?'

'Ja, she invite me into her garments. Zo I not meet you. It was good, the light and trees?'

'My friend, it was epic.' Bozzer winked at him.

'But you were alone?'

Bozzer shrugged, raised his eyebrows and raised the beer bottle to his lips, a mischievous glint in his eye.

'Ahhh … bonehead Barry was *not* alone!' Barney slapped the table, rattling the bottles of beer. 'Tell me, tell me, tell me.'

'You first.'

'Ah, man. She had bottom cheekiness.' Barney pulled a wide-eyed excited grin, his open hands held up as if weighing a coconut in each.

'So where is she?'

'Pffft … gone, into the night.'

'Prostitutes, chief – they don't count. Paying a fee, that ain't free.'

Barney sniggered. He finished his beer, spun the bottle in his palm and banged it down on the table. 'And free is not lacking of strings, ja? You know this – I am right!'

'It's a fair one, mate.'

'So, I pay …' Barney opened his wallet and fanned through a selection of currency, then jabbed a pointed finger into Bozzer's chest. 'You *pay*. Different, but same-same, ja? Zo, did you fondle secret data dongle?'

Bozzer sniggered and began rolling a joint. 'Too many secrets, my German comrade. I could tell you some of them, but then I'd have to be your friend.'

'Ha! Is true.'

The waiter delivered two fresh bottles of beer, Bozzer passed one to Barney. They clunked their bottles together. Barney leaned in, flicked his eyes around the restaurant, murmuring secretively. 'She was good sex, ja …?' Barney flicked his wrist, cocking his eyebrow as he studied his watch. 'Almost five minutes, with taxi home – you have improved endurance. You take blue pills?'

Bozzer took a swig of beer. 'You're too generous, Hanz. It was three minutes, tops.'

'This girl, you like her.'

Bozzer frowned and glanced up at Barney.

'Second time, back to Phnom Penh. You pay extra expense, just for few pictures.'

'Important pictures, Hanz. Angkor Wat is—'

Barney waved his hand through Bozzer's cigarette smoke. 'Ja, ja, important architecture, spirit temples, blah, blah. But also, you come back for material girl. I am wrong, no?'

Bozzer frowned harder, his lips silently repeating Barney's words. He returned a puzzled expression. 'I'm confused. You're right in being wrong, or—'

'You know I am saying, you like her.'

Bozzer sucked the last embers from the roll-up, plucked it from his lips and stubbed the butt in the ashtray. 'Maybe.'

'Better than Jody?' Barney pinched his thumb and finger to form a circle, and inserted a finger from his other hand, gyrating it in and out.

Bozzer laughed.

'You no dib-dab?'

'Noooo!'

'But you want it?'

'Is the grass here good smoke?'

'Is true.' Barney sighed, folded his arms and shook his head. 'So sad. No bang-bang for boring Barry.'

'Ah, you know how it goes. Easy come, easy ho.'

Barney's amusement clouded over, his demeanour becoming solemn. 'But this, not problem.' He flicked Bozzer's chest with the back of his hand.

'How so?'

Barney's solemn expression lifted. He pointed into the street. Bozzer turned to follow Barney's outstretched finger. Maddie stood in the street, a handful of tourists wandering past her.

Bozzer stared at her, his hands moving instinctively to his camera. He pressed his eye to the viewfinder, trigger finger poised.

Memory Card 3. Pic 199
'Her vulnerability, nervous excitement and fear, is it so scary to join this artistic Australian for a beer? The expectation of her unwritten journey, will it all end laying zonked out on a hospital gurney? This is truly stepping aside from comfort and stability, escaping the boredom and monotony, away from normality. She stands ready, yet unprepared, to walk her own path, away from the herd.'

Bozzer lowered the camera.

'Sure you gave me the full twenty seconds?'

'I wasn't counting.'

'You'd better not short-change me.'

'Or ...?'

Barney clasped Barry's shoulders, shook them, then ducked around him, sidestepping into the street, his arms outstretched towards Maddie. 'Welcome! Come, drink and make boring Barry happy and snappy.' He swept her up into a hug, spinning her around, catching Bozzer's eye, repeating his finger meets 'o' gesture behind Maddie's back when he plonked her down.

Bozzer held out his bottle of beer for Maddie. 'What's up, Gabby move on?'

She nodded. 'The hotel's fully booked. Some sort of national holiday.'

'Yeah, it's for King Sihanouk, signing their constitution. There's three days of celebration ahead. Place is gonna be rammed.'

'So I gathered. I've tried a dozen places, all full.'

Bozzer nodded. 'Want to try Barney's place? It's late and I'm not sure if they have a receptionist. But if you're stuck, there's floor space.'

'That where you're staying?'

'Yeah. It's cheap and convenient, now it's just me.'

Maddie glanced at Barney. 'You stay, is okay,' he said.

'Great, thanks.'

*

Ting ...

The single chime from the desk bell echoed around the small, tiled reception area. A momentary pause, then a sound of rustling emanated from behind the desk. Barney leant over the wood counter and grinned at the Cambodian man in his forties sitting up in his makeshift bed, rubbing sleep from his eyes.

'Hello. Sorry for late-time. You have room please, for friend?' said Barney, swivelling his head around to glance at Maddie, sat beside Bozzer on a plastic chair.

Bozzer watched Barney chat to the man who'd appeared from behind the desk. 'That's his bed, every night,' he said to Maddie.

'From what I saw riding a tuk-tuk to the temples, he's lucky. Lots of people sleep on the street.'

'Yeah. We're the rich ones alright.'

Barney thanked the man and passed him something. He turned from the desk and walked over. 'No rooms. He say you sleep here, or my floor.'

'How much extra?' asked Bozzer.

Barney shrugged. 'Is no problem.'

Bozzer nodded and turned to Maddie. 'Your call. It won't be that comfy, but it's a roof for tonight. Or we can look around some other hotels. But it's cracking on for two – dead time.'

'Okay, thanks. Um, Bozzer ... serious question. Are you and Barney going to be respectful?'

Bozzer turned from her to Barney. 'Mate, I know how irresistible I am, but are you gonna keep your hands to yourself? She's not into watching man fumbles ...'

'Ha! You not my type. Too tiny.' Barney waggled his little finger at Bozzer. 'We all safe. Okay, sleep?'

Bozzer looked back at Maddie. 'There you go. Bunk down with me and ze German, or out here with our host.'

'You guys.'

'Okay. Follow that pothead room-mate.'

Maddie stepped into the dim room and wrinkled her nose at the pungent musty aroma of unventilated damp walls, unwashed clothes and stale male body odour.

Amusement twinkled in Bozzer's eyes as he caught her reluctant expression. 'Betcha a hammock and mosquito net under the stars at Ta Prohm is suddenly much more appealing right now …?'

'Uh-huh.'

The door to the room swung open. Barney stepped in, sucking his toothbrush, wearing only a pair of boxer shorts.

'You have decided, who is mooning with me?' he said, flicking his eyes between them.

'He is,' said Maddie, dumping her pack in the corner of the room.

Bozzer winked at Barney, whose shoulders slumped as he cast her a forlorn puppy-dog glance.

'The bathroom is down the hall, last door on the right. I'll lay some clothes out for you on the floor, or you can zip yourself into a sleeping bag and chance it on the bed.'

'The floor would be great, thanks.'

'Sure thing, very wise.' Bozzer began laying out his clothes in a neat jigsaw beneath the end of the bed. Maddie disappeared out of the door.

'You are too much good guy, Barry.'

'Maybe … but you, my uncultured German friend, are a wolf.'

Barney chuckled, deep and nasal. 'Is true. *Oowwwllll.*'

Maddie shivered as the cold water splashed over her face. She lifted her head, staring at her reflection in the cracked mirror.

Is that really me?

She lifted her left hand, her eyes drawn to her engagement ring. She rubbed her thumb on the underside, then looked back into the mirror, leaning close to study her face. 'Is it time?' she murmured. Her gaze flitted away from her eyes, diverting to an earring, glinting under the harsh fluorescent glare. 'Perhaps, a compromise.' Her nimble fingers removed her earrings, which she wrapped in toilet paper and deposited in her purse. She glanced back at her reflection again. *Better.*

She smiled, her attention returning to her engagement ring. 'What about you?'

She shook her head, then splashed cold water on her face. After gently press-drying her skin, she rummaged in her toiletries bag for her toothbrush.

Time and travels will tell me when ...

Thirty-One

Maddie awoke with a start – something had jolted her foot. She clutched the sleeping bag under her chin, squinting through tired eyes, vaguely aware of a mumbled curse then an accented apology. Shafts of sunlight streamed in through gaps in the curtain, blindingly bright, warming her face. She shifted away, shielding her eyes as she lifted her gaze upwards, taking in a pair of feet, hairy legs, then the air gap between Barney's baggy boxer shorts and his thighs, revealing a birds nest of scraggly pubic hair, loose-skin hairy testicles and a drooping penis.

'Ugh, Barney – too much flesh!' she screeched, diving her head back into the sleeping bag.

'Ha ha ha! You like real man, not upside down AC/DC illegal?'

'Yes, correction – NO! Too early in the morning for a horror show, ugh!'

Barney reached down and clasped a hand over his boxer shorts, scrunching up the material to clamp everything firmly in place. 'Is safe, I have taken myself in hand.' Barney moved around to the opposite side of the bed and pulled on a pair of board shorts, then ducked his head into a tee-shirt.

Maddie peeked out from the sleeping bag. 'Spare a girl from heart failure, please.'

'Good wakey up, working willy – make big bang-bang. Girls always happy,' Barney mumbled, wrestling the tee-shirt over his head.

'I'm sure it does, at the appropriate time. Which is definitely *not* now.'

'Anytime is good time, ja? Pay money – time, no problem.' Barney yanked the tee-shirt down and fanned out a wedge of currency from his pocket, maintaining a deadpan expression.

Maddie flicked her eyes over at the door as it creaked open. Bozzer stepped into the room, his hair wet, a clean tee-shirt clinging to his damp skin. 'Shower's good – invigorating.'

'Hot water?' she asked.

'Hot enough to tease a warthog from a slop bog,' he replied, glancing between Barney and her. 'Bad timing? Should I return later ...'

'Cheeky git. Your friend is auctioning off his crown jewels.' She sprung up from her makeshift bed, grabbed her toiletries bag, towel, and clean clothes and ducked out of the room. 'He's not getting any winning bids,' she mumbled from the corridor.

'Barney's not fussy, don't freshen up on his account,' Bozzer called after her, sniggering.

'I swing low, for sweet Harriet. She no like,' said Barney, a hurt twang in his voice.

'She won't like the hot water situation, either,' grinned Bozzer, checking his watch. 'I reckon thirty seconds. Stand by ...'

He opened the bedroom door, standing there listening. He kept an eye on his watch as he mimed Maddie undressing. *Tee-shirt, shorts, bra, knickers. Turn water on, step into shower and* ... They both smirked at the muffled screech, drifting down the hallway.

Bozzer shut the door with a mischievous grin and stepped around the bed to start packing his rucksack, whistling cheerfully.

*

'It seems wrong for this place to exist, especially here,' said Maddie, glancing up at the long bundles of twisted wiring strung across the street and neon signs fixed to the side of the buildings.

'Yep, centuries of cultural worship meets Western decadence ... it's all about the glitz now, to bring in the bucks. We're stupid, aren't we, like a moths drawn to a bright light, unwittingly banging our heads on the pub's bar, thinking we've found enlightenment.'

She looked over at him, her forehead creasing into a frown. 'I guess ...'

'So this place we're going to instead, should offer some sanctuary from the hypocritical capitalist juxtaposition that is Siem Reap.' Bozzer flicked through Maddie's Lonely Planet guidebook.

He scanned the text and located their destination on the town map. 'Next left, then a right down the adjoining alley. I promise you, this place will offer a completely different perspective.'

'On what ...?'

Bozzer indicated for her to cross the road, leading her towards an alley between two buildings. 'Everything,' he said, easing a glossy black wooden door open, beckoning her to follow him inside to a walled garden.

She entered, her eyes panning around. A fine black netting stretched out horizontally a few feet over their heads, a sheer, near transparent canopy. It stretched out across the full width of the courtyard, joining the walled sides and merging with vertical netting fixed to the top of the wall. In the centre of the paved courtyard, the raised brick sides of a fish pond contained floating water lillies and a dozen graceful coy carp. Above the lazy fish, dragonflies skimmed across the mirror-like surface. Chairs and tables adorned a terrace area beneath fabric shades. Flitting all around them were a hundred or more different species of butterfly, attending to exotic flowers, going about their daily routine in untroubled harmony.

Maddie grinned, mesmerised by the hovering serenity of the graceful multi-coloured creatures. She held out an upturned palm to allow a turquoise and yellow-winged butterfly to land on her thumb. 'Wow, this place is beautiful,' she murmured, gently raising her hand to peer at the intricate pattern on the butterfly's delicate twitching wings.

'A fair compensation for a cold shower?' asked Bozzer, showing her to a table.

She pulled a face, then dropped her eyes back to her palm. The butterfly flicked its wings and took off, floating away across the pond's still water. 'How did you know about this place?'

'Saw it mentioned on a blog. Thought you could use some quiet time, to contemplate. After the shock, of Barney's bits and bobs.'

Maddie rolled her eyes, shook her head. 'Far too much *jungle* scenery. Doesn't he have any awareness of social etiquette …?'

'He's German, what do you expect?'

Maddie shuddered and picked up the menu. 'So what's good?'

Bozzer raised his camera to frame a shot of Maddie with the pond in the background. 'It's all wholesome.'

She glanced up into the camera lens, just as he pressed the shutter and captured her inquisitive expression.

Shh-clitch.

'What, no random, pithy observations?'

'None needed. This time the camera captures its own contextual truth.'

She looked away, a faint pink blush tinging her cheeks. 'This place, so tranquil. You'd never know what's going on, out there.'

'Away from all the glitz and vanity – travellers and their fake philosophies?'

She nodded.

'Did you notice last night, there weren't any locals eating in that part of town? Just us Westerners, being waited on exclusively by Cambodians. Not exactly integrated and multicultural ... I'd rather find the heart of the place. There's too many plastic people out there, in the corporate branding, neon abyss.'

'And yet we still go there, to socialise with other Western travellers, enjoy a drink.'

'It's true. Sometimes it's comforting to feel like you're in a little part of home ... I know, I'm a hypersensitive hypocrite. But, the camera—'

'Captures the truth?'

'Always. Which brings me neatly to you, Madeline Bryce.' Bozzer plonked his elbows on the table and peered intensely at her across the table. 'What's your truth?'

Maddie shifted on her seat. She glanced away, then tentatively pulled her gaze back to meet his. 'Me? It's still being written – isn't that what all you authentic traveller types say? The cliché that life is all about the journey, not the destination ...'

'But you don't believe that, not yet. You have to inhabit this life first. Tell me about your bloke.'

'Rupert?'

'Or the other fella.'

'What other fella?'

'Charlie pompous-chops.'

'I thought you were asking about my fiancée.'

'He likes you too – the Yankee-doodle bloke. He's a catch, for a girl like you ...'

Maddie stared at him for a few moments, then shook her head and picked up a menu, scanning it. 'Thanks for bringing me here, it's been peaceful.' She counted off several notes from her purse, then stood up. 'My treat, for renting the floor space last night. I'm sure you can think of an appropriate way of splitting it with the German chap.'

She walked away from the table. Bozzer watched her circumnavigate the pond, heading for the door. Amusement twitched at the corner of his lips.

Maddie stepped out of the quiet sanctuary of the netted compound into the narrow, dusty alleyway, the ambient noise level increasing as she walked back towards the main street.

Bozzer jogged up to her side. 'I was only asking. He's a good prospect – one more trophy for him, a sugar sonny for you.'

Maddie slid her hands onto her hips. 'Is everyone out here working an angle?'

'Isn't everyone back home?'

'No!'

Bozzer watched Maddie march away. He sniggered and checked his watch, then turned and strolled off in the opposite direction.

Thirty-Two

'*Now* you're looking like a proper traveller.'

Maddie glanced up from her book, shielding her eyes from the midday sun. Victoria slipped her rucksack off her shoulders and sank down onto the seat beside her, absently panning around the bus station before resting her gaze back on Maddie.

'I haven't changed anything.'

'It's an overall look … now you're minus your earrings. Almost completes the transformation.'

Maddie returned a startled look and touched her ear. 'Oh, yeah. I took some advice.'

Victoria nodded, looked her up and down. 'Suits you, more natural.'

'Oh, thanks. Are you catching the bus to Phnom Penh?'

'Sure am.'

'With Charlie?'

Victoria glanced away, across the bus station tarmac. She slowly shook her head, a sad look in her eyes. 'No. I mean, yes, I think he may be on the bus too, but we're not together. Never were really. It's a shame … wasn't a spark there, you know?' Victoria turned back to her. 'I guess he wasn't my type after all.'

'I'm sorry to hear it didn't work out.'

Victoria shrugged. 'I owe you an apology, Maddie … I think I may have been a bitchy towards you. It sometimes happens, when there's a bloke on the scene. Sorry.'

'Oh. I don't think you were … but okay, thanks. Apology accepted.'

Victoria nodded and lit up a cigarette, then offered the packet to Maddie.

'I don't normally, but … thanks.' She withdrew a cigarette, placed it between her lips and leaned towards Victoria to accept a light.

'That sort of day, huh?'

Maddie looked away, her eyes glazing over. 'More like several, all strung together in a continuous surreal daydream, slash reality hotchpotch.'

'Testing times soon pass.'

Maddie nodded and turned to smile at Victoria. 'Sure hope so.'

An old bus rumbled into the bay in front of them, its engine clattering to a halt. Maddie turned and looked up at the destination displayed on the front, then swept her gaze across the rest of the bus station to the old clock above the ticket office. 'I'm on this one.'

'Me too,' said Victoria, following her lead and pushing to her feet. She dragged her backpack onto a shoulder and heaved it awkwardly towards the luggage storage section, being opened by the driver.

'Where in Phnom Penh are you heading for?' asked Victoria as she settled down into a seat in front of Maddie.

'Not sure about a hotel yet, but thought I'd check out the Tuel Sleng museum.'

'S21? That's gonna be tough. It's not for everyone.'

Maddie nodded and lifted up the paperback, *Survival in the Killing Fields*. 'I've been reading about what happened to the author. It's not my normal type of book – it's horrific, but strangely compelling. Figure I need to go there, see it for myself.'

Victoria nodded and turned to face forwards as the next batch of travellers climbed aboard the bus. She scanned the new faces, homing in on one in particular. 'Oh, great.' She sank back into her seat.

'Morning, ladies …'

Maddie glanced up as Charlie sat down in the seat across the aisle from her. She looked over and met his gaze. He flicked his eyes over Victoria's side profile, then settled on her.

'Hi, small world.'

'Ha – dream world!' interrupted Bozzer. 'Hello folks, spare me your jokes. I'm back to pester you, line up girls, join the queue. Still laying on the worldly-wise traveller charm, eh, Charlie-boy? Hasn't the world got enough smarm?'

Bozzer clapped Charlie on the shoulder as he shuffled past, knocking into him with his camera case. He plonked himself down into the seat behind Maddie. 'Nice to see you again, Vicky. What's up, fallen out with golden balls?'

Victoria looked away, shaking her head as she stared out of the window.

'You too, Madeline. I missed you at the hotel. Listen, I don't want to cause any embarrassment, but I've checked with Barney, and these definitely aren't his ...' Bozzer removed a pair of cotton knickers from his pocket with "I *heart* Thailand" written on them. He pulled the elastic back against his thumb and took aim, pinging them across the coach. They bounced on the roof just above Maddie and fell onto her lap. She stared at the scrunched-up bundle, aware of Charlie's wide-eyed glare from across the aisle. She snatched the material into a fist and stowed the offending item in her shoulder bag.

Bozzer sat back and winked at Charlie, then smiled innocently at Victoria and Maddie, who had both turned to perch their knees on the seat and glare at him. He shrugged theatrically. 'If you will leave them lying around on the floor, *darling* ...'

Maddie scowled at him, then turned to sink back down. Bozzer switched his attention back to Charlie, still glaring at him. Bozzer lifted his camera and fired off a shot.

Shh-clitch.

Memory Card 3. Pic 228
'Jealous rage building a head of steam, bulging purple veins quite unattractive on this hybrid beauty queen. His angular jaw straining, wishing he could give this troublesome Aussie a good caning. Hatred burning in his eyes, with the loss of his English prize. To an annoying reprobate no less – it's futile to dabble with Scrabble, *mate,* when your foe excels at chess. But the burning question remains – did the bloke from down under deflower, and plunder? The truth will come out, given time, no doubt. Meanwhile the wallaby wanker reigns supreme – that's stuffed the water-diviner's dastardly scheme.'

The bus driver crunched the gearbox into reverse, revved the engine and began to ease out of the designated space. Bozzer lowered his camera and tucked it into its bag, all the time maintaining peripheral awareness on Charlie's tense, clenched-fist posture and snorty, raspy breaths. 'Gonna give yourself an ulcer, bud.' Bozzer turned to glance at Victoria. 'Hey, Vicky. Your boyfriend's giving me the eye!'

Victoria swivelled around in her seat and poked her head above the headrest to scowl at Bozzer. 'We're *not* together.'

'Ahhh, lovers' quarrel? That's so … unsurprising.' Bozzer's mischievous smile dissolved. 'You did seem a bit dubious, together.' He held his cold, fixed expression, then turned to glare at Charlie, unwavering until Charlie finally shifted his eyes away, rotating to face out of the window. Victoria turned away too, towards Maddie who was seemingly absorbed in her book, headphones plugged in.

Bozzer eased his own headphones over his head, watching the shops lining the main road into Siem Reap slip away behind them, overplayed by Sting, crooning the opening to The Police hit, *Roxanne*.

*

Rupert jolted awake, wincing at the crick in his neck. He peered out of the open window at Fender and squinted in the glare from the midday sun.

'Up you get, soldier. Your watch.'

Rupert eased open the taxi door, bleary-eyed. The flow of traffic past their observation point had eased considerably since the chaotic early morning clamour to enter the temple's complex.

'Still nothing?'

'No. Victoria's phone is either switched off, or she's changed her SIM. Our man at the network is doing another search. In the meantime, stay vigilant.'

'I thought we'd have seen her by now.'

'Indeed. It's not looking positive for you, Rupert. Or your family.'

'My family? What's that supposed to—'

'Remember that insurance policy I mentioned, the last time we were here? Gerald and Margaret Sullivan: Jersey Road, Osterley, West London. Lovely view from their bedroom window, out over the park. Your father, a former bank manager, took early retirement last year. Mother, a schoolteacher – deputy head in fact. Both high achievers. Home *owners*. Proud of you, are they Rupert? They surely won't be, when they have a visit from your London associates.'

'You wouldn't … don't have it in you to—'

'Me? Of course not. I've got far too much respect for my generation – they've got integrity and honour. But your Class A paymasters don't have the same respect for people's hard work – their savings and property. They'll take the lot, liquidise everything to clear your debt. And even then, you'll still be in their pockets. So keep a super-keen lookout, won't you?'

Fender brushed past Rupert, shooting him an ominous look as he climbed into the taxi's back seat and sank into the hot plastic.

*

Bozzer watched the street orientation change as the bus turned away from the wide pavement promenade overlooking the river, heading down a busy side road, wall to wall with shopfronts incorporating two-storey flats above.

'Back so soon, brother Bazza ... better hope Jody has moved on,' he murmured.

He took in the passing bars and restaurants, outside which older Western men mingled with Thai girls wearing hot pants and white blouse tops, the loose fabric tails tied in a knot above their bellybuttons. The bus rumbled on, the engine note vibrating through the seats, rattling the windows whenever it slowed to a walking pace. Bozzer glanced down to his mobile phone and swiped through several menu screens. He located the flight number, noted in his diary for a Sunday departure, in three days' time. *Cutting it fine, mate ...*

A thumb and finger reached out and pinched the plastic headphone, lifting it off Bozzer's right ear an inch from his head. 'Are you on an arsehole break?'

Bozzer flinched away from the voice. The headphones sprung away from her grip, pinging against his ear. 'Whoa, easy – treat the boys with more respect.' Bozzer removed the headphones, cradling them in his hands, shooting Maddie a faux-concerned expression.

'The boys?'

'*The* band. Too legendary to be interrupted.'

'Let me guess – an Aussie rock group?'

'The one and only. Say, do you, you know ... like AC/DC*?*'

'No.'

'Shame. I'd pay to see that live performance.'

Maddie held eye contact, fighting the mouth-twitching urge to smile at him. 'I asked you if—'

'Oh yeah, I'm still an arsehole. But it's okay, I'm on a break.'

'Meaning you're normal, at this precise moment?'

'Hey, that's a whole evening's entertainment right there – discussing normality. Sure you want to go there?'

'I wanted to ask you a question about your grandfather, but clearly you're not capable of being remotely serious.'

Bozzer laughed. 'Take a look in the mirror, honey – then define sensible.'

Maddie sighed. She turned and sat back in her seat, shaking her head. Bozzer pressed his face into the gap between the twin headrests and angled his eyes down to the right, where she rested the open paperback in her lap.

'How's the book?'

'Ten times better than having to make small talk with you.'

'Obviously.' He kept his face pressed into the gap, scanning his eyes down the text as she turned the page. 'Whoa, hang on, not finished yet—'

Maddie marked the page, shut the book and shuffled away from the backrest, opening up the angle between them. 'Are you always this annoying? Is that why Jody left?'

'Ask her, if you see her. She's probably still here somewhere.'

'Probably?'

'Yup. The book looks good. Heavy going, though.'

Maddie's expression clouded over. She dropped her eyes to the cover. 'It's … disturbing, and profoundly moving throughout,' she said quietly.

He nodded, dropped his voice an octave. 'You seen the movie, *The Killing Fields?*'

She looked up, shook her head.

'They show it here, in town.'

'I'll check it out.'

'Cool. I could tell you where the cinema is, if you like.'

Maddie studied his face, searched his eyes for sincerity. He flicked his gaze past her, out of the window, then eased back from the gap in the headrest as the bus began to slow up.

'Get ready for the gong show.' Bozzer grabbed his headphones, stuffed them into his day-pack and stepped into the aisle. 'See you on the street. Hold onto your principles out there,' he called out, over his shoulder.

Bozzer finished sprinkling tobacco into the Rizla paper, then expertly rolled it into a tube and carefully dabbed his tongue along the seam. He lifted his head to look out over the throng of people clustered around the bus, all clamouring for the attention of the Western travellers trying to collect their belongings. He could hear the calls, vying for business. 'Tuk-tuk. Tuk-tuk. Tuk-tuk …'

Maddie pressed several Cambodian Riel notes into the bus driver's palm, smiling her thanks at his surprised grin, then lifted her backpack from his hands onto her shoulders. She dropped her gaze to the floor, away from making eye contact with the twenty assorted taxi drivers all trying to attract fare-paying attention, and concentrated on putting one foot in front of the other, making for the pavement on the far side of the busy market.

Bozzer watched Maddie's exit from the taxi driver scrum. He removed the roll-up from his mouth, curled his tongue and blew against a thumb and finger pressed together, emitting a piercing whistle.

'Yo, Madge!' he yelled, waving her over. She looked up, searching for him.

Too late.

Victoria grabbed Maddie's hand, steering her away from the periphery of the market, following a young Cambodian to his waiting tuk-tuk. Bozzer watched the driver help them remove their backpacks, securing them inside the tuk-tuk as they climbed in. The driver swung his leg over the motorbike's fuel tank and fired the engine, steering away into the hectic Phnom Penh traffic.

Bozzer lowered his fingers from his mouth, making eye contact with Maddie. She began to raise her hand to wave, blocked from his view by a truck piled high with standing workers swinging across its lane.

He looked away, drawn to the remaining passengers on the bus, now filtering away through the market crowd, being led to waiting taxis and tuk-tuks by enthusiastic drivers. Bozzer's gaze settled on Charlie as he climbed into the back of a tuk-tuk. He lifted his roll-up, drawing smoke, eyeing Charlie until his tuk-tuk trundled out into main road.

'What are you up to, Charlie-boy …?' Bozzer shouldered his backpack, stubbed out his roll-up in his tobacco tin and wandered over to a group of moto-taxi riders, stood talking and smoking by the side of the market square.

'Where you go?' asked a smiley kid no older than seventeen.

'You follow my friend?' said Bozzer, pointing at Charlie's tuk-tuk. 'Three dollars, yes?'

'Four dollar.'

'Okay. But don't lose him.'

The smiley kid fired up his scooter. Bozzer hunched up his legs on the pillion pegs and grasped the hand-holds behind him, peering around the moto-rider's crash helmet, searching the busy road ahead for Charlie's tuk-tuk. He released his left hand from the pillion handhold and pointed directly ahead. The moto-rider nodded and twisted the throttle, weaving around a taxi, slipping through a gap between a group of tuk-tuks waiting to turn right. He braked hard, darting behind a battered pick-up truck. Bozzer held his palm out flat, motioned it downwards twice: *slow down.* He flicked his eyes over the vehicles stopping ahead, trying to turn left at the intersection. Red tee-shirt, angular jaw ... *there.* He pointed, leaning with the moto-rider as they weaved their way through the congestion, easing up two vehicles behind Charlie's tuk-tuk.

'Him – farang. Follow, okay?' Bozzer said to the moto-rider.

'Okay, yes.'

A brief gap appeared in the vehicles coming around the intersection. The front line of motorbikes, tuk-tuks and cars revved and pulled out, followed by a horde of other vehicles, four deep, all swarming out into the path of the oncoming traffic amidst a chorus of tooting horns.

NrrrrrrrRRRRR!

Bozzer clenched his fingers around the pillion handles, tensing his body as the moto-rider zoomed through a tiny gap between a taxi's bumper and the front wheel of a tuk-tuk, weaving through the chaos, staying tight behind Charlie. He cringed as a scooter hurtled past them, inches from their rear wheel.

*

Maddie lowered her hand, shielding the sunlight as they turned.

'He's a waste of space,' Victoria declared, lurching in her seat.

Maddie shifted around to face her, sat on the bench seat opposite. 'Who, Charlie?'

'No, the Australian *boy*. Imagine having to deal with that annoying prick every day. Jody had the right idea, bailing out.'

'I thought he left her?'

Victoria waved her hand across the gap between them. 'Whatever.'

Maddie watched her light up a cigarette, hesitate, then offer her the packet. She shook her head. 'What happened between you and Charlie?' she asked.

Victoria glanced away, her eyes drifting out over the chaotic traffic. 'Nice guy, just not very forthcoming – in the bedroom department.'

'Oh.'

Victoria shrugged. 'I like sex, I'm not ashamed of that. But it rocks my confidence when a bloke isn't that fussed. I mean, ninety-nine per cent of guys are up for it, most of the time – you know where you are with them. But Charlie … he's on this holier than thou mission. He wanted more of a *connection,* before jumping into the sack. What's that all about?'

Victoria took a pull on her cigarette, then draped her elbows along the side of the tuk-tuk carriage and shook her head, looking out over the grassy area in the central pedestrian island walkway, keeping Maddie in her peripheral vision.

'I suppose he thought he was being a gentleman.'

Victoria allowed herself a tiny smile before she turned to face her. 'Yeah, maybe. But what's the point, in modern society? Being honourable doesn't satisfy a basic human need to get laid.'

Maddie looked away and sat quietly watching the other vehicles weave around each other, beeping their horns, all vying for the quickest route through the traffic. Victoria took a last drag on her cigarette and flicked the butt into the road, blowing smoke up under the tuk-tuk's canopy, where it funnelled out of the back and dispersed in the dusky humid air.

*

Bozzer thanked the moto-rider and paid him in US dollars. He grinned, pocketed the cash and pulled out into the traffic with a screech of two-stroke engine, trailing exhaust fumes.

Bozzer stepped back to the pavement and ducked down behind a shopfront awning, turning to watch Charlie lug his backpack through the plush hotel's smoked glass entrance doors on the opposite side of the road.

He fished his tobacco tin out of his pocket and rolled a smoke. 'Gotcha, my poncy double-ducky friend. Let's see what tomorrow brings,' he muttered, smiling thinly. He placed the roll-up between his lips, then fished his mobile phone from his pocket. He typed a search for cheap accommodation.

'See you in the morning, Charlie-boy, bright and early.' Bozzer clicked on a link to a hostel and lit his ciggie, sniggering.

*

Maddie sat on the bed in the shared hotel room and toyed with her mobile phone.

'That looks like an agonising decision.'

She glanced up at Victoria exiting the bathroom, one towel wrapped around her torso, using another to scrunch-dry her hair.

'It's been mostly switched off, for …' Maddie counted on her fingers, 'over two weeks.'

'Scary, yet strangely liberating?'

'Yeah. I was thinking about what I'm missing …'

Victoria flicked her head back and wrapped the towel into a turban. She sat down on the opposite corner of the bed. 'Guess it's been a weird time for you.'

'Weird, challenging and oddly rewarding.' Maddie removed the SIM card from her purse and peered at it. 'Strange, all those people's numbers, on this little thing.'

'Technology, eh.'

Maddie nodded. 'Most of them I hardly ever talk to.'

'Before you reconnect … what if your other half is still looking for you?'

'Rupert? Oh, he'll have given up a long time ago.'

'But if he hasn't, you'll pop up on his radar.'

Maddie stared at Victoria, then dropped her eyes to the SIM card in her fingers. 'You think he's still tracking me?'

'Don't you? He seemed pretty determined. Have you thought about using a local SIM? You'd be untraceable.'

'I hadn't, but I suppose that's an idea …'

'I think I've got a spare. They were handing them out at the airport when I arrived. If your fiancée's got you tagged on a tracking website, it'll be registered to your UK number, not a new local one.' Victoria slipped off the bed and rummaged in her backpack. She produced a sealed packet with a new SIM card enclosed.

'Really?'

'Sure, it was free, so no biggie. You register it with your passport number. There should be enough credit to get you started.'

'Hey, that's brilliant. Thanks.' Maddie popped the new SIM out of its packaging and inserted it into her iPhone. She watched the screen light up and go through its familiar start-up sequence.

'You get connected okay?'

Maddie nodded absently, studying the screen. 'Just checking my emails now.'

'Anything exciting?'

'Not especially.' She tilted the phone away.

'You know, if you really want to go off-grid, you need to be bold.'

'In what way?'

'Every way.' Victoria pointed to Maddie's old SIM, on the bed. 'That's temptation, right there. Moving on means travelling light. Take nothing with you that belongs in the past. That's my motto.'

Maddie stared at Victoria, then dropped her eyes to the SIM. 'That's always been my trouble … not being able to let go.' She picked it up. 'You done in the bathroom?'

'Sure am.'

She tucked her purse into her backpack, grabbed her toiletries bag and headed across the room, taking the SIM card with her.

Maddie frowned at her reflection and flattened her hair in her fingers, peering at the dark roots protruding from her scalp. 'Going natural … wonderful,' she muttered. 'You need some colour, girl.' She smirked, then flicked her hair back and dropped her eyes to the SIM card, perched on the edge of the sink. 'Or, perhaps not.'

She brushed the SIM into the toilet. 'Oops.'

She pressed down on the flush and watched the churning water until the gurgling cleared, leaving an empty bowl. Then she grinned and glanced back at her reflection, her heart pounding. 'That bold enough?' She stifled a giggle, her stomach twinging, palms tingling.

Maddie opened the door, poked her head out into the room. 'Hey, what do you think about—'

Victoria jerked her brush through her hair, vigorously hunting down stray knots, her face turning red.

'You okay?' asked Maddie.

'Yup. Startled me.'

'Oh, sorry.'

'What is it?'

'I wondered what you think about … nothing. Image crisis, but I don't think I care anymore. Sorry I startled you.'

Maddie withdrew into the bathroom. She finished brushing her hair, ignoring the troublesome roots as she pondered why her roommate appeared to be so jumpy.

Thirty-Three

Maddie rummaged through the rucksack and held up a fake Quicksilver tee-shirt. 'Dirty washing, or good for one more day?' she pondered aloud.

She looked over at Victoria, sat cross-legged in the middle of the bed, fixated on her mobile phone. Maddie transferred her attention back to the tee-shirt and sniffed under the sleeves. She wrinkled her nose, considered for a moment, then shrugged and slipped it over her head. 'I'm going to have to get some washing done. You want me to take yours too?'

'Reckon I'm okay, cheers,' replied Victoria, stealing a look up, which Maddie caught out of the corner of her eye. Victoria dropped her eyes to the screen and attempted to shield a smirk.

What are you up to, Vicky ...?

*

Bozzer eased through the heavy glass entrance door, held open by a doorman dressed in a red jacket, pristine white shirt and black trousers. He nodded his thanks and scanned the foyer. A lone traveller sat in the far corner on a comfy couch, hunched over a tablet computer screen, balanced on his lap. Bozzer turned to his right, approaching the two attractive Cambodian girls sat behind the vast black marble reception desk.

'Hi, I'm meeting my friend here later, but I want to visit the museum first. Could I leave my bag here, please?' He slid two dollar bills across the counter, offering his backpack around the side of the desk.

The girl nearest to him swept the notes off the marble top in a smooth motion and hurried around the desk to collect his rucksack. By the time she'd dragged the pack into a back room, her colleague had already written out a label and tied it to the waistband strap. She passed Bozzer a receipt.

'Thank you sir,' the first girl said, nodding and clasping her palms together under her chin.

Bozzer pocketed the receipt and winked at them before wandering away towards the bar, on the opposite side of the grand foyer. He glanced up at the extravagant décor and retrieved his Mackenzie tartan cap from his rucksack, unrolled it and swept his loose hair back, pulling the cap firmly down on his head.

He turned to face the approaching barman. 'Hi, Chang beer, please.' Bozzer selected a low chair in the corner facing away from the entrance door towards the corridor leading to the elevator. He placed the beer bottle on an adjacent table, pulling the cap's lip further over his face as he settled back into the soft leather to wait for the afternoon's entertainment.

*

Maddie handed her bag of washing over the simple white-painted reception desk.

'Tomorrow, is okay?' the receptionist asked.

'Yes, thank you.' She pocketed the ticket stub and turned away, walking across the small lobby to the collection of mismatched chairs beside a stained coffee table. 'Any luck with the Wi-Fi?'

Victoria looked up from studying her phone. 'Yeah, I've got a Skype catch up with my folks in a few minutes. You off exploring?'

'Yup. Thought I'd head over to the museum.'

Victoria cringed. 'Good luck. Not my idea of a fun day out.'

'No. But necessary, I think.'

Victoria shrugged and dropped her eyes back to the phone's screen.

'I've left the room key with reception. See you later?'

'Sure. I'm going to bum around for a couple of hours, catch up with some online stuff. See you for a cheer-up drink. You're gonna need it.'

Maddie frowned and starred at Victoria for a long moment, something jarring in her tone. Maddie shrugged off the feeling and left the gloomy stuffiness of the hotel lobby. She stepped out onto the wide pavement, the warmth and bright sunshine encouraging her to break into a smile.

'Hey, lady. You take tuk-tuk tour?'

Maddie turned towards the voice. A young Cambodian guy in his early twenties stood by the road, grinning at her. He pushed off from leaning against a red, green and white tuk-tuk parked up by the kerb and scurried over, sweeping his hands low, tilting sideways to gesture behind him. 'Best tuk-tuk in Phnom Penh. Very sensible price.'

'Only best in Phnom Penh?'

'I say Cambodia, but no want to boast!'

She chuckled. 'How sensible a price?'

'How much tour you want? Where go? Whole day, half?'

She checked her watch. 'Um … maybe a quick tour of the city, then to this place, here. For coffee.' Maddie pointed to the small map in the guidebook.

'Okay, yes. After?'

'I was thinking of the museum.'

'Tuel Sleng?'

'Is that S21?'

'Yes, yes. S21 and Tuel Sleng museum, same-same. You must go.'

'So I've read. Okay, how much?'

He smiled coyly, comically adjusting his body posture, raising a hand to stroke his chin, portraying a man deep in thought about overcharging her. 'I do special price … for you, forty dollar.'

'*Forty* dollars? I thought you said sensible price. What's your name?'

'Rico.'

'Okay, Rico. I'm Maddie. And *my* sensible price would be twenty dollars.'

'Thirty dollar.'

'No, twenty dollars. With an extra five dollars at the end if you tell me all about the city as we drive around.'

'Like talking tour?'

'Yes, exactly.'

'My voice, it wear out. Ten dollars extra—'

Maddie raised her eyebrows disapprovingly. Rico's slender frame crumpled. He stooped, hugged his knees, giggling enthusiastically. 'Okay, okay. You tough lady. Twenty-five dollars and five dollar talking tour—'

'Twenty dollars, *plus* five equals twenty-five, total. Deal, yes?' She held out her hand. Rico straightened up. He nodded, grinning, placing his hand delicately in hers.

'Okay, good deal. We go now?'

Maddie nodded and followed Rico to his tuk-tuk. 'You speak English very well.'

'Yes, my brother, he teach. Good for me. Please, make joyful.' Rico guided her into the tuk-tuk carriage, then swung his leg over the motorcycle and pressed the electronic ignition. He glanced over his shoulder to pull out into the light traffic, grinning at Maddie's reflection in the large side mirror. 'Okay, we begin.'

*

Victoria pressed her nose up to the hotel's glass entrance window and watched Maddie climb into a tuk-tuk. She waited until it had pulled away, then headed for the reception desk. 'Room twelve.'

The receptionist smiled politely, reaching behind her to select the correct key.

Victoria pushed the door open and surveyed Maddie's backpack. 'Right then, miss prissy-perfect, where have you stashed them?' She emptied the backpack one compartment at a time, carefully checking the contents.

Six minutes later she stood with her hands on her hips staring at the empty pack propped up against the wall, the contents of which she'd spread out on the bed. 'You've either got them with you, they're in the hotel safe, or ...' Victoria swivelled around on her feet, her eyes resting on the bathroom door. 'I wonder.'

Her slender hands unzipped the washbag's various compartments, carefully removing toiletries, deodorant, a toothbrush and toothpaste. *Shit.*

Victoria stepped back into the main room, leaned against the wall and stared at the bed and empty backpack. She lowered her eyes to the pair of walking boots on the floor, frowning. She stepped over to them, crouched down and stuck her hands inside, removing the first insole. 'There you are, my beauties!' She wriggled her hand free, two balls of tissue paper held between her fingers.

She sat down on the corner of the bed, laid one of Maddie's tee-shirts over her thighs and unwrapped the thin paper, tumbling two gold and diamond-encased pearl earrings into her lap. She grinned and carefully picked up an earring, mesmerised by the shifting patterns of dancing light. 'Jackpot.' Victoria wrapped each earring back in the tissue, deposited them in her surfer's wallet and hurriedly replaced everything into Maddie's backpack. Before she left the room, Victoria turned to glance again at the pair of walking boots.

'Surely you're not that trusting …' Victoria stepped over to the boots and removed the second insole, a sly quirk at the corner of her mouth growing into a full blown sneer as she pulled her hand out, clutching the neatly flattened wedge of US dollars. 'Payday, *again*. Maddie, you're the gift that keeps on giving.'

*

Bozzer glanced up from studying his mobile phone, lifting a hand to fully obscure his face under the flat cap. He peered around the chair to see the glass entrance door swing back on its hinge, revealing Victoria. She breezed in, heading for the hotel reception desk.

'Could you ring room twenty-seven, tell my boyfriend I've arrived,' she said, strumming her fingers on the counter.

Across the lobby, Bozzer narrowed his eyes. He shifted around in his seat to sneak a proper look at Victoria, stood with her back to him. Bozzer eased back in the chair, turning away from her as she waltzed over to the bar, dumped her rucksack and ordered a drink. He sipped from a bottle of water, peering sideways across the foyer at her profile, careful to keep the lip of his cap low, shielding his face.

He waited for a few minutes, then slowly lifted his camera out of its padded bag and tucked it behind the armrest, out of sight. The lift doors at the far end of the lobby opened. Bozzer lowered his head again as Charlie stepped into view, scanned the lobby and made his way to the bar to join Victoria. She greeted him with an affectionate embrace and a firm kiss on the lips.

'How'd it go?' he asked, settling onto a stool beside her.

She grinned, opened her wallet and tipped the two small tissue-wrapped parcels onto the bar.

'Not here,' he hissed, closing his hands around the small packages.

'Yes, here – who's gonna know?' she hissed back, continuing to unravel the glinting earrings, slipping her own plain gold studs out of her earlobes. 'We're celebrating. Let's have a drink—'

Shh-clitch.

Memory Card 3. Pic 325

'Venomous, jealous greed, from this gutter-level thieving creed. The lowest of travel scams, stealing from one of your own, comparable to treason and evil to the bone.'

'What the hell!' Victoria spun round to face Bozzer, strolling across the lobby.

'Those don't look like they belong to you, darlin'.'

Charlie leapt off his bar stool and squared up to Bozzer, red faced, the veins in his forearms bulging as he glared at the camera being tucked safely away into its protective bag.

'Why so surprised, Charlie-boy? People must make you all the time, looking so shifty. Sooner or later you're gonna attract the wrong sort of attention.'

'Fuck off, kangaroo brain!'

'Ah, so nice to hear the honest guttural London-street twang in your voice, chief. What happened to the hoity-toity, freshwater-drinking multinational humanitarian superhero twat?'

Charlie launched forwards, swinging his fist. Bozzer flexed his torso, swayed his head back, simultaneously reaching up to grab Charlie's flailing arm and yank him off-balance. Bozzer snapped his knee up, whacking it into Charlie's groin.

'Yeaarrggghhh!' Charlie's eyes bulged, yelping noisily. Bozzer stepped back, allowing him to crumple at his feet in a contorted, writhing heap.

'Never try and get the drop on an Aussie, mate. We never wait patiently in a queue, especially when there's dirty deeds being dished out.'

Bozzer threw his hand out, clamping his fingers around Victoria's wrist, pinning it to the bar. 'Those, Vicky – are – not – yours,' he said with a tightly clenched jaw.

He ducked her wild cougar slap, grabbed her incoming hand, forcing it down on top of her other wrist, clamping one of his hands around both of hers.

'Calm down, or I'll headbutt you in the chops, make a mess of your pretty cheekbones. Now, breathe, relax, and release …' He held her glare and prised her fingers open, revealing the earrings. He flicked his eyes down at Charlie, still moaning on the floor, and pressed a foot down onto his back, making him groan louder. Bozzer returned his attention to Victoria, who was scowling at him. 'They'd cut your hands off in some countries, for thieving. I'll make sure these get back to their rightful owner. Where is she, by the way?'

Victoria spat in Bozzer's face. He wiped his cheek on his sleeve and scooped the earrings into his hand, depositing them in his trouser pocket. 'Lovely. So ladylike—'

'Fuck off!'

Bozzer squeezed his hand, crunching her fingers into his fist.

'Arrrggh!'

'Shh ... suck it up, you miserable, despicable, green-eyed cockroach. I have you on camera going all Gollum-like with Maddie's *precioussssss* stolen property. I reckon the Cambodian cops have a string of petty crime they could pin on you two. Tell me where Maddie went and you and laughing boy are in the clear.' Bozzer squeezed harder, crushing her fingers.

'The museum – she's at Tuol Sleng!' screeched Victoria. She snatched her hands away as he released them.

Bozzer removed his foot from Charlie's kidney and stepped away from them, the tension in his facial muscles lessening as his angry focus waned. He withdrew, his voice sombre and composed. 'Cheers. You folks have a shitty day now.' Bozzer collected his camera bag off the floor and paused. 'I'll be back later,' he said in a congenial voice. 'I can get a bit cranky in the afternoons, so best you take off. You wouldn't want to run into me when I'm in an *ugly* mood.'

Bozzer poked his index finger under the lip of his flat cap and strolled out of the lobby, leaving Charlie and Victoria glaring after him.

'You're not the only one who's interested in her!' Victoria yelled as Bozzer exited the lobby door.

'That I don't doubt,' he murmured, smiling as he stepped out into the sunshine.

*

Fender reached into his pocket and withdrew the gently vibrating phone. He glanced at the screen, a thin smile briefly creasing his lips as he lifted it to his ear. 'Miss Stevens.'

Rupert straightened his slouching posture against the side of the taxi. He unfolded his arms and turned to face Fender.

'It's about Maddie,' said Victoria, over the phone's speaker.

'Okay. Do you have—'

'Five hundred dollars, cash.'

'I'm sorry?'

'I know where she is. But another fifty isn't gonna cut it. I want—'

'A serious payday.'

'Yes.'

'Alright, Miss Stevens. You have my attention.'

'Do we have a deal?'

'How accurate is your—'

'She's in Phnom Penh. I know which hotel. I know exactly where she'll be for the next twenty-four hours. How quickly can you get here?'

Fender glanced at his watch. 'I'm still at the temples. Transportation will be slow, it's the Cambodian celebration of—'

'Yes, I know. How soon?'

'Later tonight, probably.'

'Okay. Do we have a deal?'

'We do.'

'Good. Meet me at the Pickled Parrot bar, street 104. Ring me when you're thirty minutes out. Bring the five hundred dollars in cash. You don't show, stiff me for my fee, or try anything nasty and Charlie will warn Maddie.' Victoria hung up.

Fender lowered the phone. 'Charming travel companions Maddie's befriended.' He rapped his hand on the roof of the taxi, rousing the sleeping driver from the back seat. Then he turned to Rupert. 'You've got approximately eight hours to get your *please forgive me* speech prepared. It's time to decide how badly you want your fiancée back.'

Thirty-Four

Bozzer clasped his two-dollar entrance ticket and shuffled away from the kiosk, leaving the tourist queue behind. He lifted his head and looked around the playground of the former Tuol Svay Prey High School.

He swallowed, painfully, and took several slow deep breaths as he shuffled past the three-storey grey concrete building into a dusty, dry, wispy-grass schoolyard. He panned around the perimeter, lifting his gaze to the top of the ten-foot high concrete wall, capped with rusty, wrought iron spiked railings. To his right, oxidized corrugated iron fencing, topped with spools of corroded barbed wire, marked another side of the boundary. A concrete rectangle of paving slabs sat within a grassy corner in the middle of the compound. Small trees lined one side, their fragile limbs stretching out over a row of raised tombs, painted white.

Bozzer's hands flopped by his side, heavy and useless. 'Come on Bazza, mate. There's a job to do …' he whispered, his words strained and shaky.

He stopped at the head of the first white tomb, then cast his eye up towards the far end of the schoolyard, where a heavy wood frame stood twenty feet tall, fifteen feet across. Around him, tourists mingled solemnly in the sunshine, any conversations between them spoken sparingly in muted tones. To his left and directly ahead stood the first three-storey concrete building. It had an open continuous balcony walkway on each level behind corroded wire mesh. Blue louvered doors flanked dark entrances, with rows of terracotta air bricks forming a full width lintel over each aperture.

Bozzer lifted his camera out of its bag, ducked his head to remove his cap, then eased the strap over his head.

Is this the right thing to do … here, of all places?

With trembling hands he held the camera in front of him, his finger resting over the power button.

Be professional. The book needs this context, however upsetting it may be …

He drew in a slow, shaky breath, lifting the viewfinder to his eye, flinching at the soft *shh-clitch* of the shutter each time he captured an image.

No words though, mate. Not here. Not today.

Bozzer stood facing the drab concrete building. A shiver rippled through his limbs, an advance anticipation of the cool, dank air within, drawing him inside, away of the warmth and eternal optimism of the sunshine. He ambled up the steps, hesitating, his feet heavy and reluctant at the threshold of the unlit room.

It's necessary, to try and comprehend.

To his left, bare concrete steps transited upwards to the other two floors. Ahead, parallel to the schoolyard's grassy sections and intersecting paved paths, a long open-sided corridor stretched out, past regularly spaced structural pillars clad with brown wire netting and tainted coils of barbed wire. Off of the corridor at regular intervals were rooms containing faded cream and brown square tiled floors, dusty with patches of dark brown stains.

The first room, dim and subdued, lacking any natural or artificial light, contained only a rusty metal bedframe and a sign describing the torture method employed there. Bozzer eyed the stark metal warily. He paused to read the description, his face contorted, cheeks hollow as he digested the gravity of the words.

Shh-clitch.

The faint shutter sound echoed around the room, the quick-fire resonance matching his racing heartbeat, pounding inside his skull. He lowered the camera, the image's parameters and fine detail still imprinted in his field of vision. He slowly shook his head, turned and shuffled towards the door, his very core icy, craving the warmth that lay beyond the claustrophobic concrete structure. He stopped outside the doorway, glanced to his right, towards light flooding in across the floor, asking himself whether he should he retrace his steps, or continue …?

Onwards. I have to.

Bozzer turned, padding along the corridor. He stepped into the next room, pausing to allow his heart to sink a little further, take a photograph and reflect some more, his soul suffocating, weeping away comprehension with every step.

Unlike the first section of rooms, their layout unchanged since they'd been used as classrooms, the next area had been altered by the

Khmer Rouge regime to suit their sinister, hellish requirements. Roughly built brick and blockwork internal walls with tatty wooden doors compartmentalised the previously large open-plan schoolrooms, segregating each area into a series of tiny brick cells, barely six feet by five. Tourists filtered past, squeezing by each other in sombre courtesy, ducking their heads into the cells. Some shook their heads, visibly moved by the experience. Others exchanged comments, seemingly in good humour as they snapped a continuous stream of photographs, perhaps oblivious to the true horror of this place, the segregation of humanity in the barbaric compartmentalised structures, leaving crushed human spirits lingering.

Bozzer shivered, despite the heat radiating from the mid-afternoon sun. Cold to his core, his stomach squeezed bile up towards the back of his throat, forcing him to concentrate on his breathing to keep it at bay. He reached into a pocket for his tobacco tin, clasped his fingers around its reassuring familiarity. Then he stopped, recalling a notice he'd read on the way in. He relaxed his grip, eased his fingertips away.

Last building. This is the really tricky one ...

Bozzer squeezed his eyes shut and inhaled deeply, slowly exhaling in shoulder-slumping resignation. He opened his eyes and shuffled forwards, joining the trickle of other visitors mingling towards the final building's entrance.

Whitewashed walls and ceilings brightened these large open-plan schoolrooms, minimally populated with exhibits. Paintings and photographs with placard descriptions of S21's inhumane conditions hung alongside glass-fronted display cabinets housing torture implements. But these exhibits held little interest for Bozzer. He gravitated past, towards the far wall where a row of end to end open doorways led onwards. Each former schoolroom led into the next, towards the farthest section, the one he'd read about so many times. He forced his feet to move, the action feeling remote and surreal, almost as if they were unconnected to his own body. Instead, instructions from his brain transferred through a woolly spinal gearbox, reducing his momentum to agonising slow motion. His tunnel vision saw only doorways to the rooms beyond, each containing implements of an alien, medieval, morbid world. Everyone else, all those other hardened travellers, tourists and voyeurs, filtered away to each side as he transited onwards, blinkered, unable to make eye contact. Each room he passed through faded away, merging into a gloomy background.

The surfaces around him were painted white, yet appeared so grey, so solemn, so … desperately wretched.

The final series of rooms contained only freestanding Perspex-clad noticeboards. Each section contained row upon row of faded A4 size, yellowing, black and white photographs. Haunting portrait images of the head and shoulders of men, women and children, all tortured here before being put to death in the notorious killing fields. The photographs' existence, a haunting sepia roll-call before execution, meticulously and macabrely documented. Further into the exhibition, a large black leather-bound log book lay open, on display. In it, a detailed list of all those pour souls who had trudged relentlessly through the school's barbed wire gates, never to return.

Bozzer began to tremble. He clenched his palms together, linked his fingers, entwining them in a firm grip, squeezing the tremors away from his arms, forcing them deeper inside his chest. The expressions of each person in the photographs looked distressingly familiar: solemn, fixated furrowed brows, confusion cloaking the as yet unknown fear that no doubt would have followed soon after – their appearance chilling – their final humiliation. At the end of the long rows, a cluster of photographs on one of the last noticeboards drew Bozzer over. The ghostly pale, almost transparent complexion of European and white-skinned faces stared back at him. The international admissions to this place, also forever lost amongst their Cambodian comrades.

Bozzer blinked rapidly, trying to stem the moisture from misting his vision, unable to prevent the itchy, head-spinning sensation prickling behind his eye sockets as he stared at one particular photograph.

No …

He tried to stifle a sob, barely succeeding. Tears fell freely now, breathing erratic, his entire body shuddering as he gasped for breath. He wiped the droplets away from his eyes and stepped forwards to read the short sentence:

Scott Barry Johnson. Australian. Born 15 September 1946. 32 when he was killed.

Other people filtered past, maintaining a respectful distance around him. Some exchanged fleeting eye contact with each other, others hurried through the room, away from Bozzer's living, breathing, exhibition of personal loss.

He gulped in stale air, fighting to control his hyperventilation. *Unmanly,* this reaction, he chastised, yet raw, uncontrollable … *truthful.*

A slim hand tentatively reached out, placed a warm palm on his quivering shoulder. He flinched at the unexpected contact, half-turned. She stepped up to his side, lay her arm across his shoulder, her fingers lightly squeezing.

'Hello stranger …'

Bozzer stepped back, shock creasing deeper on his red, tear-smeared face. Jody held his bewildered gaze. She reached out, her palm cupping his hot cheek, smoothing her thumb across the wetness, smearing his tears away, like a miniature windscreen wiper.

'What are you doing here?' Bozzer croaked. His voice was fractured, devoid of energy and enthusiasm.

'I'm with my friend. It's the last day before we move on.' Jody paused, casting her eyes over the photograph. 'Is this him?'

Bozzer nodded, his breathing heavy but calmer, steadier now. He turned back to face the image of his grandfather, traces of his tears gradually evaporating.

'Meet me tonight, for a drink,' she said. 'Message me later.'

Bozzer eased his gaze away from his grandfather's grainy photograph. He watched Jody leave, then turned back to the display. He allowed his gaze to linger, before he bowed his head and allowed his eyes to drift on, around the room, absently, until … *there.*

He stopped his rotation, backtracking. Maddie stood at the far end of the room, observing him. She attempted a sad, awkward smile as their eyes connected. They held each other's gaze for an endless moment, before he acknowledged her with a faint nod. He dropped his eyes to the floor briefly, then swept his gaze back up to the photograph.

Maddie glanced again at the open doorway, off to one side, then slowly walked past it, towards him. 'I'm so sorry,' she said softly, stopping short six feet away. *An appropriate distance?*

He nodded, his head barely moving.

'I'll leave you … to some quiet time.' Her footsteps retreated, seeking the reassurance of the sunlight that bathed the doorway's threshold.

Bozzer weighed the camera's bulk in his hands, alternating his gaze between it and the photograph. He glanced behind him, saw Maddie step out into the light. He hesitated, then raised the camera, twisting the lens, focusing on framing his grandfather amongst the periphery images of his fallen Cambodian brothers and sisters.

Shh-clitch.

Bozzer tweaked the focus and gently squeezed the button again, capturing another shot.

*

'I need a smoke, but I can't light up in here.'

Maddie shielded her eyes from the sunlight peeking above the concrete school house, squinting at Bozzer as he stepped out of the doorway into the courtyard. She asked 'Would you prefer to be alone, or …'

'I'd prefer to avoid bumping into Jody again, so some company would be great. If that's okay?'

'Of course.'

Maddie accompanied Bozzer through the museum entrance, into the dusty side street. He struck his lighter, waved it under the roll-up clenched between his lips. She watched him take a deep draw, pause, then blow smoke through his nose. He stared off into the distance, shaking his head in slow motion, eyes glazed, his normal sparky enthusiasm lost in a heavy straightjacket of suffocating despair.

'*Why* …? Why such barbaric, horrific violence … the complete and utter obliteration of humanity. So fucking senseless.'

'I don't know,' she murmured.

He looked away, concentrating on smoking for a while.

'He'd come to photograph the truth … tell the world what was happening here. And they killed him for it. No confiscating his camera, no asking him to leave the country. Instead … this place.' He flicked his cigarette at the museum entrance, watched it fly through the air, bounce off the overhead sign and land in a puff of sparks. 'Sheez.'

He hesitated then sighed, shrugged the camera bag off his shoulder, laying it at Maddie's feet. He walked over to the roll-up, picked it up and stubbed it out on his tobacco tin, then deposited it inside, snapping the lid shut. He walked back to her, hoisting the camera case strap over his shoulder. 'I can't wake up tomorrow knowing I've got to go through this again. I need to finish the day with all the awful, tragic, destructive stuff left behind. I'm going to go to the other place, where they took him after here.'

'Okay ... you going alone?'

He frowned, contemplating. 'I'm not going with Jody, if that's what you mean.'

'I didn't mean ... well, okay, I did wonder, having seen her in there. But I meant, do you want some company?'

'I'm surprised she even came here. It's not her scene at all.' He took a final look up at the sign over the Tuel Sleng museum and began to move away. 'If you're coming too we need to go now, to have some time before it closes.'

Maddie watched him shuffle away. 'Okay,' she said, jogging to catch up. 'How'd you get here?'

'Took a moto. We can get a ride on the main street—'

'No need, Rico can take us.'

She guided him left, down a side street where Rico lay stretched out on the tuk-tuk's back seat, staring at his mobile phone. He looked up and grinned as they approached.

*

The tuk-tuk bounced and swayed as it left the relatively smooth tarmac road, rumbling onto a dusty track of compacted mud and gravel. They began snaking past ramshackle buildings, less frequent now, the random structures eventually petering out completely to leave long periods between isolated clusters of houses in small villages.

Maddie peered through the dirt cloud billowing behind them, clasping her fingers around the tuk-tuk's carriage framework as it jolted and swayed on the loose shingle. Bozzer rocked with the motion, tensing and relaxing his muscles to brace against the sporadic rhythm. He drew his eyes back from looking outside, focusing instead on her profile. She turned back into the carriage, caught his eye.

'What?'

'Something different about you today. Something ... missing.' Bozzer dug into his pocket, pulled out a clenched fist and held it out. 'I believe these are yours,' he declared.

Maddie frowned, prompted to hold out her open palms by his raised eyebrows and nodding gesture. Bozzer used his spare hand to lift her hands up, guiding the small tissue-wrapped package into her open palms. She leant forwards and carefully unwrapped the gold-encased diamond studs.

She shot him an accusing look. 'How did you get these?'

'From Victoria and your slimy shadow.'

'What?'

'She pinched them from your room while you were sightseeing, this morning. There was always something odd about those two, the way they assessed other travellers. Took me a while to work out they were scoping us out, as potential targets. I had a feeling they had history – their body language suggested they were together, yet they made out they were both single. Got me curious. So I followed Charlie to his hotel and staked out the lobby. Figured sooner or later Victoria would show up, could tell me where you were. I got lucky with the earrings. Here's a photo of her showing them to Charlie.' Bozzer tabbed through the menu on his camera and turned it around to show her the screen. 'She was about to try them on when I stepped in.'

Maddie alternated her gaze between the earrings in her hand and the photograph on his camera. 'Cheeky cow!'

Bozzer chuckled. 'Yep. All those warnings in the guide books about scams in foreign countries, and it turns out the biggest threat is from your fellow travellers.'

'Yeah, how ironic is that.' Maddie's gaze clouded over. Concentration lines crinkled her forehead. 'These were a gift, from Rupert.'

'An anniversary?'

'Sort of, but more important …' She closed her hand, then opened her shoulder bag, removed her purse and carefully tucked the earrings into the coins section. 'Thank you for getting them back,' she said. She slipped her sunglasses over her eyes as she looked away, out over the lush green rice paddies.

'No problem. Charlie and I had a manly chat. I let him know how much you disapproved.'

Maddie turned back towards him. 'You punched him?'

'Not that satisfying – kneed him in the nuts. He's probably still digging them out from behind his eyeballs.'

She sniggered, starring at him. 'You didn't …?'

He shrugged. 'Figured those two had fleeced loads of other travellers. There's a code about that sort of thing, y'know. So I made it count.' Bozzer grinned, then looked away, sensing the tuk-tuk begin to slow. He swivelled his body forwards as they passed a road sign: *Choeung Ek Genocidal Centre.*

His smile sank, amusement drained from his face, replaced by a serious, tight-jawed expression.

Maddie turned to look past Rico as he turned the tuk-tuk into a busy gravel car park, bordered at the far end by a tall, imposing main gate and surrounding fence. Rico eased the tuk-tuk to a stop under the shade of a small bushy tree. Bozzer placed his hands onto his thighs and scrunched fingers into his muscles. Dust from the dry, gritty car park swirled and settled around them.

'You okay?'

'Yup. You step out, I need a moment.'

Maddie edged out of the tuk-tuk carriage and stepped down onto the gravel, turning to survey the entrance.

'I wait, no problem,' said Rico in a subdued tone.

Bozzer joined Maddie, walking silently with her across the gravel, heading for the entrance. She stole a sideways glance at him, something niggling her. That song. So haunting and ambiguous ... what was it? *A Whiter Shade of Pale* by Procol Harum. She stared at Bozzer's complexion, swallowed and forced herself to look away. Their footsteps slowed, scuffing wispy puffs of dust as they filtered through the pedestrian entrance. Next to them were a set of double gates beneath a multi-tiered gable roof, coloured terracotta, gold and cream. Beyond the entrance, a modern building sat at the head of a lush green area. Adjacent to the thick-stemmed grass, a light grey and white block path led to a white stone and glass stupa, its square spire a focal point. The interconnecting pathways emanated from it, neatly segmenting the manicured lawns surrounding its imposing and poignant presence.

'Brace yourself ...' Bozzer said quietly, turning to face her, his eyes lacking any trace of his normal spark. 'This is likely to be a distressing experience.'

Maddie nodded, following him to the ticket counter.

'My shout,' he said gently, paying the entrance fee. 'I got you the audio tour.' Bozzer handed the tickets to a young Cambodian museum curator, standing beside a row of headphones and control sets.

Maddie frowned and glanced at the other visitors not part of an official guided group, most of whom wore identical headsets. She nodded her thanks to the museum curator and slipped the headphones around her neck, holding the control box as she studied the instruction leaflet. 'You're not doing the same?'

He shook his head. 'I did a lot of research about this place. The audio tour is definitely the way to go, to try and understand what it must have been like. It's professionally produced, by all accounts. But it'll be too raw for me ... I need to be with my own thoughts here, because ... this place, it's very likely where my grandfather was brought after being tortured at Tuol Sleng. He probably died here. So you take your time, follow the tour. I'll catch you at the end, in a couple of hours ...'

Maddie watched him open up the killing fields exhibit pamphlet. He studied it for a moment, then ambled away. She continued to watch him for a little longer, then dropped her eyes to the audio control and pressed play.

Thirty-Five

Maddie listened attentively, proceeding to the first of nineteen walking stops that followed an anticlockwise route around the memorial site. The first narrator described the historical and political rise of Pol Pot, the head of the Khmer Rouge regime and their march into Phnom Penh, seizing power on 17th August 1975. The voice described how new arrivals were greeted by Him Huy, the Khmer Rouge guard and executioner. He *processed* them through the dark and gloomy detention building on their way to the first mass grave, less than one hundred yards away.

Maddie followed the meandering path through the exhibits at crawling speed, her feet shuffling on the shiny path. She passed the executioners' office building and chemical store room location to a mass grave, containing four hundred and fifty people. Here the narrator described how victims were killed using an array of crude implements, ranging from farm tools and machetes to the butt of a rifle, smashed into the back of the victims' heads. Every year after the heavy rains, more clothing scraps, bone fragments and teeth would be unearthed in the mud, which were carefully picked out by the site wardens and displayed in glass cabinets beside each shrine. It was estimated, the narrator stated, that approximately twenty-five per cent of the Cambodian population were slaughtered in killing field sites like this one, which were located throughout the country.

One person in four ... exterminated.

Maddie halted beside the waist-height rectangular fencing beneath a pitched bamboo and reed roof. She stared down at the fine soil, a spike of pain stabbing her tummy. She glanced to her left, reading the information sign.

Four hundred and fifty men and women, slain here.

Maddie lifted a hand to her forehead, slowly shook her head, the number replaying in her mind. She slumped down and rested her hands on the bamboo fence, steadying her trembling limbs. The narrator described how loudspeakers strategically placed around the site would play loud Khmer music and repetitive propaganda speeches, twenty-four hours a day, to hide the sounds of killing – masking yet another poor soul departing this world. All this horror, while yet more truckloads of victims arrived.

Maddie focused on her white knuckles, clenched on the fence. She summoned all her strength to prise them away, moving on to the next exhibit.

*

Did they bring you here, all those years ago? Beneath the screeching tannoy, spewing incoherent bullshit propaganda? Bundling you out of a truck in the middle of the night, into this hell? How did they finish you – was it quick? I doubt it, judging by Tuel Sleng ... this wasn't your fight, Gramps. Not your concern. But you came anyway, to try and tell the world. But did the world care? Did it give a fuck, then – does it give a fuck now? Rhetorical question. Ridiculous, stupid fucking question. Are you in there, Scott Barry Johnson ...?

Bozzer craned his neck, staring up at the glass windows in the sides of the memorial stupa. Inside, within the tiered glass sections, lay row upon row of neatly stacked human skulls.

His shoulders quivered, muscles cramping. Unable to hold on any longer, he sank into a crouch, flopping down the last few inches onto the grass. His hands draped between his thighs, head sagging over his crumpled, trembling body.

Where is the dignity, the humanity ... justification for this end? You tried to live your life honourably, respecting your fellow man. So why did you have to die like this? Why was I denied my memories of who you were ...? You lived your life, your tragically short life, as if you had nothing to lose. Yet you had so much at stake. Your photographs could have jolted people back home – around the world – so much sooner, had you not perished here. Those in positions of power, able to influence and sway governments into action, could have stopped this evil. You tried to make a difference, with your photographs – but nobody intervened. Nobody stopped this madness. By capturing the reality of what was going on here, you wanted to show an ignorant world the truth about this country, the barbarism its people waged against their own. Because you believed in your heart that it mattered. But was it worth it ... your wretched, wasted life?

Bozzer reached up with leaden arms. He rubbed sore, wet eyes with tingling fingers. Shaking his head, he looked away from the skulls behind the glass.

So what now – how do I leave this place? What lessons do I take away, for my own life? If it were me, all those years ago, what would I have done differently – what am I going to do now, from this moment on? How am I going to extract some form of positivity from this unspeakable wickedness? Try harder? Yes. Try harder, in everything I do. Focus on the photography, that's important. Capturing those special, unrepeatable moments. Develop positives from the negative forces. Yeah. That'll work ...

Bozzer drew in a long deep breath, gradually lifting his head to stare up at the stupa once again, keeping it there as he held the air inside his chest. He closed his eyes, breathed out, then straightened his torso and opened his eyes as he pushed his hands down on the ground, standing shakily, stretching his heavy limbs up straight.

Okay, Gramps. In your memory ...

He lifted his gaze to the top of the stupa, his eyes dry now, shining, resolute. He clenched his jaw, studied the glass sides and row upon row of human tragedy within, committing this moment, that image to memory, one last time.

'Gonna make you all proud. Mum, Dad, Gramps ... *everyone*. Just you watch. I *will* make a difference.'

*

All around Maddie were similarities, despite the different mixes of cultures and nationalities. Body posture, height, weight, hairstyles, skin colour, national clothing, distinctive mannerisms – a nation's *identity* and cultural uniqueness, yet still, one commonality here. An understanding amongst friends, family, travel companions, strangers ... all those wearing the headphones, carried themselves in silence. They all shared the same haunting weariness at the plunging depths of their fellow humans' evil depravity.

The tinny narrators' voices, each distinctively different, playing chillingly through the audio. Translations of survivors' stories:

Losing a child.
Witnessing a murder.
Forced to leave home.

Almost beaten to death.
The sacrifice of a stranger, saving a life ...
Maddie slowly panned her aching eyes around the lake. Zombie-like visitors stood or sat on benches staring out across the water, lost in a deep trance as they listened. Others crying openly, quietly, shaking their heads. No words. No cause. No comprehension.

Her feet shuffled on, drawn to the next location on the audio tour, compelled to keep moving, to prevent grief from enveloping her, sucking all future fun and laughter from her body.

Exhibit fifteen. *The Killing Tree.*

Hundreds of colourful wristbands and hairbands adorned the thick trunk, wedged between ridges of rutted bark. Maddie stopped short of the tree, a respectful distance from the family already stood there, silently listening to their headphones. The audio description began explaining about the atrocities committed here. She watched the family slowly move on, the mother hugging her sobbing teenage daughter, her son red-eyed and self-conscious, his bottom lip trembling.

Maddie tried to move, step forwards. She failed, remaining stuck, her feet immobile as if glued to the ground, or held there by a powerful magnetic force. The narrator described how in order to save bullets, adults were beaten to death with axe handles and bamboo sticks, then thrown into a ditch beneath the tree's roots, one on top of the other. Little children and babies were grasped by the legs, swung at the tree, their skulls smashed against the trunk.

She gasped, recoiling, her body shaking, fighting for breath. Oxygen sucked from her lungs, like an imploding vacuum.

'No ...' she croaked, tears falling down her crimson cheeks. 'Nooo!' She clutched her stomach, staring down at her hands, scrunched them tight, releasing them. She held up her shaking fingers, studying them, bewildered, then pressed her palms back on her belly.

'NOOO!' Maddie spluttered, hyperventilating as she cried out, sobbing uncontrollably. Her body convulsed in waves of increasingly violent shuddering.

'Easy there, Maddie. I've got you.' Bozzer gently placed his hands on her shoulders. He gathered her into his arms a split-second before all remaining strength failed her and she began to crumple.

'Nooo ...' she whimpered, her whole body convulsing as she wept in his arms. He reached up, slipped the headphones off her head, held them behind her back as he scooped her up in his arms and carried her away. Her body heaved in his, lungs gasping, grappling for air, her heart pounding flat out. What the hell possessed another human being to inflict such, such *obliteration?*

'Shhh ... shhh ...' Bozzer stood on the grass under the shade of another tree, far away from *that* one, cradling her in his arms. Her gasping breaths gradually began to slow. But her arms remained clutched tightly around his neck, her wet, hot face pressed into his chest. Holding onto his kindness, as it were the only thing left remotely safe and real in this shitty world.

'It's horrific, seeing these barbaric things we humans do to each other,' he murmured, 'it's beyond comprehension. There are no words to—'

'Children ... *babies*,' she blurted out, her chest heaving against his. More tears soaked into his tee-shirt.

'I know ... shhh ...' He sank down onto the grass, lowering her into a sitting position beside him. He eased her head into his neck, holding her gently, his torso rocking slowly with her. They sat there, holding each other for several long, silent minutes.

'You lost someone ... *else?*' he said eventually.

She eased back from him, her breathing steadier now, wiping away the wetness from her cheeks with the back of her hand.

'Yes, sort of,' she whispered, barely audible. 'Stefan died seven years ago ...' She took a gulp of air, lay a hand in her lap, fingers touching her stomach. She glanced at Bozzer, hesitated, then looked away. 'He rarely rode a motorbike on the road, it was too dangerous for a track racer. He died rushing to get home, to take me to hospital ... when the contractions started. We'd already agreed, before the birth, to have her, our baby ... adopted.'

Maddie shook her head, swaying the fresh trickling tears into a slalom down her prickling cheeks. 'I tried to reconsider, after Stefan died. But I wasn't strong enough. The circumstances were ... *unfeasible*. I couldn't cope without him. So I gave her away. She'll be almost seven years old now. That tree, what happened here ... those tiny, innocent, helpless children.'

She clasped her hands around her waist, doubled up, retching with emotion. Bozzer opened his arms, pulled her in close again as another bout of sobbing consumed her.

*

Bozzer wriggled his hand into a pocket and dangled a Kleenex tissue under Maddie's nose. 'I think it's uncontaminated.'

'Thanks,' she mumbled hoarsely. Sniffing and propping herself up, she leant away from him to dab her eyes and blow her nose. 'Sorry about the blubbing.'

Bozzer looked down at his tee-shirt. 'It'll dry. How you doing?'

She shrugged. 'Better, I think. That was pretty intense.'

'Yeah, horrible. But important.' He glanced at his watch. 'We should probably get a wiggle on, I think the centre shuts soon.'

Maddie nodded. She wiped her nose again, pocketed the tissue and stood up, shakily. They walked slowly back towards the entrance in silence.

'There's something I need to do, before we leave this place.' Bozzer unzipped a side compartment on his camera bag and withdrew a pen. He stepped into the reception centre and stood over the large visitors' book, taking a moment to contemplate. 'Do you want to go first?'

Maddie nodded, absently. She accepted the pen from him and leant over the page to write her comment and sign her name, handing him the pen afterwards in silence. Bozzer looked down at her neat handwriting.

Words fail me.

He nodded, glanced at her puffy, red eyes and fresh tears, then put the pen to the paper and began writing.

One can only hope and pray for the best in people. But realistic knowledge of the destructive and wasteful nature of the human race creeps in here, and I don't feel optimistic. Twenty thousand poor souls, murdered here, including one person particularly special to me. Barbaric. Inhuman. Unforgivable.

They shuffled away together, both blinking back their sorrow.

Thirty-Six

Bozzer sat opposite Maddie in the back of the tuk-tuk, their limbs juddering as it trundled along the bumpy road. Neither looked at each other. Lost in their thoughts, they stared out across the dusky fields as the last ebb of warming yellow sunlight sank below the green rice paddies, shimmering beneath the distant horizon.

Maddie shivered, tugging the waterproof jacket tighter around her. She raised her eyes skywards as raindrops began pattering on the tuk-tuk's canopy roof, strumming louder as the tempo increased.

It was raining that day, too.

Sporadic single dwellings became occasional villages, gradually appearing more frequently, eventually merging into a continuous low-level conurbation peppered with random taller buildings, which in turn gradually increased in frequency with each passing mile. The build-up of increasing traffic slowed their progress as they approached the outskirts of Phnom Penh. Multiple headlight beams tracked slanting rain, now pummelling the road in a torrential downpour.

When you arrived, and he ... didn't.

Eventually Rico swung the tuk-tuk across the road and pulled up outside Maddie's hotel.

'Go and jump in the shower, get warmed up,' said Bozzer, noting her shivering.

'What about you?'

'I'll go and collect my pack, it's stored behind reception at Charlie and Victoria's hotel – too swanky a joint for my meagre budget. Perhaps you'll let me shower in your room, I'll make a plan from there. Sound okay?'

She nodded, her teeth chattering as she rummaged in her bag and pulled out her purse, handing Bozzer some notes. 'Here's Rico's fee.'

'Thanks. Go and warm up, get some dry clothes on. I'll knock on the door when I get back.'

*

Maddie opened the door to see Bozzer shivering in the hallway, his clothes and rucksack saturated. In each hand he clutched a glass with a generous measure of dark spirit.

'Brandy, good for chills,' he said, handing her the glasses as she opened the door.

'Perfect, thanks. Bathroom's there, water's lovely and hot. Which is more than it was the last time we shared a room. Oh, and watch out for the door catch, it seems a bit temperamental.'

Bozzer nodded and stepped into the room, shrugging off his backpack. He dashed into the bathroom, hurriedly stripping off his wet clothes. She heard the spray of water. 'Thought you said it was hot?' he called out from behind the bathroom door.

'It is, after a few minutes.' The embryo of a tired smile twitched on her lips. Maddie sat back on the bed, melting into the headboard. She sipped the brandy, holding her nose over the glass lip, closing her eyes to inhale the fumes. The fiery liquid soothed her aching throat as it slipped down, warming her chest.

She picked up her book, *Survival in the Killing Fields,* and fanned through the pages. 'Not sure I can read you today, sorry,' she said, clasping the book shut and placing it carefully on the bedside table. She shut her eyes and rubbed her forehead, kneading the furrows of tension with her fingers, working outwards towards her temples. *God, what a day.*

The faint sound of singing drifted over the pattering of water in the plastic bath, drawing her subconscious mind back. She opened her eyes, listening to his voice, singing louder now as the bathroom door inched ajar with a low creak.

Maddie eased off the bed, her bare feet padding across the tiled floor towards the bathroom. She stopped short of the door, hesitating. Unable to ignore her curiosity, she leaned forwards and peered through the gap. Bozzer stood in the bathtub, his outline hazy visible behind the shower curtain, eyes shut, rinsing shampoo lather off his scalp.

She lowered her gaze, tracing the outline of his muscled and tanned torso behind the wet curtain, transparent where it stuck to his buttock cheek, hugging the curve down to his thigh where it released from his skin and disappeared behind the side of the bath. She leant against the doorframe, watched him reach down and scrabble around for the shower gel bottle, standing up straight and blindly squeezing some into his hands.

Bang!

Maddie jumped, checking herself as he cursed, his hands searching around again in the bathtub for the slippery plastic bottle.

What the hell am I doing?!

She scampered away from the open doorway, her heart racing. Plonking down heavily on the bed, she reached for her book. She scanned the pages of text, searching for a familiar place to continue from, still listening to the water thrumming against the shower curtain. Her eyes darted over the top of her book at the partially ajar door.

Close it?

Leave it.

Close it—

Maddie leapt off the bed, scurried across the room and carefully pressed the door shut, closing it with a faint *click* as the latch engaged. She settled back on the bed, lips pursed. Eyes closing, she concentrated on regulating her breathing. She heard the cascading water stop. The shower curtain whooshed back on the rail. Then …

Eeeeerrrrccchhhh.

Maddie peered through half-closed eyelids, witnessing the bathroom door slowly creak open, wider this time. She lifted her book up to her nose, darting her eyes down to the text, then glancing back up at the partially open door. The sound of Barry towel-drying himself ceased. A pause, then his head popped around the doorframe.

'This door seems a bit, er, unpredictable. One minute it's shut, then as if by magic—'

'I did warn you.' She shielded her blushing cheeks behind the book.

He held her startled stare for a moment, the corners of his mouth threatening to turn up into a smile. Then he withdrew, reappearing with a towel wrapped around his waist. He padded across the floor, unclipped the straps on his pack and began laying fresh clothes out on the bed. Maddie flicked her eyes over at the brandy glass on the side table. She reached out and held the glass to her lips, draining the remains in one swig, wincing as it burned its way down.

'Um, thanks for the brandy, lovely," she squeaked. 'Rough day, think I'd like another. I'll be down in the bar when you're … decent. Okay?'

She picked up her purse and the book, breezing past, leaving Bozzer chasing amusement across his weary, dimpled cheeks.

*

'I hope you're getting all this back on expenses …'

Fender looked up from the iPad balanced on his knee, its glow shrouding the side of his face in a greenish tint, washed white with every set of oncoming headlights zipping past the taxi.

'I'm interested in how you'll claim for paying off a Cambodian prostitute and a travelling hustler,' Rupert added.

A flicker of amusement creased Fender's mouth. He glanced down at the screen, hesitated as if weighing a thought in his mind, then he switched off the iPad. 'Is small talk, during our downtime? Your effort to humanise me?'

'You must need to switch off sometimes.'

'Alright, Rupert – dazzle me.'

'With what?'

'Whatever it is you're bursting to say. To justify your morally dubious predicament.'

'Haven't you ever made a wrong decision, regretted it?'

'Probably. Fortunately none involving a gang of east London loan sharks and a Samsonite suitcase laden with high-purity Class A narcotics.'

'Alright … so not the smartest thing I've ever done.'

Fender regarded Rupert for a few seconds. 'Is that it?'

'This a confessional?'

'Far from it.'

'I'm not all bad. I looked after Maddie for a long time, after Stefan.'

'So you said, before. You were friends?'

'Since school. I sat with him at his hospital bed, when he died.'

'With Maddie?'

'No. She was … elsewhere.'

'Was he conscious at all?'

'For a time.'

'So he made you promise, is that it?'

Rupert held Fender's enquiring gaze. He nodded. 'Stefan asked me to look after Maddie. I tried to be upbeat. I couldn't imagine Maddie being able to cope without him, they were inseparable. The society magazines loved them.'

'I read some articles, as research.'

'Really?'

'Yes. Tragic. Only twenty-four years old.'

Rupert nodded. 'He loved to race. That rush ... he truly grabbed life by the balls and rode the crap out of it.'

'You admired him.'

'We were like brothers.' Rupert looked away, a pang of stomach acid tugging at the back of his throat.

'So losing him like that, not being there at the end. That and the other unsavoury matter ... must have really messed her up.'

Rupert clenched his jaw, turned to stare out of the window. The first droplets of rain pattered on the glass, obscuring the ramshackle town rumbling past beyond the gravel road surface. 'Which is why I don't understand this – her destination, or potential travel companions.'

'No. Given the recent intel, it does seem an illogical fit.'

'Our relationship may be built more on companionship than intimacy, but it still stings.'

'Your sense of duty – up until you booked your Thailand holiday – is admirable. But this obligation to a dead friend extends only so far. Sooner or later you need to move on. For your sake, and hers.'

'Hey, have a heart, Fender – I made a promise. There's honour at stake—'

'Are you honouring him, or her, right now? In a Cambodian taxi, wearing a tagging device, in pursuit of a suitcase stuffed with drugs, and at the mercy of a notorious debt collector?'

'I was trying to make things right! Haven't you ever had family obligations, made an emotional commitment – regardless of personal cost?'

'In my line of work, it doesn't pay to develop ties.'

'What about when you were younger ... wasn't there someone special, the one that got away? There must be a reason for your detachment.'

'Sharing time travelling does not make us buddies,' Fender snapped.

'Suit yourself.' Rupert gazed out at the darkness beyond the streaks of rain juddering horizontally across the window. The parallel droplet trails occasionally spiked into sporadic, random pothole-induced pips, like lines on a stack of heart rate monitors, struggling to jolt from flat lining into a blip of something meaningful and alive.

*

Bozzer plonked down in a seat next to Maddie and placed his empty brandy glass on the bar.

'Same again?' she asked in a measured tone.

'Sure. You're thirsty.' His eyes twinkled as he studied her.

'Yeah. Today was, you know—'

'Difficult.'

'Yeah.'

He straightened up, his carefree expression glazing over. The barman topped up their glasses and withdrew to attend to a newly arrived couple, waiting patiently at the hotel's reception desk.

'That's gotta be tough on you, losing your boyfriend like that. And having to give up your kid,' he said softly, glancing at her.

She nodded, reaching into her pocket to dab her eyes.

'Motorbike, you said?'

'Yes.'

'Sorry … makes sense now – at the Angkor temples.'

Maddie picked up her fresh glass. She swilled the dark liquid in a circular motion.

'To lost friends?' he suggested.

She turned to face him, raised her glass to his, nodding. 'To friends, lost and found.' They touched their glasses together. Each took a sip, remaining silent for a while.

I don't even know your name … I wonder what they called you?

She rocked the base of the brandy glass back and forth on the bar, scrutinising the residue liquid clinging to the curved sides. 'What's next, for you?' she asked eventually.

Bozzer took another sip, taking his time to savour the taste. 'My work here is done. I've made my pilgrimage, seen what Gramps endured. Made my peace at the place he died.' He took another taste of brandy. 'So now I have tomorrow here, in Phnom Penh. The day after, I'm booked on a flight to Lima. A month exploring Peru, then a few days acclimatising to the altitude in Cusco, where I join a group trekking to Machu Picchu. From the lost city, I'm heading overland into Bolivia. Then I'm meeting up with my brother in Argentina, for his wedding. I'm his best man and the official photographer.'

Maddie nodded. She sat there for a moment, then glanced down at her fingers, mentally counting them off. She visibly shuddered, then pressed the brandy glass to her lips, finishing half the measure in a single glug. She wheezed as the heat hit the back of her throat, then slouched back on the seat, her shoulders sagging. 'Mmm. I needed that.'

'I can see. Wanna tell me why?'

'Stefan died exactly seven years ago, on Sunday. I've just worked it out.'

Barry lowered his glass, mid-taste. 'Sorry again.'

She flicked her eyes briefly over at him, then stared into the depths of the spirit bottles, stacked on three shelves at the back of the bar.

Seven years on Sunday, you were born ...

'Can you imagine me with a child, *that* age ...?' Her red eyes searched his.

'You'd be a different person, for sure.'

'Better, probably.'

'I disagree. You wouldn't be here, now. Wouldn't have seen what you saw today ... wouldn't have *felt* what you did. Difficult days like these are what *really* make you stronger inside, a better person outside.' Bozzer reached down, hoisted his camera bag up onto his lap. 'Do me a favour ...?'

She looked across at the sound of him unzipping the bag, shook her head. 'I can't have my picture taken, not now—'

'I know. I need you to take a photo of me.'

She frowned. 'Why?'

'Because where we've just been, this afternoon ... it wasn't appropriate for me to take any. I want to raise a glass to him, to Scott, my grandfather. Get it documented. You can record your twenty seconds of observation if you like, or not – it's up to you. But I'd appreciate your help.'

Maddie reluctantly accepted the camera from him, gathering it into her hands. She stared down at it, thoughtful for a moment, then straightened up and pressed the viewfinder to her eye. Bozzer wiggled around to face her, holding the brandy glass at chest height, his eyes glistening.

Shh-clitch.

Memory Card 3. Pic 412

'A painful day, dark and grey. Barry pays his respects after visiting the Genocide Centre, raising a glass in tribute to you, grandpa, his mentor. Rest in peace, Scott Barry Johnson – your grandson is doing you proud – he's one of the good guys, despite sometimes being crass enough to stand out in a crowd. But that may be no bad thing, because one day, perhaps, he'll be as iconic as you – a photographic king.'

She released the shutter button and lowered the camera into her lap.
'That'll do it. Cheers,' Bozzer said quietly, carefully collecting the camera from her.

*

'There's something I need to do, first thing in the morning,' said Maddie, resting her elbow on the restaurant table, her cheek leaning against her palm.
Bozzer set his cutlery down on his empty plate. He used a paper napkin to wipe his mouth and sat back, studying her. 'Okay …'
She stared down at the table, fiddled with her fork. 'I need to sell something, get the best price I can.'
'Drugs?'
She flicked her eyes up at his, rolled them at his mischievous grin. 'Jewellery.'
'You gonna auction off your trophy-travel-buddy, so soon?'
'Don't be stupid, I couldn't pay anyone enough to take *you* away. I'm talking about my earrings.'
'Ah.'
'Yup. I think they need to be … recycled. Into something more useful.'
'Something like hard currency?'
She nodded.
He slid his mobile phone across the table. 'Search away. There's bound to be a few decent pawnbrokers in the city.'
'Thanks,' she said, picking up his phone.
'This recycling you want to do, is it for a travel fund?'
Maddie shrugged, toying with a coy smile. 'Something like that.'

*

They walked on for a while in silence. Crossing a side road, the tarmac shiny from a recent shower, they passed a grassy area cordoned with a knee-high hedge, where Cambodian families sat in groups with picnic food spread out on tablecloths.

I wonder what you look like now?

Some groups had brought snacks from vendors, others laid out pastries and home-cooked delicacies from well-used hampers. The buzz of their happy chatter drifted across the grass, the relaxed, happy atmosphere like a summer festival.

I hope you have a nice family ... I hope they—

'You had any thoughts, about the next stage?' Bozzer asked.

She glanced across at him and smiled. 'I should probably head home, but ... thought I'd keep moving, follow your suggestion and check out Vietnam and Laos. I can get a bus from here, then a boat across the border to Chau Doc. Next stop Ho Chi Min City—'

'Saigon? You'll have a great time there. It's very different, and yet still, same-same.'

She chuckled. 'Everywhere, same-same. Peru really is going to be quite different for you – culturally, I mean.'

'Yep, that's the idea ...' Bozzer lit his roll-up, puffed on it. 'Wanna come with me?'

Maddie halted. She turned to look at him, took half a step away. *'What?'*

'It's a wild idea, I know. But think about it. Where you're at, in your life right now – would it really be such a big deal?'

'I'm not sure why you're asking me,' she said, studying his face.

'Ah, hah. What happened to enquiring when, what, how ...? Asking me why is tantamount to mistrust, paranoia and generally being risk-averse. *Okay, tell me more and I'll think about it,* would have been an adequate response. Forget I asked. It's not for you, I get it.'

Bozzer walked on, leaving Maddie standing alone on the pavement, staring after him. She scrunched her hands against her shorts, then tore her eyes away from his retreating outline to raise her palms, staring down at the glistening moisture.

How can I, now ... after today?

She jogged up to his side, panting in the evening's humidity.

'*Why* is a perfectly reasonable question.'

'No, it's not. Keep asking that and you'll never have any adventures.'

'I'm here, aren't I?'

'And how did you get here?'

'On a plane.'

'British sarcasm – great. Here, in Cambodia, with *this* happy-snappy dude. How did you get here?'

'I walked out on Rupert.'

'Exactly! And at what point in that beautiful moment of rebellious, fuck everyone else madness, did you ask yourself *why?*'

'Um … I didn't. I thought of all the reasons not to fly home with him and … just sort of did it.'

'Just for the twitchy-balls hell of it?'

Maddie stared at him, her head spinning behind a fixated expression. 'I suppose so.'

'There you go. So if you have to ask *why* to an offer of a new adventure, then clearly, that change of direction, ain't for you, is it?'

Thirty-Seven

'There was someone once, a long time ago …'

Rupert prised his eyes open and peered through the darkness across the taxi's back seat, barely able to make out Fender's vague profile. 'What did you do, buy her in the desert?' he mumbled. He glanced at his illuminated watch face and winced, mid-yawn.

Only the slightest change to Fender's regular light breathing hinted at his mood – a few short sharp puffs of what … recollection? Emotional awareness?

'No. I did the next best thing. I immersed myself in my work.'

'Kidnapping and debt management are that absorbing and fulfilling?'

'You do get pithy after hours, don't you. Work, back then was at the behest of Her Majesty's armed forces.'

'So you were a government spook.'

'That came a little later. I was in the regular army first. Intelligence gathering, mainly.'

'That where you got your nickname … *Fender?*'

'Somewhere around that time.'

'So if I ask you what's your real name, that's when you say you could tell me, but you'd have to kill me?'

The faintest chuckle echoed across the narrow gap between them. 'Fender might have been derived from several sources. *De*fender, for example, relating to the protection of corporate assets. Or from the French, *défenseur,* meaning town guard, or champion at arms – a paid post in the 13th century. Alternatively, it could be linked to my surname, or a Fender Stratocaster guitar … pick whichever explanation you prefer.'

'As in, work it out for yourself?'

'Precisely.'

'Great. I'm liking our newfound openness.'

'It works for me.'

'So where's home?'

'Home …?'

'Yeah, you know, where you keep the family photo album and childhood sports day medals, in a shoebox in a dusty loft. A man like you must have a crash pad somewhere.'

'I've had several.'

'Where?'

'They've been in many different places, over the years … Europe, Asia, the Americas—'

'England?'

'Occasionally.'

'Don't you miss not having a permanent base? I mean, what sort of life is it, constantly on the move.'

'It's been necessary, for employment.'

'What about a family?'

'What about it?'

'No regrets?'

'Only one.'

Rupert shifted in his seat to face Fender. He tried to make out more of his features, gauge the expression in his eyes, but the lack of other vehicles on the road at three in the morning robbed Rupert of the helpful illumination from their headlights.

'But that's most definitely classified. I would have to kill you.'

Rupert perked up in his seat, sharpening his focus as a lone pair of headlights appeared around a curve in the road ahead. But in the short time the twin beams briefly flooded the inside of the taxi with light, Fender had turned towards the approaching car, denying Rupert a more detailed visual assessment. The headlights faded behind them, plunging the taxi into a more intense darkness.

'What about Rupert Sullivan? He's a young, virile man. Does he have plans to start a family?'

Rupert sank back into the taxi's worn upholstery. 'Given what I told you about Maddie's issues, what do *you* think?'

'My apologies, that was insensitive of me. Nevertheless, it does require me to ask the obvious question.'

'Which is?'

'What on earth are you still doing together?'

*

Maddie slumped back against the mirror and watched the lift doors close. She stole a glimpse at Bozzer, scanning through photographs on his camera. 'Onwards and upwards,' he muttered, turning to look at her as the doors hissed shut. She looked away. The floor jolted, the lift began climbing.

'The next chapter ...' she agreed, absently.

I wonder where you are, baby girl ... do you have brothers or sisters?

Maddie swung the hotel room door open and stepped inside. She tossed her shoulder bag onto the bed and turned towards the bathroom, stopping at the sight of Bozzer, remaining stationary in the corridor.

'You okay?'

He nodded. 'Guess I'm wondering ... whether it would be cool for me to split the room rental and crash on the floor tonight? I'll pack my stuff up in the morning, take off when you go to the pawnbroker.'

'Oh. Um ... sure.'

He grinned. 'Cheers. I'll bivvie down there, if that's okay?' He pointed to a space between the wall and the foot of the bed.

'No problem,' she replied quickly.

Maddie stepped into the bathroom, closing the door firmly behind her. She scrunched her hands in her hair and stared at her reflection in the bathroom mirror. Silently, she mouthed *'What's going on?!'*

*

'This sleazy enough for you, Rupert?' Fender glanced around the gaudy, neon shopfronts lined with scooters and lush green pot plants on the wide pavement. People of various nationalities mingled, their clothing and smiles luminous in the artificial light, enticing like-minded night dwellers into the countless bars.

'And I thought Siem Reap's nightlife was overtly excessive.'

'Anything and everything at your fingertips. Including – unusually – information.' Fender threaded his way through a selection of plastic tables and chairs, mopeds and foliage, into the brightly lit entrance of the Pickled Parrot bar.

'Miss Stevens, how pleasant to see you again.'

Victoria blew cigarette smoke above her head and regarded Fender coolly, through narrowed eyes. 'Charlie's out back, watching, with the manager. The bar staff have been warned, they're ready.'

'Excellent. I assume this will appease your friends.' Fender laid a pile of dollars on the table in front of Victoria. 'I'd be offended if you didn't count this.' He sat down, motioning for Rupert to take the seat beside him.

Victoria nodded. 'So would I.'

Fender flicked his gaze around the bar, unhurried. He absorbed every detail of the layout, assessing each person mingling, drinking, schmoozing.

Victoria finished her count. She looked up and flashed Fender and Rupert a thin smile. 'It's all here.'

'But you didn't expect it to be.'

'No.'

'So …?'

'She's at The Panda Hotel, 98 Street.' Victoria transferred her gaze to Rupert. 'She's probably with Barry, the Australian. He seemed particularly interested in finding her too.'

'If your information is incorrect, I will come and find you to extract a refund,' said Fender in an even tone.

'I don't doubt it.' She smirked and stubbed out the cigarette in an ashtray. 'I can't understand what he sees in her, but you know Aussies – they have no taste.' Victoria tucked the bundle of notes into her shoulder bag. She kept a watchful eye on Fender and Rupert as she withdrew into the depths of the bar.

'The Australian – how did that happen? I thought he'd taken off a few days ago,' said Rupert, addressing the question to Victoria's silhouette, retreating into the gloom.

'Apparently not.' Fender tapped his phone's screen, mapping out a route to Maddie's hotel. He guided Rupert out of the bar. 'Does it make your decision any easier?'

Rupert shook his head. 'I don't know what to think anymore.'

Fender stepped out into the street and flagged down a tuk-tuk. 'Best make up your mind fast. You've got four minutes.'

Thirty-Eight

Maddie lay on the bed, eyes closed, hands crossed over her chest, fingers clutching the covers tucked up tightly under her chin.

Forget: When? How? Why? Most importantly: WHAT happens next?

Travelling on my own, from tomorrow ... am I sure?

Yes, I need to.

No, I don't want to.

So instead—

Him ...?

The bathroom latch clicked, creaking the door open. Maddie kept her eyes shut and listened to his footsteps pass beyond the end of the bed. She held her breath as a sleeping bag rustled and a body slumped down onto the floor. The body swished in the fabric, adjusting position, then fell silent, replaced instead with his faint breathing.

'Night Madge. Thanks for letting me doss down.'

She opened her eyes and stared at the ceiling. 'Oh, sure. No worries ... *Bozzer*.'

'You taking the piss...?'

'What?'

'With the "no worries" pun?'

'Not knowingly—'

'Sure?'

'Of course.'

'Because I'd hate to have to jump up onto that comfy bed and spank you for such colonial contempt,' he said in a serious voice.

Maddie propped herself up and glanced over the edge of the bed. She bunched up a spare pillow and threw it at his head.

'Ouch! What was that for?'

'Stop trying to wind me up. I can see you grinning.'

'That's my dazzling personality.'

'I'm tired. Lights out, please.'

'Charisma never sleeps—'

'Yeah, well, it'll be sleeping on the street unless Skippy buttons it!'

She listened to the silence for a moment, then lay back down and wiggled her head into a comfy hollow in the pillow.

'Ball basher.'

Maddie fought back an impulse to smile. 'Organ-grinding wallaby.'

His muffled sniggering drifted up from the end of the bed, its tempo and nasal squawking infectious. She giggled, tried to contain it, but instead broke into a deep belly laugh. 'You tosser!'

'I would do, quite happily. But you'd hear my sleeping bag rustle.'

'Jesus – arrrggghhh!' Maddie pulled the pillow over her head and screeched into it. She thumped the bed and sat up. 'Can't you just go to sleep?'

'Hey, I've got fifty hours of flying and plane transfers to look forward to. I'll get all the rest I need then.'

'You're saying you want to party *now*, at—' she peered at her watch, 'eleven thirty–seven?'

'Did you say party – what we waiting for?'

'I'm waiting, for you, to go to SLEEP!'

Maddie heard a heavy sigh. She listened to his sleeping bag rustle as he sat up, his head and shoulders appearing as a dark outline at the end of the bed. He rested his elbows each side of her feet, pinning the sheet across her ankles. 'Serious question.'

'Okay …' she said apprehensively. She drew up her legs, curling her knees to her tummy.

'How fucking old are you?'

'Um … twenty-six.'

'*Sixty-six*, you say? That's about right … for fuck's sake, Princess Madge, don't just go out there and get a life, get out of the casket already!'

Bozzer leapt up, darted across the room and flicked the light switch. Maddie recoiled, squealing, scrunching her eyes. She peeked out from behind the pillow. 'Can't you just lie quietly, let me sleep? Please—'

'NOOO, let's hit the town! Grab some slap, throw on your party rags and let's *do* this city before we're carted off to the friggin' morgue. We should leave this place to go our separate ways barely being able to remember how spectacular it was. I fly outta here tomorrow night. I don't wanna be sitting on that plane for the best part of two days, thinking *Aw gee, that was an okay time. I feel nicely rested* ... I want to be sitting there with a huge exhausted grin plastered over my face thinking *Fuck me – I'm wasted. That was epic!'*

*

'She's not here.'

'No, but she's not alone.' Fender pointed to the second backpack, propped up against the wall at the end of the bed.

Rupert scanned the hotel room. 'There's no suitcase. This can't be Maddie's stuff.'

Fender picked up the mobile phone off the bedside cabinet. 'This hers?' he asked, unplugging the cheap charging lead and handing the phone to Rupert.

He studied the screen, scrolling through the contacts list. 'It does look like her phone, but there's no contacts listed. None at all.'

'You've been deleted, Rupert. She's already moving on.'

Rupert shot Fender a hurt look. 'I'm not *that* bad a person.'

'Perhaps not. But you're a terrible fiancé. Keep hold of the phone and empty both packs onto the bed. Let's see who her new room-mate is.'

*

'What are you doing, *Madge* ...? It's ten past four on a Wednesday morning. You're in Cambodia with a hyperactive, degenerate, creative, eccentric Australian. It's like you're living another life ... have you completely lost your mind?'

Maddie dropped her gaze from the cracked mirror and cupped her hands in the sink, gathering cold water to slosh on her face. She used a paper towel to dab the water droplets away, then lifted her eyes to meet her reflection. She cocked an eyebrow and turned up the corners of her mouth.

'Yup. Lost it, found it. Lovin' it!' Maddie grinned at her fractured, lopsided and bright-eyed reflection.

She poked her head through the string beads dangling across the washroom doorway and weaved her way through the narrow passage, emerging in a dim smoky bar. 1990s dance music blaring from ancient speakers clinging precariously to black-painted walls.

'Drink!' yelled Bozzer, thrusting a cocktail glass into her hand.

'What is it?'

'Who cares!' He raised his glass, downed half the sunrise-shaded liquid and slouched back against the bar, flicking ash from his joint onto his tobacco tin lid.

'You're a bad influence.'

'Yeah, and not a guidebook in sight.'

'Just a camera.'

'Always. And a TV screen – you seen this …?' Bozzer pointed to the old boxy television perched on a shelf behind the bar.

Maddie turned to follow his scrutiny of the flickering image. 'What's going on?'

'I saw the story on the internet a few days ago, struck me as a novel idea …'

Maddie peered at the television screen, which showed a tall, serious-looking Westerner in his early thirties with a paunch belly, standing next to an attractive pale-skinned girl of a similar age. She had shoulder-length mousey hair and a slim yet curvy figure. The couple drifted away from two bored-looking professional photographers. They walked awkwardly, side by side with their bulky rucksacks through a glass door beneath an airport 'departures' sign. The girl's well-travelled backpack contrasted with his brand new, pristine example.

Bozzer caught the attention of the barman. 'Hey buddy. Turn it up, please?' He motioned with his thumb and finger, miming twisting a volume knob.

A British newscaster's voice grew louder: "… met today for the first time. Six months ago, business analyst Jonathan Cork booked a three-month trip backpacking around South America, securing two non-refundable, non-transferable tickets for him and his then-girlfriend, Kate Thornley. Unfortunately, with a week to go before jetting off, Kate dumped Jonathan, leaving him with an unusable spare ticket in her name. Unwilling to travel on his own due to a serious nut allergy, Jonathan decided to take drastic action and advertised on eBay and social media for someone to travel with him who had the same name as his ex. Jonathan's new travel companion, the *replacement* Kate Thornley, is thirty-two, a trained nurse and—"

The image on the screen flickered and distorted, static drowning out the rest of the newscaster's voice. Maddie glanced at the barman, who shrugged and fiddled with the television set, tabbing through the other channels, searching for a settled picture.

Bozzer turned away from the screen. 'It's a bit extreme, don't you think? He only needed to get himself out there, he'd soon pick up a travel mate.'

Maddie flicked an eyebrow, tilting her glass to swallow a mouthful of margarita. She picked the joint out of his fingers and took a toke on it, wallowing in the numbing, tingling sensation.

'Was that how you met Jody? Picked her up by charming her with your didgeridoo?'

He sniggered. 'Not all players, *play.*'

'Like the pie-eyed piper?'

Bozzer grinned and swallowed a mouthful of the potent rum concoction. 'You got a plan, after? I mean, home to the husband – back to a job?'

Maddie's eyes glazed over. 'Home is … *was,* a rented apartment. But if we're not getting married …' She shrugged. 'Guess I'll speak to one of my folks.'

'They're not together?'

'No. They separated a few years ago. One of 'em will have forgiven me by now … probably.'

He shot her a quizzical look.

'Long story. I'll be postponing *that* phone call for as long as possible.'

'Hence chasing the next adventure?'

'Uh-huh. As for the job, I sent them an email, asked for some unpaid leave.'

'You don't sound that bothered.'

'No. Right industry, wrong department.'

'How come?'

'Fashion magazine – I worked in the advertising marketing department.'

'That'll bleed the soul, alright.'

She nodded. 'Which, I suppose, is why I'm here.'

'Seeking enlightenment?'

'Or intelligent conversation. Ambitious, I know, given present company.'

Bozzer smirked and drained the rest of his cocktail. 'You should have advertised, like the eBay bloke. He's not gonna get any sort of cultural experience tucked up in a hotel room at eleven thirty-seven ... guess the new girl's paid handsomely for a share of that.'

Maddie shrugged, smiling contentedly as she offered him the joint back, shaking her head at his *so am I right, or am I right?* cocked eyebrow and lopsided grin.

'Okay, I concede. Maybe, perhaps, on this *one* occasion you might be right ...'

'Now you *see!* You were in serious danger of ageing another twenty years in that hotel room.'

She sighed, nodding. 'I don't know why I'm like that. You're right, I'm only twenty-frigging-six!'

'It wouldn't matter if you were eighty-six. Why conform to someone else's perception of how you should act at a particular age? There are no rules, only society's pre-conceived convention, all administered by governments who don't like the unpredictability of free-spirited people, of *any* age. They try to control *your* expectation of life. But right now, at this precise moment – you, Madge – are sticking two fingers up at all that bullshit conformity. And for that, Madeline Bryce, I salute you.' Bozzer stood up straight and snapped his flat palm up to his forehead, humming a 'Last Post' bugle melody.

Maddie giggled, then frowned, her lips straightening, evolving into a more sombre expression. Bozzer glanced across at her, noticing her change in mood. He stopped humming and sat back down, watching her finish the rest of the cocktail, her expression glazing over.

She leant in towards him to make herself heard over the pounding music, which the barman had just cranked up a notch. 'Today was ... seriously disturbing.'

'Yeah ... we're a pretty messed-up bunch, us humans. There's no peace to be found with so many diverse religious interpretations. Never will be, not without universal compassion.' Bozzer glanced at their empty cocktail glasses. 'You wanna stay here, or take a wander – get some shots?'

Maddie pointed to the shelves stacked with bottles. 'They've got loads of spirits in here—'

Bozzer lifted his camera case off the floor and pointed towards the street. 'I meant *shots*, for my book. Before dawn breaks out there ... lots of glimmering stars and beautiful souls to capture.'

She followed his gaze out into the street, her face relaxing into a smile. 'That sounds lovely, actually. Sure, I'm in.'

'Me too,' said an assertive-sounding voice.

Maddie and Bozzer turned towards the tall and wiry middle-aged European, entering the bar from an adjacent entrance.

'Name's Fender. Your fiancé, Rupert, I believe you know.'

Rupert stepped out from behind the stranger called Fender, like a nervous child. He had a tired, sheepish expression on his face. 'Hi Maddie, it's good to see you. We need to talk about some important, er … baggage.'

Thirty-Nine

Maddie's jaw dropped open. 'Rupert? What are you—'

'We've been looking for you, Madeline. I suggest we find a quiet corner, there's much to discuss.' Fender held his hands out, ushering her back inside the bar.

Maddie exchanged a confused look with Bozzer. He flicked his gaze between Fender and Rupert, slowly retreating with her.

They settled into a booth in a dim corner. Maddie sat next to the wall, opposite Rupert. Bozzer slid in beside her, across from Fender. A young Thai waitress scurried over, grinning enthusiastically. 'You like drinks – pitcher of beer?'

'Yes, and mineral water. Thank you.' Fender turned from the waitress to face Maddie, whilst maintaining a periphery awareness of Bozzer. 'We're here, Maddie, because your fiancé has been both foolish and reckless. He secured a loan from some rather unsavoury characters that he couldn't pay back. So to cover the debt, he agreed both of you would carry something through Thai customs and deliver it to them in London. But because you took off on your pre-marriage-jitters whim, he never completed the transaction. Dropping him, and indirectly you, up to your neck in the shit.'

Maddie stared at Fender, her heart pounding. 'I wasn't carrying anything else through customs. I checked my suitcase before we left the hotel, and I can assure you—'

'How did you get the rucksack? What happened to your Samsonite suitcase?' Fender barked, glaring at her, his eyes cold and unblinking.

Maddie tore her eyes away from Rupert to stare at Fender. 'I swapped them.'

'Why?'

'It wasn't practical, lugging an unwieldy case on and off buses. It screams *I'm a tourist – rip me off.* So I traded it.'

'With whom?'

'Another traveller.' She turned to Rupert. 'Surprised? Thought I had to have everything brand new? This is the *new* me.'

An uneasy silence enveloped the group. Fender studied Maddie's resolute expression.

'There wasn't a suitcase in your room at the Wild Orchid Villas, I checked,' said Rupert.

Maddie shrugged. 'Because I'd already … what does it matter? What did you do, Rupert? What was in the—'

'Where *exactly* did you make the swap?' asked Fender.

Maddie stared at him, her mind racing. 'What is this – you're blaming me for *his* screw-up?' She broke eye contact with Fender to glare at Rupert. 'Shouldn't you be here to apologise, try to win me back? What's so special about a bloody suitcase?'

'Maddie, please understand – this is important.' Fender lowered his voice. 'The Samsonite suitcase is important, to Rupert's creditors. We need to know where it is.'

'There wasn't anything in it! I know about the penalties for smuggling in Thailand. A woman got caught a few months ago, she narrowly avoided the death penalty. I made damn sure I checked my case before we left our hotel in Bangkok, then I locked it. There were no weird ornaments, no extra packages. No drugs.' Maddie clenched her jaw, her glare boring into Rupert.

Fender sighed and turned to Rupert. He shook his head, shoulders slumped, and dropped his listless eyes to the table top.

Fender refocused on Maddie. 'Did the case seem a bit heavy – when empty?'

She froze, her brain churning as she thought back. 'Rupert … what's going on?'

'You weren't carrying anything extra *inside* your suitcase,' said Fender. 'The Samsonite casing had been specially constructed with a double skin, meaning the suitcase itself was the transportation vessel. It contained approximately one and a half million dollars' worth of product.'

'*Product?!*' Maddie scrunched her forehead, her body trembling. She levelled her glare on Rupert. 'How is this possible – for me to be put at risk by your stupidity? You're such an arsehole!'

Bozzer sat back and shifted his gaze around the group. Maddie glanced at him as he mentally framed everyone's expressions. Her neck glowed crimson, large blotches seeped into her cheeks. Rupert had his eyes fixed on his hands, fiddling with them, like a naughty schoolboy on the receiving end of a parent's rant. Fender sat statue-like: legs still, elbows on the table, arms upright, fingers splayed and pressed together, his chin resting on his thumbs. He observed Maddie intensively, then rotated towards Rupert.

'I will speak to your masters in London. Get them on the case, so to speak.' He turned back to Maddie, his features rigid and unyielding. 'What are your travel plans, going forwards?'

'I assumed she'd be coming with us. To find the suitcase, sort this mess out,' interrupted Rupert.

'But it's not *my* bloody mess, is it?!' shouted Maddie.

'That's the logical solution, right?' Rupert countered, turning to look at Fender.

He glanced away, frowning. He removed the vibrating mobile phone from his pocket and scrutinised the screen. 'Please excuse me for a moment.' He stood up and withdrew to the far side of the bar, answering the incoming call, careful to maintain his surveillance of the group. Maddie watched his emotionless expression evolve into surprise during the murmured conversation.

'To whom am I speaking?' Fender listened, his eyelids crinkling. 'How did you ... right. Yes, I did, a long time ago. This is relevant because ...? That's unfortunate, but I don't see what it has to do with—'

Maddie wrenched her attention away from Fender, levelling a glare back on Rupert. 'What would have happened, if I'd been stopped at customs?'

'Maddie, please. I did this for us, I'd have been liable too, if—'

'There's no joint initiative here – no partnership!'

'You'd have benefitted from the payoff,' countered Rupert, holding eye contact with her as he folded his arms. 'We'd have been able to—'

'*Benefitted?!*' Maddie tensed, her breathing strained, a befuddled expression seared across her face.

'Yeah, it would have funded our wedding, for starters. Then there's the designer clothes, that ostentatious engagement ring—'

'Here, keep it!' Maddie twisted the ring, yanking it off her finger. She grabbed his wrist, wrenched it out from his folded-arms posture, pressed the ring into his palm and forcibly wrapped his fingers around it. 'There, satisfied?' She ushered Bozzer out of the booth, allowing her to shuffle over and stand up. She folded her arms, glaring at Rupert.

'You don't deserve me!'

Rupert opened his hand. He stared down at the ring for a moment, then pocketed it.

'What happened to you, Rupert? Where's the decent guy gone – the one who looked out for me, after Stefan died?'

'I wised up, you pretentious pricktease!' Rupert pushed to his feet, stepping out of the booth to loom over her.

'What?!' Maddie stared at Rupert, her body shaking.

Bozzer inserted himself between them. 'Whoa, easy mate—'

'Back off, you scavenging piece of shit!'

'That's enough, all of you,' said Fender, pocketing his phone as he approached the group. 'There's no need for this to get nasty, *yet*.' He placed his hand on Bozzer's shoulder, squeezing a pressure point. 'We can still be civil to each other.'

'I looked after you when your own family couldn't, or wouldn't!' Rupert spat the words out. He turned to Bozzer, the veins on his face bulging. 'Have you enjoyed balling my fiancée?'

Bozzer's stance stiffened. He lifted his heels an inch off the floor, flexing on the balls of his feet as he stepped back, slipping his flip-flops off. His fingers clenched into fists.

'I hope you had more luck getting into her knickers than—'

'Rupert, that's enough!' said Fender, a stern edge to his voice. He hooked a thumb into the front of his belt.

'Frigid little—'

Bozzer yanked his arm back then launched forwards, swinging a clenched fist towards Rupert's face.

Fender pressed a finger against his belt buckle. A split-second later, Rupert emitted a muted yelp. His knees buckled almost immediately, collapsing him to the floor like a brick chimney moments after a demolition charge had detonated. Rupert's scrunched-up face fell below the arc of the incoming fist, which grazed past his hairline. The inertia of the punch swung Bozzer's torso around ninety degrees, causing him to stagger forwards.

Fender snatched his free hand out, grabbing Bozzer's elbow. 'Easy, chap.' He released Bozzer, then looked down at Rupert's wide-eyed trance, regarding him with a hard, cold stare.

'Sir, sir – everything is okay …?' The young Thai manager bolted out from behind the bar and scampered over. Rupert whimpered, his muscles twitching.

Fender turned and raised his palms, smiling. 'All is okay. Our friend has had an epileptic seizure. He needs to rest. Thank you.' Fender side-stepped around Rupert and tucked a five dollar bill into the manager's hand, blocking his view of Rupert. 'Please don't be concerned. Everything is okay.'

'Whoa! What happened, chief?' asked Bozzer.

'He was being discourteous.'

'What did you do to him?' Maddie stared at Rupert's jiggling, twitching body.

'I instilled some self-discipline.'

'How …?' Maddie tracked down to the plastic cuff around Rupert's ankle, her eyes widening.

'It's a variation on a tracking device used on ex-offenders. This one's got a Taser built in. My own design.'

Fender turned away from Maddie and pinched the material of his hiking trousers above the knee to gain some slack, then squatted down beside Rupert's head. 'Take a moment to absorb what I'm saying: If you misbehave again, I will donate your most precious body parts to a Cambodian pig farm, one tiny testicle at a time. Do you understand how excruciatingly painful and inconvenient that will be?'

Rupert stared up at him, making a strange high-pitched snorting and whistling sound, while snatching rasping breaths.

'Excellent.' Fender straightened up. He glanced at Bozzer, who eyed him warily as he approached Maddie. 'Remind me of your travel plans,' he asked, cordially.

'I haven't thought that far ahead. I wondered if I should keep going for a while, work some stuff out.'

He nodded. 'Very wise. *After* this issue is resolved.'

Maddie stole a look at Rupert, still twitching by her feet. 'How much does he owe?'

'A substantial amount.'

'So what happens next?'

'You and I need to have a discussion about locating the missing Samsonite suitcase.'

'What if it stays missing?'

Fender scrutinised Maddie, taking his time before replying. 'That would be extremely unfortunate. I suggest we capitalise on my relatively good mood and arrive at a swift resolution.'

He turned to face Bozzer and offered his open palm. Bozzer hesitated before clasping his hand in Fender's firm, dry grip. 'A noble attempt at intervention, young sir. My apologies for robbing you of the satisfaction of striking your target. Perhaps you'd be good enough to plonk yourself down at the bar over there, and have a drink or two while Maddie helps to conclude a business matter.'

Bozzer withdrew from Fender's grasp and dropped his eyes to his hand, surprised to find himself clasping a ten dollar bill. He glanced at Maddie, then looked down at Rupert, still convulsing on the floor. He hesitated for a moment before he pocketed the note. 'Take it easy, Madge.' He opened his arms, inviting her into a friendly hug. 'I'll be waiting for you, to take those shots.'

She held him tightly for a brief moment before he eased back, smiling. Her hand found his, squeezing it as they parted. Bozzer winked cheekily at her, then he turned and withdrew to the bar's brightly lit serving area.

'Nuuu ... addie ...' Rupert inched his head off the floor, attempted to shake it, gurgling and grunting in frustration as he darted his eyes between Maddie and Fender.

Fender cast his eyes down, watching Rupert groan as he tried to wriggle his hands and feet. 'Madeline, do you wish to say anything to Rupert before we begin? Bearing in mind he's unable to respond intelligently for the next few minutes.'

'I can't, not yet. I'm too angry.'

'Very well.' Fender gestured with an open palm. 'Please, sit. There's much to discuss.' He guided Maddie back to the booth, then briefly returned his attention to Rupert. 'Pop yourself down over there, old son, when you're able.' Fender pointed to a vacant table and chairs, directly opposite him. 'Any more vulgarity and it's another zap from the Taser.' He waited until he saw the flicker of conformity in Rupert's eyes, then he turned towards the booth where Maddie had sat down and poured herself a cold beer. She hunched over on her elbows, arms positioned each side of her froth-filled glass. Fender stepped over Rupert and sat down opposite her.

'Ms Bryce, I have to leave shortly to attend to an urgent personal matter. Before I depart, I need your assistance to resolve this unfortunate situation.' Fender studied Maddie's pale complexion. 'Pursuing you has been relentless.' He picked up a menu from the table. 'Would you care for a bite to eat, while we discuss a suitable resolution?'

'I'm not sure I'm—' Maddie turned to glance over at Bozzer, who stood behind her at the bar. He raised his half-drunk glass of beer, his eyes lingering on her inquisitive gaze.

'Don't worry, your Australian friend can watch your back while we discuss some options.'

She blinked her eyes away, turning back to Fender. He held out a menu, smiling at her. 'Food first, for sustenance. Then the unsavoury second course. Okay?'

Maddie nodded vacantly. She dropped her eyes to the list of house specialities, a hollow, empty feeling creeping into her stomach.

Forty

Maddie stared at the steaming plate of lok lak and rice noodles, placed in front of her by a petite smiling waitress, who looked about thirteen.

'Not hungry?' said Fender.

'The opposite, actually. It's been a while since I've eaten.'

'Then please, tuck in.'

She pinched a clump of stir-fried beef between the chopsticks and popped it into her mouth.

'A whim. That's all it was?'

Maddie shrugged. 'That and Rupert draping himself over a prostitute on the last night of our holiday.'

Fender nodded, pausing to smile at the young waitress who placed a bowl of chicken lime soup in front of him. Maddie dropped her eyes, concentrating on her food. Fender watched her eat, then began on his own meal. 'The suitcase, Ms Bryce,' he said casually.

She looked up, shifted her gaze away from his. 'What about it?'

'Where is it?'

'I have no idea.'

'Poppycock.' Fender studied her with unblinking eyes. 'Who was the traveller you swapped the case with?'

Maddie absently plunged her chopsticks back into the lok lak. 'Someone I met …' She scooped a morsel of food into her mouth, chewing for a moment before she continued. 'At the hotel. They were heading home, didn't need it anymore.'

Fender drummed his fingers on the table. 'That doesn't sound plausible. Rucksacks are expensive and highly personal to traveller types.' He softened his tone. 'The truth please, Madeline. Or Rupert won't be able to thank you enough.'

Maddie swallowed, forcing a mouthful of noodles down. 'They needed the cash and I wanted an authentic travel experience.'

She watched him dab the side of his mouth with a napkin then fold it neatly, laying it on the table. 'I think you may have swapped the Samsonite earlier.' He watched her reaction.

'Why would I … *how* could I?'

'Perhaps for some of the reasons you've described. But let's set aside the why, or how, for a moment. I'm more interested in with *whom* did you swap?'

Maddie shifted in her seat, the chopsticks trembling in her fingers. Faint pink blotches began to creep up her neck as Fender's piercing stare bored into her. She clamped her hand around the glass and glugged back several mouthfuls of beer.

'All I want is the suitcase, Maddie. I'm not interested in bringing anyone else into harm's way. This person unwittingly has what Rupert's creditors want, the very same thing *I* need, to resolve this matter. So, once again—'

'I can't remember their name. It was a stressful time for me and—'

Fender laid his soup spoon beside his bowl and slipped his hand under the table. Maddie flinched at a muted gasp behind her, swiftly followed by a squeak of wood jolting on the floor and a heavy thud. She turned to see the bar's manager scurrying towards Rupert, lying twitching on the floor, his eyes bulging.

Fender casually looked up. 'It's okay, thank you. Our friend has had another seizure. He'll be okay in a few moments.'

Maddie turned and made eye contact with the bar manager, saw him straighten from stooping over Rupert, then retreat.

'I don't actually know how many hits of fifty thousand volts the human body can take in a short timeframe. Probably not that many. I'm not sure anyone's ever carried out a definitive experiment. Do you think we should console ourselves that we're advancing medical research, every time you evade my questions? Or shall we try again?'

'Her name's Liz. That's all I know,' Maddie blurted out.

Fender leaned in slightly. 'Better. But trust me, that's not *all* you know. While you're carefully considering your next answer, can I interest you in some more water?'

'More ... what?'

'Water, as in to drink. Rather than poured down your throat whilst tied to a chair with a cloth napkin held over your mouth – that's not really my cup of coconut juice.' His tone sharpened. 'Or would you prefer something stronger to loosen your tongue, before Rupert's London associates rip it out of your pretty pouty-mouth?'

'I'll stick with the beer thanks,' Maddie squeaked. She took a gulp of the cool frothy lager, then spoke quickly. 'I met Liz on the last night, at a beach bar. She found me hiding out in the ladies toilet.'

'After Rupert's fraternising with the local girl?'

'Yes. We went out for a girlie chat, had a few drinks. The next morning I saw Liz at the airport and something in me snapped. She looked so ... free. And I thought, what the hell.'

'So you swapped luggage?'

'Yes.'

'What's Liz's surname?'

'I don't know.'

'Nationality?'

'British.'

'Age?'

'Eighteen or nineteen.'

'Did you exchange any contact details?'

'Yes, she texted me. Before she got on the plane.'

Fender allowed the corners of his lips to curl into a faint smile. 'Excellent. One moment.' He slid out of his seat, strolled over to Rupert's table and returned with Maddie's iPhone. 'Please, show me.'

Maddie accepted the phone from him. She frowned as she tabbed through her messages menu. 'It's not here. Nothing is. I don't understand ... oh *crap*. I swapped my SIM for a local one, then flushed it down the loo.'

Fender strummed his fingers on the table. 'I hope you're not lying to me, Madeline.'

'I swear! I was being bold – symbolically erasing my old life.'

'What's your number?'

Maddie rattled it off, watching Fender tap the sequence into her phone's electronic keypad. After a moment, he retrieved his own ringing phone from his pocket. He glanced at the screen and raised an eyebrow. 'Different number, Thai area code. What made you decide to be bold?'

'Victoria. She gave me the new SIM. So I could reconnect, undetected by Rupert.'

'I see. That explains a few things.'

'Like what?'

'It's not important. You definitely disposed of your normal SIM?' He scrutinised her reaction.

'Erm ... yes, yes.'

'Did you back up your contacts anywhere – a cloud, for example?'

'Not since I've been in Thailand, no.'

Fender sat back, clicking his knuckles. 'Problem.'

'Why? Can't you—'

'Most likely Liz had a locally registered SIM. If I had the number, the network provider could match it with her passport, and I could trace her. Now however, your situation is somewhat protracted.'

'What does that mean, for me?'

Fender sighed. 'A simple case – pardon the pun – of seek and find, is now a significant problem for Rupert. Also for his parents, for you, and your mother and father. I doubt the London lot will be as cordial with them as I'm being with you.'

'My *parents?* What have they got to do with Rupert's financial problems?'

'Simply Rupert's connection to you. There's a debt to be repaid, and leverage must be applied – to anyone associated with him.'

'Why me, why them?'

'Because the suitcase – its contents, were in your care.'

'But I didn't know anything about that!'

'That may be, Ms Bryce. But it doesn't in any way absolve you of your responsibilities for the safe delivery of my client's product—'

'You mean *heroin.*'

'If you want to be crass, yes. Heroin.'

Maddie dropped her head into her hands. She scrunched handfuls of hair, then trailed the strands through her fingers. 'So what happens now?' she mumbled.

'Tracking down your traveller friend, Liz, isn't problematic in itself once we've identified the airline and obtained their passenger manifest. Her home will be watched. Access will need to be gained, which is risky because if the suitcase is seen being removed, awkward questions might be asked. Questions such as: what's the significance of that *particular* suitcase. There's the risk that the organisation's trafficking system could be jeopardised. In addition, what if, when Liz emptied her new suitcase, she discovered it weighs a bit more empty than she thinks it should? Has she already made this unusual fact known to someone in authority? That could mean her home is already under police surveillance. London may consider writing off the missing consignment when balanced against the probability of risk. In which case you and Rupert, *and* your respective families, will be assigned the debt. Someone has to pay.'

Maddie shook her head, scrunched her hair tightly in her hands. 'But why me, *my* family? And what about Liz? She's done nothing wrong. This is Rupert's bloody mess!'

'Ah, but the case was in your—'

'I didn't know what it contained!'

'So you've already said.' Fender reached into his compact daypack and retrieved an identical ankle bracelet to the device he'd installed on Rupert. 'This, Ms Bryce is a tracker, much like those used on convicted criminals. You will wear this whilst you and your fiancé accompany me back to the United Kingdom. London will most likely begin asset-stripping to reclaim the value of their lost product, starting with—'

'How much does he owe?'

Fender held Maddie's glare for a moment before he glanced down at the contents of her purse, spread out on the table between them. 'Considerably more than pocket change, Ms Bryce. Unless you have something more ... concrete, it's time to go home. Your left leg, please.' Fender reached out for the ankle bracelet.

'Wait. How *much?*'

'How much do you have?'

'Probably not enough, readily available. But ... what if I act as guarantor?'

'You, personally?'

'Yes.'

'Do you have the means?'

'I might.'

Fender's eyes narrowed. 'Why would you do that?'

'Because I don't want to go back. I want to carry on travelling, to be ... free.'

'You can't be free if you're vouching for Rupert's debt. There are no risk-free transactions in this life, Ms Bryce. Nothing is certain, other than birth, death and sadness.'

'I disagree. Money can't buy happiness, I've learned that much. But out here, travelling, I have a reason to get excited, and scared, every day. About life. *My* life.'

'I doubt London will be interested in—'

'I own a property.' Maddie half-turned, darted her eyes over at Rupert. She watched him hunch up off the floor, using the chair to steady himself. He slumped down at the nearby table, panting from the exertion. 'When Stefan – my previous boyfriend – died, he was … *is* special to me. He lived his life literally on the edge, every time he got on his motorcycle to race. Most of his estate is left in a trust, for his daughter.' Maddie faltered. She clenched her jaw, wiped tears from her eyes. 'It was a difficult time, for me. There was a pay-out, from a life insurance policy. Rupert didn't know. He assumed most of Stefan's estate went into the trust fund I set up, after he died.'

'Who was the beneficiary of the trust fund?'

'My … *our* daughter. She was born the day Stefan died.'

'I'm sorry for your loss.'

Maddie dabbed more tears with a Kleenex. She shook her head, then stared vacantly into the distance. 'Rupert helped me through that awful time. He was so supportive, back then. We began to grow close. But I knew how he yearned for more, more material wealth. So I protected the insurance pay-out by buying a flat, which I rented out. It was a comfort blanket, I suppose. The extra income allowed me to overspend, far in excess of my job's salary. Pretty clothes, designer labels … But the capital is all still there, the property is mortgage free.'

Fender folded his arms and sat back. He allowed his scrutiny to wander away from Maddie. His gaze settled on Rupert, slumped over the nearby table. 'That's an interesting proposition, Ms Bryce. I'll need to relay your offer on. Your daughter … you had her adopted?'

Maddie nodded. More tears trickled down her cheeks.

'I apologise for having to ask such an indelicate question, but do you have any access to the trust's funds?'

'No. A friend recommended a solicitor. He's the trustee. The fund pays out in increments, when she's old enough. It's all for her, to help make something of her life.'

'What was Rupert's reaction to the trust fund?'

'He didn't understand, at first. It was a substantial sum … which is why I kept the life insurance pay-out from him.'

Fender nodded. When he spoke, his tone had softened. 'May I ask where the property is, what it might be worth?'

'It's a two-bedroom first floor flat in Notting Hill. Six and a half years ago I paid four hundred and seventy-five thousand for it. Prices have been going up ever since. You do the maths.'

Fender's eyes narrowed. 'Rest assured, Ms Bryce, I will. The full address, please. Then you can finish your meal in peace. I need to make some phone calls.'

*

Maddie looked over at the entrance to the bar, where Fender had been slowly pacing back and forth for the last twenty minutes, embroiled in a series of intense telephone conversations. She slowly rotated in her seat, making eye contact with Bozzer. He raised his glass of beer and winked at her. Maddie attempted a weak smile, then faced forwards, aware of Fender finishing his latest call. She watched him settle into the seat opposite, her heart racing.

'Congratulations Ms Bryce, you have a deal. Subject to certain conditions, naturally. The relevant documentation is being drawn up. It will be emailed to an attorney's office here in Phnom Penh. You will sign over the deeds to your Notting Hill property. When the Samsonite case is located and successfully retrieved, ownership of the property will revert back to you.'

'So Rupert is free of the debt, and me too?'

'So long as he maintains radio silence about his adventures in Thailand, and avoids racking up any more debts with my client.'

Maddie took a deep breath, then lifted her eyes to meet Fender's. 'How soon can I move on?'

Fender glanced at his watch. 'In around six hours.' He slid a business card with a neatly printed email and phone number across the table, then flipped it over, revealing a handwritten address on the back. 'You will meet me here, at midday. The transfer of ownership will be signed and witnessed, after which you'll be free to go.' Fender took a sip of water, then picked up the ankle bracelet. 'Until then, your left leg, please.'

Maddie frowned. 'What for? I thought—'

'Insurance. I'll release it when we meet later today. If you fail to show up, attempt to tamper with the device, or stray more than ten blocks from our current location, the Taser will—'

'Zap me, like Rupert.'

'Exactly.' Fender patted the side of his seat.

Maddie lifted her left leg and watched him slip the bracelet around her ankle.

Fender tabbed commands into his smartphone, then waited for a series of electronic beeps. 'That's you activated. You've got approximately six hours of free time. Spend it wisely, be here at noon.'

Fender tapped his sinewy finger on the business card. 'Or else, suffer the consequences.' He slipped out of the booth and strolled over to Rupert's table.

Maddie watched Fender head for the door, Rupert hobbling along behind.

'You look like you could use some air.'

Maddie glanced up at Bozzer. She nodded. 'And a change of scenery.'

'Come on, you can bring your electronic friend with you.'

She frowned, then followed his gaze down to her ankle, where a green LED silently flashed on the black plastic bracelet. 'Oh, yeah. Sure you want to mix with the criminal fraternity?' she muttered.

'Hey, most of my family are dodgy descendants. You're with a kindred spirit.'

Forty-One

Bozzer and Maddie walked away from the bar's neon intensity, distancing themselves from night crawlers and sleazy money. The sound of their feet scuffing the pavement quickly became absorbed by scooters zipping by, their tinny engines whirling. Headlights drifted over sleeping tuk-tuk drivers, slumped across their carriages in shadowy side streets, their bare feet poking out beneath rain curtains. A thin, patchy-furred dog sloped past, eyeing them hopefully, his tongue lolling. A sallow man in his thirties cycled by, his knees rotating sedately, dragging a glass-fronted street food trailer.

They walked on, past a shopkeeper sweeping dust and litter across uneven, broken paving slabs. Crossing the main road was easy without having to dash for an impossible gap in the traffic, as only few vehicles trundled past. Walking under the row of palm trees evenly spaced across the promenade, the wide glassy river beckoned, fifty feet below. The vaguest hint of a lighter shade of black teased the horizon at the far edge of the sky, drawing the first light of dawn ever closer.

Shh-clitch.

Memory Card 3. Pic 563
'Sunrise over the Tonle Sap River, the fresh wooziness of a new day breaking with barely a shiver. Black sky blending into deep inky blue, promises of new adventures to carry us through. Onwards into the unknown, time soon to go it alone ...'

'Won't be long now,' Bozzer said, lowering the camera, quickly lifting it up again as he spotted an opportunity, down at the water's edge.

Shh-clitch.

Memory Card 3. Pic 564
'He casts the weighted line aloft over the river's murky water, hoping for his breakfast perhaps, or to catch lunch for him and his daughter. Waiting, watching, praying ... how much is at stake? Fishing for fun

incomprehensible to people here, no choice for them of a nice juicy steak.'

Maddie turned away from the river, watching him review the photograph on the camera's small screen. 'You have an elegance with words.'

'Cheers. Not bad for a ball-and-chain-by-birth bloke, eh?'

'Not half bad.' Maddie sat down on the esplanade wall and swung her legs over the top of the long concrete slope, which led down to the river's edge. She pushed her hands behind her, fingers draped over the curved edge of the stone, leaning back against her arms.

'Turn your head towards me, just a little …' He raised the camera. 'There, perfect—'

Shh-clitch.

Memory Card 3. Pic 566
'Material girl no longer, this born-again traveller is mentally much stronger. Her silhouette framed against the backdrop of Phnom Penh, she looks like she's comfortable here, has reached a state of Zen. Primed now to immerse herself in life's joy, despite the illusion she maintains, of acting so coy. Rise up Princess, spread those wings and soar, the winds of Mother Nature's optimism will carry you through the uncertainty of that self-imposed locked door.'

'Wow, where did that come from?' She craned her neck around to evaluate his expression.

'From you,' he said quietly, stepping over the wall to sit down beside her. He scanned the wide expanse of river, speckled with sporadic lights from small wooden boats, wallowing in the hazy hint of dawn. 'We'd never have seen this, from the hotel room.'

'No … thank you.'

'For being a pain in the arse?'

'Partly. But also for getting me out here.'

He lit a roll-up, offered it to her.

'I shouldn't, but … why not.'

They shared the smoking ritual, looking out over the vast ebbing river. She scanned the dock cranes gradually emerging from the shadows on the far bank, the first sign of light lifting the gloom, breathing life and purpose into the waterfront.

I think ... I did the best I could, little one ...

'Last night, you asked me something ...' she began, her voice trailing off.

'Something inappropriate, probably.'

She stole a look at him – saw him still scanning the horizon. She glanced away again, out over the river.

... under the circumstances.

Her gaze lingered there, before she frowned and drew back, refocusing on the plastic clasp around her ankle, the green LED blinking. 'Yes, and perhaps ... not. It was about travelling with you, to South America.'

Meanwhile, onwards.

His gentle nod drew her gaze back, away from the constraints of the past. This time she lingered a little longer on his twinkling blue eyes.

'Yeah, I remember.'

'How would it work ... hypothetically.'

He turned to face her, an amused expression twitching across his lips. 'You're asking how ... despite running into your bloke and the spooky dude. Something *has* changed.'

'Maybe.'

He nodded, accepted the roll-up from her, drawing thoughtfully on it. 'It would work if you're prepared to shed your shackles and have no expectations of anything at all. I'm talking about the country, the people *and* your new travel mate. You'd need only bring along an open mind and a sense of adventure. If you can do that, then I guarantee you'll gain a new life experience ... will have a different outlook. Who knows, we might even laugh a little along the way.'

Maddie nodded at his lopsided smile. She turned away to follow his stare as the first glimmers of daylight stretched out between the crane and the bridge structure of a container ship in dock, lying against the dark side of the river. 'How would it work, on a day-to-day basis – travelling together?'

'You want to hear about nuts and bolts?'

She nodded.

'We'd split everything down the middle, just like you would with a pal. It's cheaper travelling that way, and more fun. Someone to bounce ideas off, share the journey. There's also the probability that we'd not stay strangers ...'

'Friends?'

'Friends, foes, mates, rivals, lovers ... it's unpredictable, an unknown. Fun and scary, all rolled into one.' He exhaled smoke, passing the rollie back to her. 'Given recent events, perhaps not quite the jump for you it might have been ...'

'True. Or, we'll merely remain acquaintances, if we go our separate ways in a few hours. After ...' She lifted up her left leg, twisted her foot left, then right.

He chuckled, then looked up, studying the glowing orange, yellow and red colours blending together, pushing the dark blue sky away, giving way to aqua and turquoise higher overhead. 'That too, is a possibility. It's all up for grabs. But before you consider anything, a little while ago you asked me a question.'

'I did?' She inhaled smoke, handed the ciggie back to him.

'Yup. You asked *me*, why.' He turned to face her.

'Yeah ... I was unsure, I guess. Still am. I suppose what I really meant, is why me?'

Bozzer took a last drag on the roll-up and stubbed it out. He took his time before replying.

'*You*, because you're not phony, like many of the people out here, supposedly travelling. You're interesting, Madge, and quirky, in a spoilt-but-trying-to-break-free, unashamedly British middle class kind of way. Back at the bar, you proved that. Beyond that sheen, there's a depth to you, a deep-rooted honesty, if you'd only trust someone enough to show them more. I genuinely think you'd grow to enjoy immersing yourself in this alternative life.'

Before she could reply, he added 'When I disappeared to get my camera's memory cards from Jody, I didn't just come back to take photos of Angkor Wat, although that was important to me. I wanted to meet up with you again, try to get to know you better. Travelling together, you'd see more of my unpredictable, *live wire* personality, and what lies beneath it. And I'd understand more about who you are. Who you *were*. I like being around interesting people, and I think you'd grow into a fun travel buddy.'

They sat in silence, watching the sun peep over the horizon, a quarter of its glowing sphere visible now, shimmering light and colour across the river.

'Oh,' she said eventually. 'I thought you might be on Charlie's wavelength.'

'Hustling you?'

'Mmm …'

He grinned, a cheeky, mischievous glint in his eye. 'What makes you so sure I'm not?'

'True. Guess you never can tell with people, what their agenda might be. So Barry, am I a cash cow for your travel fund?'

'An older woman for me to use and abuse?' He held up his foot. 'Okay, you got me. Slap on the ankle cuff.'

She searched his twinkling eyes for sincerity. 'Nah, you're too wrapped up in your creativity, gathering material for your book.'

'It's true. I do sleep with a zoom lens in my PJs.'

She grinned and looked away towards the sun, now almost a full sphere above the river's industrial far bank. Sunlight pushed the deep blue higher, brightening their panoramic view.

'Of course, there's the possibility that *you're* the hustler.'

'What, lil ol' me?'

'Hey, you're wearing the jailbird tag.'

'Yeah. Trouble, with a capital T. That's me.'

They sat there for several minutes, both smiling, watching the sky change colour.

Onwards. Upwards. Outwards … it's about time.

'Okay,' she said finally, tucking her hair behind her ears, grinning.

'Okay, meaning …?'

'Meaning okay, yeah. What the hell. Let's give it a go.'

He shifted around and offered his hand. 'Travel mates?'

She hesitated for a second, then rotated fully, facing him. She reached out, clasping his hand, holding his gaze.

'Agreed. Travel mates.'

Barry squeezed her hand a tiny bit more. 'Nice one. Now hand over the family silver!' He kept a straight face, his eyes locked on hers.

She flinched, tried to pull her hand back, her convivial expression hardening. Instead of retreating further, she leant forwards and stared deeply into his eyes, squeezing his hand even tighter. 'Up yours, Aussie asshole. Hand over all your valuables!'

Bozzer's face relaxed. He beamed, releasing her grip. 'We're gonna get along just fine.' He tightened his hand into a fist, held it up. She scrunched her fingers into a ball and knocked her knuckles against his.

'Boom!' they said in unison.

'So, travel mate, tell me more about the plan – after you leave Cambodia.'

'After *we* fly out,' he corrected her.

'Of course, still getting my head around it.'

'After you shed your former life of grime, you can look forward to a shitty two days spent flying, waiting, flying and waiting, getting more knackered and irritable, before we get to Lima, Peru. From there – after a few days recovering – we hit the road. So much to see. The Nazca Lines, Sacred Valley, Arequipa ... After a few weeks we get to Cusco. The altitude is gonna hit us hard, so we spend some time acclimatising, do a bit of sightseeing. Then we start the Inca Trail. Four days hiking with a group gets us to the lost city of Machu Picchu, where a glorious photographic Shangri-La awaits. From there, we catch the train back to Cusco and make our way overland into Bolivia, taking in Puno and Lake Titicaca. Then it's a short flight into the jungle town of Rurrenabaque, which is on the Beni River. After that, we fly back to Bolivia's capital, La Paz, and catch a flight to the spectacular Iguazu Waterfalls – the Argentinean side, where my brother's getting married. We party hard at the reception, relax over Christmas, then celebrate New Year in Buenos Aires. That done, the next beautiful, unwritten chapter awaits. In whatever direction it takes me, you, or possibly – in whatever arrangement that presents itself – maybe even *us* ...'

'There's quite a few variables in that itinerary.'

'Yeah. Life wouldn't be surprising and fun if there wasn't.'

'What time does your flight leave tomorrow?' She frowned and checked her watch. 'I mean, today.'

'Ten-thirty tonight.'

'Okay. I'd best get a plane ticket sorted, if there's a spare seat. No ticket means no travel buddy, so we'd best get going. We've got a busy day ahead.' Maddie smiled at him and stood up. 'I'm ready.'

Forty-Two

Maddie and Bozzer drew up outside a plush-looking smoked glass shopfront, embossed with its name in ornate gold lettering on a polished black marble plaque.

'It's the most upmarket joint we've seen so far,' said Bozzer, peering at the shiny stainless steel watches in the window display.

'Let's give it a whirl.'

The smartly dressed jeweller peered through an eye magnifier, studying Maddie's pearl earrings.

'This is where he says they're fakes,' she whispered, raising her eyebrows at Bozzer. 'Rupert told me they were Akoya pearls, the best in the world.'

'The studs are indeed gold,' said the elderly jeweller, in a soothing, barely accented voice. 'But the pearls are freshwater, not very valuable. The diamonds too are of inferior quality.'

'Great, thanks Rupert,' Maddie murmured, adding 'Do you have a value in mind?'

'Less, unfortunately, than you would probably like,' he said, lifting his head and placing the magnifier down on the velvet cloth next to the earrings. 'Thirty dollars.'

'One hundred,' said Barry, returning the jeweller's smile.

'Too much. No Akoya, see …' The jeweller turned and reached into a drawer, withdrawing a magnifying glass. 'Imperfections. They are not matching.'

Maddie leaned over the counter, studying the pearls. 'Oh, I see.' She straightened up.

'The most I could offer would be forty dollars.'

'Sixty dollars, or we'll ask at Colombo, a few shops down,' said Bozzer, still smiling.

'Okay, you get good price. Sixty dollars.'

Barry leant his elbows on the counter and turned to Maddie. 'You happy with that?'

She shrugged. 'They're only worth the happiness they bring. But, I know Rupert, he wouldn't have duped me.'

'Which means …?' asked Bozzer.

'They're worth more. I can't let them go for sixty dollars. The extra cash could really make a difference.' She glanced up at the jeweller and collected her earrings off the counter. 'Thank you. I've decided not to sell them.'

Bozzer opened the shop door for Maddie, then followed her out onto the street. 'Travel agent, next, then the business stuff with your ex, and the gizmo goon?'

'Soon. But first, something else. There's a charity, for Cambodian kids. They have an office here in Phnom Penh, I looked them up.'

'Is that where the earrings are going?'

She nodded. 'Follow me for a long overdue dollop of spoilt-middle-class humility.'

*

Maddie squinted into the bright sunlight outside the charity café and slipped her sunglasses on.

'Happy now?' asked Bozzer, watching her tired puffy eyes disappear behind the dark lenses.

She nodded. 'I'm sure they'll be able to negotiate a better price here than we can. Meanwhile I'm two pearl earrings worth of servitude lighter. Excess baggage – jettisoned.'

'Almost.'

Maddie glanced at him and nodded, her smile fading. 'Yup. Almost.'

Bozzer offered her his smouldering roll-up.

'No thanks.'

He shrugged. 'Travel agent next?'

'Yep, I reckon.'

Bozzer fished his mobile phone out of a pocket and began searching through the list of options.

'Do me a favour … pinch me.'

He glanced up at her. 'Not convinced this is real?'

'Uh-huh.'

Bozzer whipped his hand out.

'Yeow!' Maddie leapt away from him, rubbing her bottom. 'I said pinch, not paralyse, you bloody wombat!' she yelped, smacking his knuckles.

'Hey, just doing as you asked, Princess. You want a tickle from the Taser instead? Wait till the hangover really kicks in and you wake up realising you're stuck with a strange, beer-drinking, farting, Aussie bloke with fag breath. Reality is a sore sight first thing in the morning.' He offered his mobile phone. 'There's three travel agents, half a block apart.'

*

Maddie glanced away from Kaliyan, the travel agent sat across the desk from them who was typing on a keyboard, and asked Bozzer 'What about a ticket for the Inca Trail?'

'Already emailed the company. It's a quieter time of year and a mate of a Facebook friend is working in their office. I reckon she'll be able to swing it. Even if she has to bump someone onto another tour operator.'

'You've thought of everything. When did you send the email?'

Bozzer met her gaze. His eyes crinkled as he broke into a sheepish smile. 'I asked them to hold me a spare ticket, two weeks ago. Just in case Jody decided to come with me.'

'So I'm second best, eh?'

'I emailed my mate's buddy again last night, if that makes you feel any better.'

'There's one spare seat left on that flight,' said Kaliyan, looking up from her computer screen.

Maddie continued to stare at Bozzer. 'This feels a bit like I'm walking in her shadow.'

Bozzer glanced at Kaliyan. 'Sorry, one moment please.' He turned back to Maddie. 'Nah, Jody is permanently stuck in the dark. You're stepping into the light, don't you see – striking out into the unknown. For the adventure, remember?'

She held his gaze, searching the light dancing in his eyes. 'Don't bullshit me.'

'I'm not. Let go, live a little.' Bozzer slipped his hand into hers, gently squeezing it.

Maddie felt her heart rate jolting up twenty beats. She wrapped her fingers around his, caught a breath, then wrenched her eyes away, turning back to Kaliyan. 'Thank you, I'll take it.'

'Do you have a credit or debit card?'

She nodded. Bozzer released her hand, still tingling, allowing her to retrieve her purse and pass a credit card across the desk. Maddie held her palm out flat, her fingers trembling. 'That's what stepping into the light really looks like,' she said quietly, gazing into his eyes, daring herself not to look away.

'Those nervous twinges are a good thing. You're challenging yourself, getting out of your comfort zone.'

Kaliyan pushed Maddie's card into the electronic reader and punched in the flight cost, waiting for the transaction to process. An electronic message alert drew her attention to her smartphone, on the desk beside her. She glanced at her two customers, noticed their hands intertwined and hypnotic eye contact. Then she glanced at the card reader's 'connecting' status. Kaliyan picked up her phone, scanning the Facebook notification. 'You are newly together?' she asked.

Maddie glanced at Kaliyan and blushed, withdrawing her hand from Bozzer's. 'Sort of. We're—'

'Travel mates.'

Kaliyan nodded. 'Ah. You are like the same-name eBay people, travelling to South America?' She showed them her phone's screen. 'It is a strange way to meet, yes?'

Bozzer leant over the desk and studied the Facebook discussion thread.

'Nearly a million likes and thirteen thousand comments,' said Kaliyan.

'Hot discussion topic,' agreed Bozzer.

'It is unusual, their story—' An electronic alarm from the card reader diverted Kaliyan's attention. She peered at the small screen and frowned. 'I am sorry. This card will not process payment. Do you have another?'

Maddie stared at Kaliyan, frowning. 'Oh, that's odd. Try this one.' She swapped the offending card for another from her purse.

'Maybe it's expired, or your ex cancelled it?' suggested Bozzer.

Maddie studied the rejected card. 'It's still in date.' Her frown deepened as Kaliyan shook her head and passed credit card number two back to her. 'You're sure? That's really weird. They should both be okay.' She handed Kaliyan her last card.

'Maybe your fiancé is trying to make a point—'

Maddie turned to Bozzer. 'He can't, they're all in my name.'

'Or perhaps, more likely, Charlie and Victoria.'

'How could they?'

Kaliyan shook her head and pulled the card from the payment machine and placed it on the desk in front of Maddie. 'I'm sorry, this one has been rejected too.'

Bozzer studied her confused expression. 'Did you leave your purse in the room? Did Charlie have access to it?'

'How could he? I've never shared a room, or anything else, with him,' she said sharply.

'Victoria then. She stole the earrings, so it's likely—'

'But how?'

'I reckon she photographed the cards. They could have used the numbers online, or over the phone, even had duplicates made. I heard a rumour about a scam like that, but thought it was to do with dodgy hotels, which is why I pay for most stuff in cash. Maybe it's not as bad as it seems. Your bank probably got wind of some dodgy transactions and put a stop on the cards before …' Bozzer turned and addressed Kaliyan. 'Can you tell if the cards have been stopped by the bank, or if funds are overdrawn?'

'I'm sorry sir, I don't know why they've been rejected. Please contact your bank. Do you have any other way of paying for the ticket?'

Maddie opened the sections of her purse, thumbed through the dollar bills and Cambodian Riel. She shook her head. 'I've not got much on me. There's more in the room, but it still won't be enough … oh no.'

'What?'

'My reserve cash was in the other boot. If Victoria found the earrings there, then—'

'She probably pinched the cash at the same time.'

'Bitch!'

'Wish I'd known. I could have got it back.'

Maddie clenched her jaw, scrunched her hair in her hands. 'I need to call the bank, sort this out—'

'Wait. There's only one ticket left. Let's book it. You can pay me back when your finances are sorted.'

'Seriously?'

Bozzer shrugged. 'So long as you're not scamming me.' He lifted up his shirt and unclipped his money belt, pulling the pouch out from beneath his waistband. He unzipped a compartment and handed over his credit card. Kaliyan began the payment authorisation procedure.

'I'll pay you back as soon as—'

'That's gone through, thank you sir.' Kaliyan handed Bozzer's card back to him. He smiled his thanks and turned to Maddie, reaching out to squeeze her hand.

'I don't have to pay the balance for a while. If you're gonna split, just make sure you stick around long enough to settle up.'

Maddie nodded, distracted by Kaliyan printing off and collating the flight documentation.

'Thanks, I owe you.'

'No you don't. That's what *real* travel mates are for.'

*

Maddie let the door to the phone booth swing shut behind her. She watched the teenage boy scribble an amount on a pad and show her the figure. Then she counted out six dollars. Maddie turned to Bozzer, who stood leaning against the flimsy partition, his arms folded.

'They maxed out one credit card and were racking up a bill with the other one at an electronics shop in Battambang. The guy in the bank's fraud department told me they've seen this a few times. The thieves have a dodgy deal with an apparently legitimate shop, which processes fictitious purchases on the cloned card. They hit my debit card too. There's a stop on my accounts, I have no access to any cash. But the bank's looking at unfreezing them, so I should be able to pay you back soon. Hope that's okay.'

Bozzer nodded.

'Thanks.' Maddie fanned through the remaining cash in her wallet. 'Which leaves me with around sixty-five dollars until this gets sorted out. The bank's arranging an emergency transfer which I can draw on in Lima.'

Bozzer held the door open for her, following her out of the dim internet shop. They both blinked in bright light, the traffic now rumbling by in a constant noisy, grimy, nose-to-bumper crawl.

'Guess that makes us partners. For a while, anyways,' he said, opening his tobacco tin.

'Guess so. You still okay travelling with me now I'm—'

'A risky prospect?'

'I'm still good for the money. Guide's honour.'

'We'll see …'

Maddie stifled a yawn and glanced at her watch. 'What time's check-in?'

'Eight-thirty. Allowing for the tuk-tuk journey, we need to be on our way at six.'

'Which means there'll be a chance to catch up on some sleep.'

He nodded, piggybacking her next yawn, stretching his arms above his head. 'Yeah. We'll head back to the hotel after your paperwork pow-wow, get our heads down. You ready for this?'

'No, but it's got to be done.' Maddie checked the time, then took a deep breath and walked across the road, onto the shaded part of the pavement. She homed in on a polished brass sign screwed to the centre of a glossy black door, which proclaimed: Khmerdor & Sinn Associates.

Bozzer smirked. '*Sinn*. Ironic name for an attorney.'

'Fitting though, for Rupert.'

'Yeah, figures. Ready?' Bozzer's finger hovered over the bell-push.

'No, but …'

'I'll be waiting over there, at the café. Take as long as you need.'

'You're not coming in?'

'I will if you want me to, but significant stuff is best faced alone. It'll make you stronger, better prepared.' Bozzer pressed the bell-push.

Maddie stared at him for a moment. 'Okay. I'll be as quick as I can.'

Behind the door, footsteps approached. It swung open, revealing Fender. 'Madeline, perfect timing. Please come in. I won't detain you any longer than necessary.' Fender glanced at Bozzer as Maddie slipped past him. The door closed with a clunk behind her.

Forty-Three

Maddie trudged up the stairs behind Fender's desert boots. She emerged into a bright room overlooking the street. It had a mosaic tiled floor in a faded cream, caramel and brown cube pattern that looked like endless steps, going either up or down.

'Ms Bryce, this is Mr Saru Khmerdor, attorney in law. And Rupert, of course.'

A smiling Cambodian gentleman in his early sixties stepped around his large teak desk, intricately engraved around the sides with the imposing towers of Angkor Wat. He had black hair, a short stocky frame and inquisitive eyes.

'You are fearless and wise, Ms Bryce. I am Saru and I'm honoured to preside over this formality.' He extended his hand, which Maddie shook briefly.

'I think you mean naïve, Mr Khmerdor. But I appreciate your sentiment.' She turned towards Rupert, stood in the corner of the office with his hands in his pockets, peering out of the window.

'Short chap, isn't he. I thought the stereotypical Aussie was a tall, chiselled beach-bum – six foot plus.'

'Height and stature rarely equal the same thing.' Maddie arched an eyebrow as Rupert glanced over at her, quickly dropping his eyes away.

She turned towards Fender as he cleared his throat.

'Time is pressing. Shall we begin?'

Saru picked up the document lying on top of his desk. 'This, Ms Bryce, is a deed of trust. It changes legal ownership of a property when security is required, for example when taking out a loan. Sometimes for a temporary period, occasionally irreversibly. In legal language, it states that your property in the London suburb of Notting Hill is to be held as collateral against your fiancé's debt. This is detailed as an unpaid loan in the sum of nine hundred and seventy-five thousand pounds, to Owen Goodall Holdings. The amount being the approximate value of a certain item belonging to Rupert's creditors. If and when this item is surrendered, your property will be returned to you.'

'You seriously expect me to believe there's honour amongst—' Maddie shot a look at Saru Khmerdor, then Fender.

'You may speak plainly, Ms Bryce. Mr Khmerdor's services and discretion have been secured.'

Maddie shook her head. 'We all know who they really are – London. If I get the flat back, it's a bonus.'

'Meaning you've already written it off emotionally, in order to walk away.'

'More or less.'

'I understand. But to clarify, this deed of trust is a loan agreement. It's between you and my client, certainly, but I've organised it impartially, in good faith. And I am a man of honour. The dubious circles that I appear to service notwithstanding.'

Maddie held Fender's unblinking gaze. 'What about Liz?'

'What about her?'

'She's an innocent bystander. I need your assurance that she won't be dragged into any of this.'

'Your friend will be untroubled by our business arrangement.'

Maddie folded her arms. 'Unless her home is broken into, or the police arrest her because of what they find in that suitcase.'

'Regardless, she won't be harmed in any way – physically, emotionally or financially.'

'And I'm supposed to take you at your word?'

'Of course. Integrity still exists, even in my world.'

'I don't know you. I need more.' Maddie thought for a moment. 'Your passport, show it to me.'

'It's with the hotel.'

'Driving licence, then.'

'For collateral?' Fender reached into his pocket, withdrew his photo card licence and offered it to Maddie.

'In a way.' She held up her iPhone. 'It's a shutter-stutter thing.'

Shh-clitch.

'Thanks.' She handed the ID back to him. 'Just in case anything *unsavoury* happens to Liz.'

Fender nodded and replaced the licence in his wallet. 'You also have my number logged on your mobile phone. Make sure you save it.

I'm a useful contact to have.' He turned away from her. 'Mr Khmerdor, please continue.'

'This document has been prepared in Great Britain, according to your laws. It was sent to me merely to present to you and formally witness your signature.' Saru thumbed through the top sheets and located a paragraph in the text. 'Here are the property details and conditions of settlement. Please read them carefully.' He handed Maddie the stapled pages and gestured to a leather chair beside his desk. 'Rest, please, while you study the document.'

Maddie sat down and began reading, aware of Fender leaving her side to join Rupert by the window.

'What about the rental income?' she asked, without looking up.

'In the short term you can continue to benefit from it, as per your existing tenancy agreement. Save any surplus wisely, would be my advice. Because if that suitcase isn't located after a reasonable period, London will undoubtedly foreclose the deal, and permanently relieve you of ownership,' said Fender.

'How long is a reasonable period?'

'Whatever my client deems it to be. You're lucky to benefit from the rental income until then.'

'So this is like a mortgage, in reverse?'

'In a way. Only Rupert's already had your lump sum – in that suitcase – which you gave away. My fee, by the way, has been added to Rupert's account.'

'Finally something he is responsible for in this whole sorry mess.' Maddie glanced over at Fender.

'Indeed.'

Rupert bristled. 'I'm sorry, alright. Look Maddie, this is—'

'All your fault.'

He dropped his eyes from her glare, shoulders slumping. 'Yes, okay! But if you'd not taken off, you'd never have known.' He sighed, folded his arms. 'I messed up. I'm sorry, truly. I tried to sort it out, wanted to make a fresh start. So we could build a life together.'

'By rewriting our marriage vows in your favour?'

'Maddie, come on. Be realistic. The …' he shot Fender a look, lowered his voice, 'physical side of things … you can't blame me for that.'

She bit her lip and looked away.

'Please Maddie, come home with me. I'll make it up to you. We can—'

'No. I can't, not now. You were good to me, when we lost Stefan. I'll always be grateful to you for that, but it's time to move on. For both of us.'

Rupert took a deep breath, contemplating. After a while he nodded slowly, met her flitting gaze. 'I'm grateful too, for your help sorting this mess out ... my mess. If there's anything I can do ...'

'There is, actually.'

They held eye contact.

'Before I sign, let me see your wallet.'

He frowned. 'Why?'

Maddie sat back in the chair and folded her arms. 'Do you want me to sign, or not?'

Rupert shook his head and fished his wallet out of his pocket. Fender intercepted and plucked the wallet from his fingers. He strolled over to Maddie and handed it to her.

'Still got some credit cards, I see. And a debit card. Which is more than me, right now.' She looked up from peering into the wallet's leather segments to meet Fender's inquisitive gaze. 'Victoria, probably. Sneaky cow. Some sort of duplicate bank-card scam. I could use some travel cash.'

She dropped her eyes and emptied the contents of the wallet into her lap. 'But this isn't enough. However ... that's a rather chunky-looking keepsake, Rupert.' Maddie held up her diamond engagement ring, studied the reflections of light in the stone as she rotated it. 'Beautiful. I reckon it's worth at least a few hundred. So, these cards ... they've got to be good for three hundred dollars each, right?' She tucked the currency into her pocket, then palmed the ring. 'You can have this back after going to the cash machine – I passed several on the way over. Off you go, time's a wasting.' She stuffed the cards inside the wallet, then tossed it back to him, smirking as he scrabbled to stop it heading out the window.

'I can't, I'll be overdrawn – will have to start paying interest straight away on the credit—'

'Hey, you think I give a shit about your interest?!' Maddie held up the ring. 'You can use this to cover it, when you get home. Nine hundred dollars please, in the next ten minutes. Or no deal.'

'Maddie, for Christ's sake!' Rupert turned to Fender. 'Tell her about the urgency!'

Fender smiled, his lips thin, expression cruel. 'You'd best toddle off, Rupert. You heard what your ex-fiancée said.'

'I thought you were in a hurry to get back to England – some sort of family crisis.'

'I am.'

'Unforeseen – a game changer, you called it.'

'So I d id. Quite possibly, even a regime changer.'

'Cryptic.'

'Necessarily so.'

'Then why the hell are you—'

'Take caution in your tone. My birthday cheerfulness and our pseudo-buddy banter were only valid for one day. Ms Bryce has made a fair request, given what she's about to surrender in order to save your arse. You've got eight and a half minutes left, chum, then my Taser trigger finger gets twitchy.'

Rupert stood there gaping for a moment. Then he stomped across the room and hurried down the stairs, slamming the front door as he left.

Fender glanced out of the window, the corners of his mouth creasing upwards. 'Bravo, Madeline. Adversity overcome. I do believe you're adapting to a life less plentiful.'

'I'll take that as a compliment.'

'Excellent. Exactly the spirit it was intended. Would you like some tea while you peruse the rest of the agreement?'

'Sure. It'll help to take the sour taste out of my mouth.'

Fender raised an eyebrow, his lips twitching with amusement. He turned to Saru, who withdrew, scurrying out of the room.

*

Bozzer glanced up from studying his camera's screen. He smiled at Maddie, stood resting her hands on the back of a chair opposite him.

'All sorted?'

'For now, yes.' She pulled out the chair and sank down onto it.

'You look like you need a drink.'

'Yeah. Later, maybe. Before that, got something for you …' She plunged her hand into a pocket, pulling out a bundle of notes which she counted out under the table. She folded roughly half the currency and pushed it back in her pocket, then passed the rest to him.

'What happened – you mug him?'

'I used what little leverage I had.'

'So it went okay?'

'Oh, you know ... a sordid drugs deal carried out in a business-like manner. But the deed is done. I managed to screw the cash out of Rupert, so that's half my flight reimbursed. I'll settle up the rest once we get to Lima.'

Bozzer shot her a look.

'Relax. Not *literally* screwed it out of him.'

Bozzer nodded. 'Okay, cheers.' He pocketed the cash and shifted his gaze away. They sat there for several minutes in silence.

'Want to talk about it?' he asked eventually.

Maddie slowly shook her head. 'Not really. The headlines are ... me and Rupert, we're done. He's putting my stuff into storage, I'll sort it out when I get back.' She took a deep breath and sighed. 'He was good to me, in the early days. I always felt I owed him for that. But thanks to Stefan looking after me, I've been able to repay him. I think it's helped me too, to let go.' She glanced at him and attempted a sheepish smile. 'The other stuff ... maybe some other time, when it's not so fresh.'

'Okay. Whenever you're ready.'

'Thanks.' Maddie stooped down, rubbed her bare ankle. 'This feels surreal.'

'Being released?'

'Being on my own.'

'Not entirely ...'

She straightened up and squinted into the sunshine at him. 'No. Mind if we get a move on? My head feels fuzzy.'

'Sure.' Bozzer stood up and rummaged through his pockets, depositing some coins on the table. Maddie followed him along the side street until it intersected with the main road running parallel to the promenade. 'I'll get us a ride,' he said, lifting his fingers to his mouth, preparing to whistle at the tuk-tuk drivers bunched together on the opposite side of the road.

'Actually, do you mind if we have a few more minutes? I'd like to sit and watch the river, let all this sink in before saying goodbye to ... well, almost everything I've ever known, actually.'

He grinned.

'What?'

'Don't look now, but the sleep-deprived and hungover ex-con is learning to chillax.'

She smiled. 'Maybe so.'

'Methinks you're starting to get into this traveller life … either that, or you really are hustling me – playing the long game.'

Maddie looked at him through tired eyes and managed a flicker of an amused smile before she shifted her gaze to the flow of traffic, scanning it for a gap.

'Time will tell, my reprobate travel buddy, time will – go, go, GO!' Maddie grabbed Bozzer's hand and yanked him across the road behind the back wheel of a scooter and the front of a taxi. They sprinted together, aiming for the wide-paved walkway on the far side.

'Woo-hoo!'

'Jesus, it's too early in the day for that sort of exercise,' he wheezed, staggering onto the safety of the wide pavement beside her.

'Over here, okay?' she asked, leading him by the hand to the low wall bordering the slope down to the river. 'Isn't this where we saw the sunrise from?'

'Pretty much.'

'Fantastic. I want to remember this spot, commit it to memory.'

'I can help with that.' Bozzer removed his camera from its bag. 'Are you ready to be immortalised?'

Shh-clitch.

Memory Card 3. Pic 582

'Metropolis metamorphosis. A city rising from the devastation of a generation, bustling again, full of hope and optimism. This spot by the river viewed from night through to noon, lending a changing perspective for this born-again traveller – not a moment too soon. Setting out to discover her place in the world, stake a claim on a beautiful life, so glad she didn't end up with someone else, as their unappreciated trouble 'n strife.'

Maddie stared at the camera lens from behind her sunglasses, following it down to where it dangled loose on its strap, by his side. She pushed her sunglasses up onto her head, settled her eyes on his.

'That was lovely, I think. Thank you.'

Bozzer blinked, breaking his trance. He looked away from her, busied himself with tucking his camera safely into the padded bag. *'De nada,'* he murmured, shifting his gaze back to her.

Across the wide pavement behind them, the traffic rumbled on relentlessly. Scooters weaved between cars, trucks carrying men in ragged, dusty construction clothing trundled past, tuk-tuks jostled, all vying for a better position. Pedestrians strolled by, overtaken by joggers. Tourists paused to take photographs. People continued with the obligations of their daily chores, oblivious to the stationary time bubble encompassing the two travellers, standing in the sunshine beside the river. Their world decelerating, movements slowing, a deep realisation of being right there, in *their* moment, that awareness engrossing, completely captivating.

Maddie's photo smile ebbed away, drawn to him, her heart's cadence building, a warm tingly sensation spiking deep in the pit of her stomach, prickling her palms, sparking irregular clutches of breath. Their eyes locked together, his no longer shifting away, hers gazing into a future that lacked doubt or apprehension.

Bozzer took a tentative step forwards, holding the intensity of their connection in his unwavering gaze. A boy on a skateboard rattled by, springing his foot down on the pavement, propelling the wheels faster, crouching his body, preparing to scoot his foot down to push again, his effortless mechanical movement sluggish, slowing, diminishing to half-speed, a quarter, an eighth, a sixteenth ... super slo-mo. Bozzer flicked his eyes left, transiting in the same super-slow motion as the skateboarder, gliding past, frame by frame. His eyes darted back to find hers. He took another step closer, the vehicle noise ebbing away around them, the traffic's busy resonance fading, all other peripheral movement slackening in tempo, ebbing to a complete stop.

Maddie eased her sunglasses off her head. She lowered her hand, fingers clutching the folded plastic. Bozzer took a final step to her. He reached out, his fingers slipping into her empty palm, goosebumps tingling her skin as he slid his other hand behind her back. She draped the sunglasses hand around his neck, leaning in. Their lips pressed together tenderly, torsos touching lightly, connecting, their skin warm, energised against each other.

He eased his head back an inch, his eyes searching hers, checking: *inappropriate contact, or mutual need?* She returned his searching gaze, hesitant, yet slowly leant in again, nuzzling her lips against his, the taste of coffee and alcohol and smoke lingering as they kissed. A long pause before easing apart, so slowly, still cheek to cheek, holding each other close. Outside their frozen time bubble, the boy skateboarding flicked his foot down, connecting with the paving slab, propelling the four small wheels onwards, their juddering, whirling sound resonating through the ground, vibrating up through Maddie's legs, as though she were a giant tuning fork. Their lips connected again. Energy surged, trembling through her skin, shimmering through their lips for one eternal minute of soul-searching solidarity. Gradually, they eased apart, leaving a delicious lingering tingle that lived on, long after the moment had passed.

'Mmm ... *Shutter Stutter* at its very best. Will that be in the book – that secret *je ne sais quoi?*'

'Yeah, absolutely, but it's gonna cost extra – you're a high flight-risk *in*mate.' Bozzer sniggered and drew back, a flush of red drawn up to his cheeks, mirroring Maddie's pink complexion.

'You're blushing.'

'It's the heat. Mad Aussie dogs and English girls, out in the midday sun.'

Maddie prodded his chest playfully, took half a step back, her hand dropping to her side, finding his, loitering there. Their fingers touched, caressed, entwined. Bozzer drew back, broke away from her touch to stifle a yawn. 'S'cuse me. Jeez, I'm whacked.'

'It's not the company, trust me,' she responded. 'Shall we take a walk back to the hotel?'

Bozzer nodded, blocking another yawn. 'Take me home and tuck me up in bed before I crash and burn right here ...'

Maddie slipped her hand back into his, leading him across the promenade towards the main road, heading for the shade of the buildings on the opposite side. She wore a permanent, aching grin, the sensation of his thumb skimming a circular motion on her palm sending tingles of excitement rocketing up her spine.

Forty-Four

Beep, beep, beep, BEEP, BEEP, BEEP!

Maddie jerked awake. She forced her sleepy-sore eyes open just enough to peer through the tiny forehead-scrunching gap and scan the room for the source of the noise.

'Arrrrggg!'

She forced her eyes open a little wider, rolled up onto her side and peered over the foot of the bed. Bozzer's sleeping bag jerked, his hands flapping as he desperately swept them across the floor.

'Where are you, noisy little sucker?!' His fingers clasped around his mobile phone. He held it close to his face, squinting at the bright screen, finally silencing the alarm.

'Fuck me, feels like I shut my eyes twenty seconds ago ...' he mumbled, his arm clamped across his eyes.

'I know. Horrible.'

Bozzer sat up and squinted at her, attempting a lopsided grin to match his bed hair, flattened on one side.

'Such a catch,' she remarked, 'you always look this good in the morning?'

'Technically, Princess Madge, it's early evening.'

'Last night, this afternoon ... whatever. Don't misinterpret this, but a few hours ago, when we came back here to sleep, well, I'm not saying anything was going to happen, but there was an offer for you not to sleep on the floor.'

Bozzer prised his eyes fully open and grinned. 'There was the possibility of jiggy jiggy, and I missed out?'

'No, simpleton. There was the offer of one side of a comfortable bed and your promise of no Mister Tickle wandering hands. But I came out of the bathroom and found you passed out on the floor.'

Bozzer laughed. 'Hey, get used to that. Start out the way we intend to carry on, right?' He stood up, flexing his hips to shuffle the sleeping bag down his body. He kicked it off his legs, stretched and groaned, then rubbed his face and shuffled into the bathroom.

'Cold water,' he mumbled, 'is what I need.'

'We'd better get going,' she called out over sounds of a tap running and sploshes of water. She pushed the covers off and swung her legs over the edge of the bed, dangling them into her shorts.

'Yeah, cool. Just putting in my false teeth.'

'Your what?!'

He poked his head sideways around the bathroom door, looking her up and down, catching her pulling the shorts up over her hips. She spun her back to him, yanking the zip up. 'Didn't I tell you? Same brand as the artificial hip and glass eye.'

She glanced over her shoulder, her face flushing a deep red. 'Don't do that!'

'What – joke?'

'Jump out! Being in close proximity with someone I don't know yet, it's unsettling.'

Bozzer's sideways head gravitated up and down the doorframe, like something out of a 1960s horror film. 'The first rule of travelling is don't be bashful,' he said, winking at her before pulling his head back and shutting the bathroom door.

'And the first rule of travelling with me, is – be respectful!'

'Yeah, see that's where the problem lies ...' he mumbled from behind the door, 'you're travelling with a S'tralian – it ain't gonna happen.'

*

Maddie clasped her hands together, then rubbed her tingling palms on her shorts. 'This is kinda scary,' she murmured, dragging her rucksack forwards a couple of paces, closing the gap behind the back of the queue.

'Nah, it only feels that way because you're with me. I have that effect on helpless posh English girls.'

'I, matey, am not helpless.'

'Foolish, then, travelling with me.'

'Whatever it is, it beats chauvinistic matrimony.'

'That really where your old life was going?'

'Heading that way ...'

He nodded, thought on this for a moment. 'So we agree to a banish-the-boredom treaty. Whatever this is, between us, wherever it goes –

develops, fizzles out, whatever – we agree that the moment one of us gets bored, we call it.'

Maddie held eye contact with him.

'What?'

'Just making sure you're being straight.'

'Hey, I'll always be straight with you. This is my natural happy-snappy-*happy* state.'

'Mmm.'

They shuffled on, another two paces nearer to the check-in desk.

'Look out South America …'

'Look out same-name eBay couple.'

'Think we'll run into them?'

'All things are possible … the world of the traveller is—'

'Minuscule?'

'Magnetic.'

She turned to face him, an infectious smile twitching on her lips. 'This is where my journey started, in an airport much like this one.'

'In Bangkok?'

She nodded. 'Swapping my suitcase in the ladies loos, with a girl called Liz.'

'Yeah … a Samsonite stuffed with skag. That's a shrewd swap.'

She raised her finger, rested it on his lips. 'Uh-uh. Breathe a word of that to anyone, and you're dead.'

'Having met that psychopath Fender, you're not kidding.'

'Exactly.' She leaned forwards, brushing her lips against his. Bozzer lifted her up in his arms, pressing his chest into hers. Their lips parted briefly, eyes searching, mouths reconnecting. Firmly, passionately, their tongues tentatively probing, their bodies reacting, tingling, merging together—

'Sir, madam.'

Maddie pulled back, giving the check-in clerk an apologetic look. 'Sorry, got distracted.' She slid her passport and ticket confirmation across the desk with Bozzer's. He rested his hand around her hips, his palm warm, unfamiliar and pulsating with energy.

Maddie and Bozzer picked up their passports and boarding passes, then stepped away from the desk. Bozzer flicked his passport open as they wandered towards passport control, glancing at the photo page.

'Crikey, I've aged well.'

Maddie looked over at her glamorous eighteen year old self, staring back at her from the shiny page. She opened Bozzer's passport and grimaced. 'Cheeky-looking chipmunk, weren't you.'

'Only the rare few get to change, Madeline.' Bozzer winked and held out her passport, swapping it with his own. She held his gaze.

'Yeah ... what happened to her?'

'She's no more. Picked up a backpack, grew out of herself.'

'Hmm ... goodbye Maddie. Hello—'

'Madge.'

She grinned. 'Yeah, guess so ...'

Bozzer held up his mobile phone and leant in towards her, pressing his lips onto her cheek. He simultaneously clicked the shutter icon, immortalising their happy faces on the small screen.

Shh-clitch ...

Forty-Five

Shh-shuuush ...

The ventilator hissed and sighed, the sound constant yet barely registering. Like the regular swoosh of tiny waves on a gently sloping beach. Bozzer smiled at a distant sensation, the soft tingle as their lips had slowly parted, recalled now with quick catch-up breaths. The vague taste of her first kiss, accompanied by prickly palms and heart-fluttering jolts of nervous energy deep inside. "This is kinda scary," she'd said, her voice husky and uncertain.

Scary doesn't even come close.

Bozzer stared at Madge's virtually motionless form. Occasional intermittent beeps pipped from the array of monitoring equipment. His upright posture stooped over her. Protective, yet helpless.

Particularly helpless now ...

Bozzer glanced over at the TV screen, on the opposite wall. A series of CNN images flickered: close ups of Jonny and Angel's bewildered expressions as they waved goodbye to their hordes of fans at Rio de Janeiro Airport. Their homeward-bound plane taking off, its undercarriage folding up into its belly. The footage cut back to a reporter, nestled amidst the crowd of well-wishers, many wearing *From Here to Eternity* spoof tee-shirts.

Bozzer turned away from the TV screen, his attention diverted to a louder pneumatic hiss. The door to Madge's private room eased open, revealing ... Simon Black: financial backer, rainmaker and, today, heartbreaker.

'It's time, sport.'

Bozzer flicked his eyes back to the contours of Madge's face, lingering there for a moment before he turned and nodded, his eyes listless.

The broken man, prepared to face his fate.

Bozzer shuffled up closer to the framework around the bed. He leaned over and kissed her gently on the forehead, then stayed there for a moment, gazing. Watching for any small movement, a flinch of recognition, an acknowledgement. But again, nothing. Save for the faint twitching of an eyelid. Consistent and unremarkable.

He sighed, then straightened up and shuffled towards Simon, loitering by the door.

'Don't forget to bring what I asked for.'

Bozzer turned back and reached over the chair beside the bed. He hooked the webbing strap of his padded camera case over his shoulder and followed Simon into the corridor, the soles of his flip-flops squeaking on the shiny vinyl floor.

*

Simon plucked the loose sheets of paper from the printer tray and bunched them into a tight wad, which he stapled together. He slid the paperwork across the desk. 'Here we go again. You have something for me?'

Bozzer placed two passports on the table. Simon swept them into his palm and flicked the covers open, studying the identity page in each.

'Excellent. So, to summarise: Madeline gets unlimited medical care at this hospital until such time as she can be discharged. During this time, you will tell me everything I want to know about your interaction with Jonathan Cork and Kate Thornley. You will advise them that Madeline is receiving excellent medical care, but tell them only what I instruct you to say. You will do anything else I ask of you until such time as I have them both back under my management.'

'Why not just say: Barry, you're my bitch.'

Simon grinned. 'Perfectly put. Your girlfriend's ongoing treatment, her *life*, rests solely in your hands. Because those hands are in my pocket.'

'There's the other thing,' Bozzer mumbled. 'My brother's wedding …'

Simon flicked through the contract pages. 'Clause twelve, item one. You've got twenty-four hours. You don't return, Maddie's treatment stops. You fail to dish the dirt on the eBay lovebirds, Maddie's treatment stops. I can pull the plug at any point, if you step out of line. Now, in exchange for my generosity, and to guarantee your compliance, what else have you got for me?'

Bozzer reached down to the floor by his chair. He scooped up his padded camera bag and placed it on the desk. Simon pulled the bag towards him and unzipped it. He examined the contents, checking the camera and lenses. Then he opened the smaller storage pockets, withdrawing a plastic 35mm film container. He prised off the lid and tipped several memory cards into his palm.

'Be careful with those, mate. I haven't had a chance to back them up yet. They're—'

'Priceless?'

'To me, yes,' Bozzer murmured, holding eye contact with Simon.

'Keep your word and they'll be safe. You can have the camera back the moment you return from your brother's shindig. I'll hold onto the memory cards until you've fulfilled the rest of our agreement.'

'I need the camera. I'm the wedding photographer.'

Simon shook his head. He jigged his palm, shuffling the memory cards back into the small container, then pocketed it. He zipped up the camera case and placed it onto the floor behind him. 'It's a nice bit of kit,' Simon agreed, 'looks expensive. But you might have made copies of the memory cards. You can borrow this, for the family snaps.' Simon slid a compact digital camera across the table. 'We'll do a swap when you return.'

'I can't use that, I'm a professional. I need my own equipment—'

'Then be professional enough to improvise.' Simon peeled the pages of the contract open and held out a pen. 'Save a life, sport – sign here.'

Other books in the Series

Book # 3 - The Travel Truth
ebook available Autumn 2018

Angel and JC return home from South America to a frenzy of worldwide public attention, putting their fledgling romance under the internet and media's relentless scrutiny, challenging their feelings for each other.

Meanwhile, Madge and Bozzer have issues of their own to contend with, the result of which could have serious implications for their infamous *same-name* ebay travel buddies.

Whilst Bozzer's camera never lies, cries, or sighs, the four friends soon discover that people often pry, lie, and say goodbye …

Book # 4 - The Travel Angel – ebook available Autumn 2018

Other books by the Author

The Curse of the Lonesome Mariner (Parts 1, 2 & 3)

Harry Straight doesn't want any complications in his life. Recently divorced, he's about to set sail on a small boat along England's south coast in order to reconcile with his estranged father. The last thing Harry needs is the responsibility of a mischievous and unpredictable beer-drinking dog called Lacey.

But when Harry's canine crewmate discovers he's only ever been with one woman, the fun-loving terrier takes it upon himself to educate Harry in the livelier side of life, leading him from one inappropriate liaison to the next … with disastrous consequences.

Printed in Great
Britain
by Amazon